AF435213

OWLBOUND BY WINTER'S BEAK

WESLEY E. JOSEPH

First paperback edition September 2024

Book design by Bauxxi
https://www.bauxxi.com/home

Formatting by Nastasia Bishop-McHugh of Stardust Book Services
Line art by Jonas Spokas of Stardust Book Services
www.stardustbookservices.com

Printed by IngramSpark

ISBN 978-9-4649-8160-5 (paperback edition)
ISBN 978-9-4649-8161-2 (hardback edition)
ISBN 978-9-4649-8162-9 (eBook edition)

Published by Wesley E. Joseph
www.wesleyejoseph.com

Content warnings:
Anxiety, death, animal death, grief, racism, hallucinations, misgendering, spiders, skeletons, needles, blood, bones, fantasy violence, violence toward people, violence toward animals, loss of limbs, and references of genocide.

OWLBOUND
BY WINTER'S
BEAK

CHAPTER I

BACK BEFORE YOU KNOW IT

The sun crashed into the horizon when he realised. He lost track of time. Wrestling his way through the thick snow, Tyrus allowed for less and less time between a step and the next. The cold took a much fiercer chokehold come nightfall, and last time it had almost claimed his last visible breath. He didn't wish to repeat that mistake again.

Three malicious distant howls reached his frost-nipped ears from behind and for a moment, Tyrus couldn't move an inch. He looked back, squinted, but the snowfall didn't let him see much. He tightened the straps around the firewood he had gathered on his back, and trudged ahead as fast as he could with his axe in hand. The remains of a blizzard crunched beneath his boots, while his fingers—even though he wore gloves—gradually lost any and all sensation to the raging cold. He struggled his way through that snow. Never giving up, never giving in, he kept going even when it climbed up to his knees. He felt the bleakwolves around him. He couldn't see them, nor hear them over the sound of the howling wind, but they were there. Hiding, biding their time for the perfect moment to lunge, and to tear the flesh from his bones.

One of the stalking wolves shot out from underneath the snow like a puppet jumping out of a scare box. Tyrus ducked and swung his axe upward, injuring the beast as the border of the woods neared. Salvation. He knew they wouldn't follow him past the forest's edge, as if there stood a magical border that protected his home from unwanted visitors. The relentless winter all around him aimed to freeze every muscle that tried to contract and move. It slowed him down, but despite the hardship, Tyrus crossed the threshold, exiting the woods. As he suspected, the bleakwolves didn't dare follow him beyond.

He climbed the hill that followed, and when he stood on top, he let his breathing settle before continuing. His home towered in the distance, resting below a vivid aurora borealis. Wanting to see their home and the dancing waves of colour too, Tyrus' autumn-brown curly hair peeked out from underneath his dark-green woolly hat, handknitted by his mother for his father. It had taken a while, but he had finally grown enough to wear it comfortably.

'Come on Tyrus. You've got this, big man. Almost there,'

he imagined his father saying.

Toward home he trekked, down the hill, and as the scent of the pine trees slowly left his nose, playful snowflakes dwindled down from the swirling sky above. Some perished as they landed on his light-brown skin, while others survived a bit longer on his chapped lips.

The wind picked up and birds flew overhead. Crows looking for a meal. Tyrus knew full-well they couldn't have been, but he kept hoping they were owls. Another gust of wind came along and it sang the wretched song of the never-ending cold as it dug into the scavenger boy's skin, determined to reach his bones. To take what it felt like it was owed. His warmth, any warmth, his life, any life. He wouldn't let it, and when he arrived at his doorstep, a relieved sigh escaped his mouth. The wooden door screamed as he opened it in a hurry.

'Home sweet home,' his visible breath whispered.

He wrestled his legs out of the snow, through the front door. Once inside, he slammed it shut fast, preventing the chill from creeping inside any further. The outside cold tiptoeing through his home? Not if he had any say in it.

Most people lived in cabins, cottages or huts, but Tyrus lived in a remnant; of a lost world, of a life before the cold. Life alongside magic. His home stood tall, a lonely lighthouse next to a frozen lake, surrounded by woods, hills and mountains.

His mother had told him stories about lighthouses,

about how—back when the seasons used to dance—they guided people back to land and safety. How they brought people home, sailors who were lost at angry seas or furious oceans. Occasionally, Tyrus wished his lighthouse came with one or the other instead of the lake. Even if they would have been frozen, too.

He waited by the door for a while before his head and shoulders sank, alone in his lonely lighthouse. Every time he returned from the outside, his hope yearned for their warm embraces or their comforting voices. But every time, the ruthless truth bathed in the silence. Their embraces would never hold him, their voices would never nestle in his ears, not anymore. The last time Tyrus saw his parents, he stood two heads smaller and ever since then, all the days and weeks and months, even the years, had looked the same. He didn't know it, but his sixteenth name day waited around the corner, ready to take him one step closer to adulthood. Whatever that was supposed to mean.

As soon as Tyrus managed to lift his feet out of his boots, he noticed the fireplace long for the firewood strapped to his back. He couldn't stop himself from chattering his teeth, so he gave the hearth what it craved all but immediately. Determined to banish the cold from not only his lighthouse but also his bones, he struck two rocks against each other.

Nothing. Again. Nothing. And again. Nothing.

His heart started racing, his breathing sped up, his

brows gave birth to a deep frown, and he grinded his teeth as he fought the urge to throw the rocks out the window. Instead, he took a deep breath to prevent his blood from boiling before he tried again. Sparks set the wood ablaze and the fire swayed across the branches and the logs. Heat landed on his skin like the snowflakes did before and the warmth made his chapped lips tingle. His heartbeat slipped back into the usual comfortable lento. He put his hands out forward, palms facing the flames and smiled. He liked to imagine the joints in his fingers smiling along.

The smallest things set him off sometimes, things that didn't warrant such a response. He couldn't possibly attempt to explain why. Anger always had a place in his heart, for as long as he could remember. A trait he could blame his father for.

As he calmed down while the place—and his bones— heated up, Tyrus munched on a small piece of leftover rabbit from the day before. It tasted exactly like what you'd expect leftover rabbit to taste like; dry and muffled. Yet, his stomach growled for more the second he swallowed that last bite.

'I know, but that'll have to do,' he said, hands resting atop his belly where his bowels tossed around.

He stared up at the sky through one of his round windows. The sun and the clouds up high had made way for the moons, the stars, and a whirl of colours. Like his parents, Tyrus adored the stars. They would have stargazed with him if they were there. His right hand climbed up to where his collar bones met, until they touched a totem, hanging around his neck. He wrapped his fingers around it and clenched his hand firmly. In all those years, he had never taken it off. That and his father's hat were the only meaningful physical tethers to his parents he had left. The tiny totem was carved from stone and shaped like the head of a barn owl, his favourite animal. Even after all this time, the tips of his fingers marvelled at the feeling of the detailed feathers on the totem.

'There, you'll always have an owl with you now,' said his mother when she let his hand swallow the totem for the first time. 'Keep it close, keep it safe, will you?'

He did as he was told, but he was convinced the totem kept him safe, too. He considered it both his lucky charm, and a reminder to that assuaging smile of his mother.

After letting his amber irises wander between the infinite lights in the sky, Tyrus wrestled his eyelids for a while. They sought nothing more than to slam themselves shut, and it didn't take them long before they managed to turn the tide of battle in their favour.

Tyrus fell into the treacherous caverns of his mind—where his anxieties roamed like monsters in the form of nightmares—but he unexpectedly drifted into a fond memory. A memory of that time he made a snowperson with his mom while his dad prepared dinner inside. He giggled, his mom smiled, and happiness leapt off his father's face when he called them inside for food. The smell of a hearty stew resided in his nostrils and the taste of it thrived on his tongue, the way fire danced across wood. Despite the uncomfortable cold, his father joked around, his mother laughed aloud and the corners of his own mouth rose like dough under a wet towel. Tyrus lived and bathed in that memory, for as long as he could. He stayed until his eyes opened when the sun decided it had rested enough. He woke up with a subtle smile that faded as quickly as footsteps in a raging snowstorm, followed by a single tear.

'We'll be back before you know it! We love you,' his mom had told him after giving him her totem.

Those words encompassed why he still lived in that lighthouse, because maybe, just maybe…they'd still return. Even though, deep down, he knew the cold had to have claimed them. It must have. He knew in his heart they would have done anything to make sure they could come home; they would have stopped at nothing as a matter of fact. But he also learned over the years that the cold had a knack for disregarding what a person wanted. It didn't care, mercilessly taking what it craved. He refused to accept any of it, regardless of what he knew. He couldn't. And so, he stayed with the lighthouse. He stayed, kept his head down, and avoided other people as much as he could. That's what they taught him. That's what he did.

In the morning, Tyrus abandoned the incredibly

uncomfortable position he fell asleep in with sighs and groans as he stood upright to stretch. Multiple joints cracked and a sense of relief beamed through his body. He didn't mean to fall asleep next to that window. Normally, he'd climb the spiralling staircases of the lighthouse to retreat into his room for a good night's sleep. And more often than not, he slept in for the better part of the morning, too.

His room wasn't as much a room as it was an entire floor, the third floor of the lighthouse to be exact. His towering home had four floors (five if you counted the top with the roof above it), with the floor above his room acting like a buffer between his space and the frozen outside world. At the top, just below the roof was where people used to ignite the fires of the guiding light. Tyrus had thought about lighting it for his parents, but they had explicitly forbidden him from ever lighting it, so he didn't.

Tyrus' room looked like a library. An utterly chaotic and messy one, but a library nonetheless. Books lurked everywhere, sheets of paper hugged the walls, and the scent of words on pages lingered in every nook and cranny. They used to be his mother's, the pages and the books. She often spoke of a time when seasons used to dance throughout a year as one bled into the other. A time before the Eternal Winter began. A time of magic and myth. An era filled with owls in all shapes, colours and sizes.

Owls. Utterly fascinated with them, he made it his

personal mission to know anything and everything about them. Tyrus' mother filled his mind with anecdotes of people who possessed magical abilities, fiery magic they controlled through a connection they shared with a feathered friend. People bound to owls. Tyrus would give everything to see an owl in the flesh, but he knew he'd have no such luck. No one had seen one in over a hundred years, not since they were purged from the face of the Wingspan Continent. And yet, he still dreamed. Owls went extinct, but Tyrus' hope and imagination could never.

In between all the words of wisdom, tales of magic, stories of seasons and ramblings of owls, you'd find not only a bed, but also a desk. One at which Tyrus often sat to read and learn about the past, myths, and extinct magical birds.

No matter how much he longed to do that and nothing else, right then and there, he couldn't. Low on mostly everything except firewood, Tyrus had to brave the cold once more. Perhaps, if he got back before the sun chose to crash into the horizon again, his books and words of comfort would await him with a mellow and familiar embrace.

CHAPTER 2

SILVER LINING

Tyrus had an absolute prize in his sights. He was proud of it too; he'd been tracking it for hours and all that was left, was to take the shot. The sweaty palm of his left hand held the grip of his bow while the sturdy fingers of his right pulled back the string. He tried to concentrate as the forces of the cold and his nerves teamed up against him, making him tremble. But after taking a deep breath of vigorous forest air, he managed to steady himself.

'Sorry, pal,' he said as he let go of the string.

The sharp arrowhead cut through the air like a pair of brand-new scissors slicing through paper. Tyrus flinched when he heard his arrow bury itself in flesh. He had never enjoyed hunting, but if he wanted food, if he wanted to trade and survive, he had no choice in the matter. His target ran. He was in luck, because judging by the large scarlet stains in the fresh delicate snow, it couldn't have gone far. Tyrus followed the trail of red through the forest until the trail turned into a pool. There it panted, in the middle of that pool, suffering. A heavy wild boar, an impressive creature wielding mighty tusks. It clung onto life with the cold on the sidelines, biding its time to claim it. But whether he wanted to do it or not, it was Tyrus who would claim the kill.

He carefully approached the boar and attempted to calm it down with shushing noises as he reached for the knife in his belt's holster. He looked into its eye as it laid on its side, slowly dying in a snowy carpet. Tyrus' arrow had pierced its lung. The wound throbbed and bled and hurt.

'Shhh, it'll be okay,' said Tyrus as he brought his knife closer to its head. 'It'll be over soon.'

The young reluctant hunter closed his eyes as he finished the kill and then, when his eyelids lifted, so did the spirit of the boar. Life left its bones. Tears escaped the corners of Tyrus' eyes, only to be immediately captured by the garrisons of the cold as they turned into crystals of ice.

'Thank you. Your fight is over now…Rest,' he whispered.

The meat of the wild boar would feed him for days, the hide and leftover meat could be traded for geluroots, and maybe even frostbread if he was lucky. The bones especially made for excellent trade potential. A silver lining.

'Shit!' He panicked when he looked at the sun, hanging directly above him. 'Sorry, Mom…' he added under his breath; she had never approved of cursing.

Tyrus and the trader he always met at the edge of the woods, had agreed on noon.

'Cedric will wait for me, right?' he asked himself aloud. 'Yeah, he'll wait.'

Tyrus was right. Cedric always waited because he knew the trader well. The man used to be an acquaintance of his parents. Every week, Cedric, the seasoned trader, travelled between Crownhaven and Featherburn and back to trade with local merchants and the like. And on the way to Featherburn, he'd make a pitstop by the woods for the boy with the amber eyes. This allowed Tyrus to stock up on things—mostly food—and in doing so, he avoided being around people he couldn't trust. Granted, Featherburn was only a day's travel away (by foot) from his lighthouse, but there was history there. His parents made him promise to never go back.

Alternatively, Crownhaven would take him multiple days to reach, which rendered it pointless as well. It was simply too far away to make the trips worthwhile and Tyrus didn't have a horse, let alone a carriage like Cedric did.

Tyrus walked back to fetch his sled and a tarp, which he used to wrap up the boar and make it easier to transport. Slowly but surely—and as fast as he could—

he pulled the sled carrying his game through the woods. The wind rustled the needles of the pine trees as sunrays manoeuvred between them. Every now and then, the sunshine would touch Tyrus' face, and he'd take a long deep breath. He gladly took any kind of warmth he could from the sun, because lately, it didn't seem like it had much to give anymore.

The edge of the forest came closer and closer until Cedric's carriage peeked from behind the trees. Tyrus' face burst with a joyous smile the moment he saw it. He approached it further with a skip in his step. It was a bit of a chunky clunky thing—Cedric's carriage—but then again, it held all of the merchandise the trader travelled the roads with. Six large lightly shaded wooden wheels carried what seemed like a small yet spacious cabin. It even had a slanted roof with a compact attic inside of it. And at the front, it had a bench where seasoned Cedric would sit to conduct the unimaginably massive horse that steered the entire thing. Behemoth horses they were called. They were tremendously rare, exceptionally expensive, exceedingly strong and awfully dangerous if angered. They could live for over a century and Cedric had often told Tyrus stories. Tales about how people who tried to steal his horse—emphasis on tried—usually ended up dead in a ditch. Moral of the stories? Don't mess with his behemoth horse, or any of their kind for that matter.

The exterior of the ginormous wooden carriage wore

etchings of ancient runes. Runes Tyrus couldn't read but one; the runic symbol for love. He found plenty of such runes in his books. He even studied some of them, yet he didn't recognise the rest of the etchings. One day, he'd know what the rest of them meant; this he vowed. He had asked Cedric about why he chose those runes and what they said, but all the trader had to say for himself was that he thought they were pretty. Knowing him, Tyrus figured it made all the sense in the realm.

'Cedric! I'm here! Thank you for waiting!' shouted Tyrus.

The door on the side of the carriage swung open and an odd growl escaped the giant horse's mouth. A grey-haired and kempt-bearded man climbed down the ladder that led up to the carriage door. He had a kind pale face, a cushy belly, and small round glasses rested on the bridge of his plump nose. He wore a warm long-waisted dark brown coat and underneath, a deep-blue waistcoat on top of a flannel shirt.

'Oh, calm down, Trudy, it's merely me and the laddie. Don't act like you don't know him. Or did you get hit in the napper?' He turned to Tyrus. 'You're late, lad.'

'And you're old, Ced,' he answered.

With one of his hands resting on his lower back, the man groaned, trying to hide a chuckle. 'You're only as old as you feel which, in my case, well...aye...old,' he admitted. 'What do you have there?'

Cedric's *R's* rolled, and it was as if the man spoke in melodies.

'A prize, Ced. A prize! Hunted it today,' Tyrus announced as he opened the tarp.

'Well, I'll be damned, a grown boar? Let's get it inside, laddie,' Cedric proposed and together, they lifted the carcass of the wild thing off of the sled and shuffled it into the carriage.

The inside looked roomier than you'd expect. Yes, it seemed like a ridiculously big carriage from the outside but you had no idea how big it actually was until you had taken a peek inside. Everything sat neatly organised in cupboards, on shelves and in jars, pots and crates. There was room for a table in the middle, which Cedric lifted out of the floor with an elegant sort of mechanism. Tyrus didn't know how it worked, nor did he care. He was simply glad he wasn't going to have to skin and cut up the boar himself. He tried leaving all the dirty work to Cedric as often as he could. The trader would then prepare all the hide, the meat, the bones for trade, in exchange for a small fee. Tyrus could then have his pick of what he wanted or needed and immediately traded the rest in for other goods that Cedric had with him. It was a comfortable arrangement, one that Cedric hardly ever made for anyone. He liked the kid and he didn't usually like a lot of people. Additionally, he did so out of respect for the boy's parents. Tyrus suspected Cedric made a promise to look after him, but the trader always denied it. Tyrus was never sure if he believed him on the matter or not.

Tyrus gazed around the treasure trove that was Ced's carriage. He saw many things that peaked his interests but he eyed the fresh geluroots most of all, with drool escaping the corners of his mouth. Paired with the boar, it would make for a great stew, like the one his father used to make. Meanwhile, Cedric's hands disappeared deep inside the boar's guts.

'Hey, Ced? Do you happen to have any frostbread on you this time?' asked Tyrus.

The trader looked up. 'As a matter of fact, I do. It's in a basket in the back, you can have a look if you want,' he said, pointing with a blood-soaked finger.

Cedric didn't have to say it twice. Tyrus moved to the back of the carriage in a happy strut. He opened the first basket he saw by popping off the lid and there they were. Beautiful loaves of frostbread with their signature white crust, as white as the snow outside. It was made from frostwheat. Regular wheat had gone extinct, or at least that's what people assumed but luckily, nature blessed man and elvenkind with a variant that withstood the cold temperatures. However, worryingly so, as the years kept getting colder and colder, frostwheat (and geluroot crops) all across Wingspan inched closer to the limit of their immunity to the cold. Year after year, harvests shrunk. Year after year, more and more people had to live with an ever so growing yearning in their stomachs.

'You can buy as many loaves as you want, there's enough stuff here to cover that much,' said Cedric, his hands buried inside the boar again.

'As I want? That's amazing but I don't think I can buy that many, unless it's a special kind of frostbread that never spoils?'

'Ha! Right, keep dreaming, laddie,' laughed Cedric.

'By the way,' started Tyrus. Worry surfed the waves of his voice. 'Yesterday, I ran into bleakwolves here in the woods, *again*. Can you believe it?'

'Aye, sadly I can,' answered Cedric. 'With winter getting colder year after year, they're becoming bolder. You see it with other creatures, too. They're getting stronger the colder it gets, and they venture outside their own territories, they expand.'

'Yeah, I've been noticing that...Just be careful out there,' added Tyrus, his voice lower, serious.

'I will, laddie. I will.'

It seemed like a lot of work but Cedric managed to completely pick apart that wild boar for everything it was worth in what had to be record time.

'All right, I got you nice juicy pieces of meat, real good stuff. Should keep you from starving for about a week, especially if you're planning on making that stew of yours,' explained Cedric.

Tyrus smiled at that. 'Fantastic, Ced!'

'Do you need anything else from the boar? Spare hide or a couple of bones?'

Tyrus paused, going through all his supplies in his head, but the only thing he ran low on was food. 'I'll take the spare hide, the rest I'm willing to sell or trade,' he said. A little extra hide never hurt anyone.

'Fine by me, laddie,' said Cedric. 'For the meat alone, you can take as many geluroots and frostbread loaves as you need.'

'Did you just read my mind?' Tyrus smirked.

Cedric shook his head. 'Nope, I've only known you for years, lad.'

Tyrus gathered as many geluroots as he could carry, alongside two loaves of frostbread. It would all fit nicely together for the stew he had in mind.

'For the remaining bones and the tusks, I can give you about four hundred crowns total,' suggested Cedric.

'Hmmm, four hundred and fifty,' countered Tyrus.

The trader hoisted his eyebrows at that. He was starting to think teaching Tyrus how to barter was a mistake. The boy hadn't agreed to any of his initial offers since. 'Absolutely not, more like four hundred and fifteen,' he negotiated.

'Come on, Cedric, work with me here,' said Tyrus. 'Four twenty-five?'

'Four hundred and twenty, final offer, take it or leave it.'

Tyrus hesitated and he scratched his right temple. 'I

guess that'll do. Deal,' he said after counting to five in his head.

'Oh, hold up! Almost forgot,' said Ced as he turned around, his hands roaming through one of his cupboards. 'I have something I thought you might like, laddie.'

Last time Cedric had said something like that, he offered Tyrus books about the Owlbound, which he presented to him in pristine condition. Tyrus clenched his fists in anticipation so hard they shook.

'Aha, here it is!' the trader shouted.

Tyrus' eyes started wandering already, looking for clues as to what it could be. Whatever it was, it sat wrapped in cloth. The shape didn't match that of a book, that much he could tell.

'I bought this off a scavenger in Crownhaven, said they found it in old-world ruins,' explained Cedric with wide eyes, lifting the item up high.

'Well? What is it?' asked Tyrus.

Cedric lowered his hands, gently folded open the cloth, and Tyrus' eyes lit up at the sight of it. It was a shoulder pad, a piece of armour made of leather but not any old shoulder pad, not any old piece of ancient armour. He had seen this object before in his readings, sketched in those books of his, an armour piece worn by those who were Owlbound.

'How much?' asked Tyrus immediately.

'A hundred crowns,' proposed Cedric.

Perhaps the boy had been a tad too eager asking how much it cost.

'Seventy-five.'

Cedric tilted his head at him. 'Do you think I didn't see your whole damn face light up at the mere sight of this thing? A hundred crowns.'

'Fine,' said Tyrus, and he rolled his eyes.

Cedric fetched his crown pouch and handed the kid his remaining three hundred and twenty crowns. Tyrus accepted the money and put it away without looking. He only had eyes for the shoulder pad now. It was a deep rich brown and when a mage wore it, it extended over the shoulder so that an owl could comfortably land and sit on it.

'Oh my talons!' he screamed out when he noticed scratch marks etched into the leather, marks that only talons would leave behind.

'Damnit, you should have asked for more, you knobhead,' mumbled the seasoned trader to himself.

The mere notion of owning an item that had come into contact with a living owl, compelled the boy to give Cedric a sturdy hug, one the trader welcomed like one welcomed a place by the fire after spending the day outside.

When Tyrus emerged from the carriage, it had begun snowing. The snowflakes swayed across the light breeze as he attached all his merchandise to his sled. Everything except for the shoulder pad, because he decided to wear it. After all, why wouldn't he?

'Looks good on you, laddie!' said Cedric.

'You think so?' asked Tyrus. 'Awesome.'

The boy looked Ced's way, saw the smile on the trader's face melt away into concern, and decided to stop packing his sled.

'Hey, lad…' started Cedric.

Here it comes, thought Tyrus.

'Don't you think it's time?' he asked. 'Don't you think it's time to move on? Move to Featherburn or… Crownhaven?'

Tyrus' blood began to simmer at the question; it had been a while since he had asked that. Over the years, the trader had asked Tyrus countless times, he even offered living on the road with him, help out with trades.

'Being out here alone, this is no place for a bairn,' he'd say.

Tyrus always refused and as he got older, more capable, taller and stronger, Cedric stopped asking. He always appreciated the fact that the trader didn't kidnap him. He could have, others might have, but not him, not Ced.

'This again?' He raised his voice. 'You know my answer to that, Ced.'

'I know, I know, but…'

'No buts. Besides, you know that I'm banned for life from Featherburn,' he said, consciously ignoring the

Crownhaven part of the question.

'Aye, over a decade ago, Tyrus. With your parents, when you were a toddler, for talon's sake. I doubt they would even remember who you were,' said Cedric.

'Enough!' the boy shouted. 'Mom said to never go back there. Dad too. So, I won't!

The seasoned trader opened his mouth but the words didn't follow. He stroked his beard instead.

Tyrus sighed. 'I'm sorry, I didn't mean to yell.'

'Well…there's still Crownhaven?' the trader asked after taking a few seconds. Risky, but he mustered up the courage to ask anyway.

'I don't like Crownhaven,' countered Tyrus.

'You've never been to Crownhaven.'

'I've heard of Crownhaven.'

'Hearing of Crownhaven is not the same as having been to Crownhaven.'

Tyrus sighed. 'What if what I heard about Crownhaven made me not like Crownhaven?'

'We're saying Crownhaven a lot,' Cedric noted under his breath. 'Look, laddie. I…I care about you.'

'I know, Ced. I know and I care about you too. But you have to stop,' said the boy with tight balled fists and he finished packing.

Tyrus gave the trader a big strong lengthy hug before leaving because he sensed the man needed it. After that, he walked up to the front of the carriage to give Trudy all the head pats she deserved. They turned out to be more like side-of-the-head pats since Tyrus couldn't quite reach the top of the behemoth horse's head, but he figured it was the thought that counted. When he stopped, she turned her head to follow the pets of his hand but they didn't return.

'Take care, lad. Oh, and try not to be late next time!' said Cedric while waving him farewell.

'You too, Cedric, take care, and…I'll try!' called back Tyrus and he disappeared between the trees, the snow, and the rocks.

Pulling his sled, packed to the brim with meat, geluroots, frostbread and a bag of crowns, Tyrus' hike home began. As a consequence of him being late for his meeting with Cedric, the last quarter of his journey would be witnessed by a drowning sun and then, rising moons as he laid eyes on his lighthouse. Moons, one larger than the other, accompanied by faintly twinkling stars and the aurora borealis.

In the end, the lukewarm embrace of home rewarded him for overcoming the challenge he had gotten himself into. The warmth that clung to the insides of the lighthouse earlier had nearly been expelled and replaced by a chilly presence. Tyrus longed for a portion of that stew he had been thinking about, but lacked the energy to sit down and make it. Instead, after shaking off his boots and his jacket, he put away all the things he brought with him, then roasted a hefty piece of meat in his fireplace as the fire crackled and cackled. His bones shivered, aching, begging for the flames of the fireplace, so he moved a little closer as he looked over at the shoulder pad that now hung over a chair. He took it and put it back on.

'It was worth it,' he said and he inhaled his dinner.

By the time his lighthouse heated up a bit, he decided to go upstairs and head to bed. He dragged and carried his tired bones up the spiralling oak wooden staircase. He wanted to sit down at his desk and read of seasons, magic, birds and mages but his exhaustion didn't allow it. Straight to bed he went instead.

That night, Tyrus didn't sleep through till daybreak. The sound of shattering glass upstairs abruptly woke him, while a light but chilling draft descended the steps from the floor above. Shoulder pad still strapped around his chest (of course he hadn't taken it off), he grabbed the nearest thing he could find to smack an intruder into oblivion with—a book. A thick and heavy one at that.

He climbed up the stairs and let his eyes travel the room but they saw nothing except for a broken round window and shattered glass. The moonlight landed on the wooden floor but other than that, there was nothing to see, and for a moment, nothing to hear either. Until his ears picked up a strange noise from between the boxes. When he came closer, a shadow burst out from between the crates and Tyrus fell back. Something had pecked him on the wrist. The tiny wound bled as drops of red plunged themselves to the surface beneath him.

The shadow moved. Tyrus held his book tight, ready to strike. But then, instead of attacking, the shadow hopped into the light of the moons and the boy with the chaotic curls couldn't believe his eyes.

CHAPTER 3

NICE TO MEET YOU

Tyrus couldn't move. Every muscle, frozen in time like the fish in the lake, while the book he'd previously grabbed to weaponize obeyed the laws of gravity to the letter and fell to the wooden floorboards below. It couldn't be. He pinched himself to make sure this wasn't a dream. Tyrus' mouth tried to find words as it changed shapes over and over again.

'Impossible,' was all he managed to mutter in the end.

There it stood, upright on his floorboards, observed by his very own eyes. Eyes that dared to deceive him at times, but not like this. The pain from the wound on the top of his left wrist—which still bled—fled to the back of his mind, dissolved without a trace as the remarkable reality of his situation sank in.

The majestic animal looked at him like it wasn't sure if it had done anything wrong. Its talons buried themselves in the wood beneath them. The feathered creature's wings rested beside its body while blood stained its beak. The intruder he initially feared, revealed itself to be an owl. A barn owl, his favourite bird, an impossible bird that was supposed to be extinct beyond infinity.

Instead of the usual pale brown and grey tones barn owls supposedly had, the bird's head and wings varied in shades of cyan with light purple streaks to break things up. Its white heart-shaped face shone in the light of the moons and floaty periwinkle accents bled around its eggplant-purple beak. The rest of the unbelievable creature, like its chest—which had a few drops of Tyrus' blood on it—and legs were stark white. And then there were those eyes. Large pupils as black and dark as the charcoal in the boy's fireplace. They watched him get up to his feet, and around the edges, thin irises manifested a dark magenta colour. The drawings in his books never held any colour but he read about owls having unusual colour patterns. It used to be an indication they possessed stronger magic. Whether they spoke of snowy owls, great horned owls, long-eared owls, great grey owls, tawny owls, burrowing owls, or barn owls, if they had unique and flamboyant colourful feathers, they described them as rare and immensely powerful.

He moved closer to the bird in a steady manner (and with the speed of a snail) in order not to scare it away. He breathed out softly and lengthily when she stayed put.

The closer he came, the lower his jaw dropped until you could lodge a whole frostbread loaf in his mouth.

Tyrus could tell he was dealing with a young bird by how parts of its body (like the bottom of its legs) still grew poofy and fluffy feathers. His books had taught him well. He held out his hand as he inched a little closer again. The owl started moving in the boy's direction too and they gently and awkwardly continued shifting closer toward one another, until his hand and the crown of its head met. It was soft, the softest thing he had ever felt. Tyrus bottled all the excitement he experienced in the balled fist he leaned on the floor with, as a large grin leapt off his face like a great story leaping off the page of a book. The bird closed its eyes every time Tyrus' hand came in for head rubs. The giddy boy glowed. His mouth stretched out and the corners rose until he wore the silliest, yet most genuine smile between his cheeks.

After a few minutes of gentle petting, Tyrus couldn't contain his giddiness any longer. He jumped up and broke out into a happy dance—if you could call that a dance. Surprisingly, the owl didn't so much as flinch at that. It tilted its head and stared instead.

As Tyrus' initial excitement wore off a little, he noticed the cold rolling into his lighthouse. Unfortunately, meeting an owl didn't magically fix his window.

Shattered glass laid scattered across the floorboards in what must have easily been a hundred pieces, every single one holding a reflection of Tyrus and the owl. Only the latter remained as Tyrus ran downstairs to grab a hammer and a couple of nails. He had to stop the frosty night from laying siege to his home. Roughly a hundred Tyruses joined the about a hundred dispersed owls on the floor as he stormed back into the room. He picked up spare planks from between the boxes and the crates, and boarded up the window in a fraction of the time he thought it would take. The wondrous eyes of Tyrus' new feathered friend observed every single nail that shot through the planks by means of that rusty hammer. Its body jerked slightly with every slam, but it stayed put.

'What? I had to repair that first, didn't I?' said Tyrus when he finally turned around.

The owl hooted lightly as if it apologised.

'Oh, it's all right, don't worry about it,' said Tyrus. 'Wait…Did you understand me?'

The bird stood there and tilted its head again.

'Right, maybe not…Anyways, would you mind if I took a closer look at you? I want to make sure you're not hurt,' he said and inched closer a bit.

The bird didn't care or understand what Tyrus had said (or perhaps it did, who was to say), so instead of remaining still, it opened its wings, bent its legs and lunged at him. Tyrus let out a shriek while he braced for impact with his arms crossed in front of him and eyes closed.

When he lowered his arms and opened his eyes, there wasn't a bird in sight, and for a second, he thought it was all a dream after all. A dream that spilled into the real world like a pot of water boiling over. But then, he noticed one of his shoulders felt heavier. He leaned a bit more to the left than usual and that's when he remembered. He had never taken off the shoulder pad. And as if it were destiny, on that peculiar armour piece sat the most majestic owl. Having a closer look not only revealed to Tyrus that it wasn't wounded at all, but also that he was dealing with a she; he could tell from the feathers. She looked absolutely stunning.

'Well, hi there, little lady,' he said to her in a slight whisper.

A light hoot escaped the owl's beak and she rubbed her head against his. However marvellous that was, the sting of the wound on his wrist returned and blood kept leaking out like liquor from a flask with the wrong cap.

Tyrus descended the stairs and the bird meticulously inspected the home of the boy whose shoulder she had claimed. Meanwhile, that boy walked through his lighthouse, looking like a fool, because his balance felt off. They arrived at the second floor where Tyrus usually bathed and stored his few clothes. The room had a giant chest that burst with medical supplies. The strong scents from a variety of dried medicinal herbs sprung out of the chest as he opened it, overwhelming his nostrils. Scents so strong, a rather unpleasant sterile taste swirled around Tyrus' tongue and between his teeth.

Even though it appeared to be bursting at the seams, the inside of the medicine chest had been impressively organised. Why that seemed to excite the bird was anyone's guess. The herbs rested in tiny corked-up jars, and rolled-up bandages sat neatly next to folded pieces of cloth sitting atop each other, as a pair of sharp scissors leaned against a bottle of stupendously strong liquor. Tyrus reached for a piece of cloth first. He then opened the bottle of liquor, poured an ounce or two over the cloth and used it to clean and disinfect his wound. His parents had shown him how to do it, before they…

The wound ended up being somewhat shallow, yet deep enough to eventually leave a slight scar. Tyrus didn't mind the idea of it though, because this way, he'd always carry a memory with him. A reminder of the day he met an actual owl. When he finished cleaning the wound (and after it decided to stop bleeding), the owl jumped off of Tyrus' shoulder pad to grab a roll of bandages with her beak. She brought it closer and dropped it near Tyrus' hands so he wouldn't have to reach.

'Why thank you, that's mighty nice of you. I reckon, you're pretty smart, then?' he asked but the bird simply stared at him as if nothing behind those eyes existed.

Perhaps he had spoken too soon. Tyrus wrapped his wrist tight but not too tight, just right and with that handled, his mind allowed him to fully allocate his attention to the most exciting thing ever. The bird that was supposed to be wiped off the face of the entire Wingspan continent.

The boy's gaze met the owl's heart-shaped face. 'You certainly are something,' he said. 'Where did you come from?'

The bird's empty and clueless, yet cute eyes continued their empty stare.

'Did you get lost? Do you have an owner?' he asked and then he gasped. '*Are you bound?*' The volume of his voice lowered as if he was afraid even the furniture around them would hear him.

The howling wind outside interrupted the conversation and the sun woke as it rose from its slumber. What was Tyrus thinking? That the owl would suddenly start telling him her life's story? Owls were believed to be magical, yes. But not *that* magical.

'Do you have a name?' asked Tyrus finally.

A rather disappointed hoot travelled from the owl's beak, all the way into Tyrus' ears.

'Oh, sorry, I didn't mean to upset you,' he said swiftly, and a proposal followed. 'I can find you a name if you want?'

The owl started hopping around, almost like she was copying Tyrus' happy "dance" from before. She made Tyrus laugh and the whole lighthouse sang with joy. The walls had missed that smile, especially that laugh.

'Okay, I'll think about it. I vow that by the end of the day, you'll have a name, milady,' promised Tyrus, and if owls were physically able to smile, she would have.

With the morning sun out after an eventful night, Tyrus decided to take in some fresh outside air. He prepared himself for the world beyond the lighthouse and set the owl on top of the cabinets that clung to the walls. She hooted.

'Oh, you want to come with?' he asked her. 'I don't know if that's such a good idea.'

She looked at him in a profoundly puzzled manner.

'From what I've heard, people out there wouldn't take kindly to owls. Most blame the Owlbound for winter, you know…' he trailed off.

The mythical bird lowered her crown. Tyrus reached out to pet her, to comfort her but paused.

'Then again, I've never had anyone or anything come through the woods before, I don't think. Not even Ced has ever been here,' he contemplated. His chin rested between his index finger and thumb while he looked up at the ceiling as if his thoughts were displayed there. 'You know what? On second thought, hop on!'

The boy swung open the wooden lighthouse door,

stepped outside, took in a deep breath, and went for a stroll with his new friend sitting on his shoulder. The chill air that filled his lungs made him feel indestructible and with every step, he improved his balance until he got used to the bird's weight. Tyrus thought it best not to stray too far from home but he was right about needing a hefty helping of fresh air. He didn't entirely know how to describe it but, you could smell it was freezing.

Meanwhile, the bird took in the enchanting winter displays as if she had never seen anything like it before. Tyrus adored that childlike wonder which he still possessed to a degree, and he prayed he'd never lose it.

The sun had ever so slightly moved when they arrived at a bunch of rock formations. Tyrus, in his dark-green woolly hat and maroon cloak, decided it was time for a little rest. He put his feathered pal on the ground in the snow while he sat down on a flat rock. He sighed a content sigh. It was a beautiful day. Cold—yes, always cold—but beautiful nonetheless. The owl didn't thoroughly understand how her talons disappeared in the snow and started hopping around, determined to find out how they vanished each time. In the time Tyrus had met her, she had made him smile more than he had in years.

The clouds grew a bit heavier as the boy and the bird enjoyed each other's company and then the inevitable happened. Snowflakes glided downward and the bird's eyes sparkled with awe.

'What is it?' asked Tyrus.

The wind rustled the frozen branches nearby, and this time it was Tyrus tilting his head for a change. 'Hello? Everything okay?' he added.

She gave him a soft and gentle hoot and when the snowflakes reached her, she tried catching them.

'Have you never seen snowflakes before?' he asked as he broke into a giggle.

She looked so determined that, in the end, Tyrus' giggle burst into full on laughter while his feathered companion struggled to grasp why she couldn't actually catch the flakes in her beak. A mythical creature, supposed to be extinct, chasing snowflakes; it was the most adorable and silly thing he had ever witnessed.

'Oh, praise the moons! I got it!' shouted Tyrus, louder than he expected to.

He grabbed the owl's attention but she simultaneously kept her eyes on the elusive and intricate particles of falling snow. Tyrus moved closer and kneeled as one of his knees sank in a layer of snow.

He looked right at her and repeated, 'I got it,' this time at a more pleasant volume. 'I know what to call you. Your name. It's perfect!'

It was.

'What do you think about, Flake?' he proposed.

The owl hopped around and hooted in pure, distilled excitement. She even took to the air and flew around Tyrus in circles as he stood up—taking the snowflakes with her in a spiralling motion. Was this what happiness felt like?

She landed on a rock next to Tyrus. 'I only now realised, I never introduced myself, did I?' he asked.

Indeed, he never did.

'Well, here it goes. Hello there, Flake. My name is Tyrus. Nice to meet you.'

Flake put one of her talons on the hand Tyrus had extended to her and a strange but tingling feeling erupted from the touch. She moved her head forward and Tyrus inexplicably knew she wanted him to follow her lead. His forehead touched her crown and they both closed their eyes as a deep connection buried its way through Tyrus' veins. Unpleasant and pleasant at the same time. Unnerving and calming, but undoubtedly exciting. At first, he panicked, thinking he had somehow missed something dangerous when he read about owls. However, what he felt, didn't feel remotely like danger. It was unlike anything he had ever experienced. What was happening to him? And why did it feel unmistakably thrilling? But then, the feeling stopped. Ebbed away like the seas would have before the cold.

He opened his eyes but he felt different; he *was* different, only he couldn't tell in what way. Almost instinctively, he hunched over a frozen puddle to look at his reflection. As soon as he saw it, he jumped back. It couldn't be. He slowly approached his reflection again.

This time he didn't jump. What he saw, was still there. No sign of pupils or irises in those wonderful eyes of his. Instead, flames danced inside the windows to his soul—blue flames, purple flames, *magic flames*. It was when he looked at Flake, and she opened her eyes that he realised what had happened. Identical flames danced in hers, almost synchronised with his. The impossible had happened between the two of them. In the shock of it all, Tyrus couldn't think a single thought. He sat there, looking at that enchanting owl with wide burning eyes, his mouth open.

Flake had never answered his question. Obviously, she couldn't talk so she didn't answer most of his questions, but there was only one question he asked her that was on his mind.

Are you bound?

And now? Now, the answer was yes.

CHAPTER 4

BOUND

For years and years, Tyrus had read, studied and relished in fantastical and impossible stories. He read about magic existing alongside man and elven kind in a faraway past. Occasionally, he'd get lost in his fantasies, in his hope. But ultimately, he knew it would never be real again, not anymore. He became convinced his world was devoid of magic, like it was devoid of seasons or warmth. He wanted to believe magic could return to his world one day, but he couldn't. All the signs spoke of the opposite to be true.

Until Flake.

That cute magical bird flew into his lighthouse and she fanned the flame of hope inside his heart. While meeting a living owl was as extraordinary as the words in those books of his, never in his wildest dreams did he expect her to actually come with the ancient powers of magic. Magic that some believed never existed, that *he* believed to be extinguished.

But then, in that moment with Flake near the rocks, he became Owlbound. A bonding which hadn't occurred in over a century. Because, magic was dead.

Until now.

His wildest fantasies became a reality and Tyrus felt like he burned with the energy of a thousand behemoth horses. A breeze caressed the rocks around them. It made waves in Flake's feathers and slid off of Tyrus' light brown skin.

'Flake?' said Tyrus, his voice trembling. 'Did we bond? Not like in friendship or anything, I mean also in friendship of course, but I mean, like, in the magic sense. Like, did we bond? Are we bound? Magically, I mean—'

He kept blabbering on and on, and he couldn't stop himself. He tried. He genuinely did, but he didn't stop until Flake slightly bowed her head, essentially answering yes to his question. Tyrus' heart screamed, his gut shrieked and his brain blared. His entire body sang with excitement and it sang loudly, but then his heart rate spiked. Sweat attacked his skin all over. His emotions had taken flight, scattering into all directions like a panicking murder of crows.

'I can't believe it! Flake, this is impossible! You're impossible, this is impossible, *we* are impossible!' he shouted until his lungs forced him to take more uneasy breaths.

He paced around in the snow between the rocks,

hands trembling, but not because of the cold.

'Mom and Dad would know what to do...I don't. I haven't got a clue! What the fudge am I supposed to do?!'

Flake's eyes followed him until he sank down into the snow, leaning against a rock. Whenever he got like this when he was younger, his dad would sit next to him. He'd hold him tight and breathe with him in a calm and composed manner, maintaining a regular rhythm. Tyrus' breath would fall in line and the panic would dissolve like his visible breath in the outside air. He imagined his father sitting by his side; they breathed together. Flake hopped down and sat next to him, placing her head on his lap. Tyrus' breaths grew deeper, his heartbeat slowed, the sweating stopped, and the tremble in his hands became winter's fault again. He hugged Flake and together, they returned home.

Back at the lighthouse, Tyrus shed his thick maroon cloak like a snake shed its skin, but faster. He sat down on a stool to take off his hefty chestnut boots and then reapplied his shoulder pad, he already felt naked without it.

'Come on, Flake,' he said and he shot upstairs.

Flake buried her talons into the shoulder pad as deep as she could to make sure Tyrus' sudden climb up the spiralling staircase didn't knock her off. She jumped off, onto his desk, when they arrived in her human's room. She kept her eyes on Tyrus as he started searching for something, twisting her head all the way upside down when he ducked under his bed. It looked like her head was put on all wrong.

'What if this is it, little lady?' he asked as they he crawled from under his bed empty-handed. 'What if we're the spark that brings magic back?'

Blank eyes looked into amber as Flake twisted her head back into its usual position.

'We need to learn!' exclaimed Tyrus with his arms spread wide, gesturing to the knowledge-infused papers and books around them.

He knew he had a book about using magic as an Owlbound person, or at least the basics of it. The question was: where was it hiding? Never before had his hands touched as many books in quick succession as in that moment. Flake watched, observing him search like he performed in an over-exaggerated play. Tyrus' utterly chaotic search methods sparkled in her eyes.

'Flake, I'm looking for a book with a dark purple spine and silver-looking details. Give me a hoot when you see it,' explained Tyrus. 'Don't just sit there? Look around!'

She flew atop a stack of books and merely fifteen seconds later, after dropping her focus from Tyrus, she hooted.

'You didn't. You did not find it that fast…Did you?'

Hoot.

Unconvinced as ever, he asked, 'Where?'

Hoot. Hoot.

'Flake, I don't speak owl.' He sighed with a smile. 'You're gonna have to point me in a direction.'

She flew on top of a different pile of books and looked down. There it sat. Mushed between two less colourful books, one as grey as most of the hairs in Ced's beard and the other as earthy as the dirt concealed by snow.

'Good girl!' he said, and he gave her the best head rubs she'd ever had. Her crown stayed with his hand for as long as possible when it lifted.

He took the book from between the pile, threw it down on his desk and the loud thump launched Flake into the air for a moment. He blew off the dust and opened it. The book held notes from an elven Owlbound Learnling, who trained under a human Paragon. Paragons were masters in the art of magic, while Learnlings were essentially students. It was hard for Tyrus to imagine elves and humans getting along. That time was long lost. Up until now, he had never meticulously read through it, because there was no point, no magic. In the past, he had browsed through it a handful of times, he had even learned two or three runic symbols from it, but he had never studied it closely. Never did he think he'd ever be going through it with the intent of using the knowledge in practice.

Flake watched Tyrus' eyeballs run from corner to corner and back, over and over again as he read. The notes of the Learnling described magic as dancing fire—colourful fire with shades and tints unique to every

Owlbound individual. The mages of ages lost wielded fire in the palms of their hands without getting burned. A fire that didn't necessarily seek to destroy, unless the caster intended it to. A flame that could also heal, make plants grow, and let objects float. The magical flames had the ability to provide protection and warmth as well as the potential to be used as a vicious and dangerous weapon. A smile filled the width of Tyrus' face, followed by a short-burst screech of excitement. He caught both himself and Flake off guard with it. Flake ruffled her feathers and Tyrus chuckled it away, before diving back in.

In terms of where the magic originally came from, the novice's Paragon couldn't give a clear answer. Theories differed from book to book, human to human and elf to elf. Plenty of scholars believed it came from a God and that the owls acted as conduits to wield divine power. Many other mages of ages past claimed the *magic itself* was the God. Tyrus didn't know what to believe, nor did he care, if he were honest. The magic was real, that's what mattered.

After hours upon hours of reading, Tyrus' weary eyes arrived at the first practical exercise. A simple instruction to see if a Learnling was capable of summoning the magic in their veins.

Above the description of the exercise, the Learnling had written down a warning that read, *'PERFORMING SPELLS WITHOUT THE GUIDANCE AND PRESENCE*

Flake could see it in his amber eyes; Tyrus had to try it. 'Surely, they're overreacting, right?' he questioned.

He could have sworn he got a bombastic side-eye from his magical companion.

'Don't worry, we'll start small,' he assured her, and she flew up to and landed on his shoulder pad.

The curly-haired boy then took the book with him downstairs; every step on the oak wooden staircase sounded like an odd frog's dying scream. Since the lighthouse had become rather chilly, it was the perfect time to test the first spell in the notes. He sat down next to the fireplace. It yearned for a spark and Tyrus was determined to give it exactly that. The exercise neatly described how to summon his magic, hold it in his hand, and guide it to give the fireplace the spark it craved.

'Okay, come on, you can do this, Tyrus,' he said under his breath.

He followed the instructions to the letter. It even had drawings to accompany the written words. He held his hand out with the inside of his palm facing the ceiling. He then moved his index, middle, ring, and pinkie fingers to the base of his palm while he kept his thumb extended outward. After that, he slid those four fingers as far back as he could before letting them fold open until they were almost stretched. He repeated that motion, precisely like the book told him to. The time for Tyrus to bring out the magic arrived. He needed to will a flame into existence, in the palm of his hand. This wasn't magic spoken by words, never, or cast by runes, not yet; it was supposed to be cast with intent and emotion, those were the sparks that would light the flames of his spells.

The instructions told him to close his eyes and to focus while he kept doing that same hand movement, over and over again. At the same time, he had to listen for the magic. Was he supposed to hear something? If so, what would it sound like?

'Come on! What am I doing wrong?' shouted Tyrus after a while, his leg restless.

When nothing happened, over and over—nothing at all—he screamed it out and flung an entire stack of dishes to the floor. Most remained whole, some shattered like the window upstairs had. Flake cleared out and flew on top of the tall kitchen cabinets, shaken up and trembling lightly.

Tyrus brought a hand to his forehead and breathed.

'Crap,' he said.

He looked up at Flake and inched closer to the cabinet.

'I'm sorry, Flake, I didn't mean to scare you. I don't know why I get like this.'

He put his back against the cabinet's side and slid down until he sat on the floor. A deep sigh followed.

'The smallest things get to me sometimes, and I don't know how to stop myself from exploding,' he explained.

Flake peeked down at him over the edge and he looked up at her. Tyrus' jaw was tense, his lips scowling, and he quickly averted his gaze when the bird made eye-contact.

'I'm terribly sorry,' he repeated.

She jumped down, landing on the shoulder pad and let her head hug Tyrus' curls.

Together, after a bit of rest, they got up and they tried again. This time, he stayed calm. He gave it his all, even though he didn't know what he was listening for, until he did.

There, it hummed. As clear as the glass in the lighthouse windows.

He could *feel* it, slumbering, waiting between the blood in his veins.

Hum. Hum.

Then it stopped, but the silence didn't last because then, it sang and as Tyrus concentrated on bringing that magic out, carrying it through his veins, guiding it to the palm of his hand, Flake's eyes lit up and Tyrus experienced a familiar feeling. The same identical thing he felt right after his bonding—pure magic. He opened his eyes and like his owl's, they held flames, slowly swaying in the windows to his soul. Tyrus was still performing the same set of motions with his right hand until a sudden flame hovered above the surface of his palm.

'Holy talons! Flake! I'm doing it!' he shouted, but the excitement of it all got away from him.

The flame in the palm of his hand grew and it kept growing. He tried to make it smaller but the magic didn't listen. With his concentration in the wind, the flame set the wooden ceiling ablaze. Panic spread from Tyrus' heart to his lungs and shoulders and arms and legs until he froze entirely. Ironically, not by the everlasting cold outside but by the flames of his magic. Flake snapped him out of it by means of a violent peck to the temple and the instructions of the book ran through his mind.

Intent.

There wasn't anything in the world right now that he wanted more than for his lighthouse to not burn to ashes.

'Stop!' he screamed as loud as he could.

But all his words carried was anger. Words devoid of intent. The fire grew more violent.

'No!' he screamed even louder but the flames expanded further.

Between the angry trees of his enraged forest, he sensed Flake. She felt the rage too, the only difference was that she had enslaved it. He could sense it and so, he listened to their bond. He calmed down his breathing and as he adopted Flake's control and closed the palm of his hand, he reigned in the magic. The flames that sought to burn his home to a crisp extinguished and Tyrus took the deepest breath he'd ever taken.

'Well…that was…close,' he said while exhaling.

Flake uttered a relieved hoot, but she sensed Tyrus'

blood still simmering. A slither of anger remained, anger aimed not at her, nor at the defeated flames.

'Okay, so lesson learned,' said Tyrus finally. 'Next time, let's take our practice outside, shall we?'

Flake gave him a single nod.

'It's settled then. Until we have our magic under control, the lighthouse is a spell-free zone.' And his heart relaxed.

Days passed after Tyrus cast the first (failed) spell. He and Flake settled into a new day to day routine. After getting up while the sun had already climbed the sky for a couple of hours, Tyrus would open up a window for Flake to fly through. She would hunt for her breakfast as her amber-eyed boy sat at the breakfast table, devouring his own. When Flake returned, the time arrived for practice. In between failing and failing (and the occasional hot-headed outburst), they'd have a quick lunch, and afterward, they'd enjoy dinner together before going to bed with magical lecture. When a couple of days of practice had evolved into an entire week, their magic had improved significantly enough to return to the lighthouse and finish the original spell.

Tyrus took to his knees next to the fireplace, head held high. His right hand began performing a familiar motion and thanks to practice, a flame of magic floated above his palm after the very first try. Calm and composed, he kept the reins on his magic. He had tamed it, befriended it. It listened to him and he listened to it.

Intent.

Intent was the main ingredient for every single spell in existence and while Tyrus knew that by now, he wanted to put it to the test anyways. With his left hand, he grabbed a piece of paper, one that slept on the worn wooden table in the kitchen. He told the flame not to burn it before moving the paper slowly into it. The paper didn't burn, not until Tyrus willed it, *intended* it. Armed with that same intent, he imagined a spark from the flames flying into the fireplace, finally giving it what it longed for. The magic listened. A single blue and purple spark rose up from the flame in his hand and shot to the fireplace, sparking a fire that wound up lasting longer than any regular fire would have.

Both Tyrus and Flake were pleased with themselves, but supplies began running low. With all the practice he did and with getting to know his new feathered friend, Tyrus hadn't made any time for hunting or scavenging. He was supposed to meet up with Cedric today, too. Luckily, the pouch of crowns on the kitchen table held enough to buy him and Flake food to cover the next week at least. Not wanting to show up at Ced's carriage empty-handed, Tyrus decided to hunt on the way there.

He debated himself over whether or not to take Flake with him, because people would be out to get her. But ultimately, he knew he could trust Cedric and in all those years, he hadn't ever seen anyone other than him in the woods.

And so, the owl and her boy made their way to the edge of the forest to meet Cedric. The falling snow acted mercilessly and cut into Tyrus' cheeks while the cold further chapped his lips. Flake, usually happy about snowflakes, made herself as small as possible to shield herself from the harsh weather. Besides the snowfall, it seemed as though the wind had it out for them, too. Strong gusts tested the rather limited waters of Tyrus' balance. But despite winter scheming against them, Tyrus still managed to hunt and successfully kill two rabbits and Flake had snatched up a squirrel from a towering pine tree. It had to be enough.

Tyrus swung the rabbits and the squirrel over his back and continued through the woods as the snowfall calmed down. When the bound duo approached the place where they'd meet Cedric, weird noises erupted from the distance. It sounded like a mild struggle at first but then they heard Cedric scream. They picked up their pace and Tyrus even let Flake take to the sky to see if she could spot anything. But then, a bunch of howls reached Tyrus from the direction of the carriage. Recognising those howls brought him to a full stop.

Bleakwolves, an entire pack's worth of the bastards by the sound of it. Bleakwolves were dangerous, and not only because of their sharp teeth; they also loved to bite and when they did, they secreted a poison that incapacitated their prey and if not treated in time with an antidote, that prey would die. That was about all Tyrus knew. That was all he needed to know to stay clear of them, or run the opposite direction whenever he encountered them.

He whistled to draw Flake back to him and she immediately dove into the needles of the forest and landed on his shoulder. His first instinct was to turn around, head for home. But then, an even more agonising scream reached his ears and now, Tyrus found himself running. Only not in the direction he expected to; he ran toward the danger. Toward screams, howls, and growls.

When they arrived at the carriage, Trudy had broken loose, fighting off four of the bleakwolves at the same time while Cedric tried to keep two of them away from him with a lit torch. Their fur blended in with the snowy environment except for the fact that every single strand of hair appeared to sparkle at the ends. The leader of the pack, who circled the trader, turned around. It growled and drooled as it undeniably craved the meat on Tyrus' bones.

'Lad, run! Get away from here!' shouted Cedric. His glasses had fallen into the snow, but he wouldn't have seen Flake from that distance anyway.

'Not a chance, Ced!' Tyrus called out, his voice shaky.

'Have you lost your bearings, laddie?! Get out of here, now!' shouted Cedric.

Tyrus ignored Ced's request and held his ground as he stood face to face with a bloodthirsty wolf. Dark red eyes observed every shiver in Tyrus' body and blood stained its teeth as drool mixed with red slithered from its jaws. In a single smooth familiar motion, blue and purple fire emerged from the palms of both his hands. Tyrus' eyes lit up like Flake's. Cedric only saw blurs, blurs that didn't make sense.

Intent.

Tyrus let his flames form a ball and attacked the wolf in front of him head on. It wasn't a critical hit but the wolf had no idea what happened as its fur burned. The fireball attracted the attention of the others and Trudy saw an opening. She bashed the wolf closest to her into the carriage as hard as she possibly could. It did not get up again.

Cedric's torch burnt up and for the bleakwolf closest to him, that didn't go unnoticed. It lunged at him while another one sprinted at Tyrus. In one swirling swift motion, Tyrus cast a snake of fire. It shot through the wolf that attacked Ced and circled back with the intention of stopping the wolf that lunged at Tyrus, but the young mage lost control and the fires of his magic evaporated. The bleakwolf that lunged at him made Tyrus trip and fall with his back in the snow. Flake hooted from the air but didn't know what to do to help. The rabid creature drooled on top of him now, keeping Tyrus down with its strong paws. It opened its mouth, ready to bite his head off when Trudy saved the day and rammed the beast into a sharp tree branch.

Tyrus turned his head to the massive horse. 'Good job, Trudy, good girl!' he shouted with wide eyes.

The remaining wolves of the pack had seen enough, they growled and ran. The one Tyrus had attacked head on—the leader he undoubtedly scarred for life above its snout and in between its eyes—looked right back at him before fleeing into the woods. Right as the rabid creatures faded between the pine trees, Cedric fell to his knees.

'Tyrus?' he mumbled.

Blood seeped out of his arm like water from a cracked pitcher.

'Ced!' shouted Tyrus as he got up and ran toward him.

'Bandages…inside…the cupboard next to the geluroots,' he uttered.

Tyrus used his hands to try and stop the bleeding while Flake flew inside to grab the bandages. As she came back out with the bandages in her beak, Trudy came closer and carried herself in a sombre manner.

'He'll be okay,' said Tyrus as he wrapped the wound on Cedric's arm tight in order to stall the bleeding. 'He has to be okay.'

Cedric wanted to tell Tyrus something about it being all right for the boy to leave him behind, to save himself rather than an old man. He couldn't. The paralysing toxin had already set in.

'Ced, no, stay with me. Stay with us, Ced!' shouted Tyrus.

With no antidote stashed in the carriage, his friend needed a healer. A bloody damn gifted one at that, but only one place was close enough to possibly find a person who fit those shoes. Tyrus' parents wouldn't have liked it, and neither did he, but there was simply no other choice. Their son had to go back to the place him and his family had been banished from all those years ago.

To save his friend, Tyrus had to go back to Featherburn.

CHAPTER 5

HOURGLASS

The metallic scent of blood made camp in Tyrus' nose while snow gently tumbled from the sky. He lifted Cedric into the carriage with Trudy's help. He couldn't have done it alone. Ced was a lot of things, but light wasn't one of them. Inside the carriage, Tyrus made the wounded trader a bed out of blankets and other pieces of cloth. Things he could find in cupboards to secure his friend as best he could, because if Trudy's mood told him anything, it would be a bumpy journey to Featherburn.

'Ced, if you can hear me,' he said. 'you're gonna be fine, I promise.'

He exited the carriage and Flake hopped back onto his shoulder after keeping watch to make sure there were no more surprises. He then approached restless Trudy, took her by the reins and attached her to the carriage again, before sitting in Cedric's spot on the bench at the front.

Taking the trader's place like that? It sent a shiver through his limbs. On top of that, heart palpitations beat away in his chest too; it had been a long time since he'd steered a horse. And never one as giant as Trudy.

A little window sat behind him, admiring the view of the back of his head and woolly hat. Through it, Tyrus could keep an eye on Cedric, but every time he would take a peek inside, he would wish he hadn't.

Tyrus turned toward Flake, perched firmly on his shoulder pad. It took one glance for the bird to understand as he gestured with his eyes to the sky. She jumped off and spread her majestic wings to become his lookout. And while his bird ascended the skies, Tyrus gripped Trudy's reins tight.

The journey to Featherburn ended up being exactly what the boy had in mind, an incredibly bumpy ride. Both the horse and the boy steering her were desperate to get to the settlement in no time at all. It didn't help that whenever Tyrus looked through the window behind him, he imagined the sand in an hourglass running out, faster and faster. Every grain, a valuable increment of time, gone. And with each grain, Cedric grew paler, and the bumps in the road didn't do him any favours. Tyrus wished the roads were smoother, or that he could go slower.

Unfortunately, there wasn't any time for slower.

A hefty two hours into their journey, Flake tried to warn Tyrus about what she had seen from the sky. Her magical boy didn't understand what she was trying to tell him until a deep treacherous ravine ran into view. It was as if the realm itself was an egg and a malevolent creature tried to escape its shell by cracking it wide open. A dozen trees erupted from the sides of the ravine, resembling fingertips. Tyrus thought the scene looked like it got ripped right out of a scary children's book.

The road stopped. The bridge that was supposed to be there, wasn't. Destroyed. Shattered. And by the looks of it, it didn't perish by the hands of humans or elves but rather *something* else. From what she could see, Flake felt certain that whatever it was, had to have been enraged. Tyrus' heart sank, and his mind jumped to the worst-case scenario, Ced's empty hourglass. They'd have to go around the ravine. A detour that would extend their journey by five hours they didn't have; hours Cedric couldn't afford.

Tyrus looked in Flake's direction, his eyes full of uncertainty as they attempted to ferociously hold the tears at bay. 'I have to try, right Flake?' he asked her. 'There's no other way.'

Flake nodded.

Magic offered a million solutions to his problem, but Tyrus could only think of two. He could cast a levitation spell to lift Trudy and the carriage over the ravine, which was complicated to say the least. He'd have to provide the strength to carry, the focus to move, the restraint not to burn and the endurance to see the spell through to the end. Furthermore, he lacked the aptitude to do the spell while being on the carriage himself, which meant he'd have to levitate himself across individually after.

The second option he could think of was to cast a solid bridge of magical fire to cross the ravine. He didn't know if anyone had cast a bridge of fire before, but then again, if intent was the foundation of his fiery magic, then as long as the flames listened, it had to be possible. Not to mention simpler in execution than his first idea.

After a little consideration, bird and boy agreed to go with the bridge. When they approached their towering behemoth horse, she sensed the pair of them had a trick up their thick, warm sleeves. She restlessly and repeatedly tapped the ground (and snow) beneath her hoofs. They couldn't blame her, could they? They were about to make her walk across a ravine on a fire-bridge.

'Hey, Trudy, shhhhhh. I know this is scary but I've got this, okay? I won't let us fall. I promise,' said Tyrus with all the conviction he could muster.

Did he believe his own words? Perhaps not. If he were honest, not by a long shot. He figured Trudy would have better odds at surviving if she stayed as composed as possible while she traipsed across his—hopefully gentle—bridge to be.

Nervous tingles travelled through his veins and they came together to form a sting at the top of his stomach as he steered Trudy closer to the ravine until her hoofs touched the edge of the splintered wood and cracked stone. The horse held her head high, resisting the urge to look into the abyss below, because she knew that if she looked, she'd lose all the bravery in the world.

Tyrus didn't *feel* ready but he had to be, for Ced. He procrastinated for a few grains of sand longer before his right hand performed a motion it had gotten used to by now. In the fraction of a second, his fingers slid from the bottom of his palm, away to the top, and a flame mimicked the one that sprung to life in his and his bird's eyes. He commanded the flame, which multiplied, to move toward the no longer existing bridge. His thoughts sang to the magic and it listened. The intent Tyrus gave to his flames steered them. Blue and purple flames danced a bridge across the ravine, but they weren't ready to be walked upon yet.

Solidify. The word repeated itself inside his head until it became music, the result of which would never be heard, only seen. Fuel for the fire, for the bridge. There existed only one way to know for sure that the bridge was solid now. The young caster stepped forward, gently placing his right foot on the burning bridge. It didn't hurt him, and instead of falling through the flames, he could count on the support his feet needed to stand. He remained cautious, though. Whenever his mind started to wander, the flames flickered. Plus, the weight of one boy meant nothing compared to Trudy's and the carriage.

Tyrus jumped on the bench of the carriage, grabbing Trudy's reins tight. With no time to lose, he gave the giant horse the order to step onto the magic bridge he created. Trudy neighed and huffed, but she demonstrated braveness like no other. They crossed. Nice and slow.

The boy with the reins tensed up, every muscle in his body contracted more and more with every step Trudy took. Sweat slid down his face until it froze in place and Flake struggled right there with him. They poured every ounce of energy they had into the spell, because the alternative was now death for all of them.

About halfway across, Tyrus' foot cramped under the duress and the bridge started to gradually dissolve behind them. Flake flung out a worried hoot.

'Okay, Trudy, we're gonna have to speed things up a little!' shouted Tyrus before biting down his sleeve to ward off the pain.

Against all of her instincts, she sped up as the fiery bridge started losing crumbs, like the ones a piece of frostbread would lose each time you cut off a slice. Then, the finish line jumped into view and Tyrus imagined all the moments Ced was there for him. All the times the trader helped him. And as he imagined those pockets of time, those incredibly meaningful grains of sand in the hourglasses of their lives, he let the love and friendship wash over him. It gifted him the final surge of energy and focus he needed to cross that ravine. For a little while longer, the bridge of flames stopped crumbling.

With the carriage now safe on the other side, the bridge disappeared into nothingness as if the spell was never cast. Tyrus could finally exhale fully as the fire in his eyes died out. He felt like taking a nap that would end up becoming a full night's sleep, but he couldn't.

'Trudy! Well done, girl,' said Tyrus with the energy of a dying candle. 'You too, Flake! But we can't stop now, we have a life to save.'

Flake flew across the brisk sky as Trudy's hoofs and the heavy wheels of the carriage trampled countless snowflakes. Tyrus had never ventured this far out from his lighthouse, not since he started living there and certainly not alone. That said, the road possessed a form of familiarity, like seeing someone wearing a coat you used to own. They entered another forest, one almost indistinguishable from the one near his lighthouse. The smell of the pines made its way through his nose but there was another layer there, slumbering within that scent. A layer of recognizable undertones. He was certain of it; he'd been on this road before as a little boy when his family fled from Featherburn. A hint of coal hitchhiked with the air. His nose didn't deceive him either because a few miles later, they crossed paths with an abandoned coal mine.

For a moment, Tyrus brought the carriage to a halt. It was as if something inside called for him. He even felt it in his chest, a strange trembling, a vibration. It wanted him to follow it and for a second, he considered doing so but the stern growl Trudy let out reminded him of the peril Cedric was in. His focus quickly shifted back to the road ahead as Flake came down for a quick rest on the shoulder after flying above the carriage for a while.

'Did you feel that as well, Flake?' Tyrus asked her but, as per usual, she drowned into those amber eyes of his. 'Do you think it was magical?'

Flake managed to calm Tyrus' mind down after nudging her head against his.

'Thank you, Flake. I do wish you could talk sometimes,' said Tyrus. He smirked a little as he said it but the smirk melted away quickly when his mind crawled back to the predicament of his friend.

Another hour passed, and as the trees made way for a stretched out snowy landscape, Tyrus saw the wooden walls and cabins of Featherburn etched between the hills, surrounded by a frozen river. Help was in sight, and his face birthed a slight smile.

During the last stretch, as the sun descended and the wind picked up, Tyrus' feet felt like ice cubes. He could barely move his toes and the frost nipped earlobes that peaked out from under his hat hurt. But in the end, his determination overthrew the forces of nature and the carriage arrived at the gates of Featherburn. The town that banished his family.

The walls made from pine logs stared down at them, logs that sat next to each other, jammed upright into the frozen ground. The tops of the wooden logs, sharpened like the tips of pencils, meant to deter enemies, animals or monsters from climbing over. Behind those wooden pillars, cobblestone reinforced the wall. Guards walked on top, patrolling with helmets peeking out above the pointy wooden logs. A frozen river surrounded the wall of Featherburn with a small sturdy stone brick bridge connecting the entrance to the outside world. On either side of the solid wooden gate stood two watchtowers, each one accompanied by a guard and mounted to the wooden railings, enlarged crossbow-looking weapons. Which they aimed at Cedric's carriage as soon as it arrived there. Meanwhile, Flake had already hidden herself away inside the carriage; if the guards saw her, Tyrus and Ced could kiss their help goodbye.

'Halt! Don't come any closer!' yelled a guard.

'State your business!' shouted another.

Before Tyrus could say anything useful, the first guard interrupted him. 'Wait a second. I know that carriage. You're not Cedric! What did you do to him, boy?!' she demanded, the giant crossbows ready to fire.

Tyrus pried his hands loose from the reins and raised them in the air. 'He's the reason I'm here! I found him in the forest, wounded by bleakwolves. He's badly hurt, and he needs help!'

The guards glanced at each other.

'Stay put,' said the guard that originally pulled him to a stop. 'Officers are coming down to verify your story. Do not make a move or you shall have a ginormous arrow where your face used to be.'

The gates opened and like the woman on the watchtower had told him, officers came charging toward the carriage. Three of them to be exact.

'Get off and step away from the carriage, slowly,' commanded the first and Tyrus did as he was told. Besides, he couldn't go faster if he tried. His frozen joints wouldn't let him. He moved like an old man at the end of his life.

Trudy nickered at the approaching guards but Tyrus mouthed to her that everything would be fine. An officer approached the door of the carriage, opened it and climbed the short ladder to take a peek inside.

'The kid's story checks out,' they called out with only their head emerging from the opening of the door. 'Cedric does not look good.'

'Can we please enter Featherburn and see a healer?' asked Tyrus abruptly.

'Shut it, boy,' said the officer, holding a bow to his head.

Tyrus raised his hands even higher and closed his

eyes tight while he felt his heart quicken in his throat. He imagined his father standing with him, a hand on his shoulder, in an attempt to manage his breathing.

'Enough!' yelled a guard from the tower. 'You're scaring the kid. Let them through and escort them to a healer at once!'

Tyrus sighed in relief, got back on the bench of the carriage and followed an officer into the settlement. As he moved through those gates, he couldn't help but feel flakes of anger landing on his mind. If the people of Featherburn didn't banish him and his parents all those years ago, maybe the cold would have never taken them. He'd never know what that would have been like.

Trudy pulled the carriage through the rather silent town. Most people were in their cabins at this hour and the ones he did see didn't seem particularly happy. Then again, there wasn't a whole lot in this frozen world to be happy about to begin with. They stopped near a cabin slightly bigger than most. Golden light shimmered through the vague heavily frozen windows. Tyrus couldn't fully make out what exactly stood on the windowsills inside but he felt confident they were herbs. The officer who escorted them knocked on the rather flimsy door. It groaned as it opened.

'Darren, good evening, can I help you?' said the person in the doorway, their hair short and as white and pale as the snow below their feet. Freckles spilled over their slim upturned nose and their cobalt eyes looked Tyrus up and down.

'Xylia, hello, it's not for me. This boy,' he said, pointing at Tyrus, 'he arrived this evening with Cedric's carriage. The trader is badly hurt.'

The healer was greeted by Tyrus' conflicted gaze. On the one hand his eyes had kind of narrowed, because his parents always told him not to trust anyone other than himself and Cedric. On the other hand, the narrowed eyes gave way to genuine concern, the person before him was likely his only shot at saving Ced. Two sides of him were at war. The Tyrus who couldn't trust anyone and the one that would do anything to save his friend.

'Xylia will help the trader,' assured Officer Darren.

'How do I know we can trust you, or *her* for that matter?' spat Tyrus before he full well realised it. The moment he said it, he wished to take it back. What if they didn't want to help anymore?

'Sweety, you can. But even if you couldn't, do you have a choice?' asked Xylia. 'Besides, not *her…them*,' they corrected.

Tyrus tilted his head slightly as he thought about it. 'Oh…I'm sorry. *Them*.'

'It's okay,' said the healer. 'Also, I understand. I have yet to come across a person in Wingspan who doesn't have trust issues. Rest assured though, Cedric and I go way back. He's a friend. If the stubborn bastard can be helped, I'm the one that can.'

Xylia's calming presence and convincing words relaxed Tyrus' shoulders.

'All right, let's see what that old trader got himself into this time, shall we?' said Xylia as they climbed the ladder of the carriage.

Tyrus, heart racing, followed them inside where seasoned Ced didn't move with the exception of shallow breaths. The healer immediately instructed Darren to help them carry Cedric to his own room.

'Kiddo, I'm going to be straight with you. It doesn't look good, but I'll do my best,' said Xylia. 'Bleakwolves, yeah?' they added before climbing down the ladder again.

Tyrus nodded and before he knew it, he was alone in the carriage accompanied by tears. Flake, who hid behind the baskets in the back, took the opportunity to check in on her friend. She latched onto his shoulder and rubbed her head against Tyrus'.

'Hey, Flake,' he whispered. 'Are you okay with staying here for the night while I stay with Cedric?'

Her gaze sank to the floor.

'I know, it's no fun, but there's no other way. We can't risk exposing ourselves,' explained Tyrus.

He gave her a hug which she cherished as if tomorrow didn't exist. And with that, Tyrus followed Xylia and Darren inside as the night fell over Featherburn. The healer administered the trader an antidote to the bleakwolf poison and tried everything in their power to get the fever down and clear the infection in his wounds. Tyrus slept by Cedric's side that night in a chair, hoping that tomorrow, he'd wake up to one of his friend's famous snarky remarks. Hoping to see the hourglass replenished.

CHAPTER 6

CLEVER CHAP

His curls caught the day's first sunshine as Tyrus hoisted his head from the side of Cedric's bed. The trader had regained a moderate amount of colour in his face. Still fast asleep and fighting the poison with every ounce of stubbornness he had. Tyrus didn't want to interrupt his much-needed rest and decided to head downstairs quietly. He figured he'd check up on the carriage, Trudy, and Flake.

The infirmary was rather quiet. Most patients were still asleep, and those who weren't passed the time with a good book. Tyrus tried finding Xylia, but they were nowhere to be seen. He'd have to ask about Ced's condition later.

Tyrus headed for the front door, making his way through the herb-forward corridors. In half of the hallways, it felt like walking through a sort of greenhouse, only with a lot less glass. One groaning door later, his cheeks met the sharp outside air, stinging with the blades of never-ending winter. No matter how unpleasant the shiver that shot through him, his heart warmed at the joyful neigh of Trudy.

'Hey girl!' said Tyrus with a big smile. 'I'm happy to see you too, you know…thanks to us, I think he might be okay.'

He scratched her chin and the giant horse started acting rather giddy, tippy tapping the ground beneath her hoofs. It wasn't long before they were interrupted.

Xylia's voice pierced the walls and door of the infirmary. 'I swear to talons! If you get into trouble again, young lady…I can't protect you forever, our sway in this settlement only goes so far!'

Who were they talking to?

'To hell with Yike and this orb, focus on you. Let it go, just this once, I'm begging you!' they added. 'Hey! Don't you dare walk away from me!'

The front door of the infirmary swung open as someone ran out, on a direct collision course with a boy whose curiosity got the better of him. Before Tyrus knew it, he was on the ground with his back in the snow. When he opened his eyes after closing them for the fall, they locked with those of a girl. For a moment, amber fell into cobalt and cobalt fell into amber. She quickly rolled off of him and got to her feet.

'Next time, don't get in my way,' she said, extending a hand.

Tyrus froze like the water around the Featherburn walls had. With lack of a better word, he felt *enchanted* by her. Was she magic too?

The descending snowflakes were almost jealous of her ghost-white strands of hair, which complemented her somewhat pale, yet lively skin. She wore freckles on her face too, scattered across the top of her cheeks and over the bridge of her nose like constellations. Her nose, a little bigger than most, was pierced by a stainless-steel ring in one of her nostrils.

'Hello? Did you bite your tongue off when you fell?' she asked him.

'Right, sorry,' answered Tyrus with a nervous laugh. He took her hand and pulled himself up. 'Thanks. I didn't mean to get in the way or anything.'

Trudy neighed at the nervous cracks in Tyrus' voice.

'Well, you live and you learn, chap,' she said. 'Cool horse by the way.'

'Trudy!' shouted Tyrus.

The girl frowned. 'What?'

'Trudy…name…not my name, it's her name…the horse's…Anyway, I'm Tyrus. I'm guessing Xylia is your—'

'Yeah, they're part one of the parenting package deal.'

It was the colour of her eyes that gave it away, the freckles too. That and the yelling about not getting into trouble, of course.

'I don't mean to pry—' began Tyrus.

'Then don't, great! I need more of that energy in my life. Great talk, Tyrus.' She gave him a pat on the shoulder as she walked away.

'Hold up, you never told me your name!' he called behind her.

'You seem like a clever chap; you'll figure it out!' And she vanished between the cabins across the road.

A tickle swirled inside his stomach as he was left there. Getting hit by the mystery of that enchanting girl almost made Tyrus forget why he was outside to begin with. He shifted his focus to the carriage and climbed inside.

'Flake? You there?' he whispered.

He didn't have to wait long before the young owl lunged at him from behind boxes stacked upon boxes. She immediately landed on his shoulder and started snuggling with her best friend.

'Hey there, little lady. I missed you too,' said Tyrus. 'Shall we get some practice in?'

Flake looked back with a slight drizzle of concern in her eyes.

'Only the basics, nothing fancy. We're not burning down the carriage, okay? You know…Every once in a while, we need to get in touch with the fundamentals. Or at least, that's what the book said.'

The hour flew by quickly as Tyrus and Flake practiced magic inside the familiar and comforting interior of Ced's carriage. Together, they made flames dance on the boy's palms and controlled floating embers on their path through the air.

Around noon, Tyrus decided to head back inside the infirmary and tucked Flake back behind the boxes and baskets, promising her he'd be back in the afternoon to spend more time with her. He felt a little frustrated he had to leave her behind again, but in the end, it was for her own good. The last thing he wanted was to find out what the town would do if they found out about them. He'd read too many books on the persecution of Owlbound people to risk it.

'Ah, there you are!' said Xylia when Tyrus walked into Cedric's room. 'We haven't properly introduced ourselves to one another, have we?'

'I guess with everything going on, we haven't,' said Tyrus.

'Well, I'm Xylia and as you already know, I'm the best healer Featherburn has. I've known this old geezer for a while now,' they said, pointing at the sick trader. 'I suppose it was only a matter of time before I'd have to treat him for something serious.'

Tyrus hesitated introducing himself properly, because his parents had taught him not to trust anyone, especially no one in Featherburn. However, completely starstruck, he failed to think about that when he met Xylia's daughter earlier. The ship for using a fake name had already sailed.

Hoping he wouldn't come to regret it, he said, 'I'm

Tyrus, pleased to meet you, and thank you for helping my friend.'

'Well, Tyrus, pleased to meet you too. Have you been in Featherburn before?' the healer asked. 'You look kind of familiar to me but I can't seem to place it.'

'No,' Tyrus lied as his eyes widened and his heart rate spiked.

'Guess you must have one of those faces then,' laughed Xylia.

Tyrus felt his heart beat in his throat. 'Ha-ha…Yeah, I guess.'

'I don't think Cedric will wake up before tomorrow, but no need to worry. Everything points in the right direction. Cedric is lucky to have a young lad like you looking out for him. You saved his life, Tyrus. I mean, I also had a hand in that of course, but you know what I mean.'

'Thank you, truly,' said Tyrus, hands folded together and bowing forward slightly. 'By the way, I think I met your daughter this morning? She's…'

A dozen synonyms for beautiful and enchanting popped inside his head, but he didn't finish the sentence. He wanted to avoid a weird and awkward situation.

Xylia ended up completing the sentence for him instead. 'A pain in my ass?' they asked. 'Yeah…Lyra is extraordinary, but she can also be a thorn in my side from time to time. Always getting herself into trouble, that girl.

Now, don't tell her I said this because she'll bring it up during the smallest of discussions, but...I am proud of her,' they added, as the memory of a smile clung to their face.

Lyra was her name. Perhaps Tyrus did have the makings of a clever chap.

'Don't worry, I won't tell,' said Tyrus. 'It's the least I can do.'

'Good lad,' said Xylia before heading out to help a different patient.

Tyrus stayed with Cedric a little while longer, until the late afternoon. He still had a promise to Flake to keep after all. One staircase, a couple of corridors, and a groaning door later, he was outside again. Snow slowly sank from the sky down on the roofs and roads of Featherburn. Tyrus acted casual and slipped inside the carriage, trying not to attract any unwanted attention. When he closed the door behind him, a laugh froze his hand to the doorhandle. He slowly turned around.

'Ah, Tyrus, we've been waiting on you,' said a familiar white-haired girl with Flake perched on her arm.

'Lyra?! Wha...How?! What are you doing here?!' He started sweating in places he didn't know he could sweat in the first place, while his breathing sped up.

'See? I knew you were clever. I knew you'd figure it out,' said Lyra as she smirked.

'What?'

'My name…You figured it out,' she clarified after rolling her eyes. 'Do keep up.'

Tyrus stood there, unable to say anything.

'When were you going to tell me about your forking owl?' she asked.

'What do you mean? We don't know each other; we met this morning. You didn't even tell me your name!' said Tyrus, his voice cracking a couple times.

'Calm down, Tyrus. I'm messing with you,' reassured Lyra. 'Earlier, after we met, I circled back because you seemed…interesting.' The way she said it made Tyrus wonder if she meant that in a positive or negative way.

'And I may or may not have spied on you through that little window over there,' she explained, pointing to the front of the carriage. 'And then, I may or may not have broken into the carriage by picking the lock. And look at us now, I made a new pal,' she added, petting Flake on the head.

Tyrus's shoulders relaxed a little. 'Her name is Flake,' he said. His words had a nervous edge.

'I know,' said Lyra.

Tyrus' jaw dropped ever so slightly. 'How?'

'Again, messing with you. That's a lovely name for a lovely lady.'

Tyrus came closer and sat down on the ground in cross-legged position. Flake hopped over toward him.

'No offence, but what's the meaning of all this?' asked

Tyrus, his forehead creased like freshly washed laundry. 'Why haven't you reported me already?'

'No offence, but what are you even doing here in the first place? Featherburn is the last place an Owlbound person would want to be,' countered Lyra.

'My friend needed help, and you didn't answer my question. Furthermore, why aren't you the slightest little bit phased?'

'Look, did I spend a couple hours in disbelief? Perhaps even in shock? Yes, for sure. But seeing you two together like that earlier. And then meeting Flake up close, it confirmed something I already knew. Magic isn't evil. People can be, I guess. But magic and that cute little owl? No…One more lie to add to *his* pile…'

Silence conquered the carriage interior as the conversation perished in Tyrus' speechlessness. Until screams carried their way through the wooden walls. Screams and the sound of cracking stones and snapping logs.

Lyra's gaze fell. 'I told him this would happen,' she growled.

Tyrus and Lyra opened the carriage door and stepped outside, down the ladder. They saw terrified town guards running away from the centre square, mixed in with other townspeople who were even more afraid.

'You and Flake need to come with me, now,' said Lyra. Her usual smirk had fallen away and her jaw became so tense it looked even sharper than before.

'What? Absolutely, not,' said Tyrus

'Look. Roughly a week ago, Yike, our bastard of a chief, stole a frost golem orb. He brought it here. I told him it was dangerous, but I had to mind my own business and now a golem is here to destroy us all.'

'This is what you and Xylia argued about earlier, isn't it? Hold on…Aren't frost golem orbs—'

'Eggs?' cut in Lyra. 'Oh, yes, you bet. You'd be furious too, right? Now come on, we have a town to rescue. You in?'

'I'm not helping this town,' said Tyrus.

Lyra raised her voice. 'Are you kidding me?!'

'They banished me and my family, Lyra. I can't do it. This town is the reason my parents are gone.'

'Fudge,' said Lyra under her breath. 'Look. This town, there's good people here too.'

'Good people don't banish their own into the cold,' countered Tyrus.

'Good people wouldn't fix up your friend.'

She had a point. Xylia lived in Featherburn and so did she, and from what Tyrus had seen, they were good people.

'The choice is yours, Clever Chap. Help and show this town how wrong their views are by saving them, or don't. Just know, lives are on the line. Including the lives in my parent's infirmary.'

Tyrus didn't say anything, and Lyra turned around, ready to head toward the madness. 'Wait,' he said and he looked at Flake inside the carriage. 'We're coming with you.'

With Flake on his shoulder, Tyrus followed Lyra through narrow streets to get to where the attack took place. On the way, wounded Featherburn Watch guards ran away from the danger. They must have thought the two youngsters were mad. When they arrived at the source of all the screams and destruction, the town's square, they hid behind a cabin wall.

'I have to start working on my stamina,' said Tyrus to himself, his breath swirling around in the outside air.

'Yeah, you most certainly do,' said Lyra, who barely broke a sweat.

Tyrus' head peeked from behind the corner. His curiosity needed to have a visual on the havoc-wreaking golem. Basalt rock, stone, moss, and vines moved across its rigid bulky body while crystals and ice grew out of its back like the spines on a hedgehog. Its eyes glowed a light blue and breath escaped its mouth as if it were dense fog.

Guards laid scattered across the square, some dead, others too wounded to move. Was it foolish to hope that the Featherburn Watch could still turn the tide? To hope he wouldn't have to unleash Flake and show everyone he was Owlbound? Was it too late to change his mind?

'Okay, Lyra. Talk to me, what's the plan here?' asked

Tyrus as the remaining guards on the square struggled.

'Chief Yike keeps the orb in his heavily guarded mansion. You distract the golem, while I go in and steal the orb to reunite it with its parent,' explained Lyra.

Tyrus looked at her in disbelief. 'You're going to break into a mansion full of guards, steal the guy's most prized possession, and come back alive? How?'

'My smarts, wits, and with these,' said Lyra, taking two sharp daggers out of their holsters on the back of her belt. 'If there's anyone you should be worried about, it should be you, your owl, and that enraged parent of a frost golem. Yeah?'

The golem grew more and more restless and agitated by the second. The square in the settlement's centre no longer resembled much of a square anymore. The giant creature had ravaged it beyond recognition.

'Wait a second, how long will I have to keep it busy for exactly?' asked Tyrus.

But Lyra had already taken off with the breeze that passed by. She glanced back as she ran. 'As long as it takes, Clever Chap! As long as it takes!'

'Great,' muttered Tyrus and she disappeared in the chaos.

Tyrus' eyes lit up with blue and purple flames. Flake's followed.

Lyra made her way toward the mansion quietly and swiftly. She avoided confrontation with the frost golem by taking a road that sat parallel from the square, which eventually led to a path that crawled up to a backdoor. It was locked, but for Lyra, that didn't pose as much of a problem.

She tucked away her daggers in their respective holsters at the back of her belt and two pins emerged from her cloak. She used them to poke around in the lock. After mere seconds, the door opened, and she entered the building without making a single wooden floorboard creak in agony.

Lyra had no clue where she'd find the orb she needed; she didn't get that far in her investigation. The only thing she knew for certain was that it had to be in this mansion. She had witnessed Yike head out with an escort of twelve guards and she had eyes on them when they returned. The chief had his hands on the orb; he no doubt stole it to display it in here to brag about it. That was his modus operandi. She was certain she'd find it in a spot where people would be able to see it, a place where they couldn't even miss it if they tried. Above all else, the chief's ego always needed stroking.

The mansion doubled as a maze with seemingly

endless corridors, too many rooms to count, and no way to know if you had been inside a room before or not. Occasionally, Lyra spotted flashes of blue-ish and purple-ish light coming from outside, travelling the identical hallways she wandered through. She wanted to see Tyrus and Flake in action but remained focused on her task at hand.

While the boy with the owl danced (and struggled) in battle outside, Lyra flirted and swayed with the shadows to get around unsuspecting guards. Thanks to the lightshow outside, most guards flocked to the windows in the front of the building like cats, unable to resist their natural curiosity. Lyra slid from room to room and from hallway to hallway until she finally arrived at a large dining hall.

It has to be here, she thought to herself.

A remarkable collection of valuable things gathered dust there, things that could buy the entire settlement food for a month if not two. Lyra's face creased at the thought of a single man hoarding all this wealth. And for what? Power? In the end that was always what it came down to. *Power.*

At last, while her eyes scoured the extravagant room, she spotted it. It rested on a red satin pillow; the orb, the frost golem's egg. It shone a subtle light blue glow for her irises to catch and when she touched it with her fingertips, a shiver travelled all the way through her wrist into her arm. The orb itself slept half encapsulated in basalt rock and white crystals and it was twice the size of her head. At the centre you could make out a silhouette. The shape of a small frost golem in the making, innocent and totally unaware that it was taken from its mother's lair.

Lyra didn't hesitate; she pulled out a makeshift backpack—about big enough to fit the whole thing into—and lifted the orb into the bag. She flung it over her back. All she needed to do now was get out alive and preferably unnoticed. She had to say goodbye to the latter sooner than she had hoped as a familiar voice stormed into the room.

'Come on, you dimwits! Help me move the precious stuff to the shelter beneath the mansion!' screamed Chief Yike as two of his servants shuffled into the room.

For the briefest moment, the chief's and Lyra's eyes were chained to each other. She instantaneously made a run for it.

'Guards!' screeched the chief as loud as he possibly could.

Shit. Her parents couldn't give her a metaphorical slap on the wrist for thinking the word instead of saying it out loud, could they?

Chief Yike looked red with fury. There would be reckoning.

She ran and she ran and not necessarily in the direction of the backdoor. She couldn't remember where she had come from anyway. No, she ran and followed the lights.

The lights of Tyrus' magic guided her to the windows at the front of the building and if she remembered correctly, she found herself on the first floor. *Good.* Jumping through the window from the first floor and landing without any injuries was plausible enough if you asked her.

Tyrus limped backward as Flake flew around the golem in circles. She tried distracting it so Tyrus could have a breather. He had read about the limit of magic; his own magic was no different. Every mage possessed a pool of mana, a sort of energy reserve deep within their own being and his, his ran low. He kept praying to whatever it was that would listen for Lyra to make it back with that godforsaken orb.

The frost golem slammed Flake out of the air, like a swatter hitting a fly and Tyrus lunged to catch her. She acted a bit hazy from the smack when Tyrus cradled her in his arms, but soon enough she sat upright on his shoulder again, ready for what would have to be their last stand.

The enraged creature grew boulders of ice out of its hands, lifted them above its head and catapulted them at Flake and her human. Tyrus destroyed the first one that came for them with a fiery fist, but after evading the second and third ones, his knees fell to the snow below. The golem shrieked out in rage.

'What! Is that all you got?!' shouted Tyrus at the distraught creature as he panted.

He shouldn't have done that.

Tyrus' eyes widened when the golem flung its arms to the ground. For a fraction of a second, the fresh snow around her colossal fists became airborne again as the ground shook. Tyrus felt something move below the surface. It was large and coming his way. He stood somewhat near the cabin where the young girl in the window cried. He ran toward the centre of the square with everything he had; he couldn't let the girl become collateral damage.

In anticipation, Flake, once again, took to the sky. The movement in her wings looked erratic, like she had to fight harder to stay airborne, but she managed. The humming beneath Tyrus' feet signalled him to jump and as he did, a gigantic spike of what looked like mossy ice sprung from the ground. The icy thorns that formed around the thing longed for nothing more than to bury themselves into Tyrus' skin. And they did. Three cuts stung from his left knee down to his ankle as his right arm broke his fall. He stayed down. He couldn't possibly get back up and golem slowly moved in on its next victim.

Flake tried everything in her power to slow the beast down but was eventually forced to land beside Tyrus. She tried helping him find the strength to get up by pulling at his clothes, gently pecking his hand. His pool of magic, his mana, had run out and the energy within him had withered.

But then, a smile graced his bruised-up face. Behind the golem, Tyrus' eyes picked up on Lyra, jumping through a window on the first floor. In stark contrast to his fall just now, she landed perfectly and elegantly. He could have sworn he saw her face wearing a smirk.

Meanwhile, the golem closed in on Tyrus to finish the job. At full speed, Lyra ran across the square. The golem made icy spikes grow around her fists, essentially creating morning stars. She lifted both up in the air to strike down the feeble human and bird beneath. Lyra opened her makeshift satchel to take out the orb as she sprinted, slid underneath the golem's legs and came to a stop right next to Tyrus. Together, Lyra and Tyrus lifted the orb up for the golem to see, revealing what the frost golem so desperately sought for; her orb, her egg. Safe.

The expression on the golem's face changed. Anger made way for relief and gratitude. She lowered her morning star fists slowly after the icy spikes melted away. The rocky hands of the now gentle golem wrapped around the orb. It glanced back at both Lyra and Tyrus and closed her eyes. Lyra closed hers too and Tyrus did the same. The frost golem straightened itself before simply walking away. She did so peacefully at a steady pace as if it hadn't laid waste to the town's square. The loud thumps faded and faded with every step until the creature was nowhere to be seen.

Flake hopped onto her shoulder pad as Tyrus and Lyra

helped each other stand up. He had helped save the town that banished him. Together, they saved Featherburn.

'Thanks for getting out here when you did,' said Tyrus, drawing deep heavy breaths.

'Yeah, you would have been Tyrus mash right now if I didn't,' answered Lyra.

He realised he couldn't fully open his right eye but smiled anyway. 'I think so, yeah.'

'Good job, Clever Chap!' Lyra turned toward Flake. 'And you too, of course!' she said and reached out a hand to pet her. 'Well done, Flake.'

'Great stuff, little lady,' added Tyrus.

The freckled girl meticulously observed every movement Flake made. 'Would you look at that. An owl and magic in Featherburn, never thought I'd see the day.'

'Quite the story, isn't it?' said Tyrus. 'By the way, a girl with daggers and a quarrel with the chief. How did that happen?'

Lyra smiled. 'You said it yourself, quite the story.'

They laughed while slowly, folks from the town emerged from their cabins and surrounded the square. Things had quieted down considerably and so; people were curious to see what had happened.

'The boy!' shouted the little girl Tyrus had seen in the window before. 'And the owl, and the girl! They saved us!'

The people of Featherburn didn't dare come closer, not with that owl on Tyrus' shoulder. Except for the little girl.

'Thank you, Mister! Thank you, birdy! Thank you, Miss!' she said, and she gave Tyrus a hug.

The sting in his left leg made him flinch, but he smiled anyways. He even let her pet Flake and the crowd around the square gasped. When the little girl saw her mother, she ran toward her, letting her know all about Tyrus', Lyra's, and Flake's heroic tale.

Then, an intense vibe washed over the crowd as a squadron of guards arrived from within the mansion. Lyra started looking around for a possible way out but there wasn't one. Tyrus wondered why; hadn't they saved the entire settlement? What was she so afraid of?

The crowd split and made an opening. One man paced through the corridor of people, surrounded by guards. Lyra immediately hid below the dark green of her hood and took a step back in an attempt to fade away behind Tyrus and Flake. Somehow, Tyrus felt Lyra's ferocious heartbeat behind the sensation of his.

An older man eventually stopped in front of the boy and the bird. The one and only Chief Yike. The man responsible for his family's banishment years ago, towered before him, fully dressed in armour as if he had ridden into battle. The entire square was soon shrouded in silence, before at last, Chief Yike gave an order.

'Guards! Arrest them!'

CHAPTER 8

REWARD OR PUNISHMENT

Cuffs closed around Tyrus' and Lyra's wrists. The arresting guards even brought in a cage for Flake. Tyrus could see the fear in her eyes. Yet, she refused to leave her best friend's side. He wanted nothing more than to burn those cuffs to ash, to blast that cage out of existence but his magic needed to recover, and he'd only feed the anti-magic narrative that conquered Featherburn. He would only be sealing their fate, at least now there lived a slither of hope. A quarter of the townspeople around the square protested the arrest, a quarter cheered, but most didn't know how to feel.

'What is the meaning of this?!' the chief shouted to the crowd.

'That boy and the bird, the girl!' shouted the little girl from before. 'They saved us all!'

Her mother held her closer all of a sudden. To keep her from stepping—or rather speaking—out of line further, even if it was the truth.

'False! The boy is a diabolical sorcerer! I saw it with my own eyes! Evil, wretched magic!' shouted a different villager while pointing at Tyrus with greasy fingers, their teeth so rotten, Tyrus imagined that while they talked, they'd fly through the air like the golem's icicles did.

The people around the square argued as camps for and against magic formed. Some wanted to celebrate their heroes, while others went as far as suggesting to burn Tyrus and Flake at the stake.

'Silence!' demanded Chief Yike as he rose a balled fist into the air.

The breeze was the only sound left standing.

'This boy and his impossible bird clearly committed acts of witchcraft! Need I remind you that witchcraft is the source of all evil? Need I remind you that witchcraft has no place here in Featherburn?' he said. 'As for the girl, she's nothing but a foul thief who used this whole affair to steal a valuable item from my mansion!'

Tensions simmered amongst the crowd.

'What the little girl speaks of is true!' shouted a familiar voice from behind the chief's squadron of guards.

Chief Yike turned around, and his guards split. None other than Darren, a soldier of the Watch, limped to the centre of the square. His helmet no longer protected his head and his armour had dents, scattered everywhere like the freckles over the bridge of Lyra's nose. Tears welled in his eyes, blurring his vision.

'The boy and his—I can't believe I'm saying this—his owl…they saved my life!' he announced. 'That golem was ready to smash me to pulp when a wall of fire saved me. This boy's kind wall of fire.'

Darren looked Tyrus' way and knelt in the trampled snow. His charcoal hair sat partially frozen (as sweat from the fight with the golem had soaked it) and the fawn in his cheeks bled and bruised, while one of his small and long eyes looked swollen.

'I owe you my life,' he said.

The crowd held its breath.

'Preposterous!' exclaimed the chief, his face red with rage, and his brows furrowed beyond repair. 'Magic is evil. We all know this to be true!'

'What if it isn't though?' asked Darren.

Now, the crowd gasped.

'Do you even hear yourself, young sir?' countered Yike. 'My dearest townsfolk, that monster was bewitched! I assure you! This boy must have put a spell on it to do his bidding. This is deceit hidden in plain sight and of the highest order! This despicable mage wants us to think he saved us but has anyone stopped to think *he* is the one who orchestrated all this in the first place? All a distraction, so the girl could steal what was mine!'

The Featherburn settlers muttered amongst themselves, but Lyra decided to raise her voice after trying to stop her mouth from talking. She couldn't stay quiet. 'You should be grateful!'

Heads turned, gazes locked, and for a few seconds, words left both the air and the many ears around the square alone.

'What did you say to me?' said Chief Yike, narrowing his eyes.

'You heard me,' she said, puffing up her chest, holding her head high. 'If it weren't for Tyrus, the bird, and myself, you'd be sleeping with the frozen dead right now.'

Lyra's eyes refused to run from the chief's stern stare while whispers and mumbles scattered among the townspeople like wildfire.

'That frost golem didn't come here because it had been hexed. It came here because our leader—the great Chief Yike—stole its orb, its egg, its child!' exclaimed Lyra to the crowd. 'Wouldn't you all do anything and everything in your power to get your child back?!'

The crowd grew restless.

'Preposterous!' announced the chief again; it was shaping up to become one of his favourite words. 'What other wild fantasies swirl around in that head of yours, girl? Maybe imprisonment will do wonders for your mind.'

'Maybe you should own up to your mistakes, Chief,' said Tyrus. His body ached with every word he uttered. 'I fought that thing and it felt scared, it felt enraged, it would have levelled the entire settlement if it meant getting its child back. The child you stole!'

While the crowd disagreed and squabbled among themselves, Yike squinted at Tyrus.

Oh no.

He shouldn't have said anything. The only plausible reason people would ever squint at him the way Yike did would be because they thought they recognised him. Seconds later, Tyrus saw the crown drop behind the chief's eyes.

'Fair ladies, gentlemen, and fellow townsfolk! I recognise this boy!' he exclaimed.

Tyrus sank like a brick thrown in water. Flake let her head hang a little, too.

'You have lived here before, haven't you?' he asked with the most annoying grin in existence; it was the kind of grin you wanted to punch.

The crowd looked at the boy for an answer, but Tyrus didn't move or say a word. Between his heart that raced, his breath speeding up and his entire body still aching as hell, he couldn't.

'Answer me!'

Tyrus struggled to carry the weight of all the gazes while anger and fear simmered inside his bones.

'Yes,' he said with his teeth clenched and jaw locked.

The chief continued, 'Years ago, you and your family were banished, were you not?'

'Yes.'

'That's right, we banished them! And guess what for, my dear people?' He looked at Tyrus. 'Will you tell them, or should I?'

Yike didn't believe his eyes when the young mage presented him with a genuinely puzzled expression.

'Oh, they never told you...' He smiled. 'They were banished on the account...of witchcraft!'

The words spread through the crowd like fire through a dry old wooden barn. Tyrus wanted to let all his frustration, all his anger out but he had no energy to spend. His parents had never told him the reason they were banished, neither did Ced. He never knew. Why didn't they tell him? Lyra saw the tears well in Tyrus' eyes and put a hand on his shoulder, the birdless one.

The chief continued to accuse Tyrus of bewitching the golem, even going as far as insinuating he used a spell to brainwash Darren and the little girl he saved. He claimed that the evil wretched magic ran in his family. Tyrus had just fought a giant enraged creature, and his wounds hurt, but none of them hurt more than Chief Yike's wordy attacks. He felt untamed anger rise in his chest, and yet, he didn't have the strength to wield it. Perhaps, it was for the best, too.

Lyra observed how much the chief loved the theatrics of all this, he thrived on the spotlight he put himself in. He kept going and going until confusion about the entire affair conquered his settlers, and that was right where he wanted them.

'I propose a vote!' said the chief finally. 'A vote to punish this boy for his heinous acts of witchcraft! And since banishment didn't do the trick last time, I call for a death sentence!'

Voices cheered, voices protested. But a loud whistle from the back of the crowd silenced all of them. Tyrus looked up. He'd recognise that whistle out of a thousand.

The crowd split and supported by a single crutch on one side and by Xylia on the other, none other than Cedric the seasoned trader passed through the crowd.

'Cedric!' shouted Tyrus as he ran the man's way. He wanted to go in for a hug but with his hands cuffed, he pressed his cheeks against Ced's red tartan flannel shirt.

The trader closed one arm around the boy while simultaneously in awe of Flake who looked into his eyes with her adorable stare.

'Banishing this lad and his family all those years ago was a foolish and utterly uncivilised decision, and anyone who had a part in it then should be ashamed!' shouted Cedric. 'This young lad lost his parents because of you lot. They died out there in banishment and *still* he stepped up to save your arses. He could have let you all die and perish, gotten revenge. But he didn't because he's a bloody hero. He saved my life yesterday, and today, he saved yours. Be grateful for talon's sake!'

Tyrus' eyes were waterfalls by now, a never-ending stream of tears.

Cedric continued, 'You lot are always talking about how diabolical magic and witchcraft are, but I'm pretty sure Tyrus here, proved you all wrong, didn't he?'

Contemplation washed over the townsfolk as they seemed to be taking Cedric's words to heart but Chief Yike didn't have ears for them.

'Clearly his feelings for the boy are clouding his judgement, fine folk of Featherburn. Let's not forget that magic brought us this wretched Eternal Winter. These people are all talk. Where's the proof the boy isn't to blame? Hmmm?' continued the chief in an attempt to still steer the crowd's opinions.

'You say we're all talk, but I haven't heard or seen any evidence supporting those ridiculous claims of yours!' spat Lyra. 'You have no proof Tyrus put a spell on that thing and if he did, why would he let it beat him up this badly? Why not only a few scratches? Not to mention the fact that we have two people that confirm our story, one of whom is a member of your own Featherburn Watch!'

Xylia gave their daughter a stern look. What she was doing was dangerous, but Tyrus recognised the sparkle of pride hidden inside those eyes. Underneath the worry, underneath the shock, they were proud of their daughter.

More and more angry faces shot Chief Yike's way and Lyra relished in them. Tyrus couldn't find the courage to speak but he appreciated Lyra's words deeply and gave her a grateful nod. She looked at him and then charged into battle again, armed with words that spoke the razor-sharp truth.

'The frost golem came here because *you* stole its egg, it came to get it back from *you* and *your* greed. It's protective like that. Maybe you could learn a thing or two from its kind when it comes to protecting what you vowed to?'

Lyra's words stung and, together with Ced's, managed to convince the majority of the crowd to side with her, Tyrus and Flake. The townsfolk had always been fed a black and white story about how magic was the root of all evil. They questioned all that now, Lyra and Tyrus could see it etched on their faces.

However, the chief—stubborn as ever—still wanted his way and called for the vote anyway. Any other day, the entire town (with the exceptions of a few) would have voted Tyrus and Flake on the stake and Lyra in prison. But not today. Today, next to no one raised their hand. Today, they had snatched a glimpse of what went on behind Chief Yike's curtain. Today, they had seen people stand up to him, a man they usually feared. Both Lyra and Tyrus took enormous pleasure in the look on the chief's face when he realised his plan failed.

'Fine,' accepted the chief, his face looked like a piece of paper that had been folded seven times, full of chagrin and scorn.

The crowd turned on their chief. Insults flew around like murders of crows and if it weren't for the guards, half of the townsfolk would have gladly given their leader a couple of punches. To add extra spice and flames to the fire, Tyrus and Lyra granted Chief Yike the pleasure of perceiving two unbearable smirks.

'Settle down, everyone! Settle down. We all make mistakes, don't we? Let's forgive and forget, shall we?' said the chief, sweat freezing into small pockets of ice on his brow. 'As an apology, I'll be granting everyone in Featherburn a gift! Come by the mansion tomorrow and you'll all receive fifty crowns each! What do you say? Ice under the bridge?' He slowly backed up toward the mansion, surrounded closely by his guards.

Things always came down to money for Yike. Lyra should have known; it didn't matter what pickle he found himself in, his crowns would always get him out of it. The crowd cheered. Not as much as the chief probably would have wanted, but at least they let him retreat to the comfort and warmth of his corridor-forward mansion in peace. But the look he shot at the Tyrus, his enchanting owl, and the thieving girl drooled revenge.

The crowd dispersed. Some offered Tyrus and Flake frowned faces, others kept their distance despite knowing they saved the town, and a few lovely people stayed to thank them and Lyra for their bravery. But with Tyrus feeling like he could sleep for days, his eyes so heavy, his body so bruised, it didn't take long before he decided it was time to get back to the infirmary. Xylia supported Cedric, and Lyra supported Tyrus and Flake as they walked back together.

The infirmary door closed behind them with its usual groan.

'Lyra, what were you even thinking? Do you have any idea how dangerous that was?!' asked Xylia all but immediately. 'You could have…died!' Their voice cracked.

'Well, good thing I didn't,' their daughter fired back.

Xylia's eyebrows folded in on themselves. 'Damnit, Lyra, this is not a game!'

'Are you seriously angry with me, Ren?' asked Lyra.

Ren. Tyrus hadn't heard that word before. Lyra used it as short for parent.

'I helped save the town, for talon's sake!' continued Lyra as her eyebrows mimicked the healer's.

Xylia's hands crawled up into their white hairs. 'No one asked you to and again, you almost died!'

'Almost maybe, but I didn't,' said Lyra with her index finger aimed at the ceiling. 'I feel like that should be the main takeaway from this, the fact that I didn't die.'

'See, Tyrus?' Xylia looked his way. 'Pain in my ass.'

Tyrus and Cedric stood awkwardly by the door, unable to give parent and daughter privacy to talk. Xylia and Lyra blocked the hallway and so, Tyrus and the seasoned trader became an unwilling audience, occasionally trading glances.

'Listen here, young lady—' started Xylia.

'No, you listen, Ren. No one had to ask me to step in. I chose to because I couldn't sit on the sidelines and hope for a miracle, especially because I knew exactly how to fix it. You and Dad raised me better than for me to stick my head into the snow at the first sign of trouble.'

Xylia stiffened.

'You taught me to be strong and brave,' added Lyra.

'Oh, don't you dare.'

Lyra beamed. 'So, technically…'

'Don't you say it,' warned Xylia again but a smile hid behind their frown.

'If, anything…'

'Lyra…I'm warning you…'

'When you *really* think about it, this is kind of your fault,' said Lyra eventually.

'Wipe that grin off your face and let me tend to those cuts,' answered Xylia as they hugged their daughter tight.

Lyra smirked. 'I'm proud of you too, Ren.'

They disappeared into the first examination room to the left and closed the door. Tyrus and Cedric shared a perplexed look before heading upstairs. Tyrus helped Cedric to his room and onto his bed, putting the one crutch next to the bed against the beige wall.

'So, tell me laddie, is this real?' asked Cedric, pointing at Tyrus and Flake, his index finger going back and forth between the two. 'Or am I still in a sort of coma, waiting to wake up, stuck in a land of dreams?'

Flake felt like she had to be the one to resolve Cedric's reservations, so she jumped off Tyrus' shoulder, leaping onto the trader's bed and gave him a small gentle peck in the leg.

Cedric flinched. 'Definitely real, ey?'

'This is Flake, and yes, she's definitely real. I checked if I was dreaming too, but she's real all right,' said Tyrus. A nervous smile with a lot of teeth lived between his cheek and his toes were squirming in his boots. He knew deep down Cedric would be thrilled his magical owl, but it felt scary, all the same.

'When I first woke up in this wee bed, I couldn't make sense of what I saw when you saved me. All I had seen were blurs, you know? Impossible blurs, and I thought maybe it was the poison. But it was…'

'Magic.'

'Aye, magic. You, Flake, and magic,' said the seasoned trader. 'You're going to have to give me a demonstration soon, you know that, right?'

Tyrus laughed. 'With pleasure, Ced.'

'Thank you for not listening to me and saving my life, laddie. I owe you the world.'

Tyrus went in for another hug.

'Cedric, you don't have to thank me. I saved you because you're important to me,' answered Tyrus.

'Oh, I'm important to you…Good to know, lad. I'll keep that in mind next time you try bringing my prices down.'

'I mean you're not *that* important to me, old man,' joked Tyrus.

'Is that right, eh?'

Dusk waltzed over Featherburn like an overeager dancer at a tavern and torches lit the streets. And as candles burned in the cabin windows, greeting every gaze they attracted, silence filled the room for a moment until Tyrus needed to get something off his chest.

'Hey, Ced, why did my parents never tell me we were banished for witchcraft?' he asked.

Cedric sighed. 'They never explained it to me, but for whatever reason, they didn't want you to know. Or better yet, they didn't want to burden you with it.'

Tyrus sat down in the chair next to Ced's bed. 'And why didn't you tell me? Especially after they…'

'Because, it simply wasn't my place, laddie,' said Cedric.

Tyrus' face dropped into his own thoughts. He had to ask, right? He had to know. 'Was there any…truth to the matter?' asked Tyrus, his voice softer.

'Not that I know of,' shared Cedric. He sighed deeply

before continuing, 'Your parents…they didn't believe the Owlbound were evil, that magic was evil. Their only crime I think was being vocal about it where they shouldn't have been.'

A knock stopped their conversation. 'Am I interrupting?' said Xylia on the other side of the door.

After seeking confirmation on Tyrus' face, Cedric told the healer to come inside.

'Ah, there you are,' said Xylia, referring to Tyrus. 'Lyra is all patched up, so it's your turn. Through the hallway, down the stairs, first door to the left. I'll be right over.'

'Wow, Ren. What are you, a general?' said Lyra, popping her head in the door while saluting her parent. She then waved goodbye and went on her way.

Tyrus meant to say goodnight to her but as soon as he entered the hallway, there was no trace of her. He couldn't believe how quick and light on her feet she was. He wielded fire for magic, perhaps what she did was her own kind of magic.

With Tyrus out of the room, Xylia shot Cedric a look he knew would come.

'You haven't told the lad, have you?' he asked. 'I don't want to put the extra weight on those broadening shoulders of his.'

Xylia came closer and sat on the side of the trader's bed. 'I haven't and I won't, that's up to you, but I need you to tell me you understand.'

'I do,' said Cedric, looking straight at them with tears in his eyes.

'I need to hear you say it,' pressed Xylia. 'With how long you were exposed to the Bleakvenom, the next time you get bitten by one of those wolves, there isn't an antidote in the world that could save you.'

'I understand, Xylia. I need to stay clear of those things,' he said and started smiling, the tears ebbing away. 'As if my life depended on it.'

'You're a bastard, you know that?' asked the healer with narrow eyes, yet they couldn't hide their smile.

Cedric laughed. 'Oh, I'm aware.'

CHAPTER 9

THANK YOU FOR YOUR TIME

Tyrus sat upright on the table in the centre of the examination room. Herbs and scary-looking tools witnessed him wait for Xylia. He put Flake down next to him on the coarse cloth covered table surface. Her eyes canvassed the room, taking in the various potions that relaxed on the many shelves clinging to the walls, like spiders fused to their webs.

'So, Tyrus, I guess we now know why I thought you looked so familiar, don't we?' asked Xylia as they stepped through the door. They moved a chair closer to the examination table and sat down. 'I knew your parents.'

On top of wearing bruises and a couple of grazes and cuts, his face also wore the look of confusion. He felt a brick form in his throat, too.

'I was rather fond of Sibyl, Mykel too. They were kind and loving, but I suppose I don't have to tell you that, do I?'

Tyrus remained silent. His eyes stung, announcing tears. He didn't outright know what to say and Flake leaned on his elbow in an effort to console him.

'My apologies. We don't have to talk about them if you don't want to,' said Xylia eventually. 'I would like to say though, they'd be incredibly proud of you for what you did today. That can't have been easy, not with the history between you and Featherburn.'

'Lyra roped me into it actually,' said Tyrus, pushing away his feelings.

Xylia broke into a giggle. 'Yes, well…That doesn't surprise me in the slightest,' they said while reaching over to a cart to grab a flask of vinegar.

They poured the vinegar on a clean, soft piece of cloth and gently pressed it against the cuts on the boy's cheeks. Tyrus winced at the sudden sting, and reluctantly showed Xylia the cuts that sat slashed on the inside of his right leg. The slashes travelled from his knee to his ankle. Most were shallow and merely needed a splash of that vinegar, but three of them had dug deeper.

'Uh, what are you planning with that?' asked Tyrus as his healer grabbed a needle and thread. A sudden burst of sweat erupted all over his body. Didn't he face a deadly frost golem earlier? Why, of all things, did a needle warrant such a response?

'See those wounds?' They pointed to the three deeper cuts. 'They need to be stitched up. Is that a problem?'

They tilted their head.

Tyrus mumbled before ending with, 'Is the needle necessary?'

'Unless you have an alternative in your professional experience as a healer, then yes, the needle is necessary.' Xylia smiled.

Definitely Lyra's parent.

Tyrus took the owl head totem out from underneath his shirt and held it tight while Xylia closed the wounds like they would holes in trousers or socks.

'Scared of needles? Or is this the first time someone is sewing you up with one?' asked the healer.

'Can it be both?' asked Tyrus while flinching.

Xylia laughed. 'Definitely.'

'Do me a favour, though…Can we not tell Lyra about this?' asked Tyrus. 'She would never let this go, would she?'

If Tyrus could see the faces he made in a mirror right now without context, he'd think he was possessed by some kind of demon.

'Oh goodness no, she wouldn't. Your secret is safe with me,' reassured Xylia as they finished closing up the deeper gashes in the boy's leg.

Tyrus sighed in relief and let go of the totem around his neck as he let towel-wrapped ice rest against his black eye. 'Thank you.'

Xylia's eyes widened at the sight of the owl head

around their patient's neck. 'May I?' they asked, pointing at his totem. Their fingers travelled across every little detail. 'Your mother used to wear this. She was rather fond of it.'

Tyrus took it back from the palm of Xylia's hand. 'She gave it to me a few weeks before she…' His eyes twinkled in the candlelight for a while but then, he snapped out of the mournful thoughts that fired through his mind and looked at Xylia. 'Did you mean what you said before? About my parents, that they would be proud of me?'

'Every word.'

Tyrus stood up, gave Xylia a hug, and Flake flew back onto his shoulder pad. 'Thank you for patching me up,' he said.

'Are you okay, Tyrus?' asked Xylia.

'I will be,' he answered with a light smile at the end. 'I will be.'

They wished each other a good night and Tyrus traded the examination room for Cedric's quarters. The man was already snoring and Tyrus put his gorgeous owl down on the makeshift bed Xylia had made him below the window. Tyrus imagined his parents proud as he admired the almost weightless snow descend from those shimmering stars in the sky. Until the moons and his dreams took him into the night.

Tyrus loved a lot of things. But one thing he held dear the most was naturally waking up in the mornings without anyone's or anything's help. It had been remarkably easy at the lighthouse, took no effort whatsoever. Today, waking up according to his own rhythm was never an option, because as soon as the beige walls of Cedric's room caught a stripe of sunlight, Lyra stormed in. Loudly.

'Rise and shine, Clever Chap!' she shouted.

'Go away, I'm still sleeping,' mumbled Tyrus into his pillow, the words muffled but still somewhat comprehensible.

Cedric laughed from behind his book. He sat in a chair on the other side of the room.

'Not anymore you're not, because you, Sir Sleepy-face, are coming with me to the market,' said Lyra.

Tyrus turned around, sat up and scratched his head in the curly mess that was his hair. Flake opened her eyes too, which took visible effort. They were clearly bound to each other. When his brain finally caught up to what Lyra had said, the idea of going to the market made what felt like a rash travel through Tyrus' veins. He felt utterly depleted after interacting with so many people the day before. He wasn't used to it. He loved being alone, isolated. He had convinced himself he was simply not built for too much social interaction. However, Lyra tried convincing him anyway. Since Xylia forbade Cedric from selling his inventory at the market himself, Lyra decided to help the old trader out. She even dusted off her puppy eyes and made an excellent point of having Tyrus and Flake there to boost sales. After promising him he could have the entirety of tomorrow to himself, Tyrus caved. And so, together they went to the market to set everything up for a day of many trades and sales.

Tyrus had never noticed, but Cedric's carriage had a rolled-up tarp built into the side of the large coach. A long slim wooden trim spanned the length of the carriage, a trim you could slide down to reveal a dark purple tarp. With Lyra's help, he rolled it out and attached it to the poles at the market of Featherburn, essentially creating a stand out of Cedric's travelling warehouse of goods. They carried the merchandise outside and stalled out the various products for customers to spend their hard-earned crowns on.

The townsfolk's eyes would start their journey at the graceful snow-white appearance of crunchy loaves of frostbread, jump over to take in the various shapes and colours of the widest range of odorous herbs, before arriving at a splendid display of meats—waiting to be smoked, cooked or baked. If people so desired, they could continue. This time, following their nose, which would take them to baskets filled with geluroots, frostwheat and rare dried fruits from all across Wingspan. And finally, roaming hands could travel antique tools and objects, which were either up for trade, or for sale in return for a hefty pouch of crowns.

'Do you always look like you were forced to drink a glass of sour milk when you try and sell things?' asked Lyra. She crossed her arms at him as she said it, leaning against the roughed-up wood of the carriage ladder that climbed up to the door.

'Very funny,' said Tyrus, smiling as Flake decorated his shoulder. Her head turned toward whoever spoke. 'I'm not much of a morning person, that's all.'

'Oh, that's the most shocking news. Hadn't noticed!' she teased, every syllable, every word drenched in sarcasm.

'Has anyone ever told you, you are infuriating?' asked Tyrus.

'Oh yeah, all the time. It's how I show people I care,' said Lyra with a wink.

Tyrus blushed before launching himself off the stool he sat on to tend to their first few customers. The frostbread and geluroots in particular were in high demand. Tyrus commended the townsfolk's choice. As expected, the meats and dried fruits performed well, too. After about an hour, one of Cedric's pouches was already full of crowns, and they still had plenty more to offer. Lyra was right (of course she was), having Flake and Tyrus there didn't hurt the sales.

Things went well, but something irked Tyrus. Something other than desperately trying not to tear his nails from the social interaction overload he experienced. He couldn't put his finger to what else bothered him. Until he saw Lyra, lifting crowns out of people's pockets. When she came back from mingling in the crowd, Tyrus took her by the arm as they turned toward the carriage, away from the faces. 'What do you think you're doing?' he whispered.

'Being infuriatingly good at almost everything I do. Not sure how I do it, though,' said Lyra as she scratched the temple on the left side of her head.

'I mean the stealing,' clarified Tyrus. 'You're picking pockets. Why?' His eyes looked fierce, filled with judgement. 'Well?'

Lyra's hands rested as fists, sinking in her sides. 'First of all, you're sounding like my ren. Second of all, what's wrong with balancing the scales of wealth?' she asked him.

Tyrus frowned. 'Wait, what?' Now that he thought about it, she did only steal from clearly rich customers as opposed to ones who had to count their crowns to make sure they had enough to buy what they needed.

'In case you hadn't noticed, this entire town is corrupt and rotten to the core. I only steal from the rich bastards who won't even notice a few crowns went missing. The people with the thick fur coats, the ones wearing fancy elven jewellery. What I nick, I give to people who need it.'

Tyrus apologised for jumping to conclusions. 'Won't

this get you in more trouble than it's worth, though? The chief and the Watch already don't seem so fond of you.'

'Nice work, detective. But I can handle myself, thank you very much,' she said before turning around to help a customer.

In a way, Tyrus respected what Lyra was doing, but he wasn't sure if stealing was the best way to go about it.

The morning hours slipped away as Tyrus and Lyra sold and traded their way through every minute. Throughout the morning, Tyrus had noticed something strange, or rather, someone strange. A shady character roaming the market of Featherburn. It seemed like the mysterious figure kept returning to their stand. Never coming close, let alone buying anything. They simply observed him from a distance, face hidden underneath a black hood, and their left hand wearing a silver ring with a dark-purple rock. Every time the hooded person was in view, Tyrus felt their eyes on him, and a deeply unsettling chill travelled through his entire body. He didn't think much of it at first, but the figure kept returning, avoiding Tyrus' glance when he looked their way. Is this what his prey felt like when he went hunting? He couldn't shake the feeling that something was wrong with that person. Maybe this was the kind of person his parents warned him about, the kind you can't trust.

Close to noon, unable to shake his unnerving feelings, Tyrus had enough. He (and Flake) slowly left the carriage behind to see what the figure would do. When this mysterious person started running away, Tyrus knew something had to be up and went after them. The chase was on and Flake took to the sky, leaving Lyra to tend to their last customers alone.

'Tyrus?! What the heck?!' she called out after him, but the sorcerer boy was gone in a flash, running the heart and lungs out of his body without looking back.

'Stop right there!' he shouted as he gained on his black-hooded stalker.

After a brief chase, which according to his stamina had been long enough, Tyrus cast a spell. One that would have made jaws drop if there had been anyone near to witness it. The boy's eyes caught fire and commanded the magic inside and around him to burn a barrier in front of his stalker, essentially trapping them in an alleyway. He didn't let the barrier spring from the ground, neither did he catapult it from his hands. Flake—who flew above the alleyway, a little ahead of the person they chased—dived down and breathed a wall of blue and purple flames on the ground as if she were a dragon. Tyrus had no idea if it would work, but it did. Their stalker stopped dead in their tracks, right before they'd hit the wall of roaring magical fire.

'Who are you and what do you want from me?' Tyrus demanded.

The shady figure turned around and lifted their

hood, revealing a middle-aged man. Silver threads ran through the charcoal black strands of his slick hair and subtle crow's feet dangled from the corners of his eyes. A slight stubble clung to his face, as dark eyeliner brought out his handsome and fascinated gaze. The gentleman's fingernails were painted in the same black as his hood, which made Tyrus a little jealous, if he were honest.

'Remarkable,' said the stranger, his voice soothing the atmosphere around him.

'I asked you a question,' threatened Tyrus.

The man held his hands out in front of him. 'I'm a traveller. I didn't mean to upset you, young man,' he said, looking down at Tyrus' boots, avoiding eye-contact.

'Why are you following me?' pressed Tyrus, his eyes still lit with flames. He steadied his pose and summoned a fireball above the palm of his right hand. 'Stalking me?'

The man looked at the swaying flames in Tyrus' eyes and then at the blazing fire in his hand, emerald-green pupils taking in burning purple and blue.

'I merely wanted to see if it was true. I didn't want to bother you until I knew it was true, but this...' He turned and looked up at the burning wall of flames behind him. 'Well, this...definitely resolves my doubts.'

'What are you talking about?' urged Tyrus.

'You're possibly the last Owlbound person alive. There is important information I need to share with you,' said the traveller.

'Well? Out with it,' ordered Tyrus.

'Do you mind if we talk about this somewhere less… unpleasant? A quiet tavern perhaps?' The wall of flames melted away like ice would have during spring centuries ago. 'I swear, I will tell you everything.'

Tyrus wanted to hear what the traveller had to say and considered going with him right away, but he couldn't do that to Lyra, could he? What if the man wouldn't agree to meet up later and ran off? Then, his eyes popped with an idea.

'Stay right there,' said Tyrus to the stranger.

Tyrus took a piece of wrinkly paper out of the inside pocket of his maroon cloak as Flake returned to her shoulder pad.

'Astonishing,' said the stranger, referring to the bird, not the paper.

The curly autumn-haired boy closed his eyes as Flake's lit up with familiar blue purple-ish flames. He held the wrinkled piece of paper in his left hand as small sparks danced on the fingertips of his right. He let his hand hover over the paper, moving his fingers, intending the magic to write. Magical burns formed words on the paper. When his eyes opened, the flames disappeared, and an impressed expression sat trapped on the strange traveller's face. Tyrus rolled up the piece of paper as if it were a cigarette and gave it to Flake who held it, gently in her beak. She opened her wings, took to the sky, and flew away. Silence enslaved the boy and the man in the alley as they waited. Tyrus' untrusting stare was met by the stranger's intimidated and awkward look. The man didn't dare say anything and Tyrus figured he'd let him sweat a little before Flake eventually returned to his side.

'So…' said Tyrus when Flake sat on his shoulder once more. 'A quiet tavern?'

Lyra felt proud. Most of Cedric's wares had sold out, multiple bags of crowns were filled (including her own, albeit through less honest practices), and the market came to an end. But there was no sign of Tyrus to help her clean everything up.

A few minutes passed before Lyra saw the other vendors in the corner of her eye, looking and pointing up to the sky. Before she full well realised it, Flake landed on her lap, holding a tiny wrinkled rolled-up piece of paper. Lyra rolled it open and her pupils feasted on letters.

Lyra, I'm sorry. Something came up. I'll meet you back at the infirmary.

'Something came up? Yeah, right,' she said under her breath.

The damn boy ditched her right before they needed to pack things up, convenient. As soon as she read it (and ripped it apart), Flake flew away again. She had done her job.

'What are they up to?' Lyra whispered to herself. A slight sigh followed and as soon as her irises picked up on none other than Chief Yike passing by various vendors. A big sigh outplayed the slight one that came before. Most of the vendors showered the chief with gifts in exchange for honouring them with his presence. Only a handful of vendors had the self-respect to treat him like any other customer.

Don't stop here. Don't do it. Don't stop. Not here. The thoughts repeated in Lyra's mind when with every step he came closer and closer and closer.

'And what do we have here, if it isn't the thief,' spat Yike finally arriving at Ced's carriage. 'Selling stolen goods, I take it?'

Lyra rolled her eyes as he said it. 'If it isn't the manipulative bastard that calls himself a chief,' she replied swiftly. 'Buying people's opinions with money, I take it?'

'I'd watch that tongue of yours if I were you,' warned the chief. He leaned, hovering over the stalled out open crates and baskets that sat between them, and looked her in the eye.

Lyra got to her feet, moved closer to the chief, and leaned in. 'And I'd stop threatening a girl who helped save the town in front of everyone if I were you,' she said in a whisper next to his hairy ears.

Chief Yike scoffed. 'You're nothing in this town and you never will be.'

Lyra smiled at that, which infuriated Yike and that's exactly why she did it. He turned and walked away.

'Thank you, chief,' called Lyra after him.

He glanced her way. 'For what?'

'Oh, nothing, just…thank you for your time,' she said.

He refused her the satisfaction of saying another word and walked off, for real this time. When he finally left Lyra's view, her hand folded open to reveal why she'd smiled and smirked. A golden pocket watch rested on her palm. This, she didn't steal for the poor. This, she stole for herself.

Thank you for your time.

CHAPTER 10

TALES OF AGES LOST

The Hound's Bow smelled of rather curious ale. Cedric had told Tyrus about taverns before but he never imagined they could smell so terribly uncomfortable; his nostrils thought it a crime. Stepping foot into that tavern for the first time felt like entering an ill-kept barn full of farm animals after a refreshing walk in the forest air. Flake didn't enjoy herself either, restlessly repositioning herself on the shoulder pad every few seconds.

'Right, we're here now. Spill it,' fired Tyrus.

'Can't a man order a drink first?' asked the stranger, and he called the handsome bartender to their table. 'A plain ale for me, please.'

The beardy bartender's eyes moved to Tyrus next.

'Oh, nothing for me, I'm good,' he said.

'I'm buying. Are you sure?' asked the strange traveller. 'We might be here a while.'

Tyrus stared at him without saying a word.

'All right, one plain ale, coming right up,' said the bartender as he shot a wink to the traveller and returned to the various liquors in the back of the tavern. The stranger smiled at that wink. He still had it.

'Hello?' snapped Tyrus at the man in front of him, clearly distracted by the biceps of the bartender as they poured an ale. 'Last time…Spill. It.'

'My apologies, my thoughts were…elsewhere for a moment,' spoke the stranger, that last part rather sultry, more than it needed to be. 'My name is Malum and I'm a traveller from Talonstead. Pleased to make your acquaintance, Tyrus.'

'I never told you my name.' The boy's hands became fists and Flake clacked her bills.

'The settlers are an extraordinarily chatty bunch, especially about a boy wielding magic to save the town, you know,' explained Malum.

Tyrus relaxed his fists again. 'I suppose that's true… Talonstead, you said? That's fairly far away from here, isn't it? Why are you here? What do you want from me?' asked Tyrus, his patience wearing a little thin.

'Where do I even start?' Malum scratched his head in his slick black and slightly silvered hair.

'The beginning maybe? Just a thought,' proposed Tyrus.

The bartender brought over Malum's ale to the table,

accompanied by another wink. The drink sat in a wooden goblet. Tyrus thought it looked (and smelled) disgusting; Malum could gather as much from the faces the boy made.

'The beginning would be rather confusing, I'm afraid,' began Malum. 'Let's start with how I got here and why instead. I've dedicated my life to learning about magic and owls from a fairly young age and somewhat recently, the old-world ruins near Crownhaven have piqued my interest.

'I had been spending a lot of time there and a little while ago, I drank at the local tavern when I overheard a trader talking with a man about…well…a trade,' the mysterious traveller continued.

Cedric.

'It wasn't so much the trader that interested me, as much as the object he wanted to buy off the other person there.'

'Let me guess…this shoulder pad?' Tyrus pointed to the one Flake sat on, to which she bowed down, thinking Tyrus would pet her. He didn't plan to, but did it anyway as gentle hoots warmed his heart.

'Precisely. Rather sharp, young man. Indeed, worn by the Owlbound in a long-lost age. I overheard the trader say something about a contact being interested in it and that intrigued me so much that I decided to follow him,' said Malum.

'Why?' fired Tyrus.

'Because the prospect of meeting a soul as invested in Owlbound research as I am, was compelling. There aren't many who consider magic an interesting topic. Most want nothing to do with it,' the traveller said. 'Now, sadly, along the way I lost track of the trader, blasted behemoth horses.'

'Yeah, Trudy is fast,' confirmed Tyrus as he got slightly more comfortable talking to the strange man in front of him.

'Anyways, I picked up a trail of tire tracks from the carriage, which I followed up to an area near a forest where I suspected he'd stopped and ran into trouble, judging by the bloodstains,' said Malum. He drank a sip of ale every time he paused. 'The peculiar thing was that the scene showed signs of something impossible. I've read about magic, real magic in my books and the burn marks I found were, well, not possible.

'As you could imagine, my curiosity grew and having seen what I've seen now, my wildest dreams were true. It was magic, *your* magic,' he said pointing at both Flake and Tyrus.

'So then, after going around a ravine, I arrive at Featherburn and I hear stories about a kid saving the town with magic. I followed that trader in the hopes of finding a person with similar interests, but I must say, finding a boy who is both interested in magic and a real mage is infinitely better.'

There wasn't a drop of ale left in his goblet.

'And why is that?' asked Tyrus as he leaned over the table a bit, his fingers interlaced.

'Because, Tyrus. Magic was dead. It was gone and now, it's alive somehow, which means there's hope after all.' Malum's mouth produced the words but the way he swung with his hands in the process, those hands told his story just as well.

'Hope for what?' asked Tyrus.

'To save the world,' said Malum dramatically and his eyes sparked as they grew larger. Tyrus thought they would pop out of their sockets.

Flake looked as bewildered as Tyrus did. 'I'm sorry, what?'

'Wingspan wasn't always this cold place, almost devoid of life. It was once an oasis where life sprung from every inch. Plants and flowers thrived and the seasons, the seasons were real and they flowed in a perpetual holy cycle. Magic undid all that, magic can bring it all back. *Your* magic can bring it all back,' he explained. 'This is why I needed to see if you were real.'

Was the man telling him the truth? Or was he lying through his perfect teeth? The details he described about his journey to Featherburn, it was all true; it made sense. Tyrus asked Malum what he meant when he said magic undid the seasons, to which he answered with a question of his own after signing the bartender to bring him another ale.

'What do you know of the Owlbound Council?'

Tyrus flinched backward slightly, and Flake turned her head to look his way while the bartender brought a new goblet of ale over to their table.

Tyrus leaned back in and said, 'I've heard of them, read about them. They're a myth.'

'That's where you're wrong. They were real.' Malum grabbed his newly filled goblet and began telling the story. 'Long ago when the Owlbound gave our world the most extraordinary gifts, there was a council of Paragons. They made the most important decisions on all things magic. They wrote laws, guided the academies and decided all the big things concerning magic within the realm.

'However, well over a hundred years ago, a dark entity infested our world at its core and if left unchecked, it would have destroyed us all. So, when the council figured out the entity's weakness was cold and frost, they decided contain the beast in a frozen prison within the core of our world.'

Tyrus already puzzled things together. 'But by freezing the core of our world, they froze the rest of it with it.'

'A rather unfortunate side effect. The council decided to maintain the prison until the entity was dead, which after all these years would have already happened. The plan was always to let the seasons return, to let spring free us from the cold but they never got the chance. The

Unbound culled your kind for causing the Eternal Winter until no one was left. No matter what explanations were given, those without magic wouldn't listen and ultimately, they ended up dooming our world in thinking they were avenging it,' explained Malum carefully. 'Our world will grow colder and colder until all life will cease to exist. You know it's true. We're seeing it happen already with more and more cold-resistant crops dying off. Our realm was doomed beyond oblivion, Tyrus. Until now. Until *you two*.'

Tyrus froze. 'Where did you learn all this?' he asked after silence had swallowed their table for five or six breaths.

'These stories were carried over from generation to generation within my family. We're a family of Owlbound admirers,' answered the traveller. 'That and too much research, research I've dedicated my life to.'

The late afternoon crept up on them like an owl stalking their prey, and even though Tyrus wanted to hear more, he told the man he had to get going. He needed to let all this new information sink in. Besides, he didn't mean to worry anyone over at the infirmary and he figured Lyra would be slightly annoyed with him for ditching her.

Malum rose to his feet as he poured the last gulp of ale into his mouth and swallowed. Initially off-balance for a second, he let his goblet rain down on the table below like he was a judge who'd reached their final decision—

although a goblet would make for a rather lousy gavel.

'Well, Tyrus. If you decide you want to hear more, I'm staying at the Feathering Inn, room twelve,' he said.

Tyrus held out his hand. 'Thank you, Malum.' And the man shook it.

Palms let go of each other and behind Tyrus, footsteps across rotten wooden floorboards faded slowly until a door opened and closed. When the boy turned around, he saw the bartender smiling after the mysterious traveller had walked out, falling into the roads of Featherburn.

Dwindling snow peeked inside the Hound's Bow through the windows while welcoming Tyrus outside. The tavern's sign swung a little in the wind, it depicted a hound holding a bow and arrow in its teeth.

Deeply lost in thought, he walked as every crunchy step in the fresh snow, brought him closer to the infirmary. Then, without realising, as if a chunk of time had fallen between the cracks of the world, he saw Trudy and the carriage in the distance. Lyra hung around, leaning against the ladder as Cedric stood on a small stool, brushing Trudy's manes with one hand, the other still bandaged.

'Cedric!' shouted Lyra as Tyrus got closer. 'Tell my ren to stop crafting missing posters! The missing mage has graced us with his return!' She could have been an actor for the weekly plays at the square.

'Okay, that's fair,' said Tyrus as he handed both her and Cedric a smile.

Trudy neighed, her manes rustling in the wind.

'Ced, shouldn't you be resting?' asked Tyrus.

The trader paused. 'Don't you worry, Xylia gave their okay, laddie. Besides, they assigned me a guard to make sure I don't overdo it,' he said, looking in Lyra's direction.

'What was so important that you had to ditch me, Clever Chap?' asked Lyra with a sharp stare that almost pierced his skin and nearly tickled the vital organs underneath.

'Before I explain, I think we should all sit down for this. Perhaps inside?' proposed Tyrus.

Lyra snorted. 'Way to make it ominous.'

In the company of warm flames (and with Flake on his shoulder), Tyrus told his friends—including Xylia—what Malum had told him earlier. From the Owlbound Council to the festering blight at the core of the world, everything. By the end of it, no one knew what to say.

Cedric scratched the grey in his beard. 'Tyrus, this all sounds fascinating, but have you considered that this man is lying to you? I mean, this man comes out of nowhere? It's suspicious to say the least, no?' he said eventually, Xylia agreed.

'Not to mention the fact that it all sounds like it's made up, like a fairy tale,' added Lyra as she came away from the rest of her chair and leaned into the conversation.

'Listen, I know this sounds suspicious, and perhaps even ridiculous. But the way he talked, the details of his story…it felt like he was telling the truth,' defended Tyrus. 'What if it's true? What if I have the power to rid the world of the cold?'

'Lad… Is this about what happened to your parents?' asked Cedric.

Tyrus flashed red with anger while holding the welling tears in his eyes at bay, like they were inmates stuck in a cell. 'So, what if it is, Ced? So, what if it is?' He breathed in deeply to not lose control. 'Don't I owe it to them, to everyone who has ever perished at the hands of winter? Don't I owe it to the world to at least see if there's any truth to the matter? He's staying at the Feathering Inn, he said to come see him if I wanted to know more.'

Flake stroked her head against his to help him calm down.

'You know what? I say, let's hear him out. If he's full of sh—'

'Lyra,' Xylia cut in, firing a stern look their daughter's way.

Lyra rolled her eyes at them. 'If he's full of *bogus*, we'll know. And if not, which—again, for the record—I think is highly unlikely…we'll know too, everyone happy.'

'What exactly do you mean with "*we*"?' asked Tyrus.

'Obviously, we're coming with you, laddie,' said Cedric. 'You're clearly biased toward this whole thing, and I don't trust the gadgie.'

Xylia and Lyra both nodded in agreement.

'I'm capable of taking care of myself,' said Tyrus, still all bruised over from the fight with the frost golem.

'Have you looked at yourself in the mirror? Besides, it's not only you getting physically hurt that scares me, laddie. It's what someone can do to your roaring heart, to your boundless mind, to your kind soul,' said Cedric with his right hand covering Tyrus' chest.

'The fact that you told us all of this should tell you that part of you also doesn't know whether you can trust this man, no?' added Xylia.

Tyrus' eyes were sweating a little because of what the trader said earlier. 'I guess you're right,' he acknowledged.

Tyrus' parents had told him to not stray from the lighthouse and to stay away from people as much as possible, to not trust anyone but himself (and Cedric). But Tyrus started thinking they might have had it all wrong. Ever since he left the lighthouse behind, he hadn't been bored for a second. He had met Xylia and Lyra, two amazing people. Cedric would be dead if he hadn't left. He wondered if Malum was trustworthy like these new friends he had made. Or did what his parents taught him apply in this case?

The next morning, Tyrus, Cedric, and Flake woke up unexpectedly. Screams seeped through their door, coming from downstairs. They didn't waste a second as they dashed through the hallway and shot down the staircase. Cedric held his crutch as if it were a broadsword and Tyrus held a fireball in each of his hands. Instead of facing danger, however, they watched as a tight hug took place.

Lyra let go and turned around. 'Father, meet Tyrus and Flake! And Cedric's here too!'

Silver eyes looked Tyrus and Flake up and down in disbelief, as fireballs vanished in the blink of an eye.

Lyra's father was lost for words. 'Is that…?'

'An owl, a magician boy, and an old man?' fired Lyra quickly. It could have been the start of a joke. 'Yes, that's exactly what that is.'

'You and your ren never sit still while I'm gone, do you?' he said with his hands in his hair after rubbing his eyes.

He'd been out hunting for days and ran straight home when he arrived back at Featherburn, well before any stories about a town-saving mage could reach him.

He took a step forward toward both Tyrus and Flake. 'My name is Silas,' he said. 'Pleased to meet you,' he added and held out his hand.

Tyrus shook it as he noticed where Lyra got her nose from. Silas stood tall and carried broad shoulders, the kind you'd find on experienced warriors. A scar crossed his left eye. It erupted from his skin about halfway into his cheek and crept up his face before eventually, getting lost in the fields of the short blonde hairs on his head.

Cedric gave the man a sturdy hug, the kind brothers gave each other. No such relation ran through their blood, but family isn't always found in blood. Sometimes, it's found in friendship. Tyrus couldn't explain it, but he brimmed with hope. He knew he would never see his birth family again save for in his dreams and memories. But seeing the brotherly connection between Ced and Silas, it filled him with the hope he might find a new family.

'Sorry about the crutch and the fireballs, brother. We're a bit on edge it seems,' apologised Cedric. 'How was the hunt?'

'Oh, no need for that. I'd rather you be ready for danger whenever it comes, it's a valuable skill to have in this world,' assured Silas with a smile. 'The hunt was good, great even, but what in talon's name happened to you, you old sod?'

'A story to tell over eggs and sausage, perhaps?' asked Cedric.

'Agreed,' said Silas, patting his friend on the back.

Tyrus followed everyone into the actual home of Lyra's family for breakfast. It wasn't long before Silas' face lit up like a campfire in the evening when Xylia welcomed them all inside. They hugged their husband, they kissed, and hugged some more.

The rest of the morning was spent at a lively breakfast table. Tyrus felt like he belonged for the first time in a long time. Maybe he'd been wrong to decline Cedric's proposals to come with him. His heart felt warm, like his stomach after inhaling delicious eggs. Tales about Flake and her magic, Cedric and the bleakwolves, and Lyra and the frost golem orb swept over the table. Even Flake— barely tall enough so the breakfast table bathed in her eyes—hooted along between everyone.

After the family had caught up with one another, Silas retreated to his chambers to get much-needed rest. Breakfast melted away, like the snow outside never would. Unless Malum spoke the truth. And so, Tyrus and his merry band of friends, new and old, made themselves ready to pay the Feathering Inn a much-needed truth-seeking visit.

CHAPTER 11

KEY AND LEGEND

Tyrus felt his heart race throughout his entire body, down to his smallest toe. A sharp ache stung his stomach from within as if a sapling spread its roots through his gut, growing and paining the host. He waited in the lobby of a rather fine establishment after the key master had fetched Malum from his room, telling him the mage that saved the town wanted to see him. When the mysterious man eventually strolled into the lobby, he found Tyrus waiting to hear him out. However, to his surprise, the boy didn't wait alone. Cedric, Xylia, and Lyra waited with him.

'Uhm, Tyrus, I'm pleased to see you, but…are these friends of yours?' whispered Malum as he came closer to Tyrus' ear.

'They are, and I trust them completely,' said Tyrus.

'We simply don't trust you,' fired Lyra without hesitation.

Tyrus turned back to face Malum. 'They think you're full of…' He glanced at Xylia. '*Bogus.*'

'Very well,' said Malum, his eyes narrow and his index finger resting over his lips, below his nose. He sighed and he led the way. 'Follow me…everyone.'

The entire gang entered room twelve of the Feathering Inn, one by one. Malum didn't mind the compact space before but reconsidered his position on the matter when four people and a bird joined him.

'Right, I assume you told your friends about our chat yesterday,' said Malum.

'I did and they don't believe you. They don't trust you, which is why they're here with me,' explained Tyrus, pointing at his friends. He then paused for a second. 'And the truth is, I don't know if I can trust you either. I believe that you believe you, but that's not enough.'

Malum's left hand rested at the bottom of his throat. 'That's fair, I suppose,' he said.

'Right, let's cut to the chase, shall we?' said Lyra, narrow-eyed and her arms crossed.

Everyone gathered around a solid oak table. A large thick book slept on top of it, one that had been incredibly hungry for pages, carrying words and runes and drawings. Roughly in the middle, a bookmark peeked out, biding its time for anyone to gaze at the pieces of paper it marked. Malum clapped his hands together once. It made sure everyone's attention was accounted for.

Not knowing what Tyrus had already shared with them, he started with a quick summary of how the world became the way it was. As he spoke, everyone thought the same thing; the man had a way with words. The way words rolled off of the traveller's tongue, effortless, elegant, rather posh and somehow soothing too. Cedric's fingers scoured the strands of his beard, Xylia bit their already short nails, and Lyra leaned with her palms flat on the table. All of them listened carefully. Malum gripped the giant book on the table with one hand and used the other to support his words by waving it around.

'Somewhere out there is a place,' he said, almost like he performed a serious monologue on the stage of a theatre. 'The place where the Owlbound Council cast the spell that trapped the blight. After years of research, I've learned that after completing their magical ritual, they sealed the site to prevent anyone from releasing the blight before it had died.

'The location of this place is still a mystery; however, the only way to get inside is with a key. If we find the key, I am confident we can use Tyrus' magic to locate the seal and break the prison that trapped and killed the blight, releasing us from winter's beak.'

Cedric squinted. 'This is a lovely story and you're telling it well, but do you have anything to back up those pretty little words of yours?'

'Fair question, sir,' said Malum. 'You're looking at it.

This book holds almost all of my research. You're welcome to go through it, but what I wanted to show you was this.'

Malum swung the heavy book on the table open and the bookmark could finally breathe. 'I don't know where the key is, but I do believe I have an accurate depiction of what it looks like,' he said. 'Perhaps, using the owl, we can find it somehow.'

A sketch covered the page, not made in pencil or ink; it had to be charcoal. The depiction of an owl lived on the coarse paper but it didn't resemble a real one. It looked more like a statue—a tiny one at that. The palm of a hand that was drawn behind it could swallow it whole in a balled fist. Tyrus couldn't shake the notion that it looked familiar, while Xylia's eyes widened.

'Wait, why do you two look like you recognise this?' asked Malum, his eyes sparkling with delight.

Cedric pushed his glasses a bit higher up his nose, and neither Xylia nor Tyrus could find the words to speak. Tyrus' heart pounded its way up his throat as if it wanted to jump out. He pushed his coat aside and stretched his shirt away from his chest to take out his owl head totem. He lowered his head a little—leaning forward slightly— and removed the string from around his neck. He then carefully placed his totem down next to the drawing in the book with a trembling hand. Shock conquered the faces inside room twelve with overwhelming force as the fireplace crackled and the wind outside howled. The owl head totem—aside from a few scratches, your average wear and tear—looked exactly like the head of the stone key in the book.

'Fascinating,' whispered Malum as he inspected the owl head closer.

With the aid of a magnifying glass, his emerald eyes noticed markings at the bottom of the totem. It looked like the head had been severed.

'See these cuts?' said Malum eventually. 'There's only one thing in the entirety of Wingspan that can cause this kind of cut.'

Tyrus straightened himself. 'Magic.'

'Magic indeed,' confirmed the Talonstead traveller. 'Tyrus, could you focus on this totem of yours and listen for the song of magic for me? If this is what I think it is, it will undoubtedly sing.'

To Tyrus' knowledge, he had never sensed magic coming off of his owl head totem, ever. Then again, up until a fortnight ago, he didn't possess any magic at all, so he did what Malum asked.

The room went silent until Lyra asked, 'It will sing? Are you high?'

Everyone shushed her into silence while Tyrus did as the traveller instructed. He heard the floorboards creak below Cedric's feet, he listened as Xylia's breath entered and left their lungs over and over. He focused as he registered Lyra's heart beating away and felt Malum's eyes blinking. The clock in the room ticked, the wind outside wanted to be invited in but then there was something else—a noise. A hidden layer. A familiar presence, yet new at the same time, lurked beyond it all. Between the fibres of its being, the owl head oozed with energy. *Magic.* It hummed; it sang. It sang a song no one but Tyrus and Flake could hear. How did he not notice this before?

'I can hear it! The totem, it's infused with magic. I...I've never noticed it before...What does this mean?' He had asked the question but already knew the answer.

Malum put a hand on the boy's right shoulder. 'It means you're in possession of a part of the key. A key that has been cut into pieces, *splinters*, waiting to be found!'

'Why did Sybil have part of the key to save the world?' asked Xylia.

'Either she came into possession of it illegitimately, or...' began Malum, pausing as he dug through his knowledge. 'She could have inherited it. Many Paragons on the Owlbound Council had children. It's possible she was a descendant.'

It was a real possibility and the longer Tyrus pondered it, the more it felt right. It explained so much. It explained his parents' passion for the Owlbound, it explained the tales of magic and seasons, the books, everything.

'Sibyl didn't have an owl, she didn't have magic,' mentioned Cedric, leaning over the table. 'Did she?'

'Being a descendant of an Owlbound person, doesn't

mean you automatically possess the gifts of magic,' explained Malum. 'Magic doesn't follow blood. It chooses you. It's how many children of Owlbound people survived the purge.'

'When my mom gave this to me,' began Tyrus, tears welling up. 'She and Dad had to leave suddenly. She told me to keep it safe. And then they disappeared. I think... She knew they wouldn't come back. I think this might be why they warned me about straying from the lighthouse.' He looked at Cedric. 'It couldn't fall into the wrong hands.'

'I'm so sorry, Tyrus,' said Lyra all of a sudden. She'd been unusually quiet, biding her time for when she had a meaningful to contribution to add to the conversation. 'If what Mister Malum here says is true, then Tyrus' mom carried an artefact that could doom the entire world if it was used before its time. Did something scare her?'

Malum sank away in the quicksand of his thoughts, after which he suddenly started looking around in a suitcase, one he had dragged from underneath his bed. For a moment, everyone looked at each other and only the wind outside dared to open its mouth.

'Here it is!' exclaimed Malum. 'The Renegade Paragon!'

'Oh, yeah, that sounds jolly,' said Lyra.

They all felt it, the time for another story dawned on them, another legend Malum would eloquently paint a picture for with every word that leapt off his tongue. And he did.

A few years ago, Malum had travelled all the way to Beaksworth, the biggest human settlements in the realm, ruled by a queen. There, after plenty of reconnaissance and research, he had gotten a hold of a series of notes. Notes that told the story of a powerful mage called the Renegade Paragon. A ruthless and wretched Paragon of the Owlbound arts, an individual that wished nothing more than to plunge the realm into nightmarish chaos, an ally to the blight at the core of the world itself, someone who wanted to free it.

'At first, I didn't think much of it,' said Malum. 'After all, there's plenty of stories about powerful mages out there; Merlin the Mighty, Johanna the Seeker, to name a few. But if this Renegade is real...' He looked at Tyrus. 'Or your mother had reason to believe they were real, that they were after her and the key...'

'So,' began Lyra, 'a nefarious entity at the core of our world was trapped by this council in an attempt to starve it, accidentally plunging the world into a never-ending winter. But there was also this Renegade, who basically wanted to free the entity before it died, so that it could continue to devour our world? And somehow, this person might still be around?'

'Precisely,' said Malum. 'That is the current hypothesis.'

Cedric started laughing. 'Are you all hearing yourselves? This is impossible!' he said.

'Cedric, I know how this sounds,' said Malum. 'But I believe, Tyrus' mother, and by extension his father, were tasked with guarding their part of the key until someone came along with the ability to bring about spring. Someone who could do so once enough time had passed.

'I believe that back then, when they gave Tyrus their splinter of the key, the time wasn't right. Bringing about spring wasn't safe, not yet. However, if my calculations are correct, now is the time, and with Flake by the boy's side, we can!'

Tyrus had been listening to the conversation but the knives of his grief hadn't gone dull yet. All of them, talking about his parents and what they were up to back in the day and why, it stung badly.

'What's the next step?' asked Tyrus finally.

'Well,' began Malum, 'my original plan involved figuring out how to track down the key, but since we have an actual piece of it, that shouldn't be an issue. Using the splinter we have, combined with your magic, maybe we can find the other splinters! Do me a favour…hold your totem and hold it tight.'

Malum used his hands to close Tyrus' around his owl head piece. 'Close your eyes and listen, listen to it humming…listen to it sing like before.'

Tyrus did, and like before, he found the hidden layer of sound only he and Flake could hear. Flames sparked behind his closed eyelids, behind Flake's too.

'Yes, good. Now follow it. See where it leads, Tyrus. Where does it flow to?' whispered Malum.

Could he follow it like a dog tracking a scent? The song of magic carried Tyrus' mind outside the Feathering Inn, he was above the settlement now. Meanwhile, everything in room twelve around Tyrus' body began to shake as if an incredibly local earthquake led an attack on the inn. His mind took off, flying over Featherburn's gate, back toward the forest, above the road Tyrus, Flake, and Trudy had taken to save Cedric's life. The totem started vibrating in his hand and that's when Tyrus knew where the next piece of the key hid, because those vibrations, he had experienced them before. A few days ago in fact, on that road to Featherburn, in that forest. It wasn't his chest that hummed outside that cave they encountered; it was his totem. It was his splinter of the key.

Tyrus' eyes shot open. He found himself on the floor, back in room twelve of the inn. The faces of his friends hovered above him, Malum's too. He couldn't possibly begin to explain it, but he knew. He knew the location of another splinter, the body to his owl totem. It slept at the heart of an abandoned coal mine in the forest outside town.

Tyrus could feel it in the magic; everything Malum had told them had to be the truth. They had a real shot at ending the never-ending cold. Xylia and Lyra were fully on board, too. The former felt a bit uneasy at how excited their daughter had been about all of it, because even as a child, Lyra had always dreamed about getting out of Featherburn, to see the world. And as Lyra's parent, that scared them. They knew full well this adventure wouldn't stop at an abandoned coal mine outside of town. Lyra being who she was, would want to see things through, no matter where it would lead her. Malum even managed to win Cedric over to a certain degree. The trader still didn't trust the mysterious man, but he did think he told them the truth.

'Are you all right, laddie?' asked Cedric as he helped Tyrus up from the floor.

'Yes, I'm fine. Thank you,' he said.

His head felt heavy, perhaps partly because Flake sat on top of his hat now, tilted forward, peering into those amber eyes of his, making sure he was unharmed. Tyrus explained what he had seen and where they would be able to find the chest splinter.

'The abandoned coal mine...interesting,' noted Malum.

Cedric turned to Malum once Tyrus found his footing again. 'The coal mines are dangerous. There's a reason they were abandoned.'

'Yes,' the traveller agreed. 'The perfect place to hide a splinter of the key. Wouldn't you agree?'

'Even the old miners in town think those mines are haunted,' added Lyra.

Xylia looked up at that. 'How do *you* know that?' they asked.

'Because, *they* told me,' said Lyra plainly. 'They've been having a hard time ever since Yike closed the mines after part of it collapsed. I help them out from time to time.'

Xylia sat on a chair, visibly confused. But Tyrus knew exactly how she helped those miners out; he doubted anyone else knew.

'So, what happens now?' asked Lyra.

'I go and get that splinter, that's what,' said Tyrus, his volume raised.

Malum held his hands out in front of him. 'Hold on now, Tyrus. Let's calm down for a second. We have to assume these splinters of the key are protected,' he said, slowly lowering his hands. 'It would be wise to tread carefully.'

'Besides, we didn't let you go at it alone before, we're not about to start now, laddie,' said Cedric, his voice cradling worry.

'May I propose an idea?' asked Malum.

Everyone nodded.

'Tyrus is without a doubt the one that will need to enter those treacherous caves. However, he doesn't have to go in alone. Since I possess an extensive range of knowledge about magic, I propose I go with him. Make sure things are safe,' he said.

'I'm coming with as well,' announced Lyra.

Xylia couldn't say they didn't expect this. They moved in front of Lyra, as if to protect her from Cedric, Tyrus, Flake, and Malum. 'The hell you are! Absolutely not, Lyra. It's way too dangerous.'

'Why is the boy allowed to go but not me?' fired Lyra.

'The lad has magic, you don't. Your ren is right, young lass,' agreed Cedric.

'That and the boy isn't my son. I'm not the boss of him,' added the healer.

Cedric straightened himself. 'I will join Tyrus and Malum. We can take Trudy and the carriage to get there.'

'But Ced, your arm, and you still limp,' said Tyrus.

'Don't be ridiculous, Cedric. You're in no condition yet to traverse caves,' said Xylia, immediately sliding back into their role as healer.

'You know who's in a perfect condition for that?' teased Lyra, even though she knew it wouldn't work. She had to try.

As Xylia told Lyra to cut it out, it became rather clear for Tyrus that Cedric didn't trust Malum alone with him. He wanted to be there, to make sure that there were no malicious intentions from the mysterious man. After all, Cedric supposedly had a promise to keep.

'We could use a lookout though, no?' proposed Tyrus as he decided to help his friend out.

No one disagreed and Cedric's only job would be

staying by the carriage, then be their eyes and ears outside the cave.

'It's settled then,' concluded Malum.

Tyrus, Flake, Cedric, and their new acquaintance would adventure to the abandoned coal mines in the early morning of the day that followed to retrieve a splinter to the key that could save the world.

Chapter 12

Nightmare Hex

The early morning washed over town as the sun slept for a few hours more. Several townsfolk on the other hand were already up and about. A few by choice, most less so. Some were awake because they couldn't for the life of them fall asleep; many got up at the crack of dawn because the chores had demanded so; and some, like Tyrus, had woken up early (albeit reluctantly) to embark on a journey to save the world. Malum and Cedric had left their respective beds roughly an hour before Tyrus managed to crawl out of his. They prepared the carriage with food, water, and medical supplies. They needed to be ready for anything and everything.

Ced and Tyrus had already said goodbye to both Xylia and Silas the night before, and both wished them all the luck in the world. Lyra, however, hadn't shown up. Flake had seen the girl sneak out during the night as if she were a blur, nothing more than a shadow cast by the light of the moons, carrying a pouch full of crowns. To help out villagers with what life at Featherburn ultimately came down to; coin.

A yawning Tyrus, a rather awake Flake, a grumpy Cedric, and an excited Malum were about to leave when a familiar no-nonsense voice stopped them in their tracks.

'You weren't gonna leave without saying goodbye again, were you, Clever Chap? I'm not waiting for a note this time,' said Lyra, every syllable as sharp as fangs.

Her words cut his blushing cheeks. 'Of course not!' said Tyrus, his right hand resting on the back of his neck.

'Be careful out there, Tyrus. You too, Flake,' she said as her silver hairs rode the waves of the chill wind. She pulled a strand back behind her ears.

'I will be,' said Tyrus. 'We will be.'

'Promise?' she asked.

'Promise,' he said.

She leaned in and the butterflies in Tyrus' gut burst from their cocoons when Lyra kissed him on the cheek. She took a step backward after, letting her hands rest on her lower back.

'Goodbye, Lyra,' said Tyrus. He wore his goofiest smile.

'No. Not goodbye,' she said, smiling back at him. 'See you later.'

And as the snow craved a chilling life on the various

surfaces of the world, the carriage moved away from a door that closed and toward a gate that opened.

The way to the caves they sought wasn't long, it would only take them a couple of hours. However, it felt lengthier than that because of the awkwardness in the air. Cedric steered Trudy while Tyrus and Malum sat in the carriage but instead of keeping the little window that peered inside closed, the seasoned trader insisted on leaving it open. He didn't admit it but ultimately, he wanted to hear if they talked. And if they did, he wanted to hear what they talked about. The frostiest draft crept inside alongside intense distrust and Malum didn't dare say a word. He understood the trader's feelings toward him, but if he were honest, this was getting slightly ridiculous.

The entire way over to the mines, Tyrus tried to start conversations because he couldn't bear the crushing weight of the dead air, but no matter what subject he picked, Malum brushed his attempts off in fear of Cedric's watchful eyes and stellar ears.

'Want to hear how I was bound to this little lady?' he asked him eventually; he figured magical talk would do the trick.

'I don't think you've mentioned it,' replied Malum as the seasoned trader peered inside once again.

And so, Tyrus told him his story. Sure, it wasn't the conversation he'd hoped for as much as it was only him doing the talking, but at least it had made the journey to the cave slightly less uncomfortable.

'Fascinating.' The word escaped Malum's mouth a couple of times.

'Extraordinary!' That one a few times too, while he wrote some things down in his notebook.

When the carriage came to a halt, an unnerving feeling travelled through Tyrus' veins; the mysterious mines called him inside through the vibrating totem around his neck.

He left the large coach with Flake after Malum did and climbed down the short ladder before putting his boots down into snow. Snow that also tumbled down from the heavens. It didn't take long before the boy noticed a cold and wet feeling, harassing the toes of his left foot.

'What's the matter, laddie?' asked Cedric as he tended to Trudy.

Tyrus turned and hoisted his left foot into the air, catching it with his hands, balancing on one leg. 'Nothing, it's a hole in my boot.'

'You know, a simple repair spell could fix that,' mentioned Malum.

'There is a repair spell?' Tyrus lowered his foot into the snow again, amber eyes wide and mouth open.

'Of course there's a repair spell,' grunted Cedric as he

bound Trudy to a tree, not that it would keep her from running away; it helped her understand she had to stay put.

'Well, that would have been handy to know for the bridge, wouldn't it, Trudy?' said Tyrus.

Trudy neighed.

'Hmmm, something as big as a bridge would be quite the feat, but I guess it wouldn't be impossible,' noted Malum. 'Find the hole, concentrate, guide your fires to it and will them to bridge the gap in your boot. It's no doubt easier said than done, but feel free to give it a go!'

Tyrus followed Malum's instructions to the letter. It took him a couple of tries, and he almost set his foot ablaze once because of that temper of his. He hated his flare-ups of rage, which only added more heat to his already simmering blood. He often wished he could borrow a snowsnail's patience. But eventually, after some positive reinforcement from both Malum and Cedric, he'd done it. The hole in his boot stitched itself back together.

'Awesome! Thanks, Malum!' said Tyrus before he looked up at the mountain the coal mine dug into. 'Hey, Ced, did you climb this one?'

In all the time they had known each other, the trader had mentioned his fondness of mountain climbing. He used to climb all sorts of mountains back when he had fewer grey hairs.

'As a matter of fact, I did, laddie,' answered the trader.

'Wasn't much of a challenge if I remember correctly. I bet I could still do it, too.' He laughed.

The mountain held the entrance to the abandoned coal mine at the base, surrounded by the woods. Sounds crawled out of it, nothing you could make anything out of, but Tyrus understood why the old miners thought the coal mines were haunted nowadays.

'So, what's the plan?' asked Tyrus as the owl head splinter hummed on his chest, a feeling he mistook for coming from his heart before.

'Well, we go inside,' said Malum. 'With caution, our eyes and ears open wide.'

'Okay, well, let's do this,' said Cedric as he stepped toward the entrance.

Malum frowned and Tyrus took Cedric by the arm (the one that didn't hurt) to stop him from going in.

'What do you think you're doing, old man?' asked Tyrus.

'Look, lad. I'm not letting you go in there alone with *him*,' said Cedric.

Malum rolled his eyes at that. The disdain in the trader's voice bordered on disgust.

'Roll your eyes at me one more time, ya bastard!' threatened Cedric and Tyrus intervened, getting in between the two his arms stretched on either side.

Malum backed away. 'I'm not the enemy here, Cedric! I merely want this miserable eternal winter to end, for talon's sake! Same as you I'd hope!'

'Seriously, Cedric, talk to me. What's the matter with you?' asked Tyrus.

The seasoned trader took a step back and looked down.

'He's jealous,' said Malum. 'Jealous of how we talk about magic with each other, jealous of how your face lights up when you talk to me about the world from ages past. That's what this boils down to, isn't it? Jealousy!'

'You shut your mouth!' warned Cedric, shooting forward past Tyrus, pointing a finger in Malum's face. It almost went up his nose.

'Enough!' shouted Tyrus. 'The both of you.'

Cedric took a step back and looked the other way to avoid Malum's gaze and funnily enough, he did the exact same thing. Tyrus felt like the only adult in these woods.

'Look, Ced, I'm sorry you don't trust Malum, but he's not going to replace you. No one can. And Mal.' He paused. 'That wasn't classy either now, was it?'

If there was one thing Cedric and Malum could agree on it was that they hated being lectured to, especially by a sixteen-year-old boy.

'I'm sorry, I shouldn't have said what I said,' spoke Malum in Tyrus' direction.

Tyrus shook his head, standing there with his arms crossed and he looked toward Cedric. Flake looked fierce too, to which Malum repeated his words, this time addressing the trader.

'I was angry at the way you've been treating me. My apologies.'

Cedric turned to Malum, albeit reluctantly.

'Apology accepted…I'm…sorry too, I shouldn't have been this cold to you.'

Tyrus let out a deep breath. 'Great, now can we get back to saving the world?' he said as everyone agreed to stick to the original plan. Cedric would stay and keep an eye out, while Malum, Tyrus, and Flake entered the mines.

'Take care of him, will you?' asked Cedric, one hand on Malum's shoulder.

'You have my word,' he answered, and he decided to give Ced and Tyrus space.

Cedric put his hands on Tyrus' shoulders, one arm lifted more easily than the other. 'I am sorry; I'd forgotten exactly how jealous I can get. This is going a bit fast all of a sudden and I promised your pa—'

'It's okay,' Tyrus cut in. 'I understand and hey, again, no one could ever replace you, old man.' He smiled and Cedric smiled back.

'I'm proud of you, lad,' he said. Tears lounged in the corners of his eyes behind those round glasses of his. 'Now, go and get that splinter.'

They hugged. Tyrus always figured that hugging the people you cared most about was like sharing in their emotions; it felt like exchanging memories of each other, with each other, in the comfort of a warm embrace.

And then, the time had come. Tyrus, Malum and Flake entered the cave and as soon as darkness swallowed them whole, Ced's leg wouldn't stop shaking until they'd return to the light of the snow, glistening in the sunshine.

'Now, Tyrus. Remain vigilant. These tunnels and caves are treacherous and who knows what obstacles await us in search of this splinter,' said Malum, who treaded carefully behind the magical duo, his words echoing off the sides of the mine.

Tyrus, Flake, and Malum, started in an eerie mineshaft. Rusty rails for minecarts led the way into the unknown, and the tunnels they traversed were held up by worn-down wooden pillars and beams. Unlit lanterns hung from the pillars, holding the ghosts of flames from long ago. Tyrus wondered what these tunnels would have looked like when they were still in use. As they went deeper, the tunnels turned in an elaborate network, but thanks to the owl head around Tyrus' neck, they didn't have to worry much about navigating. What Malum did worry about was finding their way back after collecting what they came here for. Tyrus and Flake made quick work of extinguishing those worries by lighting the lanterns in the tunnels they walked through.

At a certain point, the rails on the floor ended. The tunnels became more irregular, more cave-like, no lanterns could light the way anymore. Tyrus held his signature blue and purple-ish flames in his right hand to provide a source of light. The sounds emitted from deeper within the cave became louder and clearer until they circled them, disoriented them. They surrounded them. Slowly, steadily and most of all, creepingly. With his empty hand, Tyrus soothed Flake who sat trembling on his shoulder. Every inch of that cave was drenched with eeriness, even worse than the mineshafts before.

'Stay focused, Tyrus,' he heard Malum say.

Despite standing right behind him, he sounded far away. Tyrus even turned around to see if he was right behind him. He was. When he turned back, the cave ate his fire, feasted on it, including the flames that burned in the eyes of his bird and his own. His fire wouldn't light and by now Flake had practically glued herself to the side of Tyrus' head.

'Mal?! Are you there?!' he shouted, and his question echoed and echoed until it came back like a boomerang.

No matter what Flake or Tyrus tried, their magic wouldn't flow, until it did and a bigger flame than anticipated sparked out of the boy's palm, making him trip and fall to the slippery rock-hard ground. When, eventually, a more manageable light shone from the palm of his hand, the walls of the mines weren't right; they appeared to be moving, like snakes shedding their skins. The walls formed faces and they shouted despicable, heinous things. The voices, warped at first, changed. They turned into voices Tyrus recognised, voices he valued, voices he missed.

'We're dead because of you,' he heard his mother say.

'I've always wanted a son, but not one like you,' said his father.

The voices lied, but they stabbed Tyrus' mind as badly as they would if they were truths. His parents had never said anything remotely like that, and they never would have. But hearing those words in their actual voices, voices he hadn't had the pleasure of hearing in a long time, hurt more than he could ever put into words.

'Your father and I, we're glad we're not alive to see what you have become!' his mother screamed as he cried and cried.

Tyrus closed his eyes, trying to ignore it all. He started shouting, attempting to drown out their voices, but when he finally found the strength to get to his feet, a figure grabbed him tight. His eyelids lifted and he stared into the tearful face of his father.

'You let us die! You didn't try to save us; you could have saved us!' he shouted.

'I was barely a teenager when you perished!' screamed Tyrus as he pushed the twisted shape of his father away. 'What was I supposed to do?! Mom told me she'd be back before I knew it. She told me to stay put, to stay with the lighthouse!' He sobbed. 'Why did you not come back?!'

'Because we'd rather die than come back home to you, boy!' shouted his mother.

The maniacal laughter of his parents echoed throughout the cave.

'No! Lies!' shouted Tyrus.

Despite Flake being there with him, he couldn't feel his connection to her at all. The bird found herself unable to move, and no matter how hard she tried, unable to reach out to her human.

Meanwhile, rage continued filling Tyrus' lungs, his gut, every fibre of his being, even as sharp sounds pierced his eardrums. Between that sharpness, between the hurtful words and hateful syllables, between his rage and evil itself, somehow a different voice persevered. It pushed through. Somehow it reached him. It was Malum.

'Tyrus, none of this is real, it's spell work. Genius spell work, forbidden spell work, but spell work nonetheless. This is all in your mind!' he shouted.

Suddenly, everything went quiet and Tyrus, still panting out his rage and sorrow, didn't trust it. He found himself in emptiness, or so he thought. Out of nowhere he felt a tingling sensation in the back of neck. He slapped it because, it felt like a bug had crawled up there. It stuck to his hand. He didn't dare look. Was this still part of this nightmare or was it real? He glanced at his hand, against his better judgement. He shouldn't have.

A huge dead spider clung to it and as he tried to get rid

of the eight-legged carcass, thousands of spiders like it—
alive ones—erupted from the walls. Tyrus screamed and
screamed and screamed, feeling every leg that crawled
across his body while Flake flew to the ceiling of the cave
to save herself. He begged for help, drowning in a sea of
hungry spiders. Was this where his story ended?

'Tyrus, the magic, it has a hold over you. It uses your
fear, but you have to fight it, you have to fight it!'

It uses your fear.

It made sense. Tyrus had spent years wondering if he
could have done something. Perhaps he could have saved
his parents, but what he'd told this shadow version of his
mother was true. He was only a child, barely a teenager.
There was nothing he could have done, and his own
parents had told him to stay put. There wasn't any magic
to aid him, not back then.

And then there were the spiders, Tyrus had been
terrified of spiders since always, the memories of him
being afraid of the eight-legged bastards dated back to
one of his first. But Malum kept reaching out because he
had read about spell work such as this; it was rare and
cruel but there was a way out. He believed the boy could
fight his way through this deep nightmare and Tyrus
started believing it too. Tyrus unleashed all the anger
he had inside of him, every ounce of pure distilled hate
burst out of him in the form of a wave of fire. A fiery wave
that washed over the spiders, burning them all to a crisp,

reuniting him with his bird.

Tyrus opened his eyes, eyes that he had never closed in the first place. He knew he was free when Flake's large eyes and Malum's upside-down face hovered above his.

'Oh, thank goodness! You did it, Tyrus! You did it!' he exclaimed.

'What in the world was that?!' said Tyrus breathing heavily.

Malum stood up and held his hand out to Tyrus. 'That, young lad, was magic that the Paragons of the Owlbound Council had forbidden. A nightmare hex, they called it.'

'I wouldn't wish that upon anyone, not even scum like Chief Yike,' said Tyrus as he got to his feet with Malum's help. 'Did it get to you too?'

'Oh yes, it did…Unfortunately, it did.'

Tears welled behind Malum's eyes. Tyrus offered to talk about it but he kindly declined. Whatever the spell showed him, he didn't want to relive it again.

'How did they even do this?' asked Tyrus.

'It's an outright diabolical use of magic, it uses runes to inscribe and infuse nightmarish magic into an object or a place.'

'Right, so the old miners were kind of right, this place *is* haunted.'

Malum, Tyrus, and Flake travelled deeper and deeper into the mine and the atmosphere grew grimmer with every step they took until a blue light shone bright in the distance like the fire in Tyrus' eyes would. They followed it to an open carved out space with at the end of it—and in the middle of the coarse wall—the next piece of the key. The owl body splinter sat frozen in ice and the head piece around Tyrus' neck longed for it. It shone in a dim pastel blue light.

'Extraordinary,' said Malum once he caught sight of it.

The entire opening seemed like it was hollowed out by pickaxes. Once upon a time, it had to have been a coal ore deposit, and a big one at that. The narrow spaces they followed to this place, were likely the veins that had led to it. Here and there, a few pieces of coal still sat lodged in the walls and ceiling, but they glowed too, an unmistakenly magical glow.

Tyrus wanted to run at the chest splinter immediately, but Malum stopped him, because in the middle of the room on the floor sat runic inscriptions in what seemed like sand.

'I'd be careful if I were you,' warned Malum. 'These are the runes that made our minds the most nightmarish of prisons.'

They looked elegant, refined, and yet the source of all that wretchedness. They basically spelled out what the caster wanted the hex to do. Malum noticed something in the runes other than nightmares, though.

Tyrus noticed it too, even though his runic reading had been rusty. 'Malum, do you see what I'm seeing?' he asked as they walked past the runes, hugging the walls on either side. 'Flake, are you?'

Flake hooted affirmingly while Malum took a moment to study the runes more closely.

'The last line of defence,' he said eventually. 'If anyone were to run through it, disturb these runes'—he looked at Tyrus—'the cave would collapse in on itself to protect the body splinter. Remarkable.'

'So, be careful. Got it,' said Tyrus as he inched closer to the frozen chest piece, encapsulated in ice until he stood in front of it.

'Okay, melt the ice gently,' instructed Malum as he joined Tyrus' side.

The young mage held both hands around the ice as blue and purple danced across his palms. The intent he gave it made it heat up slowly and steadily. The ice melted away until the body splinter came free. Tyrus and Malum looked at each other as excitement leapt between emerald and amber. Flake, however, felt like something wasn't right, she wanted to try and tell Tyrus, but she was too late. Tyrus' hand had closed around the chest piece already and sadly, the bird was right. The failsafe in the runes wasn't the last line of defence, it was *a* line of defence. The true failsafe was the splinter itself.

A powerful pulse broke free from the chest piece and the three adventurers were flung backwards, causing Tyrus to let go of the splinter in the process. Thanks to her manoeuvres in the air, Flake was able to land elegantly by the opening through which they came, but Tyrus and Malum had no such luck. They landed in the sand of the runes. Malum instructed Tyrus to get up carefully, and for a handful of seconds, nothing happened. They thought they were in the clear, despite having disrupted the runes. However, as soon as Tyrus sighed deeply in relief, the pieces of coal that lit the carved-out space lost their shining quality, and the cave and mining system sighed back with a violent shake. The damage was done, the runes disturbed. The ground beneath their feet suddenly felt instable, it felt like they found themselves inside the bowels of an enraged colossal monster. Tyrus, Malum, and Flake shared frightful looks as the walls began crumbling.

'Tyrus! The body piece!' shouted Malum.

The boy had almost forgotten to pick it back up from the floor and luckily, the pulse was a one-time thing. He then slid the splinter in the inside pocket of his cloak and started running. Flake flew because she'd only slow her friend down. Together, they ran and ran, and the bird flew and flew. The cave crumbled around them but the white light of the snow outside closed in.

'Tyrus! Malum!' they heard Cedric shout, the panic in his voice spread through the collapsing cave when a heavy boulder, the size of two owls, struck Malum in the back.

He fell to the ground, but he was behind Tyrus, who

didn't see until he cried out. Tyrus turned around and saw Malum, laying on the floor struggling to get up.

'Go, Flake! Get out of here!' commanded Tyrus but she refused and started kicking falling pieces of rock out of the way with her talons to protect her humans.

Outside, Cedric felt like he couldn't breathe, the ground shook. Trudy panicked and the trader hoped he'd see that dumb smile on Tyrus' face again. Shortly after the trembling had started though, it stopped. Smoke and dust fled out the cave, but nothing and no one else.

'Tyrus?! Flake?! Malum?!' repeated Cedric as he fell to his knees but no one answered.

He lowered his head, preparing to feel the unimaginable pain inside his heart but right before he would burst out into inconsolable tears, Flake landed in front of him, hooting at him in distress. Two coughing people reached his ears.

'Oh! Laddie, Flake! Thank the heavens!' exclaimed the trader.

Tyrus struggled keeping Malum up. Every time they took a step, the man screeched out in pain. Tyrus tried to hold in his coughs to take their steps as stable as possible, but it was only when Cedric ran over to assist that Malum was able to fully keep his shoulder stable as they walked toward the carriage. Free from carrying Malum out a collapsing mineshaft, Tyrus began coughing out his lungs because of all the dust. Not only magic and blood ran through his veins at that moment, adrenaline too, lots of it.

'Are you okay, laddie?' asked Cedric, hugging him tight, and then inspecting him for any major injuries.

Tyrus looked at him with wide eyes. 'I got it,' he said. 'We got it, Ced!'

Cedric smiled. 'That's great lad, but that's not what I asked, was it?'

'Right,' answered Tyrus. 'A bit beat up, but I'm fine. Don't you worry.'

'I'm fine too, you know…Thanks.' Malum coughed, followed by another fit of straining pain in his shoulder.

Ignoring Malum, Cedric asked to see what they had just risked their dear lives for. Tyrus folded open his right hand and there it sat, the body splinter that belonged with the owl head, a splinter of the key to save the world from the cold. Malum and Cedric watched as Tyrus took the owl head totem from around his neck and brought it closer to the chest piece until both pieces got loose from his grip and smashed into each other, merging into one, floating in the air. For a moment, Malum forgot all about the pain he was in.

Tyrus grabbed the merged splinters and as he did, his mind was transported, the way it had transported itself when he was in room twelve of the Feathering Inn. He flew over the landscape but this time he flew much farther, soaring through the sky until he arrived at an island, surrounded by a frozen sea, an island off the coast of Crownhaven. That's where the next splinter to form the key hid.

When Tyrus came to, the first thing he noticed was that the sun had moved a considerable bit, an impossible bit, in fact; it was already sinking. Had he been out like an extinguished candle for that long?

'How long was I out for?' he asked.

'Oh, not long, a minute at the most,' said Malum.

'Wait, how long were we in there for then?' asked the amber-eyed boy, pointing at the mine.

Cedric stroked his beard. 'Oh, I don't know, seven? Perhaps eight hours? Why?'

Magic, what a peculiar thing.

'What did you see?' shot Malum, grabbing his hurt shoulder.

Tyrus revealed the location of the next splinter, but before they could start their journey there, they'd have to head back to Featherburn.

'If we leave now, we can make it before the sun sets completely,' said Cedric.

He had the right idea, they did not want to spend the night in the forest outside town, and as for a journey to Crownhaven, they were simply not prepared. Besides, Malum hurt his shoulder pretty badly, he couldn't move his left arm at all. Xylia would have to take a look at it for sure.

Together, Tyrus and Cedric carried the injured traveller into the carriage and this time, Cedric kept the little window closed, but no conversations were had, because the entire ride back to town, Tyrus and Malum napped and snored until they woke to the sound of opening gates.

'We did it, we got the body piece of the key!' announced Tyrus as he swung open the door of Xylia's living room.

Hoot!

Both Cedric and a slightly crooked Malum stood proud behind the magical duo but their return wasn't met with the enthusiasm they'd expected. Silas got up from his armchair as Xylia remained sat in front of the hearth, peering into the seemingly endless flames.

The hunter sighed. 'That's wonderful news, but…'

Tyrus frowned. 'What's the matter? What happened?'

'It's Lyra,' said Xylia. The words chilled everyone to the bone.

Cedric pressed on. 'What about the lass?'

'They took her.'

CHAPTER 13

THEY TOOK HER

'Goodbye, Lyra,' he said.

He wore his goofiest smile.

'No. Not goodbye,' she said, smiling back at him. 'See you later.'

While the early morning plunged fluffy snow down to Featherburn's walls, roads, and rooftops, the white-haired girl saw the carriage moving away from the door she opened and closed. A door that led to same old same old. It would lead Lyra toward a perfectly normal day. Or at least, that was what she thought. But what she thought couldn't always come to be.

A few hours after she went back to bed to sleep for a few hours more, a pounding disturbed the infirmary door. It was loud and rude.

'Healer Xylia, Hunter Silas! Open up! This is the Featherburn Watch!' shouted a town guard.

Xylia travelled down the stairs to open the door, even though the infirmary wouldn't officially be open for another two hours. The guard kept pounding. It sounded urgent and as soon as the healer moved the bolt out of the front door lock, the Watch wrapped in brown leather armour and metal helmets barged in. An entire garrison of them, but none of them seemed injured.

'I beg your pardon? What's the meaning of this?' demanded Xylia. They expected to treat cuts, stabs, burns, or frostbite, not for them to barge in like this.

The guard commander ordered the others to look around, to search the entire infirmary from top to bottom, including private quarters.

Xylia fumed. 'What right do you think you have?' they asked.

He turned their way. 'I'm sorry, Healer. But we have reason to believe a stolen object, finds itself to be in this building.'

Xylia looked around frantically, but in the back of their mind, a question burned. *What did Lyra do now?* Silas joined his partner downstairs, asking the guards the same questions and a couple of moments later, Lyra also descended the stairs.

'The girl, grab her!' ordered one of the broader guards.

Lyra's eyebrows lifted her forehead like arms lifting weights. Were they here because of the pocket watch? She wanted to run back upstairs and escape through her window, but another guard had already blocked the staircase and grabbed hold of her arm.

'Search the girl's bedroom.' The order spread through the room like wildfire and two guards followed it up the stairs.

'What in the bound and unbound is going on here?!' shouted Silas. 'Let her go, right this second!'

Any and all sounds that carried through the ground floor of the infirmary were sucked out of the air the moment Chief Yike stepped through the front door.

'Chief?' Silas hesitated. 'What's…going on?'

The chief looked concerned but a smirk hid behind the façade. 'It pains me to bring you this news on this fine morning but I believe your daughter stole from me.'

'This again? Lyra helped save this town!' argued Xylia.

Yike brushed the snow off of his armour. 'Oh no, this is not at all about that,' he said with a smirk. The façade had dropped.

'Then what is it about?' spat Lyra from across the room. There was no way they were going to find her secret stash, right? She hid it away under the loose floorboards below her bed.

The two guards that had gone upstairs to search Lyra's room returned. The girl's heart raced and sweat conquered her armpits. The right one carried most of the contents of her hidden stash, the other held the golden pocket watch she stole from the chief at the market. Chief Yike smiled.

'Well…that's what it's about, thief. What was it that you said to me at the market? Thank you for your time? Clever… I'm afraid it's *time* to pay for your crimes!' he spat, his nose closing in on hers.

Lyra couldn't help herself and spat in his face. He deserved worse but that was all she had in the moment.

'Get her out of here!' ordered Yike.

Xylia started crying and Silas' disappointed stare stabbed her heart. She never intended to cause her parents pain or shame. The simple truth was, she should have known better than to rob the chief of their town *again*. She should have resisted the urge.

Chief Yike turned toward Xylia and Silas. 'I'm deeply sorry, but your daughter is under arrest on various accounts of thievery. Her punishment shall be determined soon,' he said and he followed his men out the door, dragging a cuffed and struggling Lyra with them.

'Mighty talons, is there anything we can do?' asked Cedric.

Silas' hands balled into fists he tried hiding in his pockets. 'Nothing…at least not until we know her punishment,' he said.

Tyrus read how defeated the hunter felt, right off the pages of his face. The powerlessness nagged at him like a rat at an open wound.

Silas let his now trembling hands cover his face. 'I should have been here. If I was not out hunting all the time, maybe I could have—'

'Don't do that to yourself, brother,' said Cedric as he sat down next to the man. 'What Lyra did couldn't have been prevented and you know it.'

Meanwhile, Tyrus inched closer to Xylia who sat there in silence, paralysed by what had happened that morning. Malum—even though he found himself to be in quite some pain—didn't want to disturb them by asking if they could fix up his shoulder, but Tyrus thought he'd try. Maybe it could keep the healer's mind occupied with something other than their daughter's arrest.

'Hey, Xylia?' he said quietly. 'I know this is stressful, but everything will be fine. We'll make this right, I promise.'

'Don't pretend like you know what's going to happen,' they snapped. 'Don't pretend like you know for sure this will all end well, because you don't. No one does. So please, do me the courtesy of being honest with me. Now, what is it you need?'

Tyrus felt taken aback a little. 'I'm sorry, I didn't mean to—'

'What is it you need?' repeated Xylia, their words blunt like an ancient knife.

'Malum injured his shoulder while we got the splinter, could you take a look at it?' the boy asked, his voice shaky.

'Sure,' answered Xylia, standing up.

Both Malum and Tyrus followed them down to an examination room, while Flake stayed with Cedric and Silas. She attempted to comfort the distressed father, tried to cheer him up by walking around all silly-like. It turned out to be the most difficult and impossible of tasks that had ever existed.

Once seated on the table—ready to be examined— Malum took off his coat and removed his sweater and shirt for the healer to look at his aching shoulder. He struggled and both Xylia and Tyrus helped him. His shirt had been the hardest piece of clothing to get off and eventually, Xylia lost their patience. They grabbed a pair of scissors and cut the thing off Malum's body. The skin on his entire right shoulder had turned into a mix of dark and light purple with hints of brown and yellow. It also looked like it didn't sit right. Xylia recognised they dealt with a dislocated shoulder as soon as they saw it. Malum's back wore a large tattoo in the shape of an owl, and Tyrus' jaw gaped at the thing. The artist had only used black ink. Malum didn't opt for a realistic depiction. Instead, he had chosen the runic symbol for the bird, a more abstract rendition of an owl's features: the wings, the talons, the beak, the eyes; all the ingredients of what made a bird an owl were present. The tattoo made Tyrus think of the one his mother had; it looked similar. Hers was smaller though, and it lived on her upper left arm.

'When did you get that tattoo?' asked Tyrus to distract Malum. Xylia prepared to put his shoulder back in place.

'Tyrus, I see what you're trying to do,' said Malum before he shouted out in agony as Xylia relocated his shoulder.

After, it still felt sore but at least it could heal properly now.

'Thank you, Healer. Now, do you by any chance have a spare shirt for me?' he said with a painful smile.

They did and after Malum got dressed, everyone hunkered down. Waiting for the verdict about Lyra's punishment, they prepared themselves for the worst. They waited and waited, because after all, there wasn't anything else to do. Or at least, nothing that would help Lyra's case.

The news didn't arrive until the next day. The chief had had his meeting with his board and delivered a letter with the verdict to Xylia's infirmary in person, escorted by a security detail.

Dear Xylia and Silas, parents of Lyra,

We regret to inform you the evidence found in your daughter's room confirmed her to be the perpetrator of a dozen pickpocketing incidents. It was hereby declared that a simple slap on the wrist wouldn't suffice. While banishment and the removal of hands were on the table, the Featherburn Board decided on imprisonment. Lyra will be held in the town's jail for an undefined amount of time, until Chief Yike is convinced she has learned her lesson. Like any other prisoner, she will be granted one family visitation per month until she is released.

Sincerely,
The Featherburn Board

'This isn't fair! It's outrageous!' screamed Xylia after reading through it. 'You hate her, despise her! You'll never let her see the light of day again!'

The chief folded his hands together. 'Xylia, I understand you are angry, but the girl made her choices. Those choices have consequences. It pains me you think so little of me that I'd never release her. She will be free when I know for sure she won't cheat the fine people of our town ever again!' he said as a dastardly smile thrived between his cheeks.

And that was the end of it. Lyra would be allowed one family visit every month like the other inmates, the thought of which weighed heavily on the minds of both her parents. Xylia fell to the floor and started crying, while Silas wrestled his tears and hugged his partner tight. Neither of them could bear the idea of seeing their little girl only once a month. Furthermore, the fact their daughter would rot in a prison cell for possibly the remainder of Yike's time as chief gave them a nauseating headache they were sure to never recover from. Xylia tried pleading, even going as far as offering to take their daughter's place, but Chief Yike declined. His mind was made up.

After Yike had left, Tyrus said, 'No, this isn't over. We can't let him get away with this.' The fires of rage burned and roared inside of him; he owed it to Lyra to help her. After all, he did tell her he'd see her later, and not goodbye.

'What do you propose we do, laddie?' asked Cedric. He sounded genuinely interested in what Tyrus was thinking, but at the same time, his eyes widened ever so slightly with worry. Worry that one day, that rage might ruin the boy's life.

'We stage a prison break,' he said. 'I'll blast her cell open with magic and we all run.'

'Surely, you're smarter than that, boy.' Silas after uttered a deranged laugh. 'You can't go ahead and break my daughter out of prison with your magic! They'll hunt the two of you down and kill you!' he added with balled fists.

'What if there were no clues to hunt them down with?' posed Malum from the other side of the room. 'It would require practice, but there is a spell that could help Tyrus get Lyra out of that cell without the guards noticing until it was too late. It's a spell that would allow Tyrus to become the magical flames themselves and phase through the prison wall. It would allow him to take Lyra and phase back through.'

Did he hear that right? 'Holy talons! I can do that?!' asked Tyrus.

'As I said, it would require practice, but…yes. Ideally, casting portals would be perfect in this scenario, but you're not strong enough for that yet.'

'Even if you pull this off without leaving evidence, where will she go?' countered Silas, now watery-eyed.

Tyrus hesitated to speak his mind, almost certain both Silas and Xylia wouldn't like it in the slightest. But then, he found the courage. 'We still have to find the other splinters of the key, however many more there are. She'd be more than welcome to join us,' he said.

'Her talents would certainly be useful,' noted Malum.

'Enough!' shouted Silas, his face red and fuming. 'My daughter is not coming on your beyond dangerous quest to save the bloody world!'

'Do it,' said Xylia as they turned around.

They hadn't been participating in the conversation, but they had tuned in. Their cobalt blues looked Silas in the eyes.

'This way, our daughter can at least be free. You don't want her to rot inside those cells for the rest of Yike's tenure as chief, do you?' they asked.

Their argument seeped into his bones.

'I'm being selfish, aren't I?' he asked finally.

Xylia let their hands cup Silas' face. 'I want her close too, but not like this. Besides, you know as well as I do she wasn't going to let this whole magical saving the world adventure go. She would have found a way to go with them regardless. She'd have snuck out under the cover of night and left us a note.'

Silas let out a deep sigh as tears ran into Xylia's hands. 'How is it you're always right?' He turned to Tyrus; determination drenched his irises. 'Okay, do it.'

An entire week of preparations flew by in the blink of an eye. Tyrus trained with Malum every day, and phasing through a solid wall proved to be a great challenge for him. It was a week filled with Malum pushing Flake and Tyrus to the limits of their powers. Tyrus had to first become the flames of his magic themselves before being able to move and phase through a wall. It took him two whole days to be able to turn into those flames, and the days after were mostly spent running into walls. And as if that wasn't enough, through practice, Tyrus quickly learned he'd be able to execute his phasing spell twice before running out of mana. He would only be able to phase through the jail wall to get in and back out. But there was another wall that stood between them and freedom, the wall surrounding Featherburn itself.

Because Tyrus and Lyra wouldn't be able to walk through the gates, Silas spoke with a friend on the Featherburn construction team, a friend who owed him a favour. Under the guise of the frost golem attack from earlier, they managed to create a hole in the Featherburn wall, large enough for Lyra, Tyrus, and Flake to escape through. There was only one problem. The construction team was immediately ordered to fix it as soon as possible, which meant Tyrus was suddenly on a tight schedule for learning his spell. It was only around noon on the day before the prison break when Tyrus finally managed to successfully phase for the first time. He didn't feel confident, and the only thing he could do was practice more and hope he was ready.

Malum approached Tyrus a few hours before the prison break. 'Necessity and urgency have often driven human and elvenkind alike to do the things they thought they could never do. Perhaps tonight, your spell work will exceed your expectations,' he said in an effort to calm the kid's nerves. 'In fact, I'm sure it will. I believe in you two.'

Tyrus hoped he was right, because there was no more time for practice now, whether he had mastered his spells or not, they were breaking Lyra out of her cell at midnight.

Two full moons graced the night sky as the hour struck midnight and Tyrus and Flake snuck their way through the empty streets of Featherburn. Their quest to free Lyra had begun.

Everyone had taken their positions. The only hiccup that saw the light of the moons was when Xylia discovered the hole in the wall was guarded, something Silas' friend had forgotten to mention. Ultimately, it didn't matter. Xylia came prepared, because in the days leading up to the prison break, while Cedric gathered supplies, Malum trained Flake and Tyrus, and Silas helped out where he could, they were in the infirmary poisoning darts with sedative, mixing the same stuff into cookies (they couldn't be sure what they'd need and what not). They even laced a couple of daggers with the sleepy mixture to be sure. When push came to shove, Xylia ended up feeding the guards the cookies they had made. The two watchers of the hole in the wall would sleep for the entire night and as a bonus, not remember a thing.

Meanwhile, Cedric and Malum had stationed themselves outside Featherburn. They left through the gates as soon as the sun went down and positioned themselves roughly a mile's walk from the hole in the wall, ready to sweep Tyrus and Lyra off their feet and journey to Crownhaven. But for now, everything was up to Tyrus and Silas.

Tyrus snuck up to the back of the guard-post, ready to (hopefully) run through the wall of Lyra's cell. He felt her quaking behind the bricks with his magic. Tyrus' heart quickened with anger. The punishment Lyra was receiving, did not fit her crime. And even if they had criminals that had done something so wrong to end up in a cell, no one deserved to be left in the cold. Yes, they needed to be punished, but as far as Tyrus was concerned, robbing them of their freedom was enough. He waited until he heard Silas arrive, because the hunter would serve as the distraction to make sure the guard wouldn't be an issue.

Luckily, Flake and her mage didn't have to wait long before Lyra's father arrived, pretending to be drunk beyond reason. He blurted out the most incomprehensible kind of gibberish, but it worked. The guard left their post to assess the situation.

Tyrus took his chance as every fibre of his being, and every fibre of Flake's, caught fire and morphed into the flames themselves, swirling in purple and blue. Together they moved toward the wall of Lyra's cell. Tyrus laid his fiery palms flat on its surface until they started phasing through and just like that, the wall swallowed him whole. It also spewed him back out on the other side where Lyra was supposed to be chained to the moist floor of the gloomy cell. Instead, she had broken free from her chains, trying to pick the lock of her cell using a paperclip of sorts. One she undoubtedly nicked off a guard. She turned around as the cold ruled over her body in shivers. The purple bags under her eyes had never weighed more and her beautiful eyes muddled in confusion at the flames before her. But then, the flames became a boy and an owl.

'Clever Chap? Flake?' she whispered, her greasy hair pointing at every wall. 'What are you doing here?'

'What am I doing here? I'm busting you out,' said Tyrus.

'I was busting me out,' said Lyra.

Tyrus nodded. 'I can see that, impressive. Now, care to get out of here?'

'No, I'm good honestly,' she joked. 'Of course, I want out of here, dummy.'

Tyrus reached out and she took him by the hand. For her the touch was warm, for him the opposite but both of them found comfort in it nonetheless. He then closed his eyes and as he did, he became embers, Flake followed and lastly, Lyra as well. For a moment, flames in the shapes of a boy, a girl, and a bird danced in a prison cell that night. Tyrus wondered what Lyra was thinking, what she was feeling. She hadn't made a sound either, perhaps she was speechless, perhaps she didn't want to get caught in an escape attempt.

Outside, Silas struggled keeping the guard distracted. The guard told him to get lost, to find a different person to dump all his drunken thoughts with. It came to the point where Silas threw himself onto the guard, acting like he was going to throw up. An attempt to give his daughter, Tyrus, and the bird more time. It wasn't enough. The guard pushed Silas to the snow on the ground and kicked him in the stomach.

'Get away, you pathetic prick!' he shouted.

Inside, Tyrus leapt toward the wall with full confidence but instead of going through, his face met solid brick. Within seconds, both the boy's and the girl's backs hit the floor. The embers had gone as they heard the guard and their clamouring armour heading back to their post. Tyrus' heart threw a massive tantrum. He laid on the ground breathing rather fast and heavily. He couldn't do it. What was he thinking? They were doomed now, right? His plan would fail, the chief would lock the three of them up…or worse.

'Tyrus, come on get up, we need to try again,' whispered Lyra. 'Breathe.'

'I don't know if I can,' spat Tyrus, fuming, panicking.

Lyra got up to her feet and held out her hand. 'Don't give me that *bogus*. I'll be damned if I let me be the reason you're in a cell as well. You can do this! I believe in you, Clever Chap. You got this.'

Tyrus' parents laid beside him, only for the boy with the curly hair to see. He closed his eyes, took a deep breath, held it for three seconds, and let go. His parents were gone, never there, but they made sure Tyrus pushed through the panic. With Lyra's help, Tyrus got to his feet, and Flake hopped back on his shoulder, ready to try again, and this time it had to work; he already felt the magic in and around him waver. The sound of the guard opening the door, returning to their post reached him and lent him the extra push he needed to phase through that wall with Lyra holding his hand tight.

Fresh air thrived in Lyra's lungs as the two moons looked into her eyes and the gentle snowfall clung to her hair. They were outside, but Tyrus felt a little light-headed. He struggled to keep his balance and so, Lyra swung his right arm over her shoulder to support him and together they made way for the hole in the wall as Silas proceeded to keep the guard away from the actual cells; they needed to delay the sounding of alarms for as long as possible.

Twelve frighteningly cold minutes passed until Tyrus, Lyra and Flake arrived at the hole in the wall. Xylia met them there, accompanied by two sleeping guards.

'Oh, my little girl!' they whispered and Lyra dove into those arms like there was no tomorrow. 'Thank you, Tyrus,' they added as they embraced Lyra tightly.

'I don't think I could have made it back here without Lyra's help, so she also saved me,' said Tyrus. 'Again.'

'Your modesty makes me want to puke at times, you know that, Tyrus? Then again, I almost got out on my own, so there's that,' fired Lyra. 'Anyway, let's say we're square now? Great. What's the plan?'

'Cedric and Malum are waiting beyond the wall. We head for the carriage,' explained Tyrus while he caught his breath a smidge.

'Okay, then we'll go as soon as Dad gets here, right, Ren?' asked Lyra. The hope in her voice broke Xylia's heart.

'Lyra…we're not coming with you,' said Xylia.

'What do you mean?' asked Lyra. 'You have to come with.'

'You go on your adventure. We'll see each other again, I promise,' they added.

'I'm not leaving without you,' she said while trying desperately not to cry.

'This is what you've always wanted. You're going to travel across Wingspan,' said Xylia.

'But this is not *how* I wanted what I've always wanted,' said Lyra, now crying. 'It isn't fair.'

'Me and your father, we'll be fine, but you can't stay in Featherburn, and we can't get up and leave out of the blue. We both have duties upon which people's lives depend,' explained Xylia. 'You do understand that, yes?'

'I do but I don't have to like it,' cried Lyra.

Xylia hugged her tight. 'It's okay. We'll meet again. As soon as we can leave, we'll find you.'

Then, Silas arrived, on time by a hair's breadth, to say goodbye to his daughter, his Lyra. The man had run as fast as he could and the three of them shared a hug so warm, Tyrus swore he could feel the heat landing on his face.

'Godspeed, Tyrus and Flake. And be careful, Lyra… Don't get into too much trouble,' said Silas.

'You know me, Dad. I wouldn't dare,' said Lyra with tears freezing to her cheeks.

The stars and the moons bore witness to the trio escaping Featherburn, traversing the snowy landscape and reaching the carriage. They bore witness to Lyra's tears, to Tyrus' tired eyes, and Flake's exhausted wings. They bore witness to a wailing alarm that came from the settlement, a settlement now far behind the travelling coach.

Tyrus and Malum slept, and Flake kept Lyra company while her sadness moved into acceptance. Cedric sat proudly at the front, completely wrapped, battling the cold and steering Trudy through the night. The behemoth horse pulled the carriage toward their next destination as every mile led them closer and closer and closer to the frozen port of Crownhaven.

CHAPTER 14

A FROZEN PORT

Cedric steered Trudy and the carriage through the first night of their journey to Crownhaven, through a ferocious snow shower, in case the Featherburn Watch was on their tail. The following morning, Tyrus took over, while Flake accompanied Cedric for warm and cosy naps. The seasoned trader appreciated both the rest and the warmth after the night had made a home in his bones for the cold.

Lyra joined Tyrus at the front of the carriage; they talked and talked about magic and owls, seasons, and their parents, while Malum buried himself in research inside, as far away from Cedric as he could. Tyrus told Lyra he lived in a lighthouse; hidden behind forests they passed a while back and she frowned at that. He explained it to her the way his mother had explained it to him. And as he did, a smile rested comfortably between Lyra's cheeks like it was a person, bathing and relaxing in a natural hot spring. The conversation took her mind off being away from her parents and Tyrus simply couldn't get enough of her smiles.

'What if we all lived together with you?' asked Lyra. 'When this is all over, I mean. Build our own settlement at your lighthouse; it sounds like it's the perfect spot to do so. We'd be better at it than Yike ever was and will be till the day he kicks the bucket.'

Tyrus had never entertained the thought. He had always been alone, not trusting anyone. Not even Cedric had ever been to his lighthouse, let alone seen it. That's how he was raised. But the more he thought about it, the more a settlement around his lighthouse filled his soul with a pleasant warmth, the kind you'd receive from a fireplace after an entire day out in the cold, the kind you'd get from a soft family hug. In spite of what his parents had taught him, he made friends, he found trust. Besides, Lyra wasn't wrong either, it would be a safe place to build a town.

'Your parents could join us,' he said eventually.

Lyra looked his way with that enchanting smile of hers. 'Yeah, they could. That'd be nice,' she said.

Chapped lips braved the icy, whispering and howling wind as the humongous wheels crushed fresh snow and trampling hooves did the same.

'So, Crownhaven, huh,' said Lyra eventually, looking out to her right away from Tyrus. 'How did you find out the next splinter is there?'

Tyrus alternated between looking out to his left away from Lyra and keeping his eyes on the road. 'Uhm, the totem, I mean the key, it showed me,' he said. 'I saw it in a vision.'

Lyra's giggle tickled his ears. 'Of course you did.'

Wind brushed Tyrus' auburn curls and moved Lyra's white hairs as the sound of Trudy waltzing through the snow brought a sense of calmness to them both. A sense Tyrus hadn't experienced since the bleakwolves, a sense Lyra hadn't been familiar with since a boy with an owl showed up at her door. And then there was the snowy landscape. Breathing danger, treachery even, but it was also so beautiful. Tyrus guessed that the mercilessness of winter, its brutal nature, was the price the world had to pay for its beauty.

The early evening dawned on Tyrus' group of travelling friends, and Cedric, after his much-needed rest, resumed his task of steering his behemoth horse until it was time to set up camp for the night. They had ridden through the lands under the blanket of the dark icy night the day before, they weren't going to do it again. No need to push their luck. And even if the Featherburn Watch was following them, by now they'd be hopelessly behind.

The group shared a meal around a campfire. Malum had cooked a simple, yet tasty rabbit stew. A stew that hid the dryness of the meat and complemented the rabbit's gamier flavours. It couldn't hold up against the stew Tyrus' father used to make but then again, none ever would.

'Hey, Cedric,' began Malum after staring at the side of the carriage for a while. 'Is there a reason why the runes on your carriage spell out *"I love eating sand"* on the sides?'

Tyrus broke out into uncontrollable laughter, almost choking on a piece of rabbit. Lyra followed his lead.

'Oh, haud yer wheesht! You're messing with me,' defended Cedric.

'I'm serious! You have the runic symbol of self, the one for love, then eating and lastly the one for sand,' explained Malum. 'I love eating sand.'

'Oh my talons, you're right!' shouted Tyrus, laughing some more.

'Hey, Ced,' said Lyra. 'What kind of sand do you like most?'

'Is that how it's going to be from now on? Great. Thank you, Malum. Thank you for giving them ammunition,' said Cedric.

Malum smiled. 'You're welcome.'

As lovely as it was to see Cedric and Malum bond a little, Tyrus took an early night as his eyes yearned for dreams. And by the time Tyrus had drifted off to a world beyond his own, a world in which everything was possible, Lyra decided to hit the hay too. Or at least, she pretended to. She wanted to see what would happen if she left Malum and Cedric alone. More specifically, she wanted to *hear* what would happen if that came to be. Would they attempt to sort out their differences? Would they bury their hatchets? Or would they sharpen them? And so, Lyra hid herself beside the door that she didn't entirely close and left the night owls—both figuratively (the two men) and literally (the bird)—to enjoy each other's company. She happily put up with the invading claws of the chill night.

'So, it's only us two then,' she heard Malum say after an agonising long time of closed still mouths.

'Aye, us two and Flake,' answered Cedric.

Malum scratched the slick black and silver hairs on his head. 'Ah yes, how dare I forget,' he said and patted the bird's crown. 'Cedric…I would like to thank you.'

A frown sank into Cedric's forehead as he poked the campfire with a stick. 'What on Wingspan for?'

'For aiding us in our quest,' said Malum.

Cedric put his stick to the side and peered straight into the man's vivid emerald-green eyes. Malum started twisting the ring around his ring finger on the left with his thumb. He resisted the urge shake his leg as he waited for Cedric to say something.

'I'm not doing it for you, am I? I'm doing it for the lad.

Heck, for the world. Not for you,' said Cedric finally.

Malum got up to his feet. 'Seriously, with the hostility again? What is it that bothers you about me, Cedric?' he asked as he walked beside the fire.

'I don't trust ye, Malum,' said the trader as he also rose to his feet. 'I don't trust ye.'

Lyra started thinking she made a mistake.

'I made a promise. A promise to protect that lad in there, and I failed when the bleakwolves attacked me. He was never supposed to be the one to take care of me, and then you come along with your stories. And while I see now that there's truth to them, it doesn't change you putting the lad in danger, *my lad*. Besides…I'm convinced you're hiding something, too.'

'Tyrus' decision to go on this quest is his and his alone, I didn't force him to do anything about the state of the world. He made that choice on his own. I did not put him in danger,' said Malum firmly.

Cedric squinted and leaned forward. 'That may be, but you didn't do anything to stop him either, did ye?'

Malum took a step back at that.

'Why would I? I want to bring an end to this disgusting Eternal Winter, this never-ending cold that has a hold over every living thing in this realm! Don't you?' he countered.

Cedric's eyes watered. 'Of course, I do! I'd like nothing more than this miserable cold to end, but not at the cost of him!'

'You know, I am hiding something, Cedric,' said Malum. His voice broke. 'Something I keep buried, something I'd rather not discuss, but maybe when I tell you, you'll believe me when I say that I will do my darndest to make sure nothing happens to that kid.'

The two men sat back down, next to the fire, surrounded by the woods and the snow, the starry sky, Lyra's ears and the moons.

'Long ago, I loved someone. I loved him with all my heart, and he loved me. We married under the light of those moons,' Malum said, pointing at the sky.

Cedric noticed the cracks in the man's voice as he spoke.

'However, I was also in love with my research. Now thankfully, he understood that. He did. But then, this cruel world struck and took him from me and…he died,' said the traveller through his teeth.

'I'm so sorry,' said Cedric as he saw tears dangling from Malum's crow's feet.

The slightly less mysterious man tried composing himself a little but didn't manage to make it work. 'I could have spent more time with him, I could have been there more with him, I could have lived more in the moment with him, instead of sinking my teeth into the past, instead of losing myself in magical stories.

'If I'd known, I would have devoted myself to him completely instead of partially. That's why I'm so obsessed with this, Cedric. That's why I followed your carriage when I overheard your trade in that tavern when any other man, woman, or person would have ignored it, because if I can't do this, if I can't help save the world, then the time I spent with my nose between books—instead of spending time with my lips on his—would have been for nothing. And I can't bear that, Cedric. I can't.'

Cedric stared at the fire and then at the ground before his gaze settled on Malum again, the man he didn't trust. 'I don't know what to say.'

'There's nothing to say. I admire your passion and I respect your commitment to protect the boy, but I'm not the threat here.'

He lifted a heap of snow up from the ground in his dark purple gloved hands.

'This…This is the threat.'

In the end, Lyra felt bad for eavesdropping because what Malum had shared with Cedric was the kind of thing that ran so deep, something so delicate she felt like she pickpocketed Malum's deepest darkest most personal thoughts. So, when the man announced he'd hit the hay, Lyra joined Tyrus in the land of dreams, for tomorrow would be a big day. Tomorrow, they would arrive in Crownhaven.

The sun managed to climb up to the last step on the staircase of the bright blue sky when the travelling troupe exited the woods and laid eyes upon the settlement with the frozen port. When he looked up, smudges of clouds accompanied the sun in Tyrus' amber eyes and a breeze—as chill as ever—ruffled Trudy's manes as she picked up the pace for the last couple of miles.

Crownhaven sat right next to a frozen sea and in the olden days it had the biggest port of the realm. Now, most of the docks were lost but the remnants were still there as broken piers reached into the icy still sea. A wall surrounded the settlement too, more sophisticated than the one around Featherburn. It was made of bricks carved out of stone, and while the walls weren't as high as those in Lyra's hometown, they looked and felt way steadier and sturdier. Technically, Crownhaven's wall didn't surround the entire settlement as much as it left the side toward the sea mostly open. It did extend a tiny bit into the water, a sea tamed by the never-ending winter. Once upon a time, that wall extended all the way to the small island a little off the coast, with giant gates on either side of the isle for the ships. Not much of that was left now, because on both sides of Crownhaven, the battlement heavy stone brick wall crumbled into the sea until it disappeared into and under the ice and then, on either side of that little isle, echoes of that same wall climbed back up.

Within the walls resided many charming neighbourhoods of cosy cottages—and to the contrary of how things were where Lyra hailed from, the settlers there seemed happy. She didn't think she would ever see people live like this. People in Crownhaven didn't live in fear. They lived in joy. They were hungry, like everywhere else, but they somewhat seemed to enjoy life.

'So, now what?' asked Tyrus as Cedric instructed Trudy to park the carriage in the commercial district.

Eyes everywhere fell on Flake; she inched closer to Tyrus' face.

'I shall check the local inns, see if they have room for us. My treat, if you don't mind,' said Malum.

'Hold on, what's wrong with me carriage?' asked Cedric.

No one had the guts to tell him it was somewhat cramped in there with four people, and they didn't dare talk about the fairly horse-forward smell that ruled the interior. Their mouths were as still as a lifeless pond on a windless day.

'Fine, check the inns,' said Cedric eventually, admitting defeat.

'And what do we do in the meantime?' asked Lyra. Tyrus and Flake wanted to know the same.

'Discover all that Crownhaven has to offer, I'd say,' said Cedric. 'Since I'm back here later than anticipated...' He pointed to his bandaged arm, the bites slowly fading into scars underneath. 'I need to tend to long overdue trades.'

Malum looked at the kids. 'While you're at it, maybe the two of you can find out more about the island off the coast.'

With the excitement of arriving in Crownhaven flooding their brains, Tyrus and Lyra had almost forgotten that the isle was the reason they were there. This wasn't a road trip; it was the next stop on their quest. They needed to get their hands on the next splinter of the owl key.

'Be careful, you two,' said Cedric.

'Yes, especially with Flake gracing your shoulder, young man,' agreed Malum.

'We promise we'll try to not get into any sort of pickle.' Lyra smirked.

Cedric's face sank behind his hand and Malum rolled his eyes.

'We'll meet back here in, let's say an hour?' asked the Talonstead traveller, after which Lyra pushed a thumb in the sky as they walked away.

Crownhaven brimmed with life. Everyone was busy, everyone knew what to do and the air felt thick with positive and cheerful energy. The town had taverns, a butcher, a fruits and vegetables merchant and a cute little bakery, which was where the famous frostbread Cedric usually had with him always came from. At first glance, you'd think the settlement prospered but all the stores had to ration the wares they sold. They had to make sure everyone had at least something. The effects of freezing winter didn't stop at the gates.

Tyrus, Flake and Lyra took it all in as stares followed them everywhere. Tyrus had tried hiding Flake inside his jacket (which she did not enjoy in the slightest), but as soon as people caught glimpses of the owl, the whispers started all but immediately. The effort of hiding her became redundant. Strangely enough, people didn't seem as scared as they were in Featherburn. But they didn't dare to approach, though.

They finally arrived at the coast where the people of Crownhaven took to the ice. A dozen people moved across the frozen coastline, some with speed, finesse, and expertise. Some less so. People sped across the ice in wooden shoes with steel skates attached to the sole. There was even a shop where you could buy them, handmade, carved from wood by the vendor themselves. A shop on the frosty sand next to the frozen sea. There was something in how easy a handful of ice-skaters made it look, how utterly effortless, that made both Lyra and Tyrus want to try it. Flake felt delighted at the people who rushed and danced over the ice in the reflection of her eyes. Many of the townsfolk's kept staring at the magical bird, but to the frosty trio of travellers, the ice-skating was the magic.

One person on the ice caught Tyrus' attention. It was a handsome boy, skin darker than his, wearing a burnt orange sweater, covered by a stylish navy coat. The coils of his charcoal hair hoped to one day reach his shoulders.

He had to have been about Tyrus' age and he showed tremendous skill on his skates; it seemed as though no one else on the ice was even remotely a match. The way he moved, it was like a second nature to him, as if he was born for the ice. There was something about that boy that the other townsfolk didn't seem to appreciate, and it wasn't until vibrant amber crossed that boy's dense blue eyes that he realised. The boy was an elf. Tyrus had never seen an elf in real life, only drawings.

Then, as the clouds thickened in the sky and light snow began its journey to the surface, the black elven boy winked at Tyrus. He didn't expect the blush that erupted inside his cheeks. The feeling felt familiar, the exact same sensation as when Lyra kissed him on the cheek. It was an infuriatingly good feeling, so good it made him uncomfortable, so good that it was annoying. He winked a clumsy wink back and Lyra shot a jealous glance his way.

While Tyrus' mind wandered through the maze of what he felt, he hadn't registered the young elf skating in their direction. Lyra squinted him up and down, she didn't know what to make of him, not even when he stood right in front of them. She hadn't ever seen an elf either, she had only heard stories.

'Hi, uhm, w…w-welcome to Crownhaven,' said the elven boy, ears so pointy Lyra wondered if they could pierce skin. 'Nice c…c-cloak.' He aimed his words at Tyrus.

One of Tyrus' hands travelled to the back of his neck

to scratch the place where his curls stopped. 'Thanks.' He paused briefly. 'You're great on those skates,' he added after not being able to think of anything else to say.

'Oh, thank you,' said the elven boy avoiding Tyrus' gaze.

Lyra rolled her eyes and Tyrus gulped, louder than he wanted to. 'I'm Tyrus, pleased to meet you,' he said after what had to have been long agonising minutes.

'L-l-likewise,' said the boy. 'My name is Kellan.' He then looked at Lyra.

'Oh, right, I'm Lyra, I'm his...friend, and honestly, I'm waiting for you to start asking about the figurative elephant in the hypothetical room, also known as the bird on his shoulder.'

'W...w-ell, I didn't want to b...b-e intrusive or rude or anything. The rumours are true then, there was a mage in Featherburn. What's their name?' asked Kellan, pointing at Flake. 'They're b...b-beautiful.'

Astounded, but not surprised, by the fact those stories had already reached Crownhaven, Tyrus introduced Kellan to his owl. Kellan asked if he could pet her, and while Tyrus wasn't too sure about that, Flake looked at him with a pleading look in her eyes. Who was he to deny her pets? Besides, Kellan seemed like a kind person, and so, Tyrus agreed, hoping the looks weren't deceiving.

'So, what b...b-rings you three to Crownhaven?' asked Kellan.

'Banishment,' answered Lyra plainly. 'What brings an elf to Crownhaven? To any of the human territories, come to think of it? Are you here to feed on us humans?' She pulled up her hands as if she was telling a scary story to children.

Tyrus gave her a small shove with his elbow. His parents had told him about the stories people made up about elves, as if they were savages, or in any way lesser. Kellan's disappointed look cut into Lyra's heart deeply, she didn't think, she just blurted it out without thinking. She had meant it as a joke, but she realised it wasn't a funny one. Instead, it was downright hurtful.

Tyrus knew from his books that humans and elves had never mixed well, especially not in recent history, and Lyra knew that too. Despite her parents always saying she shouldn't listen to the vile things people had to say, she had almost exclusively heard demonising stories about elves. Seeing Kellan stand before her now, those stories weren't rooted in any sort of reality. The people in Featherburn clearly had no idea what they were talking about.

Lyra stared at her feet. 'I am so sorry, I...didn't mean to...'

'It's okay, I g...g-get that a lot,' said Kellan. 'Well... n...n-not so much the feeding part, never heard t...t-that one before. Creative. I live here, it's a long story. But m...m-most people don't pay attention to me; others aren't very kind.' He looked at Lyra.

Lyra's eyes sank. 'Again, I'm sorry. People are asshats,' said Lyra. 'Including me apparently. I shouldn't have said that.'

'Apology accepted.' Kellan smiled.

'We're here for that island over there,' said Tyrus. His finger pointed across the sea, to the island with ruined walls on either side, shrouded in gloom and mist.

Kellan frowned while giving Flake chin scratches with his right hand. 'W…w-ait. You're here for Alula Isle? That place is haunted and unreachable.'

Alula Isle was called that because back when the walls still erupted from the sea, combined with the edges of the water where the sea met land, you could make out the shape of an owl's wing. The place where the island sat was exactly where the alula feather or the winglet of an owl would sit.

'What do you mean by haunted?' asked Tyrus with his experiences in the old coal mine in mind.

'What do you mean by unreachable?' asked Lyra.

'Well, there's tales about Alula Isle, or W…W-Winglet Isle if you want to call it by a less exotic name.' He looked at Lyra for that last part. 'Tales about the dead ruling there, the dead that were claimed by the rimewhales and winter.'

'Rimewhales?' asked Tyrus. 'Those are real?'

Kellan slightly tilted his head at that. 'Why wouldn't they be? They're the reason we b…b-lock off the ice of the sea. Beyond those markers, the rimewhales get you. They're fast c…c-creatures, too fast to outskate. Trust me on that one,' he said as he held his left arm close. Tyrus wondered what that was about but decided not to press the young man.

'They're fascinating, but they b…b-break through the ice and kill…or mutilate,' he continued, now hiding his left gloved hand in the pockets of his navy coat. 'There used to be a c…c-competition up until a decade ago or so, where ice-skaters were tasked to skate all the way to Alula Isle and back and whoever was fastest won. B…b-but with the never-ending winter getting colder and colder, the rimewhales grew in numbers. It has made it impossible to get to the island in one piece, let alone get back alive. You'd have to be mad to try and go there.'

'Challenge accepted, right Tyrus?' said Lyra, lifting and lowering her shoulders.

'Hold on, I'm telling you it's impossible. It c…c-cannot be done,' warned Kellan. 'Why is it you want to go there anyway?'

'It holds an artifact we need, Kellan,' said Tyrus. He sounded way more ominous and mysterious than he needed or intended to be, but it did something for Kellan.

'Anyway, Tyrus, I'm afraid we'll have to go now and tend to your…uncles,' said Lyra, grabbing hold of Tyrus' arm.

Tyrus didn't follow. 'Uncles?'

'Yes, they're so old and they love to bicker…you know,' she said.

And then the crown dropped. 'Oh yes, of course, my uncles, yes. See you around Kellan!' he shouted as Lyra dragged him with her. Flake took to the sky and followed.

'Nice to m…m-meet you! You know where to find me!' shouted Kellan as the peculiar trio disappeared between the people of the town.

As the wandering kids (and Flake) returned to where Cedric had parked Trudy and the carriage, Malum also arrived, and a few minutes later the seasoned trader himself followed.

Malum had a wide smile on his face. 'I got us a room at the Feathering Inn of Crownhaven! Can you believe it? I asked about the establishment in Featherburn and apparently the owners are franchising, whatever that means,' he shared.

'Good for them…I guess? We also have news!' announced Lyra. 'Right, Clever Chap?'

Tyrus' thoughts were with Kellan and then with Lyra and then with Kellan again before he registered what the white-haired girl had said. 'Uh, yes…There was this kind elven boy at the shore, ice skating, and he told us a lot about Alula Isle.'

Cedric and Malum both noticed it, the subtle blush in Tyrus' cheeks. Tyrus and Lyra looped the *"uncles"* in on everything they had heard.

'Is every single cursed splinter going to make this such a dangerous hassle?' asked Cedric when he'd heard it all.

Everyone then looked over to Malum, because surely, he had to have a plan, right? Somehow, he'd know of a spell that would aid them in their quest, right? A tense vibe gathered around the travelling troupe as Malum sank into his thoughts. His one arm in a slingshot, the other, bringing his index finger to rest on his chin. It took a while, longer than the time he came up with a spell for Lyra's escape. But then there it was, an idea.

'Tyrus, Lyra, how great are you two at ice skating?' asked Malum at last.

'Weren't you listening? The rimewhales would kill us, Malum. And I'm pretty sure neither of us has skated before,' said Lyra.

'Hey now, speak for yourself, I've skated on ice before with my dad,' said Tyrus. The pitch in his voice rose toward the end of his sentence.

Lyra eyes grew so narrow everyone wondered if she could still see. 'Is that so, huh? How many times?' she asked.

Tyrus lifted his shoulders. 'I don't know. How is that relevant?'

'Very.' Lyra's nose entered Tyrus' personal space. 'How. Many. Times?'

'Okay, maybe once but he did say I showed promise,' explained Tyrus as Lyra laughed so hard, she thought she'd pass out.

Cedric raised his voice. 'Okay, enough.'

Lyra tried her best, but her muffled laughs still made it out.

The seasoned trader continued, 'We can't dismiss what the lass said before. There's no way they can get past those rimewhales unscathed.'

'That's why Tyrus is going to enchant their skates,' stated Malum.

'Enchant them?' said both Tyrus and Lyra at the same time.

'Yes, enchant them. It's time you learn runic magic, Tyrus,' said Malum and the boy's amber eyes lit up, figuratively this time around.

Malum continued, 'The only thing we need is someone to teach you two how to become semi-competent ice skaters. Preferably in a short time frame.'

'Why don't you come with us, Malum? I mean Cedric is old and still recovering but you're not *that* old right?' asked Lyra, smirking as ever. Cedric shook his head slowly.

'Firstly, I may not be *that* old. But I have tried ice-skating in the past. I'm afraid I'd only slow you down. Especially with this,' he said, pointing at his damaged shoulder.

Cedric put his hand up. Everyone stopped talking in an instant and looked his way. He heard something skulk from behind the carriage. Whatever it was, it had to have knocked over a couple of crates. What if they were listening? He walked to the back and found a boy hiding behind crates. The seasoned trader grabbed him by his burnt orange collar that peeked out from underneath his worn navy coat and dragged him in front of the rest of the group.

'Kellan? What are you doing here?' asked Tyrus, while Lyra had her daggers out already.

'You two know this lad?' asked Cedric.

'Yeah, we met at the shore. He's the average-looking elf who told us about the isle! I knew something was up with this one,' she spat as she clenched her daggers so hard, they'd lose consciousness if they could.

Both Tyrus and Kellan frowned when Lyra said he was average-looking.

'C...c-calm down now! I don't m...m-mean you any harm! I may or m...m-ay not have overheard things and p...p-perhaps I followed you, b...b-but only because I want to help you! I'll do it, I'll teach you how to skate the ice,' Kellan said.

'Why would you do that? What do you want?' asked Cedric, because everything came at a price.

Kellan looked them all in the eye as Cedric loosened the grip on his collar. 'I only have one c...c-con, one condition.'

'Well, young man. Name it,' ordered Malum.

'I get to skate to Alula Isle with you.'

CHAPTER 15

RUNES AND SKATES AND ICE

Confusion ruled everyone's faces—Kellan's being the exception—with an iron fist.

'What? At the shore you told us it couldn't be done, that we'd have to be mad, that it's impossible?' asked Lyra. 'What changed?'

'Tyrus and Flake did,' he answered. 'Normal people can't cross it, but with magic. M...m-magic changes everything!'

They could all agree; magic *did* change everything. Tyrus knew that better than anyone because if it wasn't for magic, Cedric wouldn't be alive, and he would have never met all these wonderful people.

'It's one thing to teach us, but to come with? Why?' asked Tyrus.

Kellan's gaze fell to the footsteps in the snow below and his right hand shifted to his left arm. 'The w...w-why

213

doesn't m…m-matter. You need someone to teach you and I'm the b…b-best ice skater in Crownhaven.'

Tyrus sensed Kellan didn't want to talk about it. So instead of pushing, he corroborated Kellan's claim to the others. And even though he could only speak from what he saw on the ice that one time, the elf did outperform all the other skaters without breaking a single drop of sweat.

'If you insist, young elf,' said Malum, 'we will accept your offer.'

As soon as the words left the traveller's tongue, Kellan felt like he could breathe and Tyrus smiled a big goofy smile. Lyra pouted slightly with crossed arms, but that may have had more to do with the energy between Kellan and Tyrus than anything else. Was Kellan the Malum to her Cedric?

'Hold on, why can't we let Flake fly over there, let her steal the splinter, and have her bring it back to us? That way we won't have to risk our lives!' suggested Lyra proudly as Flake shook lightly with a hint of terror.

Tyrus turned to face Lyra. 'We can't send Flake in there. We have no idea what awaits her there. What if she got hurt?'

'Yeah…You're right…You better make sure those ice skates pack a punch or I'll pack one for your face,' said Lyra, her eyes narrowing.

That same evening, Tyrus ventured into the art of inscribing objects with runes and therefore, magic. In the old days, runic magic was taught by Paragons to their Learnlings in the first year of their training. Malum figured that imprinting the ice skates with runes and distilling them with magic, essentially enchanting them, was perfect practice for Tyrus and Flake's magical abilities.

The first step to runic magic was knowing your runes, and while Tyrus had learned a few of those already, he spent the first few days studying. In order for a runic inscription to work well with magic, Paragons of ages lost thought it wise to utilise runes that had a strong correlation to the thing you wanted them to do. Pouring magic into runic inscriptions was a straining process that worked better when the runes and the intentions had a connection. That was why most runic inscriptions formed sentences. The caster would then repeat those sentences over and over as they poured their magic into the object (or the place) they were enchanting.

Malum bought three pairs of skates from the merchant at the shore for Tyrus to enchant once he was ready to do so. He thought it best to have Tyrus practice on pieces of rock first, so that he wouldn't have to buy skates again and again. After almost burning down his lighthouse, Tyrus figured it a safe bet. While Tyrus submerged himself into the art of rune carving, the three youngsters used the so far unenchanted skates to practice on the ice. When Tyrus wasn't carving, he'd join Lyra and Kellan for ice-skating practice. To Lyra's surprise, Kellan turned out to be an adequate instructor. The pickpocket prodigy picked things up rather well while the last of the Owlbound struggled.

'I thought your dad said you showed promise, Clever Chap?' teased Lyra, a couple days into practice.

'Yeah…well…I'm starting to think he was only being nice,' said Tyrus after falling for the twentieth time.

Kellan had to laugh. 'Don't w…w-worry, Ty. You'll get the hang of it.'

Ty. Lyra threw up inside of her mouth while Tyrus kept blushing more intensely. *Did he call him Ty? Nicknames? Already?*

Kellan reached out to Tyrus with his right hand and the auburn-haired boy took it. Their hands touched, Kellan's skin a tad darker than his, slightly warmer too and just like that he was up on his feet again. Drunk on a different kind of magic he was used to.

'Thank you, Kell,' he said softly while Lyra figuratively threw up some more.

'Okay, now…Try staying low and k…k-keep your knees above your toes,' said Kellan. 'Your shoulders should be above your hips, like so.' He aligned Tyrus' body to fit the perfect ice-skating posture.

Kellan's advice sounded like swirling symphonies, dancing toward Tyrus' eardrums and it made his stomach tingle with the same vigour as Lyra's quick quips. Lyra, who kept squinting at the two from a distance, felt something she hadn't ever felt before. Was it jealousy?

With Kellan's tips and tricks in mind, Tyrus tried again and again and again with the handsome elf holding his arm for support, until he no longer needed it.

'Good, Ty! Great even, now k…k-keep those feet about shoulder-width apart!'

Tyrus listened and as Flake flew above Crownhaven's shore—admiring her friend's skating from the winds above—her human successfully managed to turn around and skate back toward Kellan.

'Yes, Tyrus! Awesome!' the elf shouted.

'All thanks to you,' said Tyrus as they hugged.

Tyrus wished the embrace lasted longer. Perhaps Kellan did too. In the meantime, Lyra went off on her own, skating by the shore. She'd seen enough of the two boys for a while and Tyrus and Kellan decided to take a break.

'Thank you for doing this,' said Tyrus as snowflakes stuck to his woolly hat and the curls that peeked out from underneath.

'It's my p…p-pleasure,' said Kellan. 'My grandfather would have been proud of me.' A sombreness settled on Kellan's face, one that felt powerful. The kind Tyrus felt when he thought about his parents.

'Your grandfather?' asked Tyrus.

'Yes, my grandfather always t…t-took me ice skating. He taught me and he'd always tell stories about the Alula C…c-competition. He competed once. He didn't win, but he did make it back, third place!'

Tyrus let his hand land and rest on Kellan's shoulder as Flake landed and rested on his. 'Well, he taught you incredibly well,' he said.

'Thank you, that m…m-means a lot,' said Kellan with a slight smile.

After a while, Lyra joined them again after skating along the entire shore and back. Together they moved and danced and laughed on the ice until the isle off the shore (and the frozen sea) devoured the sun.

In the days that followed, Tyrus dove back into runic magic alternating with more ice-skating practice, until both Lyra and Tyrus were fairly competent and felt confident on their skates. From then on, Tyrus had to spend more time with his runes as opposed to with Lyra and Kellan. He didn't like it. Quite frankly, he thought it sucked, but it had to be done. After all, the fate of the world didn't care about what Tyrus wanted—all it cared for was being saved. As a result of working closely together, the group learned to trust Kellan. Cedric and Malum agreed the elf was a good lad. Even though Lyra didn't like the way he looked at Tyrus, she couldn't deny the boy had a good heart. And above all, everything she had ever heard about elves were confirmed to be lies. Slowly and steadily, they introduced him to the specifics of their quest, explaining the magic, the splinters, all of it.

It taken him roughly a fortnight, but Tyrus' hands

had made the act of inscription their second nature, the first being creating magical flames from thin air. They had been in Crownhaven for a little over two weeks now and that's when Malum saw it: perfection inscribed in rocks, Tyrus' rocks.

'Now, listen carefully,' spoke Malum. He sounded as wise as an old sage. In other words, he sounded every bit as himself as ever. 'The carvings you made, the inscriptions, they are a vessel for your magic. They will hold your magic, if you tell your magic to allow itself to be held,' he explained.

Tyrus understood now more than ever why Learnlings used to practice only under the watchful eyes of Paragons. How was anyone supposed to figure all this out on their own? He felt grateful for Malum. Even though he wasn't Owlbound, the knowledge he had gathered about magic over the years, allowed him to be a great mentor regardless.

The runes Tyrus had inscribed his rocks with, told the rocks to be devoid of weight. With instilling them with his magic, he hoped they'd float on their own. Tyrus listened to the chaos of his magic. Magic that would listen to him like an invaluable friend. For a while, not even the floorboards of Crownhaven's Feathering Inn dared to creak until the magical duo's eyes thrusted open, carrying the purple and blue flames the two had grown rather close with. Fire sat comfortably on Tyrus' open hand, and he guided it.

And like a shepherd, herding their cattle, leading them to safety, he led his flames straight to the crevices he created in the rocks. The inscriptions caught ablaze while Tyrus whispered an almost incomprehensible gibberish, as if he spoke backward. He told the magic it wanted to be kept within those markings, he told it that it was its own wish and after shortly refusing to do so, it gave in. The magic bowed to its caster and seeped into the crevices of the rocks until the markings glowed with a faint blue and purple shine.

Tyrus looked at Malum. 'So? Did it work? Did I, do it?'

'I don't know, you tell me, young man,' said Malum as he pointed back to the rocks.

The boy turned his head, and the corner of his right eye already noticed them before they came into view entirely. The rocks hovered above the table, truly weightless like Tyrus and Flake had intended. Malum didn't see the hug coming but he welcomed it, nonetheless.

'Well done, you two. Well done. Now, let's try that again a couple of times. Let us also add more complexity to the runes before enchanting the skates,' said Malum.

More practice wasn't exactly what Tyrus had longed for, but Malum was right. The skates would be more of a challenge, one he needed to be ready for. Lyra had suggested making the skates capable of flight so that they could "sky-skate" across the sea. While a Paragon of the

Owlbound arts would be able to pull that off, a Learnling like Tyrus, wouldn't. He and Flake didn't possess that kind of power yet. Instead, Tyrus and his owl would make the skates faster and capable of higher jumps. That, paired with Tyrus and Flake casting spells along the way, crossing that icy frozen sea, should get them to Alula Isle in one piece.

The stars and the moons shone bright as three pairs of ice skates were brought to a room in the Feathering Inn of Crownhaven as yet another week of relentless practice had further seeped through the hourglass of time. Tyrus and Flake gave it their all as they let their magic flow into the runic symbols, inscribed into the sides of each and every skate. The primary runes stood for speed and nimbleness, both accompanied by markings that illustrated height and jumping. The fiery magic was poured into them as people from outside the inn saw blue and purple flashes of light dance through the windows. And when the lights in the windows went out, Tyrus and Flake had successfully enchanted their first magical items. Soon, they would take them out for a spin.

Roughly an hour after the enchantment, Tyrus felt like he needed a good old Cedric chat. He'd been pondering something between practicing runes and ice-skating, something about the feelings in his stomach and the blush in his cheeks. He needed advice. He exited his room and knocked on Cedric's door, which the seasoned trader opened a few seconds later.

'Oh, Tyrus, Flake. Come in, laddie 'n wee lass. Everything all right?' he asked as they walked in before closing the door behind them.

They went up to the balcony which looked out over a good portion of Crownhaven as slowly but surely, the lights in all the windows went out.

'Ced, how do you know when you like somebody? Like, *really* like somebody?' asked Tyrus. 'And how do you know they feel the same?'

'Oh, that's a few big questions right there, lad. Is this about Lyra by any chance, ey?' asked Cedric in a whisper while poking the boy with his elbow.

Tyrus looked away. 'Yes, and no…I think,' he said.

Cedric frowned and asked him what he meant.

'Is it possible to like two people at the same time? A girl and…a boy?' asked Tyrus finally.

'Aye, of course it is,' answered Cedric with a smile. 'Why wouldn't it be?'

Tyrus looked down at the street below, avoiding eye contact with Cedric. 'I don't know…am I weird for that?'

'Lad, look at me,' said Cedric. 'A couple of centuries ago, people may have bat an eye or two, but boys who like more than only girls? Or boys who only like boys for that matter? That has never been weird. Never.'

Tyrus smiled as a weight lifted from his shoulders. He had only ever seen his mom and dad together. He didn't realise that for some people, liking someone, didn't look like any one way. What he felt for Kellan had surprised him. Deep down, he knew it wasn't wrong or anything, but ever since discovering his crush on Kellan, and after feeling the same about Lyra, he wondered if he was alone in that.

Tyrus dropped his head in his hands. 'What do I do with these feelings?'

It was the sort of thing children asked their parents. He wished so terribly hard being able to pick their brains about it all, and it was in moments like these he missed them all the more. But just like love, family didn't look any one way either, so he asked Cedric.

'Look,' said Cedric in a low, warm, and comforting voice. 'These feelings are new for you, aye? All I can say is, explore them. Love is a lot of things. It can be confusing, messy, sometimes cruel, but most of all, beautiful, no matter what form it takes. You owe it to yourself to explore, see where they lead. Whether they lead to Lyra or Kellan, or whether or not their feelings lead to you, explore.'

Cedric gave Tyrus a big lengthy hug, and the boy let go of the tears he'd been holding onto ever since the conversation started. They weren't sad tears, though. He cried because relief had avalanched across his body and mind, and the joyous tears disappeared into the trader's flannel shirt. There wasn't anything wrong with him or how he felt, better yet, there never was.

'This world is cruel enough,' said Cedric. 'So…be unapologetically you, whoever that may be, and love whoever you love. You hear me, laddie?'

Tyrus sniffled and wiped his happy tears away. 'I hear you, Ced. I hear you.'

After a good night's sleep, Kellan, Lyra, Tyrus, Flake and their two older geezers didn't hesitate to give their new toys a try as soon as the first rays of sunshine fell on Crownhaven. The six of them stood by the town's shoreline on the cold and dense sand. Cedric and Malum were buried in thick coats, thicker than usual as the wind at the shoreline was armed with sharper, even icier gusts. In front of them, the three teens sat down to put on their skates.

Tyrus' feet dug themselves into his brand-new skates. They still smelled of freshly carved wood with smoky hints from the magical inscriptions. They fit him perfectly. Kellan was first to notice it; the skates felt rather strange. Strange in a good way, but strange, nonetheless. He helped Tyrus up from the cold sand and that's when Tyrus felt it too, the familiar humming of his magic, living and thriving inside the skates, inside those runes, patiently waiting to be used as the energy ran up his legs.

'All right, Clever Chap. Let's see if you fudged this up or not, shall we?' said Lyra. She had barely uttered the words before she zoomed away.

The speed the skates gave her was astonishing and Kellan couldn't fully grasp what he had witnessed. The only thing he knew was that he had to follow her lead immediately. Trudy at full speed and power would lose a race against a human or an elf on those skates and Cedric's jaw had fallen so far down, Malum was sure it would tumble to the sandy ground below. Ced wasn't the only impressed person on the shore, because many of the Crownhaven townsfolk wore shocked and flabbergasted faces too, as a small crowd started to form.

Lyra needed to fall to the ice a dozen times before she got the hang of how sensitive the skates were, while for Kellan, falling merely twice was enough. Tyrus on the other hand took a little longer, but eventually—after losing count at how many times he'd lost his balance—he got used to it, too.

'These should make us jump higher than usual as well, right?' asked Lyra after about ten minutes on the ice.

'If the runic magic I did is up to snuff, then yes, they should,' said Tyrus with one hand on the back of his neck, unsure about whether he did a good job or not.

Kellan's right hand landed on Tyrus' right shoulder

as he came to a stop beside him. 'W…w-ell, I'm sure you did w…w-wonderfully,' said Kellan as he built speed and attempted to jump as high as he could.

'Extraordinary,' uttered Malum when he saw Kellan essentially taking to the sky.

'Laddie!' cheered Cedric. 'I think you did it!'

Now, it was Lyra's turn, and then Tyrus', and as the three teenagers gave their new skates a proper spin, Flake enjoyed the view from the restless sky above. But gloom, darkness and danger lurked across the icy sea, and it was hungry. Hungry for new flesh.

CHAPTER 16

WINGS ACROSS ICE

Together, Tyrus, Lyra and Kellan welcomed a guest. It was none other than time itself. Time to cross the frosty sea in which danger roamed free. The wind felt like it was armed with millions upon millions of tiny daggers as they stung into the skins of everyone at the shore—and even though the water of the once tumultuous sea sat frozen, salty air made its way through noses and lungs alike.

'So…This is it then,' said Lyra, chattering her teeth.

'Lads and lasses, if you're not comfortable and you'd rather wait a few extra days, train a wee bit more perhaps, you can,' said Cedric, every sound from his mouth oozing worry.

Malum said nothing. Even though he wanted them to go as soon as possible, he also wanted to make sure they were positively ready.

The three youngsters looked at each other before Tyrus

said, 'No, I think we're ready.' He sounded confident, too.

'I hate that I can't do anything to help the four of youse,' said Cedric after the biggest sigh of his life.

'It's okay. We've got this,' said Tyrus, touching the seasoned trader's elbow.

Cedric pet Flake under her beak. 'You'll keep them safe, won't you?' he asked her.

Hoot.

'I know you will,' he said, patting her crown.

Lyra had her daggers ready to face whatever dangers got in her way. She also carried a rucksack filled with the trios' boots, to change into once they reached the isle. Kellan wore a sword in a sheath, strapped to his back above his navy coat. He didn't think he'd be of that much help with a sword in combat, but it beat going without one. At last, Tyrus' weapon sat atop his shoulder, not to mention that it flowed through his veins and hummed in every one of his cells. His magic was ready and Flake, too, as noon subjected Crownhaven to the sun, shining through light clouds directly above everyone's heads.

Word had already spread. The town gathered where the beach met the town roads to see the three kids off to Alula Isle. Many people didn't think they were going to go through with it and most believed that if they did, even when aided by a magical owl of old, they'd never make it. The villagers didn't know what to make of the bird. They weren't afraid or against the creature like some in

Featherburn were, but they weren't sure Flake was safe either. They stayed at a distance, curious, yet careful. The townsfolk came prepared, too, with binoculars of all shapes and sizes.

Meanwhile, Cedric and Malum hoped—with the power of all the Owlbound that ever lived—the young ice-skaters would be okay.

'Kellan, are you sure you don't want to say goodbye to anyone?' asked Tyrus.

'No, I'm fine. I haven't had anyone here for me…f…f-for a while now,' said Kellan.

'I'm sorry,' said Tyrus.

'Oh, it's okay, I've got all of you now. Let's get this done,' he said with a dapper smile.

The crowd gasped when Tyrus and his bird, Lyra, and Kellan headed for the barrier on their skates. As Flake took off from her best friend's shoulder to survey the ice from above, the three adventurous and brave skaters jumped over the small barricade, crossing the boundary. They left safety behind.

Not even a minute had passed before Flake spotted the first of the rimewhales below the ice. They looked exactly like whales except for the heads, which were shaped like hammers. Kind of like the hammer Tyrus had in his lighthouse. They also wore white scales, difficult to pierce like a knight's chainmail armour. Their hammer-shaped heads weren't smooth either; spiky crystals grew out of them, crystals so sharp, they could cut through the thick layer of ice whenever they desired.

Tyrus was their first target. The rimewhale underneath the ice below his skates readied itself to attack, hungry for human flesh. Flake hooted loudly, signalling her magical boy to brace himself. The frightening sea monster burst through the ice the way volcanoes violently erupted with lava. Tyrus jumped away just in the nick of time and before he knew it, the whale had already buried itself back into the freezing waters.

'Ty, are you okay?!' shouted Kellan, moving forward fast.

'Yes! Let's keep going!' he shouted back.

'Oh, I thought we were going to take a break and have a little picnic on the ice! Seems like the perfect place and time!' shouted Lyra.

There wasn't any time for laughs because Flake now hooted above Lyra. Fifty meters away from the white-haired girl, a rimewhale burst out of the ice, wanting to pierce her with crystal from the side. Reflexes took the reigns as she ducked but not before a sharp crystal grazed her cheek.

Kellan figured he would be next, and he was right. The biggest whale yet shot out of the ice, straight up in the air in front of Kellan, forcing him to a full stop. The blades of his skates touched the edge of the hole in the frosty surface as the ice-cold water longed and reached to steal his heartbeat away. The rimewhale, now in the air, turned, ready to smack back down right into the brave elven boy, but the best ice skater of Crownhaven wouldn't have it. He swiftly circled around the hole and continued heading for Alula Isle, and as the rimewhale plunged itself back into the sea behind him, they all knew it. They felt it in every muscle they moved, in every bone that shivered, in the air that stung their lungs. The rimewhales were furious now.

Flake was the first to see it from overhead. Not one, not two, not three, but a dozen of them lurked below the ice. And as if things weren't dire enough, the clouds grew darker as if they were cross. Lightning randomly struck around them with bellowing thunders trailing behind and the snow that came down turned into ferocious hail.

Tyrus, Kellan, and Lyra fought the wind. They clung onto dear life while they dodged rimewhales to the left and the right, below them, above them—all around them. Flake struggled too, flying through the menacing hail that sought nothing more than to bring her down. To her relief, the hail quickly turned into snow again. But the snow made it difficult for her to see and the consolation she felt, melted away like ice-cream in the summer-sun of old. She had lost sight of her pals. They were on their own now.

The next quarter of an hour was brutal, merciless and utterly devoid of compassion. Fins cut calves, crystal hammer-shaped heads bruised and pierced skin and the snow and the cold, chapped lips further and farther. The ice beneath Tyrus' skates quivered before a rimewhale erupted from the frozen sea behind him. It shot through the air above the surface with impressive speed, determined to devour the boy. As he skated and skated, Tyrus used a trick he'd learned when he got Lyra out of her cell; he turned into flames and let the whale phase through him. Waves of confusion washed over the rimewhale, or was it the chill water of the sea as it dove back into the ice?

Tyrus leapt over the crater the creature had left and astounded he was still alive, he continued and found Kellan. They stayed close, skating side by side, trapped in a treacherous dance between life and death. But then, Tyrus' skates had to get stuck, caught between the cracks of broken ice. Kellan could have left him behind but there wasn't a hair on his head that had that intention, so he turned around and brought himself to a halt where Tyrus sat pinned down. The mage's maroon cloak suffered rips and holes and frostbitten scratches decorated his cheeks as the rimewhales charged for them.

'Tyrus! Cover us while I get you loose!' shouted Kellan.

Shooting and zooming magical fire wounded the aggressive sea creatures. Tyrus screamed, fighting off the rimewhales. He let his anger roam free while Kellan used the blades of his own skates to hash into the ice, trying to get Tyrus's skates free.

Meanwhile, Lyra arrived at the shore of what she

hoped was Alula Isle. She was bruised and cut all over and once she closed in on the actual beach, she noticed the rimewhales backing off. The water had become too shallow for them and the ice perhaps too thick. The first thing she did as the blades of her skates hacked into the cold gravelly sand, was plunge herself to the ground, trying to catch her breath.

Not long after, Flake emerged from the thick mixture of mist and clouds. Lyra called out for her loudly as she waved her hands and arms around as if the bird hadn't already spotted her the moment, she left the fog behind. Flake sought comfort on Lyra's shoulder, leaning with her crown against the side of the girl's head and for a moment only the howling wind spoke.

'Where are Kellan and Tyrus?' she asked.

The sigh of relief Lyra wanted to sigh didn't allow itself to come until—after what felt like an eternity—Tyrus and Kellan skated out of the brutally dense mist. Both pretty banged up, but they were alive. In the end, that was all that that mattered.

'You made it!' shouted Lyra and she swung around Tyrus' neck.

The embrace only lasted a second because as soon as the girl caught herself doing what she was doing, she stopped.

'Well, someone was worried,' said Tyrus between huffing and trying to catch his breath.

Lyra slid a slither of hair behind her ears. 'Of course. Without you we can't save the world, you know,' she said as Flake hopped from her shoulder to the pad on Tyrus'.

'Oh, hi there, little lady. Are you okay?' asked Tyrus.

Flake hooted affirmingly as she received pets and scritches. Kellan looked up at the ruins of the walls, the worn-down guard tower and the decaying building attached to it. He had a smile on his face and tears made their way down his cheeks. Lyra and Tyrus came closer.

'Kellan? Are you okay?' asked Lyra.

'Kell?' asked Tyrus. 'What's the matter?'

'Nothing. It's…I m…m-made it,' said Kellan, after which he sniffled and sniffled some more. 'I c…c-can feel him, Tyrus. I can feel my grandfather.'

Tyrus gave him a hug, a sturdy one. Lyra, unsure what to do, patted his shoulder.

'Sorry,' apologised Kellan, wiping his tears away.

'Nothing to be sorry about. I mean, I have no idea what your deal is, what this is about but, nothing to be sorry about!' said Lyra. She sounded genuinely sincere, which Kellan had to admit, came rather unexpected.

'He would have been proud of you, Kell,' said Tyrus.

The elf composed himself and thanked them both for their kind words. Lyra changed into her boots and wandered off a little, leaving Tyrus and Kellan to themselves.

'You tried it before, didn't you?' asked Tyrus finally.

'Getting here before.'

Kellan pulled away, leaving the Tyrus' hand to hover in winter's breath.

'I'm sorry,' said Tyrus. 'I shouldn't have blurted that out. It's none of my business.'

'No, you c…c-caught me off-guard is all,' said Kellan. 'Shortly after my grandad p…p-passed away, I tried crossing the sea,' he added. He then carefully lifted his left hand out of his navy pocket and as Tyrus suspected, it was a wooden prosthesis. Most people had to look thrice to notice it.

Kellan continued, 'After he died, I wanted to feel close to him. So m…m-much so, I tried to reach Alula Isle one night, as he once did. Foolish of course, it ended up costing me my hand and p…p-part of my forearm.'

'Not foolish at all,' said Tyrus. 'When I lost my parents, I did anything that made me feel close to them and if that would have involved crossing a dangerous frozen sea on ice skates, I would have done it too.'

'Thanks for saying that,' said the elven boy, letting his hand rest on Tyrus' hand.

They both blushed. Tyrus couldn't keep his eyes off the elven boy's lips. They started out in a rich dark brown around the edges, changing into a more pink-ish hue where they touched. Despite being slightly chapped—not unlike his own lips—Kellan's looked full and gracious. Why did he feel like kissing him? It was hardly the appropriate time? Did Kellan want him to kiss him? Why did this butterfly stuff have to be so complicated? But then, Lyra interrupted their moment. Tyrus felt relieved the tension had been broken, the moment ruined, but at the same time he couldn't help but feel disappointed, too.

'I think I found an entrance!' she shouted.

Kellan and Tyrus turned around to face the building that hid the next splinter, broke away from each other, and put on their boots. Lyra figured she'd do something useful while the boys were too busy pining for each other.

The architecture of the complex almost made it look like a temple, complete with pillars and statues and shapes of Owlbound people etched into the walls. Crownhaven used to be the most important port of Wingspan and before the never-ending cold it was protected by mages from all across the realm. Tyrus felt positively giddy at the prospect of entering this gargantuan historical building. He was about to walk through halls that were once filled with countless Owlbound magicians, both Paragons and Learnlings. A large smile thrived between his two reddened cheeks. However, that smile was quickly overshadowed by the fact that he didn't know what would await them there. His experience with the last splinter was anything but pleasant, what if somehow, this was going to be worse?

'So, the next splinter is in there?' asked Lyra, her eyebrows raised and her pupils dilated. Her voice had a minor tremble to it too, and no one could blame her; the building that stood before them had an intimidating quality to it.

'It should be,' said Tyrus. 'Let's be careful when going in, though. We have no idea what tricks await us inside. We need to stick together.'

'I envy how you make everything sound so delightful, Ty,' said Lyra.

Kellan giggled at that.

'Yeah well, you two weren't around for the nightmare hex that protected the last splinter,' defended Tyrus. 'I want us to be careful.'

The three of them (and Flake) walked up toward the entrance Lyra had found. The structure housed a giant wooden gate. The edges of the wood, supported by steel frames to give the door more structural integrity. In the end, it didn't matter because Tyrus flung it open with ease using his fiery magic.

The hallways behind those doors had an eerie vibe to them. They were dark and damp as drops of water dripped from the ceiling and it smelled like death itself had died in there. Their noses craved the outside air as much as Tyrus craved to have the next splinter in his possession. The further they went into Alula Isle's fortress, the more bones they encountered. Bones upon bones upon bones. Entire skeletons humans, elves, and owls. Every single one picked clean. Flake made herself as tiny as possible, a little ball of feathers. When they found the first full skeletons, Lyra gasped so loud she could taste the smell around them.

Tyrus had closed his eyes right after they had been the widest they'd ever been. 'What happened here?' he asked.

'They say a d...d-dark mage came and slaughtered everyone after winter began,' said Kellan with the shakiest voice as he continued stepping through the hallway as carefully as he could. 'But I don't know how m...m-much of that is truth.'

Tyrus and Lyra shared a look. Had this been the work of the Renegade Paragon?

Eventually, they made it to a large dining hall. As they stepped through the door, a dozen of odd-looking bats glided away from their nest which hung above the doorframe.

'Woah! C...c-cool! Those are snowdrift bats!' shouted Kellan a little too loudly. 'Sorry,' he whispered. 'Those are snowdrift bats.'

'How can you even tell?' asked Lyra. 'They just look like weird bats.'

'Well, as opposed to regular b...b-bats, they're light grey, have more of a fur and they basically drift along in the air. N...n-not so much flying,' explained Kellan.

'How do you know all that?' asked Tyrus.

'You c...c-could say knowing about animals is my own less-fiery magic.' Kellan winked.

The tables were broken, the walls peeled, and holes were scattered across the ceiling like freckles on a face. In the middle of the end of the large hall sat a pedestal and atop it rested wings carved out of stone. The next splinter. The partial key around Tyrus' neck started humming, the way it hummed outside the abandoned coal mines. The wings splinter on the pedestal didn't sit there unprotected, though. A cage embraced it, locked.

'Tread carefully,' said Tyrus, looking up. He sounded almost like Malum.

Flake noticed them too, runes etched into the walls, below the ceiling. The stench didn't only come from all the death, although all the armoured skeletons that once had human or elven meat around them undoubtedly didn't help the case. The runes on the walls enhanced the foul stench, no doubt to deter people from entering. The inscriptions were also to blame for the extreme weather conditions around the island. Nothing that related to the growing population of rimewhales, though; the eternal winter made sure of that herself.

As they slowly inched closer to the cage atop the pedestal, Tyrus noticed more runic magic in the metalwork surrounding the cage. He tried making sense of them as Flake hopped on top of it.

'We've gone through all this trouble to be c...c-confronted with a lock? W...w-where are we supposed to find the key?' asked Kellan.

'No need, I can lockpick this baby,' said Lyra as her nimble fingers emerged from her coat with pins. Right before inserting one of her pins into the lock, a hand stopped her.

'Don't!' shouted Tyrus.

'What? You don't want the wings?' asked Lyra. 'Because if you want them, you'll have to let me pick the bloody lock.'

'It's the runes. Look,' he said as if they supposed to mean anything to her, or Kellan for that matter.

'Ty, you're gonna have to explain,' said Kellan, and Lyra agreed.

Tyrus' stare intensified. 'Pick the lock, fight death, pick it fast, before death takes you at last,' he said.

'First of all, that's a horrible rhyme,' said Lyra. 'Second of all, what does that even mean?'

Tyrus raised his shoulders and Kellan gulped loudly.

'All right, fools. This is what's going to happen,' said Lyra finally, because the silence was too infuriating. 'I'm going to start lockpicking and you two are going to protect me from whatever will try and kill us. Does that sound good?'

Tyrus figured there was no point in arguing with Lyra. Besides, what else were they going to do? 'Okay, let's do it,' he agreed.

Kellan nodded. 'Sure...I guess...' His legs started shaking.

'Here goes nothing!' proclaimed Lyra as the pin went inside the lock. 'And? Anything happening?'

'Not yet,' said Tyrus as fire danced above his palms and inside his eyes.

'You know, m…m-maybe the magic has an expiration date?' asked Kellan as he unsheathed his sword.

'That's not how magic works,' said Tyrus.

Kellan readied his sword. 'How should I know?'

A sound interrupted them. It dragged itself through the corridors, hitchhiking on the unpleasant odours. It sounded like the clanging of bones but what would an enemy want with bones? But then the bones in the big hall, the skeletons, they started shaking, clanging against each other.

Pick the lock.

'Um, Lyra? How is that lock coming along?' asked Tyrus in a trembling voice.

Fight death.

'Yes, Lyra, how l…l-long until you got it?' asked Kellan, unable to hold his sword steady.

'It's a quality lock, it'll take a while,' she said.

Pick it fast.

The bones in the dining hall assembled. They got up on their feet until standing and walking armoured skeletons surrounded the gang. More sauntered their way from the corridors too. Bright pink flames burned in the sockets of their eyes as they grabbed hold of the many weapons that rested on the floors or leaned against the walls. Tyrus and Kellan shook in their boots and the former could hear Flake's heartbeat race in his ear. Sweat ran down Lyra's until the drops froze in place.

Kellan shrieked. 'Lyra, p…p-pick it faster please!'

'Fun fact: telling me to pick it faster isn't going to make me pick it any faster!' she shouted.

Both Tyrus and Kellan screamed like little children waking from a nightmare as their battle with the dead commenced. Kellan didn't know what he was doing with that sword of his, but it appeared as though the skeletons missed the brains to avoid his terrible attacks. For now, he stood his ground, but greater numbers were coming.

Tyrus and Flake fought with the flames in their eyes and with the fire that burned in their hearts. They made sure the enchanted bones regretted ever getting up. Together, Tyrus, Flake, and Kellan protected Lyra with everything they had and everything they were. But inevitability showed its face when Kellan fell backward. A skeleton got on top of him, strangling him with its bare bones while another passed him by and limped Lyra's way. She hadn't heard it coming, either. She was lucky she checked behind her to see how her boys were doing. She kept her hands by the lock. She was too close to picking it to let go and ended up blocking the skeleton's attack by launching a foot into the air.

Lyra was in an awkward position now, picking the

lock with her hands, standing on one leg, with the other up in the air, blocking a skeleton holding a sword at the wrists. 'A little help here?!' shouted Lyra.

Tyrus, turned around without hesitation, used his magic to envelop the skeleton that attacked her in flames and as he intended for the bones to become ash, they did. He wished he had enough mana inside of him to do the same thing to all the other skeletons. There were simply too many.

'Thanks, Clever Chap!' said Lyra.

While Tyrus and Flake had dealt with that, the light in Kellan's eyes dimmed. His right hand scavenged around the floor around him, desperately searching for something to turn the tide but nothing was in reach. Lyra saw him struggle in the corner of her eye and quickly let go of her lockpicking with one hand and used it to throw one of her daggers right into the skull of the skeleton that attempted to squeeze the life out of the elven boy. Kellan gasped for air as he got to his feet.

'How long, Lyra?' shouted Tyrus.

'I'm almost there, I think!' she shouted back.

'You think?!'

'Yes, I think!'

Tyrus steadied his pose. 'I hope you're right!' he shouted as he made a giant wall of flames erupt from the floor, shielding them from the dead for a little while.

'Thanks, Lyra. Thanks, Ty,' said Kellan as he looked

around for another sword.

'No problem,' said Tyrus, the threads of his magic wearing thin. 'Lyra?'

'Yes?' she answered.

'Please…tell me you…have it,' said Tyrus straining himself, keeping the wall of flames up.

'Maybe if you two stopped interrupting me for two whole seconds, I would have gotten it already,' she snapped.

'I can't hold this wall for much longer!' shouted Tyrus.

'Again! Not helping!' roared Lyra.

The glowing wall of fire held off the armoured skeletons, but other bones had awoken too. Kellan gasped as undead owl skeletons flew over the wall of flames. Flake immediately took to the sky to handle this threat by spewing fire at them from her beak.

Kellan readied his new, yet old, sword once again, preparing for the worst. And Tyrus held out till the last of his mana ran out. The wall he had conjured extinguished itself within a single blink of the eyes. A couple extra blinks later, Tyrus and Kellan faced their dreaded dead once more. This time both wielding swords, both exhausted. Flake did her part by keeping the airborne attackers at bay, now putting her sharp talons to good use. Death itself won more and more ground every second, until the two defending boys couldn't inch backward any further as their backs hugged Lyra's.

Before death takes you at last.

Tyrus and Kellan closed their eyes, convinced this was it. Tears escaped the corners of their eyes. They accepted their fate and then…*nothing.*

Did they die? Tyrus and Kellan had prepared for swords and daggers to cut through their skin, for weapons to strike them down, for pain to come and then go. Instead, they opened their eyes to bones and armour crumbling, falling and clanging to the ground.

'You could say I got it,' said Lyra proudly.

The three of them hugged as Flake landed on Tyrus' head, burying her talons in that woolly hat of his. She spread her wings and attempted to wrap them around the three heads. She didn't exactly manage but it was the thought that counted.

As the four of them let go, Tyrus and Kellan's eyes crossed each other, and they locked in. Their noses almost touched while their lips longed to be as near to each other as they could. But once again, they lacked the conviction to do anything about it. Lyra saw them, and she full-well knew what she saw. Connection. Perhaps even love? Either way, she let out a loud grunt and diverted everyone's attention back to the splinter in the now unlocked cage. The wings were ready to be taken and Tyrus let his hand travel inside, slowly and carefully as if he expected another trap, another trick but nothing came. The wings splinter was in theirs.

Lyra, Kellan, Tyrus, and Flake made their way back to the beach where they had left their skates. They decided to sit there for a bit, catching their breaths, gathering their strength for the way back to Crownhaven's shore. All they did was breathe for a while, staring at the frozen sea.

'I'm glad we met you, Kell,' said Tyrus eventually. 'Without you, we wouldn't have been able to do this.'

'I think we could have,' said Lyra, wearing the smile of a chaotic gremlin.

'Y…y-yeah?' asked Kellan.

'It would have taken longer sure, but we could have done it,' she said.

'I appreciate you too, Lyra. I appreciate you too,' said Kellan.

After resting for a few minutes more, they took off their boots, stuffed them back into the rucksack and changed into their skates. At the very least, the stormy, gloomy weather that had challenged them before had dissipated. Their trip back to the mainland would be a little safer.

And so, their journey back to Malum and Cedric began, and it began calmly. Once they passed the area where the water was too shallow and the ice too thick, the rimewhales came back and they craved revenge. Thanks to the wonderful weather and with the sun setting behind Alula Isle, painting the sky pink and orange, they evaded and eluded the persistent sea creatures at every turn and at all eruptions from the ice.

Malum and Cedric watched from the Crownhaven shore with binoculars, and they watched with pride. They bested the vicious whales and while there were still a few close calls that made the two seasoned men tense up, the kids arrived safely back at the shore. Most of Crownhaven had gathered and cheered them on. No one had made it to Alula Isle and back in decades. Multiple warm embraces took place on that beach that evening.

'I'm so proud of you three,' said Malum. 'Four, I mean. My apologies, Flake.'

'We're glad you're all okay,' said Cedric, his voice a tad gravelly as always.

Lyra saw Malum looking at Tyrus a certain way and she knew the traveller wanted to ask him about the splinter, but she also knew he didn't want to seem rude in immediately asking about it. 'Malum, spit it out,' she said after giving Cedric and Tyrus a second or ten.

'Well…did you get it?' asked Malum. 'Did you find it?'

Tyrus buried his right hand in one of his pockets and dug out a pair of wings, carved out of stone. Wings that fit perfectly with the rest of his totem, the key around his neck.

'Extraordinary! Exceptional work!'

Tyrus proposed to go back to the Feathering Inn, and everyone agreed.

Lyra led the way. 'Wait till you two old geezers hear about what we went through over there! Strap in!'

CHAPTER 17

WHAT REMAINS

The wings splinter inside Tyrus' clenched fist longed to be reunited with the rest of the key around his neck. It hummed, violently almost, but it would have to wait until all tales were told in the safety of the warm rooms of the Feathering Inn.

Before they would get there, they had to face the townsfolk of Crownhaven. In the time Tyrus, Flake, Kellan, and Lyra had been gone, the crowd that had gathered had tripled in size. People were still arriving, too. The villagers had been shouting about the teenagers' return, not many could resist seeing it with their own eyes.

As the group got off the beach, and onto the roads of Crownhaven, they were surrounded by cheers and toasts in their name. They even seemed to show Kellan appreciation now that he was an official Alula Isle champion. His heart felt lighter than ever, filled with hope for his future in the human territories of Wingspan.

Lyra relished in the attention of course, while on the other hand, Tyrus felt a bit overwhelmed at the ecstatic response from Crownhaven's citizens. He felt relieved when they finally arrived at the doors of the Feathering Inn. The telling of tales could begin.

Once the brave adventurers had finally told Malum and Cedric all about what had happened on Alula Isle, Tyrus brought the two pieces together. Closer and closer, until they acted like a magnet in the presence of a piece of metal, unable to stay clear of one another.

The moment the pieces joined, the room around Tyrus disappeared, every bit like last time. He soared up into the sky like an owl and flew further east. He crossed forests and rivers and creeks and hills, until he arrived at a quaint little town that climbed up and into a mountain. A mountain that longed for the sky, perhaps it even craved to see what was beyond it. Tyrus could feel it though, that peak, the peak of that mountain. They were there, the talons to his key. The location of the next splinter revealed itself and it all went dark.

Tyrus heard a mix of voices as the hard half-rotten wooden floorboards clung to his spine. He took a moment to catch his breath. These visions were no joke; they were way more intense than they had any right being. Malum and Kellan eventually helped him get up on his feet. His head rocked a little as if he were standing on a boat out on an unfrozen ocean.

'Ty, are you okay?' asked Kellan, checking his friend for any bruising that hadn't been there before.

'Talonstead,' answered Tyrus as he steadied himself, determined as ever.

Cedric was caught in his signature move, stroking his grey beard. 'Talonstead? Isn't that…'

'Where I was born! It's where I live!' exclaimed Malum. 'You're telling me a splinter of the key was right there in my vicinity the entire time?'

Tyrus felt grateful the room had stopped spinning when he registered what Malum had said. 'Yes, the *talons* splinter is in *Talons*tead,' he confirmed.

'Hold on,' said Lyra. 'The talons splinter is in Talonstead? A little on the nose, don't you think?'

It most definitely was, whoever divided and hid the splinters unmistakenly had a sense of humour (depending on who you asked). Tyrus found it quite amusing, and at the same time, he felt thrilled at the prospect of visiting the place where Malum grew up. What sorts of wonders would he get to see next?

'Rather fitting indeed,' said Cedric, and he put his hand on Malum's shoulder. 'Looks like you're going home.'

Everyone felt eager to prepare for the journey immediately, especially Malum, who hadn't been home in ages. Tyrus didn't hesitate asking Kellan if he wanted to tag along. He was more than nervous to hear the answer.

'I think I've st…t-stayed here for long enough. I stayed because this was my grandfather's home, and I missed him t…t-terribly. But getting to go to Alula Isle, m…m-made me realise, there's n…n-nothing here for me anymore,' said Kellan. 'So, I'd love to join…if that's okay with everyone.'

Lyra was the one who stepped forward and said, 'I think I speak for everyone when I say welcome aboard.' The elven boy turned out to be nothing like the stories she'd heard. She'd even go as far as to say he became a friend, despite her nasty initial comments.

Everyone agreed, no objections, and they all started packing for the journey toward Malum's hometown. The next morning, they already waved the settlement of Crownhaven goodbye, and for Kellan, it was a bittersweet moment. He'd called the town his home for so long. And even though he never fully fit in, he felt a bit frightened about leaving it behind. Luckily, he had found a new family. One where he didn't need to hide his ears, one where he could fully be himself.

At one point, the road to Talonstead seemed endless. Snow and snow and snow, for miles and miles and miles, followed by frigid forests, frozen rivers, dying creeks and white-tipped mountains that climbed up as they attempted and succeeded to pierce holes in the sky.

Everyone was in the carriage except for Malum and Cedric, who were in the front guiding Trudy through the winter landscape. Cedric had never been to Talonstead because he usually stuck to his journeys between Featherburn and Crownhaven, minus a few exceptions here and there. When he was younger, he travelled a lot more, mostly around western Wingspan, but never this far east. He found himself in uncharted territory and so, he didn't know the way. He despised not knowing, mostly because it meant following Malum's directions, but it also meant they only travelled by day, because both Malum and the trader needed sleep.

Even though the two of them seemed to finally get along(-ish), there were still things Malum did that infuriated the seasoned trader. For one thing, Malum possessed this insatiable need to always be right no matter what. That brain of his housed valuable and impressive knowledge, but the problem was that he also had an opinion or hypothesis on things he knew nothing about. They would argue and Cedric would be right, but Malum would never admit it. He'd blow it off and start talking about anything else. Every time, Ced squeezed his reins tighter while simultaneously taking it as a win.

For Tyrus and Flake, the journey had been great. Cold as always, but great. Flake had changed a great deal since she flew into Tyrus' lighthouse. The poofy feathers had disappeared and she'd grown a smidge taller. You could still tell she was a young owl, but she started looking more like an adult bird with every passing day. Together, they spent heaps of time with Lyra and Kellan. They shared stories, had a laugh, and Lyra taught the two boys how to play cards. And while things were positively lovely, every time Tyrus found himself alone with either Lyra or Kell. It didn't happen often that he could be alone with either of them, mostly during stops, when gathering or hunting food for example. But every time it did happen, his heart panicked, stuck in a tug-of-war. There were moments where his heart longed for Lyra, but then Kellan would step in to sweep him off his feet again. It drove him wild, and it hadn't gone unnoticed for Lyra. On their last stop, the day before they would arrive at Talonstead, she volunteered to go and find firewood together with Tyrus. And so, as the evening dawned, they headed out into the woods together. Alone.

Tyrus' familiar dark-green woolly hat rested comfortable on his head, but he had traded his maroon cloak for a green one that matched the hat. His previous cloak sat riddled in holes and rips and he couldn't be bothered to fix it all with his magic.

He noticed Lyra wearing all black. She said it was her favourite colour, even though Kellan told her repeatedly he felt pretty confident it was a tint, not a colour at all. Tyrus blushed thinking about him, or was it because he was looking at her?

'You and Kellan, huh,' began Lyra out of the blue, and straight to the point.

Tyrus froze as he crouched to pick up two perfect branches; a bunch of awkward and incomprehensible noises followed.

'Oh, come on, I have eyes, Ty. You like him,' she continued. 'I don't blame you, he's cute. It's more about the person for me, but you know, good-looking is a nice bonus.' She winked.

Tyrus blushed some more and remained speechless, shocked.

'You like us both. And you can't tell which one of us you like more?' asked Lyra. 'That's the issue, right?'

Tyrus' eyes widened. 'How did you know?'

'Because it's painfully obvious, Clever Chap,' answered Lyra. 'Like, you can't miss it, to be honest. Kellan is oblivious to it, of course.'

Tyrus let his gaze fall to snow below their boots. 'Do you like me too?'

'Infuriatingly so? Yes. I do like you too,' answered Lyra. 'The butterflies are *so* annoying.'

Tyrus laughed. Lyra came closer. 'I don't know how to determine if I like you more or Kellan. I can't figure it out,' said the young nervous mage in all honesty.

Lyra bit her nails. 'What if we kissed?' she asked.

The white in Tyrus' eyes had never been more prevalent, the blush in his cheeks too.

'I'll be frank with you,' said Lyra. 'I'm pretty sure I know who you like more, but I feel like a kiss would help you see it.' Lyra came even closer. 'Can I?'

Tyrus nodded. The feeling in his stomach exploded as if millions of butterflies came out of their cocoons. Chapped lips kissed chapped lips and it felt even better than he had imagined. But when the warmth of Lyra's lips left his, he knew. She was right, the kiss helped him see what he already knew deep down.

'It's Kellan, isn't it?' whispered Lyra with her forehead against Tyrus'.

Tyrus' gaze dropped to the snow below them. What if he hurt her?

'You can say it, it's fine, Clever Chap,' she said. 'I'll be fine, I promise.'

'I think it is Kellan, yeah,' confirmed Tyrus. 'I mean, not that the kiss was bad or anything. The kiss was great! Amazing even! Genuinely…Not bad at all…It's…you know…'

Just before Tyrus could start embarrassing himself even further, Lyra stopped him from trailing off completely. 'I know,' she said. 'I'm a stellar kisser.'

They both laughed.

'Are we okay, Lyra?' asked Tyrus.

'More than okay,' she answered. 'I came out here with you to know, and now I do.'

Tyrus gave her a hug. 'Thanks, Lyra,' he said.

'Glad to be of service? Now, if Kellan is foolish enough to not like you back. I want you to know I've sharpened my daggers recently.' She winked.

Together, they continued collecting firewood, the thing they set out to do in the first place. Once they had collected enough, they returned to where they had set up camp. Tyrus was initially afraid what that kiss would mean for Lyra and him going forward, but it seemed like nothing had changed. To the contrary, even. The quips and jokes remained, and surprisingly, things didn't get awkward between them either. Lyra needed the closure Tyrus' rejection offered her to move past it, to accept being friends would be enough. And as it turned out, it was.

A marvellous campfire and a wonderful night's sleep later, the gang was on the road once more, until they made a rather ominous stop. Cedric stopped the carriage near eerie ruins, a few slippery roads before the climb up to Talonstead would begin. The few trees that stood there were more like husks, charred and pitch black. A thick layer of fog clung to the snow.

'Bloody hell…What the hell happened here?' asked Cedric as everyone stepped off and out of the carriage.

'What is this p…p-place?' asked Kellan, closing his thick navy jacket.

'You mean: what *was* this place?' said Lyra behind him, leaning against the carriage wheel behind the ladder.

'This used to be Ravencreek, a settlement my hometown often traded with, in a distant past,' said Malum.

'D…d-did an avalanche do this?' asked Kellan.

Piled up snow tried hiding the cabins. The rooftops popped out here and there, but most of the settlement had been eaten by winter.

'It seems that way, doesn't it?' began Malum. The way he said it, he clearly knew more than he was letting on. 'However, what happened here happened over a century ago. Winter merely claimed what was left. It's what the snow hides that reveals the truth.'

Tyrus conjured flames into his hands and spread his arms wide. Lyra felt the warmth conquer her cheeks, the tips of Kellan's ears felt again, Cedric's frost nipped nose tingled with delight, and the snow around them melted away until a thin layer remained. Everything the group wanted to say remained unsaid as their eyes took in scorched cabins and charred bodies, all frozen and preserved by winter's beak. When Tyrus saw the damage, he knew there was only one thing that could have done this. *Magic.* Tyrus walked forward and inspected one of the countless burnt down houses. He sensed something peculiar.

'Uh, laddie? What are you doing?' asked Cedric.

Tyrus didn't answer; he felt confident there was magic

nearby. He could sense it and concentrated on the echoing humming it left behind. He stepped inside the burnt cabin, Flake confidently gracing his shoulder. Everything was scorched by magical fire, but it wasn't that he was sensing. He forced open a charcoal-black door, which revealed a bedroom. A charred unrecognisable body laid partially buried in the ash of what would have been the bed. Tyrus could sense the magic coming from there and then he saw it. The body clenched something in its hands. Something shiny.

He didn't take any pleasure in it, but Tyrus wrestled the fingers open, and after unpleasant cracks and a couple of fingers disintegrating into ash entirely, Flake managed to pry the magical object loose with her beak. She dropped it in the palm of Tyrus' hand. It was a pearl, a shiny peculiar pearl. It looked cracked, damaged, but in between the cracks, you could see swirling purple and green flames.

Tyrus emerged from the burnt cabin and showed everyone what he had found. 'Malum, what do you think this is?' he asked as he held it forward in between his thumb and index finger.

'Tyrus! No, wait!' shouted Malum but it was too late.

The pearl started glowing and everything started burning in those same purple and green flames. Panic jumped between everyone until they realised the fire didn't hurt them. It painted a picture of what happened.

The fire became silhouettes of people, Ravencreek villagers most likely.

The fires showed Tyrus and his friends the grim fate of those who lived in the destroyed settlement. People were struck down by the flames of magic, wielded by a hooded mage in the distance. There weren't any details visible, and their face was mostly covered underneath the hood they wore. One thing was for sure; a scary large owl graced their shoulder. The Renegade Paragon.

As sudden as the fires had poured out of the little pearl in Tyrus' hand, they disappeared. 'What was that?!' shouted the young mage.

Everyone was in shock. Even though what they saw didn't look real, it managed to rattle everyone to their core.

'That...was an Echo Pearl,' said Malum. 'I never thought I'd ever see one. Sometimes, magic leaves such an impression, whether it's trauma or intense moments of happiness that it leaves behind a concentrated pearl. These Echo Pearls hold powerful memories, like the one we saw. Sometimes, they're so strong they can cause real damage when activated.'

'Which is why you shouted,' said Tyrus.

'Precisely,' said Malum. 'We were lucky.'

'That Renegade fellow seems to be the cause of every vile and evil thing we've encountered so far,' noted Cedric.

'Like the d...d-dead on Alula Isle,' said Kellan.

'Everywhere we go, we encounter what's left in the wake of their evil,' said Tyrus through his teeth. It got him thinking too. 'What if the cold didn't take my parents, but they did?'

Cedric knelt down, took hold of Tyrus at his elbows. 'Don't go there, laddie. We can't let this twisted figure get into our heads.' The way he said it, the way he looked away when he said that first sentence, it seemed as though he had experience with overthinking what if scenarios.

'Let's pray we never encounter them,' said Lyra. 'Right?'

'Very much so, young lady,' said Malum. 'This mage wields powerful magic. I mean they're a Paragon. No offence, Tyrus. But you'd be no match for them right now.'

'None taken,' said the amber-eyed boy, hoisting his shoulders.

'There's still the possibility they're long gone, though? Right?' asked Cedric. 'As in, they may have kicked the bucket already, no?'

'For all our sakes, let's hope so,' said Malum.

The pearl still shone in the palm of Tyrus' hand, he decided to hold on to it. Being conscious about not accidentally activating it this time. He didn't know why, and he couldn't possibly begin to explain it, but he couldn't help but feel like he needed to hold on to it. And so, he did, sliding the thing into the pockets in his coat.

CHAPTER 18

HOMECOMING

Trudy's might and force, in addition to the weight of the carriage, made travelling up the narrow road that swirled around the mountain dangerous. Cedric decided everyone should walk in front of his behemoth horse, so that he could focus on slowly getting his moving home up to Talonstead without the added burden of passengers.

The path they walked sat decorated with pine trees and frozen shrubbery, while the dazzling view swam in the reflections of the travelling troupe's eyes like rimewhales under the frozen seas. They took in the hills, the forests, the still steams and the rivers they had passed before, along with what had remained of Ravencreek.

In approaching Talonstead, Tyrus, Lyra, and Kellan noticed they hadn't yet seen any gates, guards, or patrols, nothing of the sort. Malum informed them that Talonstead didn't have need for any of those things. The mountain range itself was the settlement's first line of defence, and as they kept walking up the spiralling path—passing a few quaint cabins and cosy huts—they arrived at the settlement's next line of defence when the town seemingly stopped in front of the entrance to a cave.

At first, you'd think the town ended there and something in the vein of a mine would continue but, nothing could be further from the truth. Talonstead continued inside the cave. It exploded, flourishing into a dense, yet homey commune. Over the centuries, the people here had hollowed out part of their mountain, all the way through to the other side to nest their homes into. A giant and impressive mechanism of stone and sturdy wooden cogwheels hid behind the entrance to the cave, a contraption that could push a gargantuan metal door to seal the cave. The same monumental apparatus was copied on the other side of town. The townsfolk didn't have to use it much, but when they did, they sure were happy their ancestors had built it.

Everyone walked through the cave in awe, except for Malum. They couldn't believe their eyes. The ceiling of the ginormous cave was lit by chandeliers, light that a designated squad would extinguish by nightfall and enkindle by daybreak. It seemed magical but Tyrus felt there wasn't any magic involved. It seemed that way initially because the ceiling wasn't made from ordinary rock. It was more of a reflective surface, a material crystal-like in nature and it dispersed a variety of colours through the lively settlement streets.

'Malum, how come you never talk about this place?' asked Tyrus.

'It's marvellous here!' agreed Lyra.

Malum knew his hometown was amazing for outsiders, but he had lived his entire childhood there (and a reasonable amount of time beyond that). He supposed he'd gotten used to the splendidness.

Eyes followed them everywhere, whispers too. This time it wasn't only because Flake graced Tyrus' shoulder, the villagers were also weary because an elf walked among them.

'Don't worry, everyone. They're with me,' repeated Malum a few times as they walked through the narrow streets.

To the surprise of Tyrus and his friends, Malum appeared to be a respected member of Talonstead's community, even if he wasn't physically there most of the time.

As they walked, Malum eventually asked Tyrus a question, who couldn't take his eyes off his surroundings, distracted by the beauty of the place. Kellan had to nudge him.

'Are you sure the talons splinter is at the peak of Talonstead's mountain, Tyrus?' asked Malum for the second time.

'Right,' said Tyrus as he let his attention flow into the

conversation. 'The vision I saw put a lot of emphasis on the peak. I'm sure it's up there.'

'That's…rather unfortunate,' said Malum as his companions followed him further through Talonstead. 'A slither of naivete within me hoped you had been mistaken.'

'How so?' asked everyone at the same time as they walked closer together.

Worry welled up to the surface of Malum's face. 'If it's up there, we'll have to climb the mountain, an extremely dangerous climb, I might add.' he said while looking up. 'Well…*you* would have to climb it.'

'Okay,' said Lyra, the word drawn out like the string of a pulled-back bow. 'First of all, why did you say *"you"* like that? Secondly, surely this time Flake can fly up and take a look, no? She's a bird with functional wings!'

'Absolutely not, Lyra,' said Tyrus. 'For the exact same reason as last time,' he added before Lyra could ask why.

'I was kidding,' she said rolling her eyes. 'Mostly.' She then looked at Malum. She had asked him a question and her eyes demanded an answer.

'I'm not climbing, not even to save the world. I'm not particularly fond of… heights,' he shared.

Lyra snorted loudly and stopped after Malum's stern stare.

'Don't worry,' said Tyrus. 'You won't have to come with us because we already have an experienced rock-climber in our midst! Tell them, Ced!'

'Aye, I may have dabbled into mountaineering here and there,' said Cedric. 'When I had significantly fewer grey hairs.'

'Interesting,' noted Malum with an index finger in front of his mouth, his elbow supporting his right arm.

'Dabbled?' asked Tyrus, blinking twice in rapid succession. 'If you call climbing Crown's Summit dabbling, then sure.'

'That's the largest m…m-mountain in the known realm, no?' asked Kellan. 'Near Beaksworth?'

'Holy schnitzel!' shouted Lyra. 'Cedric, you're a living legend! That's wild!'

Cedric spent a great deal of time around Beaksworth in his younger years. The mountains there stood tall as giants. If the mountains around (and above) Talonstead aimed for seeing what was beyond the sky, Crown's Summit considered it done with its highest peak.

'Cedric, that's extraordinary,' said Malum. 'You can lead the expedition! Why haven't you shared this before?'

'Because modesty fits him like my gloves fit my hands perfectly?' suggested Lyra.

While Malum was happy they wouldn't have to go looking for someone to lead their perilous expedition, he did have more worries highlighted on his face.

'Malum, please, for the love of the spring we hope to see one day, spit it out,' said Lyra.

The man hesitated but eventually said, 'Cedric's experience climbing Crown's Summit will undeniably help our case. However, while Crown's Summit was higher, the mountain ranges around Talonstead are infamous for their hazardousness.' He paused. 'I didn't want to worry you on the way here, but it's not only because of the rough terrain.'

Just as Malum stopped talking, he invited everyone inside a rather boring-looking house, his house. Were they getting a peek behind the curtain of the Malum show? Would they get the chance to peel away a few mysterious layers as if he were an onion—or an ogre? Their excitement set them up for disappointment, because when inside, they were greeted by the dullest, barely decorated, dustiest and emptiest house they had ever seen.

'My apologies for the dust and the cobwebs, I haven't been home in a while,' said Malum simply.

'You take the mysterious, charming professor act far, don't you?' asked Lyra. 'Couldn't you have done *something* to decorate? Anything at all?'

'What's the point? I'm rarely home these days. More things mean more stuff to clean when I am here,' he explained, and Lyra couldn't fault his reasoning; she imagined doing the exact same thing if she were in his shoes.

To no one's surprise, there was a bookcase. If anything, there was going to be a bookcase. Filled, overflowing with books about magic and Tyrus' brain fizzed with eagerness because while he knew—and had already read—some of the books back at his lighthouse, most of the books here were completely new to him. Borrowed and old, yet brand new.

'Right!' yelled Malum and he clapped, after lifting a book out of a worn chest. 'My current theory is that the next splinter is in the Nest.'

'The N…n-nest? Nest of what?' asked Kellan.

Malum looked the elf's way. 'Unfortunately…No one knows.'

Cedric sighed. 'I swear, none of these splinters are going to be easy, are they? Not a single one!'

'There's plenty of tales, stories, and legends that describe the peak of this mountain as *The Nest* and the creature that guards it…the Beast,' explained Malum.

Lyra sighed a sigh that complemented Cedric's. 'Sounds snuggly.'

'It is said that the Beast was the reason our Talonstead ancestors built the giant doors. Furthermore, no one is mad enough to go up there to see what's the matter,' said Malum. 'Those who *did* go up there, were never seen again.'

'Have there been no d…d-descriptions of this Beast?' asked Kellan. 'None at all?'

Malum shook his head. 'The only thing people seem to recollect is that it flies,' he answered.

'That d...d-doesn't narrow it down, does it? It could be any n...n-number of things. A dragon, a griffin, a peryton, a wyvern, it c...c-could be any number of things,' said Kellan.

Tyrus loved seeing Kellan nerd out over creatures, especially in this case where it had to be a legendary or mythical one. The first time he noticed it was when the young elf talked about the rimewhales, and then again with the snowdrift bats. The jealousy that conquered his face when Lyra and Tyrus told him they had fought a frost golem, was a sight to behold.

Lyra joined Kellan in brainstorming what the Beast could be. She mainly pitched made-up creatures to annoy the elven boy, but he seemed to appreciate the out-of-the-box thinking.

Malum clapped again. 'Children, let's not get ahead of ourselves. We should focus on preparing this expedition.'

'Children? Ew, okay gramps,' sneered Lyra.

'Malum's right,' cut in Cedric, Tyrus could see he hated admitting that. 'If we're going to do this, and this climb is as dangerous as advertised, we're going to need the best gear. Ice axes, ice tools, screws, pickets, rope, harnesses, helmets, quickdraws, the whole affair.'

'Ropes we can easily find at the market, as for the tools, we have a solid blacksmith in town,' said Malum. 'She can provide us with everything we need.'

And with that, Cedric and Malum decided not to waste

any time and set out into Talonstead to get all the equipment they needed, leaving the kids to their own devices. They had asked them to do some digging regarding the Beast even though they probably wouldn't learn anything new. However, Lyra had an idea for making their interviews not completely worthless. This was their chance to see if any of the townsfolk had any juicy gossip about Malum. So, while the bickering uncles gathered the gear for their expedition, Tyrus, Flake, Lyra, and Kellan set out into the town to gather intel on the Nest, the Beast, and because they couldn't help themselves, Malum.

As expected, they didn't gain valuable intel surrounding the creature they wanted to know more about. The only thing villagers had to say about the matter was that it could fly, it had wings, and it was dangerous, thirsty for human and elven blood alike. Some didn't even want to talk about it at all, claiming it would bring them ill tidings.

They also asked about Malum, and those conversations turned out slightly more fruitful, though they unearthed nothing surprising. Most villagers talked about how they didn't know a lot about him, that he kept to himself, but that his family had always been a constant in Talonstead's history. One of Malum's direct ancestors founded Talonstead, which explained his sway within the community despite them not knowing a whole lot about him. Most townspeople figured him a bit of an odd bird, but all of them could agree that he was the spitting image of his father, Malum Senior.

The people of Talonstead described Malum exactly as Tyrus, Flake, Lyra, and Kellan knew him: bright, charming, wise, polite, and private. Lyra almost told Tyrus and Kellan what she overheard him share with Cedric at the campfire when they travelled from Featherburn to Crownhaven. About how he loved someone. About how he lost that someone. How it broke him and how that's why he's so obsessed with ending the Eternal Winter. But ultimately, she decided against it. If he wanted to share it with them, he would have and perhaps one day, he still would.

The day flew by faster than Flake ever could, and the teens met Cedric and Malum back at the house. The house without flavour, the house that smelled of dust and absence. Ced and Mal had found everything they needed, and Kellan told them about how their questions didn't get them many answers.

Malum turned around after placing the supplies they had gotten on his table. 'Tyrus, we'll need you to inscribe these tools with runes, instil them with magic, make sure they're extra sturdy. We have magic at our disposal, we might as well use it. Especially since we still don't know what will await you all up there.'

Tyrus agreed, so he let an evening of inscribing and instilling in Malum's study wash over him like Kellan and Lyra welcomed sleep with open arms. The boy enchanted the harnesses, the helmets, the ice picks, and most of the other things to make sure everything was the sturdiest and the most powerful they could be. The only things he couldn't inscribe with magic were the ropes. He couldn't possibly carve any runes into the threads.

When he was done, Malum approached him. 'Tyrus, this is stellar work,' he said. 'You know, I'm proud of you. You've come far. If you were a Learnling studying under a Paragon, they'd be proud, too.'

'If we're telling Tyrus we're proud of him, count me in!' shouted Cedric from the other room, the one that housed an ugly pink couch. 'And *they* would be proud of you too, laddie,' he added as he shuffled into the study. 'I know it.'

Tyrus appreciated the words, gave the both of them a hug and made his way to the guestroom where Lyra and Kellan already snored. Sleep called Tyrus' name, Flake's too and they gladly answered the call.

CHAPTER 19

THE BEAST OF THE NEST

The ginormous mountain that disappeared into the clouds weighed on Malum's stomach as if it had punched him in the gut with everything it had. He felt incredibly grateful he didn't have to go up there with the others.

They wouldn't even be a quarter of the way there and he would have passed out, leaving Cedric to carry him up the rest of the way. If the monster at the top was as ferocious as the legends made it out to be, he'd be helpless against that, too.

It had been a week since they gathered the gear and the tools. A week since Tyrus had inscribed and instilled them with magic. Cedric had taught the kids all he knew about rock climbing, or at least the things they needed to know to survive as they prepared for the climb.

As per usual, Lyra picked things up rather quickly while Tyrus struggled a little and Kellan struggled right there with him. However, practice made adequate. They had to make do with that because for perfection they'd need years, years they weren't sure the world had left. They had seen it everywhere they went, the hunger on faces, the growling of stomachs, ferocious animal populations growing, and death tolls rising at an alarming rate.

Tyrus had made a special attachment for Kellan to temporarily replace his usual prosthesis. One that extended his lower arm into a pickaxe instead of a hand to help him climb more comfortably. Kellan cheered when he got it, saying he appreciated. He gave Tyrus a peck on the cheek, something that came accompanied by luscious blushes between the both of them.

Then, the time came for the climb. Cedric rubbed his hands together at the prospect of mountaineering again, like a child in front of a cake on their name day. However, he figured it best to keep those feelings to himself, because Tyrus, Lyra, and Kellan were as nervous as they were brave. Even Malum, who didn't even dare go up there, wore a contracted face merely thinking about the whole endeavour.

Cedric made sure all the harnesses were up to snuff and that everyone wore them correctly before linking them all together with the ropes. That way, if one of them fell, the others could act as a tether, utilising the enchanted ice picks. They could bury those into the side of the mountain to hold on to. Helmets sat on heads, hands gripped ice picks (and talons gripped a shoulder pad) tight and Cedric led the way.

'See you around, Malum!' he shouted as he started climbing.

Lyra felt compelled to weigh in. 'Yeah, have a good one!'

'Be careful all of you!' shouted Malum from the safe and sturdy ground.

Flake—perched on her human's shoulder—responded with a gentle hoot, while Tyrus yelled, 'Always!' and off they were, ascending to the peak above.

The climb progressed slowly, yet steadily and Cedric wouldn't have it any other way. He'd rather be slow and careful, than fast and reckless. After all, the lives of three teenagers were in his hands. A responsibility he didn't feel entirely at ease with.

The cold had already reddened and numbed noses and Tyrus' cheeks felt like he had severely grazed them by slipping and falling face-first into sandpaper floorboards. The others felt it too winter laying siege to their bodies. Tyrus wanted to use his magic to warm himself and his friends up a little, but he had to save his strength for a possible encounter with the monster at the top. Whatever it would turn out to be, he needed his mana pool charged and at the ready, not hungry and depleted.

The higher they got, the fiercer the wind became—both in force and icy sting. The oxygen in the air thinned too as they needed to draw in considerably deeper breaths to stay conscious. Tyrus kept telling himself to not look down. He didn't think the height would bother him so much as it did. Luckily, he had Flake with him. She'd give him a gentle peck to the temple every time his gaze attempted to fall. Kellan, on the other hand, felt his heartbeat in his throat pound more vigorously with how the fog around them became thicker and denser. Lyra and Cedric had no thoughts. They focused on the task at hand; getting to the top of that mountain in one piece, nothing else, nothing more and certainly nothing less.

Everyone climbed at a snail's pace, but they made satisfactory progress. Until a sound threw everyone off their game. A loud grunt barged into the ears of the climbers. The kind that exerted dominance and demanded fear. It didn't stop with the grunt either. A certain presence stayed with them. It hung near them, skulked around them, stalking them, scaring them, intimidating them to make a mistake. Hoping they might slip and fall. The sound of flapping wings lurked in the fog too: they didn't sound like your average ordinary wings either, especially Flake could tell the wings they heard were far larger than hers.

Kellan's spine shivered. The possibilities as to what

the Beast could be flew through his mind. Could it be a dragon? Fighting an undead army of soldiers was one thing, the prospect of fighting a fire breathing, impenetrable, scaly dragon was another. Kellan couldn't know for sure, not yet.

Whatever it was, it grunted louder and louder at their presence in short rageful bursts. The Beast poured the distilled essence of fear into their brains by being all around them at once. Not long after the first time they'd heard it grunt, it decided to actively thwart their quest by attacking the ridge they climbed. It sounded like it smacked into it above them with sharp claws. Snow and debris fell, and while Cedric managed to evade a large falling brick by the skin of his teeth, smaller rocks grazed Lyra's shoulder.

Kellan noticed the sudden musky smell fill the air. It ruled out the possibility of a dragon and it couldn't be wyvern anymore either. It thrived on the tip of his tongue now.

Without warning, two sets of sharp talons and two sets of hoofs shot out of the mist as they aimed to bring Lyra down. Flake warned her from Tyrus' back with precautionary hoots, making sure she was able to move out of the way early enough to not be crushed or torn into shreds. The rope that tethered Lyra to Cedric and her Clever Chap, however, had no such luck. The talons had severed the rope.

Lyra and Kellan were now only tethered to each other.

'Lyra?' called out Kellan. 'Are you okay?'

'No, but yes!' she shouted back at him. 'Let's keep going!'

And so, they did. But another attack was imminent, and the Beast grew slightly more aggressive, attacking the trespassers at increasingly shorter intervals. Evading crashing debris, and staying clear of sharp and speedy talons, became as much a part of the experience as the enchanted ice picks that buried themselves into ice and rock, time and time again.

Fear had made a home in their hearts, but at the same time, their curiosity still thrived in the guest room of their thoughts. What in the last of the Owlbound were they up against?

They weren't far from the peak of the mountain now. They were only a few meters away from reaching their goal when their mystery monster dove for Lyra once again. Her final tether, connecting her to Kellan and her equipment, was cut. And she would have been thrust off the ridge entirely if she didn't hold on to her enchanted ice pick with everything she had and everything she was. She hoped that was enough. It wasn't. While the pick sat sturdily stuck in the mountainside thanks to the magic instilled within it, Lyra's grip slipped away. She hyperventilated, not knowing what to do. As the realisation of falling to meet death settled, she couldn't even bring herself to shout for help.

Kellan saw it all happen as Lyra struggled a couple of metres above him. He tried getting closer to her to help, but there was no way he could have made it up there in time.

Lyra fell.

This is it, she thought. *This is the end.*

She heard Cedric and Tyrus cry out from above. The latter hadn't ever felt more powerless. All his magic at his disposal, but he could barely see anything to take concrete action.

Lyra had accepted her fate and closed her eyes, but Kellan and Flake didn't. Flake dove down, breathed fire around Lyra, somehow slowing her fall. Kellan then tied his rope to his ice pick and let go, relying on the tether he made to hold him as he swung himself over to meet Lyra's slightly slowed-down freefall, to grab her hand.

He caught her.

Lyra was in shock. The rope held, or at least it did for the time being. Silence conquered the two teenagers and they both froze in place like the water that used to flow in rivers and creeks, water that used to make waves in the seas.

After letting what had happened sink in a little, the two prepared to climb once again while Flake returned to Tyrus' side. Lyra crawled up over Kellan's body to the ice pick, after which she helped him get to it as well. Everyone had brought spares on their backs, which turned out to be a great idea. It allowed Lyra to get back to her original one and climb the rest of the way.

'Oh, thank the gods!' uttered Cedric once they reached the top.

'Lyra!' screamed Tyrus in relief. 'Am I glad you're still alive! For a moment we thought we had lost you!'

'I have Kellan and Flake to thank for that,' she said as they all shared an embrace.

The embrace didn't last long though because Cedric interrupted them to bring their focus back to the quest at hand. He figured they could let things settle once they were back on the ground.

Dense fog surrounded them, but they could make out two shapes, lurking in the distance.

'What's that?' asked Lyra, voice still shaky.

The shapes didn't move, not even a little. They looked like ovals. Ovals that stood still, and they stood as tall as they were. The closer they got the clearer the shapes became; giant eggs.

'Of c…c-course! I know what we're dealing with. The m…m-musky smell, the wings, the talons, the hoofs, the eggs. We're d…d-dealing with a peryton,' Kellan announced, back straight, chest puffed.

'A what now?' asked Lyra.

'A peryton, and it is p…p-protecting its eggs. It thinks we're here to steal them,' explained Kellan. 'They get aggressively t...t-territorial when trying to hatch their babies.'

Just as the words left his lips, giant wings flapped in the distance, getting closer and closer and closer until they made the dense fog around them clear out. Except for Kellan, no one had a clue as to what to expect. The elf stood on the cusp of describing the creature, but he no longer had to. They had expected a thoroughly scary beast, a creature that would chill them to the bone like the icy wind. Instead, they were met by a meticulously elegant and majestic being. Towering before them, stood a peryton, a white peryton to be precise.

The creature stood with a rather pompous frame; a true royal beast as proud as a peacock. Four robust feathered legs, the two front ones ending in fierce talons, the hind legs ending in deer hoofs, both invading and cracking the black rock below. They carried the rest of its body like it was nothing. The wings were twice as long as the creature itself and its head and body were that of a wild buck. It stared at them with stern determined eyes and it wore its antlers like a ruler wore their crown. Antlers strong enough to break bones and talons that could easily cut through flesh, even rock. It grunted at them and put itself between them and its eggs.

'Look, Tyrus,' said Kellan, pointing at the peryton's neck.

The talons splinter hung strung around its throat.

Cedric felt compelled to calm the creature down, to try and make their intentions clear. They weren't there for the eggs, not at all, and while the seasoned mountain climber carefully stepped forward with his hands out—palms facing the creature—Lyra slithered back behind the rocks. Tyrus and Kellan looked her way and knew exactly what the plan was; they agreed too. They would distract the peryton while she found a way to snatch the talons splinter.

It became rather clear, rather fast that Cedric's tactic didn't work. Instead of the peryton calming down, it got more restless until it resorted to an attack. It lunged at Cedric with its antlers, attempting to stab holes in that gut of his. Tyrus and Flake had conjured up a shield of fire to protect him. The peryton's antlers met the fiery barrier after which it flapped its wings in confusion, pushing Cedric, Kellan and Tyrus and Flake backward.

'Whatever you do, d…d-don't look into its eyes. They consider it highly disrespectful, like f…f-flipping someone off!' warned Kellan.

'You could have told me that before, lad,' answered Cedric.

Tyrus didn't want to fight it, but like with the frost golem in Featherburn, he knew he'd have to enter a dance. A dance of distraction and evasion and so he did, once again waiting for Lyra to swoop in.

Cedric and Kellan thought it wise to hide behind the

irregular rock-formations around them while Tyrus kept the enormous beast busy with fire.

'Be sure not to hurt it, Ty!' shouted Kellan from the sidelines. 'And try and keep it from getting airborne, that's where it can do the m...m-most damage!'

Every time Tyrus saw Lyra move and the peryton's gaze attempting to spot her, he'd shoot a ball of fire directly at its head. Every time, the fire drew its attention back to him and every time, he told the fire not to hurt, not to harm. The creature didn't have to suffer for simply protecting its spawn and territory.

In a stroke of arrogance, Tyrus thought he had things covered and got a bit greedy with his attacks. The peryton sought to humble him and knocked him down by spinning around and letting its unexpectedly long tail slam right into his chest. The attack flung him backward, his back hitting rocks and the pores on his right cheek practically breathed in the cold black basalt of the ground.

'Right, should have w...w-warned you about the tail,' added Kellan.

With Tyrus down for the count by the surprise attack and Lyra now exposed, Flake decided she'd take over the distraction act by harassing the peryton's antlers. She did the best she could to annoy it into not spotting Lyra as she made her jump.

She landed on the white peryton's shiny back. The creature's response was to take to the sky as it flapped its gigantic wings. Flake wrapped her talons tightly around the antlers to not be flung off, and Tyrus tried to stop the creature from taking off. He cast chains of fire around its hoofs and talons, but the peryton was too strong. His fiery chains shattered, and Lyra's screams disappeared into the clouds above.

Lyra hung onto the beast as tightly as she could, her hands gripping the feathers that decorated the creatures back in between its white fur. Every single feather shone silver and every single one was about as sturdy as her enchanted ice pick. No matter the moves the peryton made in the air, Lyra refused to let go. And so, the Beast of the Nest crashed down to the basalt ground in between Tyrus, Cedric, and Kellan.

Lyra let her hand guide one of her daggers to the peryton's throat but, to the contrary of what the creature believed to be true, she didn't have any intention to kill. She cut the band and removed the talons splinter from around its neck. Lyra jumped off the back of the creature and carefully stepped back.

'Show it the splinter!' shouted Kellan. 'Show it we m...m-mean no harm!'

Lyra did what Kellan recommended. She continued inching backward with her hands out in front of her, showing off the talons splinter. Slowly, slower, slowest.

'Perytons are smart, intelligible b...b-beings...if I remember correctly,' added the young elf.

The anger in its eyes disappeared like a spell that was lifted. And that's when the peryton saw; that's when it understood. They weren't there for its eggs, its children. They were there for that silly little talons-shaped rock that had hung around her neck for years and years. The great white peryton rose to its talons and hoofs and stood up tall before them, as it graciously bowed down and presented the climbers with its antlers.

'Kellan, what do we do?' asked Tyrus.

'It wants us to touch them with our bare hands,' said Kellan. 'It's how they express gratitude. Or in this case, it's how they offer their apologies. T…t-touching the antlers will reassure the creature that it is forgiven,' he explained.

Everyone followed Kellan's lead and removed one of their gloves. The tips of their fingers battling the early beginnings of frostbite. Together, they took hold of the antlers in one swift motion, almost synchronised to the millisecond. The white peryton then retreated to its eggs to provide them with the warmth they craved.

'Can the n…n-next splinter be hidden underneath a flowerpot, please? Like a spare key type deal?' asked Kellan.

'Delightful thought, but wishful thinking, lad,' said Cedric.

Kellan sighed. 'Well, it's important to have dreams, no?'

In the meantime, Flake had found markings on the

back of one of the large boulders on the mountain peak, runes instilled with magic like with the other places they visited.

'Clever,' said Tyrus. 'Incredibly clever.'

Like over at Alula Isle, the runes were responsible for the horrible weather around the mountain peak, but they also acted as a sort of prison for the peryton. Not only did Tyrus get another splinter back, they also set a wild creature free.

With every fibre of his being, Tyrus commanded the fires of his magic to undo the runes, to wipe them away. He sang a song to it, hummed to it. Singing no one heard, humming no one registered, and as the runes and his magic quarrelled, fought even, his magic reigned victorious. Whoever had carved and instilled these runes had powerful magic at their disposal.

The descent ended up being much easier than the climb. For one, they weren't attacked by a murderous peryton. Secondly, there were no extreme winds or fog to battle with, and lastly, the laws of gravity came in handy for rappelling back down toward the settlement of Talonstead in a swift manner.

They were back on solid ground—no longer clinging onto rock for dear life—before they knew it and Malum awaited them there, shrouded in anxiety (and curiosity).

'You all made it back!' he screamed. 'You did it!'

Lyra smirked. 'You missed a breathtaking view,

Malum. You should have joined us,' she said.

'Glad you didn't leave your sense of humour up there, Lyra,' said Malum as he rolled his eyes.

'We're alive, we made a friend up there, and we have the talons,' said Tyrus proudly.

He held the talons piece above his head as he felt it hum, craving to be reunited with the rest of the key.

'If you ignore the fact that Lyra and I almost d...d-died, you could call this a ten-out-of-ten trip,' added Kellan.

Malum took the courageous mountaineers back to his house for a few cups of hot tea. Nice warm beverages to heat up their aching chittering bones and their frostbitten fingers.

Once everyone managed to expel the cold from their bodies, Tyrus reached under his shirt to reunite the key with the talons splinter. Lyra and Kellan had made preparations and gathered every soft thing they could find and piled everything up on the floor behind Tyrus. That way, when he had his next vision, the pillows and the blankets could catch him.

Tyrus always felt a slither of anxiety when putting the key and a splinter back together again, because the sensations of the visions were anything but pleasant. In those visions, everything looked so real and tangible, it freaked him out a little every time.

His heart started to race and as soon as the pieces

touched, it skipped a few beats to then double down and beat faster than before. Every beat sounded like someone hitting a drum with all their might as everything around him melted away, like ice during the long-lost springs and summers of the last age. It was as he feared. For the last splinter, they would have to travel even further east, which meant they would need to cross a border. One that divided the realm, one that found itself to be in a state of constant conflict. The border between the human territories and the Elven Kingdom.

Tyrus flew high above snowy landscapes. He crossed the Wall of the Humans into the Void Lands, before gliding over another wall entirely. He surfed the skies above the Elven Kingdom, straight toward its capital, where an impressive palace sank away in his rich amber. The palace of an old queen. The queen of the elves. It was there where the tail feathers splinter waited. Tyrus fell and crashed down into the cobblestone in front of the elven palace. Luckily, the rocks changed into pillows and the streets around him became the faces of those he knew, valued and loved as his vision ebbed away. The final splinter hid inside the halls of the royal elven palace.

CHAPTER 20

DISTANCE TRAVELLED

When Cedric noticed the blood creeping out of the boy's nose, his face changed wardrobes as it slid into a coat of worry. Everyone had noticed it; Tyrus' visions were getting way more intense.

'Everything all right, laddie?' asked Cedric as he gave the boy a hug.

'Ty, you're b…b-bleeding,' said Kellan, his voice creaked like Malum's floor.

Tyrus wiped the red away with the dark green of his sleeve. 'It's fine, I'm fine, I promise.'

Flake and her human could already see it on Malum's face, the longing to learn the location of the final splinter.

'Our next destination is Mantlecrest,' announced Tyrus, holding a piece of beige cloth to his nose as it drank his blood.

Kellan gulped. 'M…M-Mantlecrest?'

Cedric's hand already strayed into beard. 'The elven capital?'

'Indeed, but that's not all,' added Tyrus. 'It's not just in Mantlecrest, it's inside the royal palace.'

'The final splinter in the royal palace?' asked Malum like he couldn't believe it. 'Are you sure?'

Tyrus nodded. 'No doubt about it.'

'Extraordinary!' shouted Malum, of course he was excited.

Lyra scratched her neck. 'So, let me get this straight… Not only will we have to get through The Great Walls and the Void Lands, we'll also need a way into the royal palace of the Elven Kingdom?'

As she said it, everyone heard how absolutely mad that sounded. Then again, battling a frost golem, skating over ice avoiding murderous rimewhales, fighting off walking skeletons, climbing the most infamous mountain of the realm, and facing a peryton had sounded mad as well.

Cedric immediately went to work and started plotting out a course on his maps while Malum lost himself in thought. Crossing the borders and going through the Void Lands wouldn't be a jolly ride, but it wouldn't be incredibly difficult either. Getting inside a royal palace on the other hand, that would require an audience with the queen herself.

Meanwhile, Kellan had gone silent. And the way he

carried himself, something was the matter. Kellan usually stood upright elegantly, but now his shoulders had caved in, and his gaze fell to the tingling toes in his boots. When Tyrus asked if he was okay, Lyra noticed it too. She put a hand on the elf's left shoulder, while Tyrus did the same on the other side, and Flake jumped onto his lap as they all sat down.

'I'm okay, guys. I d…d-didn't expect we'd need to go to the Elven Kingdom, let alone M…M-Mantlecrest,' said Kellan.

'Is there history there?' asked Lyra. 'You don't have to talk about it if you don't want to,' she added. 'We can sit here with you in silence for a while too if you like. Well, not too long though, I'd get bored.'

He smiled. 'That was almost kind of you, Lyra,' he said. 'My grandad said I was born in M…M-Mantlecrest. When my p…p-parents fled the Elven Kingdom, they fled from the capital. Going back there, it's…'

'Scary,' finished Tyrus for him. After all, he knew all about what that felt like.

Tyrus, Lyra, and Flake gave him a most welcome hug. One that Kellan appreciated beyond everything in the world as they exchanged warmth between their hearts.

'You know, you don't have to come if you don't want to,' said Tyrus. 'I'd understand if you chose to stay here, or if you went back to Crownhaven… Not that I want you gone… Obviously. I don't want you gone at all…but you have to do what's best for you… Again, not that I don't want you here, I do…of course.' The more he trailed off, the more awkward it became.

Lyra rolled her eyes extensively and eventually had to tell him to stop.

Kellan gave Tyrus a modest smile, then shook his head. 'Thank you, Ty. But no…I'm coming with you.'

Tyrus, Lyra, and Flake then decided to give him space, and by the time they would commence their journey to Mantlecrest, Kellan was already doing a bit better knowing he had the support of his friends. So much so in fact, Tyrus was thinking about asking him out for a date. It would entail a stroll through the woods and a picnic underneath the stars with a campfire-cooked rat for dinner, but it would be a date, nonetheless. Tyrus had only one problem; he had no idea on how to organise it, let alone ask. He decided to ask Lyra for advice as the mountain of Talonstead shrunk behind them and Trudy pulled the carriage further east. He was sitting at the front next to her and Cedric, Malum, and Kellan were taking power naps.

'What do you mean, "how do I ask"?' said Lyra. 'You just do.'

Tyrus looked at her as if she were missing a couple of screws.

She picked up Flake, put her on her shoulder, prepared to do an impression and said, 'Hey, Kellan. Look at me.

I'm Tyrus, I'm a mage and I have an owl. I was wondering if you'd like to go on a date with me?'

'I don't sound like that at all,' said Tyrus.

'I thought it was spot-on, laddie,' said Cedric, weighing in on the matter. 'Lyra's right though, go for it and ask the lad. What's the worst that can happen?'

'Oh, I don't know, he could say no and stop being my friend, shattering my heart into a million tiny stinging pieces?' said Tyrus.

'Life's too short, Clever Chap,' said Lyra. 'Ask him.'

'Ask who what?' said Kellan from the tiny window behind them. He had only caught that last bit.

'Nothing! No one!' panicked Tyrus.

Lyra buried her elbow into his side. 'Dude,' she said, giving him a stern look that reminded him of Xylia.

Confusion ruled Kellan's face like the elven queen ruled over her kingdom, while Tyrus gathered the courage to ask the boy out.

'Kellan,' he started, stress stinging the top of his stomach. 'Would you...consider...to maybe...I don't know...' He ended up mumbling the rest in what sounded like gibberish.

'Would I c...c-consider what?' asked Kellan.

'Oh my god!' exclaimed Lyra. 'I can't do this! He's failing miserably to ask you out, Kellan!'

Kellan looked Tyrus' way with a blush that burned in his cheeks. 'Is...that true?'

The same blush blossomed inside Tyrus' cheeks as he nodded.

'I'd love to,' answered Kellan. He was caught off-guard by his own voice. He didn't mean to say it that loudly. 'W…w-when?'

'How about tonight, lads?' asked Cedric. 'I hear the stars will be absolutely splendid.'

Lyra and Cedric gave each other a high-five when both Tyrus and Kellan agreed. The white-haired girl felt excited for her boys. Thanks to Tyrus' rejection from before they arrived in Talonstead, her jealousy could make way for genuine happiness in shipping the mage and the elf. Her feelings didn't simply disappear, but she was able to place it. She even went on helping Tyrus prepare for his date.

Malum's home became tinier and smaller until it appeared to be the size of a marble, then a speck of dust and eventually it was gone entirely, as if it was never there to begin with. Swallowed whole by distance travelled as the early evening fell on the Wingspan Continent.

When Cedric stopped the carriage for the night, two campfires were made instead of one. One for Lyra, Cedric, Flake, and Malum, and one for Kellan and Tyrus' date. Tyrus built the campfire on a hill in the clearing of the forest they were travelling through. The sky was open, ready to be admired by two boys on a date. Lyra had arranged a red piece of cloth and filled a basket with frostbread and thinly sliced squirrel meat. Not the most romantic thing in the world, but for a realm shrouded in Eternal Winter, it had to do.

'Have fun, you two,' said Malum as Tyrus and Kellan walked from the carriage toward the picnic spot.

Lyra and Cedric put up their thumbs, and he swore he saw Flake wink at him.

It was silent for a bit as Kellan and Tyrus walked toward their campfire and the food that came with it. Neither of them knew what to say as they were both incredibly nervous, until they both wanted to speak at the same time.

'Sorry, you go first,' said Tyrus, trying to avoid eye contact.

'I w...w-wanted to say, I was surprised when you asked,' said Kellan. 'I mean, I'm happy. I just d...d-didn't think you were interested in me.'

For a handful of seconds, Tyrus considered what he was going to say before taking a deep shaky breath. 'I've been interested since day one, if I'm honest.'

Kellan smiled the most electric smile. 'Good...me too.'

Once at the campfire, they told each other stories. They talked about their parents, what they remembered from them. Kellan especially opened up about his past. He told Tyrus how he ended up living with his grandfather in Crownhaven.

Long before he was born, his grandfather left the Elven Kingdom behind, dissatisfied with the way Queen Sarela ruled. He travelled the human territories, searching and studying fantastical (and less fantastical) creatures. It was a shared passion. When he was still a toddler, his parents fled Mantlecrest. He didn't know why, but what he did know was that just like his grandfather, his parents weren't fans of the elven royals. He only remembered blurs, but Kellan's parents died getting him to Crownhaven, to his grandfather. The only thing he could remember about them was a sweet short lullaby his mother always sang for him. Whenever he'd whistle it, his grandfather would cry, but he would never talk about any of it. This was why the prospect of going to Mantlecrest caused Kellan pain. The unknown history there felt intimidating, and the young elf wasn't remotely ready to go discover it. He chose to come with for the quest, and perhaps one day he'd return there, to find out the truth. But it wouldn't be now.

After the hefty talk about their parents, they also gossiped a little about Cedric and Malum to lighten the mood, while they ate their remarkably average roasted squirrel. But that didn't matter, because most of all, they enjoyed each other's company. Flake couldn't stand her curiosity and so she secretly flew over to Tyrus' date and observed everything from a branch high up in a pine tree.

Cedric had been right. The stars were beautiful, and when they came out in full force, Tyrus and Kellan laid down next to each other on the red piece of cloth Lyra had put down.

The stars bathed in their silence for what felt like a bliss eternity. 'You know, I always thought you were m…m-more interested in Lyra,' said Kellan eventually.

'To be completely honest with you, I was into Lyra at first,' admitted Tyrus. If they were going to do this, he wasn't going to lie. 'But then you came along, and for a while I was confused.'

Kellan remained silent, and he could feel the warmth of Tyrus pinkie next to his on the cloth.

'Lyra actually approached me, saying she liked me too,' said Tyrus.

'Yeah, that s…s-sounds like her,' said Kellan with a giggle.

'Full disclosure, Lyra and I kissed that day,' confessed Tyrus, blurting it out rather fast as to rip off the bandage. He paused and then rushed to add, 'But it immediately confirmed what I already knew.' He looked straight into Kellan's eyes now. The elven boy's gaze seemed relaxed; he didn't seem surprised, neither did he seem offended or upset.

'That's okay. Thank you for being honest,' said Kellan.

Their pinkies now touched and metaphorical butterflies swirled around them.

'Has anyone ever told you your eyes are beautiful?' asked Tyrus as amber gladly drowned in dense blue.

The wind composed a melody of wiggling branches, as the bright moons in the sky staged the most gorgeous of scenes together with the uncountable stars. Tyrus and Kellan were holding hands now, but they weren't looking at the marvellous scene in the sky. They only had eyes for each other as the both of them leaned into each other. Both smiling dorky smiles.

'Can I kiss you?' asked Tyrus.

'I'd like that,' answered Kellan in a whisper.

Their mouths slowly approached one another until fireworks. The real deal. The elf's lips were softer than he expected, both chapped of course, but the cold stood no chance to destroy the heat between them. Tyrus didn't know how to explain what he felt, and neither could Kellan. Lightning struck at the right place. Millions of their butterflies swirled around their campfire.

Not only magic could feel like magic.

Together, they looked at the stars for a little while longer. They talked a few more conversations into existence. They kissed again…and again.

The day after Tyrus' date with Kellan, the both of them slept well into the afternoon, undoubtedly dreaming of each other. When they finally did wake up, they refused to give out any details to the rest of the gang. The only thing they all knew was that their date went incredibly well, the constant hand holding kind of gave that away.

In the late afternoon, Tyrus and Flake enjoyed the classic bickering between a wise traveller and a seasoned trader. Him, Kellan, and the two uncles sat squished together on the bench at the head of the carriage, while Lyra followed along from inside, her head popping out the little window.

'We're almost there, we're almost there, but not entirely. We're almost there, we're almost there, just not quite yet,' they heard Malum of all people sing.

Lyra rolled her eyes so far back, everyone thought they'd be lost forever, while Tyrus smiled and Cedric breathed through his nose, trying not to lose his nerves.

'Who even came up with that?' asked Cedric. 'I thoroughly hate it.'

'No idea, all I know is that when I was a kid, we used to sing it while we were on the way to somewhere,' explained Malum.

'I k...k-kind of like it,' said Kellan after and before giggling.

The same annoyance Cedric wore proudly could also be read off of the pages of Lyra's face. 'You'd sing that the entire way?' she asked.

'Naturally,' said Malum.

'Come on, Mal,' said Cedric. *Mal? Mal.* Progress. 'It doesn't even have any other lines! Where are the rest of the lyrics? Was it only that and nothing else on repeat?'

Malum looked over to Cedric. 'We repeated it, yes.'

'Are you sure you didn't forget the rest of it?' asked Cedric.

'We're almost there, we're almost there, but not entirely...' continued Malum.

'We aren't even remotely close to Mantlecrest yet!' shouted Cedric.

Malum kept going to annoy him. Cedric smiled though—Tyrus saw it—and it made him happy. And as he held Kellan's soft hand in his, he realised everyone had grown closer to each other, warming up to each other. Most in friendship, him and Kellan in love.

Pretty neat, he thought.

'Ugh, this is going to be a long ride,' sighed Cedric eventually and everyone laughed.

Trudy pulled the carriage further than any of them (except for Malum) had ever been, in search of the final splinter. The final splinter that would complete the key, the same key that would help them save everyone. Every single human and elf, every adult, every child, every beast, every plant.

'We're almost there, we're almost there, just not quite yet.'

CHAPTER 21

PASSAGE

Time slipped away like the sand in an hourglass, slowly but quickly at the same time. Every grain of sand, a fleeting moment in the lives of the travelling gang, flushed away. Never to be seen again. Only when they remembered would those moments spring to life again, viewed through a filter of who they were and how they felt at the time. Time's passing and Trudy's pulling brought them closer and closer to the border with the Void Lands, sandwiched in between the human territories and the Elven Kingdom, like the peanut butter and jelly between two (albeit vastly different) slices of bread.

The carriage approached a human checkpoint along the border line, one of many. Tyrus saw Kellan hide his appearance in the shadows cast by the hood of his coat. It made him feel safe from the history they were about to journey through.

'All right, lads and lasses,' announced Cedric from the little window that peered into the carriage interior. 'We're arriving at the checkpoint, but they'll want to check the cargo.'

Malum jumped in, 'Stay calm, keep your mouths shut unless you're spoken to. Checkpoint control…they can be somewhat jumpy. Trust me.'

With that, expectations were set. Expectations that became people in Tyrus' imagination. His mind birthed strict and unbribable people, ready to search the carriage from top to bottom. They would interrogate every single passenger to make their intentions clear. In his imagination, they'd even resort to torture if they refused to cooperate. Reality was far less interesting and far safer, because the carriage arrived at the checkpoint and no one was even there to stop them.

Cedric thought it odd and called out. 'Hello?' he asked. 'Someone there?!'

A short, stout, red-haired woman in worn down leather armour emerged from the guard post. 'What do you want?' she asked.

'We seek passage through the Void Lands to enter the Elven Kingdom,' said Malum who sat next to Cedric at the front of the large coach.

'Well, go on then,' said the woman, already turning around.

'You're not going to check our cargo?' asked Cedric.

He couldn't believe it.

'No one cares, mate. If you want to go, then go. No one's stopping you. Either they turn your ass around or it's your funeral, not mine,' she said.

Cedric frowned at that. 'What do you mean?' he asked.

'It's been a while since those bastards let any humans in. They either turn them around or they murder them if they sense nefarious intent, good sir. They want nothing to do with us smelly humans. And to be fair, we want nothing to do with them either,' the guard explained. 'Now, I'd personally reconsider your travels, but by all means, go if you want to.'

The gang inside the carriage couldn't believe it either. They were just going to let them go? No search, no interrogations, nothing. Was what they said true? Did the elves at the border kill humans seeking passage?

'A lot has changed it seems,' said Malum. 'And not for the better, I'm afraid. It seems like us humans are almost looking for ways to start a war. Spoiler alert: right now? We'd lose.'

Cedric had often thought people overexaggerated when it came to stories about the border. In recent years, people had been telling tales detailing friction and aggression at the Great Walls. Mostly, they talked about how the Elven Kingdom had become stricter, more ruthless. They would soon find out if those tales bore any truths, and with no other choice than to accept that the guards at the border simply didn't care what they were doing or why, Cedric instructed his behemoth horse to keep going, to cross the threshold.

No one (except for Malum) had ever seen the Void Lands, and since the elven border was merely a few miles away, they decided to continue on foot. However, the Void Lands weren't all that special in the slightest. Lyra had overheard people talk about it like it was a hellish no man's land, but the reality was far duller. Trees were cut down and only the stumps remained, scattered all over like stars in a constellation, freckles on a face. A few meagre bushes remained as well, peeking out from the snow, but nothing that seemed too alive. These lands had something about them though, a serene quality, beauty in all that emptiness, a certain kind of rest could be found there.

A couple of miles later, they arrived at the elven border. Immediately, you could tell that the elves took the security of their border more seriously. As opposed to the corroded human battlements, the wall on the elven side looked like it was in excellent shape, like it had been renovated the week before. The wall itself stood taller as well and it had fully-fledged watchtowers and a gate, whereas the humans essentially had a few holes where the checkpoints were. The two walls were always referred to as *the Great Walls* but when it came down to it, only one was deserving of such a title and it wasn't built by human hands.

'Halt!' The words came from above, from an elven

soldier in the watchtowers, donned in shiny polished iron. 'Not one more step, humans!' Their armour was adorned with golden vines and flowers, even the spear they held was delicately decorated with intricate runic symbols. Contrary to most of the runic symbols they had encountered on their travels, these weren't imbued with magic.

Tyrus suffered from déjà vu and Cedric made Trudy stop immediately. No one dared move a muscle.

'State your name and your business!' shouted another guard, wrapped in the same beautiful armour.

The gang hadn't formed a detailed plan as to how to get through the elven battlements, but one thing was for sure: Malum would speak. Only Tyrus beat him to the punch by stepping forward with his arms in the air.

'We seek an audience with the queen,' he said. 'And as for who I am…I am Tyrus. And I am Owlbound.'

Cedric's and Kellan's hearts raced, Malum's too, despite being impressed by the boy's bravery, or was it foolishness? Lyra felt a sense of pride, but she'd be lying if she said sweat wasn't growing everywhere. The words echoed up the wall, over the gate and that's when the guards saw her. Flake.

An owl.

An animal they'd only seen in history books. They didn't believe it. It had to be an illusion. The looks on their faces said it all. They didn't think the owl was real, let alone bound to a human boy capable of commanding the forces of magic. So, as one guard started laughing, the others followed.

'Owlbound, yeah sure and I'm the wealthiest elf in the realm,' scowled a guard. The laughing continued.

'Tyrus, get back,' whispered Cedric.

He refused. 'They're not going to let us in under the guise of wanting to trade or whatever, surely you realise that, right?' he asked. 'Malum can't *say* anything to make them open those gates…I can *show* them.'

Tyrus sounded determined, and Cedric couldn't flaunt his logic. They would order them away, and if they refused, they'd open fire on them. Their crossbows were at the ready, the ones they had at Featherburn looked like toys in comparison.

'Turn around and pull your pranks elsewhere, boy,' spat the guard that originally told them to halt. 'Or prepare to perish.'

'No!' shouted Tyrus.

The guard took aim. They pulled the arrow in the crossbow back, it longed for flesh and blood and pain.

'We are here for an audience with your queen, and you will bring us to her,' demanded Tyrus. 'All of us.'

'Tyrus, w…w-what are you doing?' whispered Kellan from the back, distress carried the words. Worried for the boy who was on his mind all the time.

Tyrus looked back at him and said, 'Trust me, Kell.'

Another soldier considered the conversation over and fired a bolt straight at Tyrus, who evaporated it the moment it would have hit his face. Tyrus pulled his hands up like they were wings, like he was a bird as his eyes (and Flake's) had given birth to fire. They conjured those same flames behind them. They grew larger as they morphed into the shape of an enormous burning barn owl, armed with spectacle for intent.

The soldiers on the wall and in the watchtowers couldn't believe their eyes. Jaws dropped as they realised the boy spoke the truth. He was Owlbound. With one smooth motion, Tyrus let his arms sway to the front of him, aiming at the gate of the wall and in doing so, the giant owl of fire flew toward it, inevitably crashing into it. Tyrus didn't blast the gate open though. He merely wanted them to know that if he wanted to, he could have, but chose not to.

'As I said, I'm Tyrus. I am Owlbound and we have urgent matters to discuss with your queen. We request an audience with her majesty and refuse to take no for an answer.'

'You tell 'em, Tyrus!' shouted Lyra before covering her mouth with her gloved hands. She didn't mean to blurt that out but was too late to stop herself.

The mechanisms behind the gate turned as the border opened itself to the travelling troupe of friends. Trudy pulled the carriage through and Tyrus and Flake, Lyra,

Malum and a hooded Kellan followed. Gazes were locked on the magical bird. Most of them filled with awe, some with fear. Once they passed through the gate and it had closed again, the commander of the soldier's battlements graced them with her presence.

'Hello, Tyrus the Owlbound. I welcome you and your friends to the glory of the Elven Kingdom,' she said. 'My apologies for earlier, our orders are to not let any human enter. But this, I'll admit, is a peculiar circumstance.'

'We understand,' said Tyrus.

'We've sent a…' She looked at Flake. '…raven to the palace to inform them of your arrival and your request,' said the commander.

'Excellent, thank you,' said Malum.

The commander looked at him with this look on her face, a look that screamed *and who are you?*

'Anyways,' she said, addressing Tyrus again. 'You're provided an escort which will bring you directly to Mantlecrest, to the palace's doorstep.'

'An escort to protect us or an escort to keep an eye on us?' asked Cedric.

She looked him up and down. 'Both…Fair, no?'

'I suppose so,' said the trader, and off they went.

The road to the elven capital, to the palace, was as smooth as the butter Tyrus liked to put on his frostbread. It wasn't as rocky and uneven as the roads in human-controlled territories. Humans didn't have any obligations to maintain their roads, unlike the elves. In the Elven Kingdom, they had districts and each and every one of them had a duty to maintain the roads and if the need arose, to repair them. It made for a comfy journey with plenty of rest for everyone in and on the carriage. Tyrus stayed close to Kellan, who had difficulties being in the Elven Kingdom, a place where he might have truly belonged, among his people. Then again, he felt at home with his new friends, too. His curly-haired boy kissed him on the cheek, saying everything would be okay, and it made all the difference in the world.

It took them a few days of being surrounded by elven soldiers, but eventually, Mantlecrest towered into view. A city of architectural wonder. The city hung above a steaming hot water reservoir, carried by ginormous robust pillars. Legends said they were once sculpted by giants. They were decorated with runic symbols all over (once again devoid of magic). A long slender bridge—wide enough for two carriages to pass one another—connected the elevated city to the mainland. The miracles didn't stop there either. Plants grew without issue, trees blossomed, flaunting their green leaves in the sun and most noteworthy, there was barely any snow there. The steam of the lake made sure it either melted away or didn't even reach the various surfaces of the city to begin with. It felt strange too, cold yet warm at the same time. If Tyrus and friends were entirely honest, it was a shock seeing them live without thick coats, gloves and hefty boots. The only one who didn't seem all that impressed was Malum. Clearly, he'd been here before, how he had managed that was anyone's guess, but he did agree to it being a truly miraculous place, for the most part.

Regrettably, while they did have warmth, Mantlecrest wasn't spared from failed harvests and hungry bellies. Here and there, they saw elven patrols needing to break up fights. And while the capitol bathed in the pleasant warmth of steam, the rest of the Elven Kingdom had as much trouble surviving as their human counterparts.

Kellan felt kind of relieved there wasn't any time to have a proper gander. He didn't think himself ready to dive into his history, to explore what life is like for elves outside the human territories. Nonetheless, he wasn't thrilled by the fact that their audience with the queen awaited them either.

The royal palace itself looked magical too, nothing like the human palaces Tyrus had seen drawings of in his books. In human eyes, it had the look and feel of a temple, a place of worship and in a sense, that's what it was; a place to worship their queen.

The palace erupted from the city like weeds that sprung from a neglected garden, armed with large looming towers of marble. The windows displayed impressive colourful glass work and golden rooftops proudly watched over the city, standing tall, shining bright.

When they arrived near an arched entrance, they were asked to leave the carriage and Trudy in the care of the palace's guardians. Not a single scenario existed in which they could have refused. They were forced to accept it in order to continue onward. Cedric kept scratching his beard after leaving Trudy in the care of strangers, He had given her a sturdy hug before he headed inside together with the rest.

The corridors of the palace exuded the same extravagance as its towers and rooftops, filled to the brim with expensive art, and decorated with chaotically patterned wallpaper. The floor clashed with it all as large checkerboard stark-white marble and black basalt tiles relaxed beneath their feet.

'They should consider hiring someone else for the inside, maybe the person that did the outside may want to weigh in on how it should look,' whispered Lyra.

Malum shushed her. 'No matter how much we may or may not love the interior, this is not the place nor the time for your quips, Lyra,' he said.

Their escorts bumped into Lyra as they brought everyone to a stop in front of closed doors. She gave them an angry frown when they didn't even apologise. She guessed it was what she deserved after slamming their interior.

'Wait here,' commanded the leader of their escort. 'The doors will open when the queen and her council are ready to receive you.'

The queen and her council. Tyrus had clearly sparked the sovereign's interest. He grabbed Kellan's sweaty hand with his sweaty hand, hoping it would lend him the courage he required for their next encounter.

They waited. They stayed put. And they waited a bit longer until the heavy doors that led into the royal hall opened, with the throne of the elven queen, eager to be introduced to the last of the Owlbound and his friends.

Chapter 22

A Risk Worth Taking

Queen Sarela had ascended the throne of the Elven Kingdom at thirty-one years of age after her father, King Eobard, died at the mercy of the wounds he had sustained by ending the previous dynasty. Eobard the Usurper's original plan was to install none other than himself on the throne after ending the reign of Gol the Mad, but when things didn't work out as planned, he was forced to crown his only daughter instead.

King Gol had turned the Elven Kingdom into a tyranny after giving into his paranoid thoughts entirely, much to the disdain of his own blood. Even so, out of precaution, Eobard hunted and extinguished the blood of the royal family of the bygone dynasty. Most of the elvish people didn't agree with this course of action, and many called it an overcorrection. Unfortunately, any such claims were always silenced one way or another, and any protests squashed without mercy. With no one left to challenge the throne, and having established an iron grip over his new kingdom, Eobard the Usurper crowned his daughter queen. All of that happened over sixty years before Tyrus and his travelling band of friends set foot inside the sacred royal halls.

Malum had taken it upon himself to inform his friends of this rich history in the time it took to get to the palace from the Void Lands. He did so in hopes to avoid anyone saying anything that could get them killed while they addressed the queen.

Now, a frail and old elven woman sat on the throne; Queen Sarela, daughter of Eobard the Usurper. She was over ninety years-old now, her nose as crooked as the crown on her head, pointy ears that gave in to gravity at their tips and a battlefield of wrinkles that draped her brave face. The years had worn her out, but they had also made her a benevolent ruler. One that did the opposite of what her father would have done. One that chose peace over war and death at every turn.

Tyrus' message at the border had made sure the entire Queen's Council sat by the ruler's side, including—but not limited to—her grandson, Crown-Prince Drec, who wore a face deserving of a punch. Or two, maybe even three. Left, right, uppercut. Where Sarela was benevolent and level-headed, her grandson Drec was ambitious, impulsive, rude and aggressive, not unlike her father.

Meanwhile, the humming above Tyrus' chest, below his sweater and shirt, swelled. The splinter had to be nearby.

'Tyrus,' whispered Malum as they approached the council, approached royalty. 'Look…inside the crown.' His hands and their painted black nails pulled off a subtle point.

Tyrus' eyes searched and while they didn't find anything at first, there it was. Locating the tail feathers splinter was no longer an issue that needed resolve, for the final splinter sat right in the middle of the golden crown. Surrounded by silver thorns, bronze roses, and brass details, carried by the queen herself.

'Is that lady still alive or did the servants dive way too deep into taxidermy?' asked Lyra to Kellan in a whisper.

'Lyra, n…n-not now,' said Kellan, who was understandably not in the mood for jokes.

'I think it's the former, lass. But it does look like the latter,' whispered Cedric back.

Things were rather awkward because the way from the doors to the actual throne was long, uncomfortably long and for the most part, they had to shuffle through the hall in eerie silence. They passed a pillar after pillar, and another, and another. Flake tried counting them but after a while she got bored of it and let it go in favour of paying attention to the otherwise gorgeous and impressive throne room that thrived in tints of green.

'What is it you want?' spat Prince Drec as their visitors

arrived before the queen and her council.

The throne and the queen sat elevated on a massive marble platform with statues carved into the sides. The chairs for the Queen's Council were also elevated but none sat higher than her majesty. All of them looked down at the travellers, the bags of their belongings still in the carriage outside, and the bags of exhaustion hanging under their eyes.

'We're here for your crown!' exclaimed Lyra.

The council gasped. Tyrus sighed.

'Not in the we're-going-to-overthrow-you kind of way, we're not going to dispose of you or anything, there's something inside your crown that we need is all,' she trailed off.

'Don't worry, Grandmother,' stepped in Drec. 'I'll have her tongue for that.' He stood up, pulled a sword out of the sheath around his waist and walked Lyra's way, descending the steps of the elevated platform.

Lyra began looking around for possible ways to escape at once, eyes wide, but she didn't see many feasible options.

'You…shall do no such thing,' spoke Queen Sarela, draped in white expensive fabrics, intricate flowers embroidered all over.

It was a fierce struggle to get the words out, but her majesty managed it in the end and so the prince returned to his seat, his face smitten with rage. Lyra smirked. She couldn't not and it only made the fires of rage behind the prince's grey eyes grow.

The rest of the council, which consisted of generals and the heads of powerful elven families, restrained themselves from saying anything that would oppose their queen, but they clearly agreed with Drec on the matter.

'My apologies, your majesty,' said Malum, bowing as he did. 'The girl forgets herself occasionally. Forgive her transgression.'

The frail queen nodded toward one of her councilmen.

'Proceed,' said the councilman, a general encased in silver adorned armour.

Malum continued. 'Well, you see, Your Highness—'

'No,' said the queen, followed by a lengthy pause. 'Not you.'

Tyrus had sought for an audience with the ruler of the Elven Kingdom and so he—and he alone, no one else—received one. His friends were merely allowed to be witnesses, nothing more, nothing less. They weren't allowed to speak unless spoken to.

'Spit it out, Tyrus the Owlbound,' said Drec. He emphasised the word *Owlbound* both in tone and by signing quotation marks in the air around his annoying face. 'We don't have all day to listen to you and whatever fantasies you bring into these halls,' he added.

Tyrus laughed, and Drec leaned forward as his eyebrows contracted underneath his huge forehead.

'What's so funny, human?' he asked.

'Nothing,' said Tyrus. 'You don't believe a single word in that letter the raven delivered. Do you?'

Prince Drec leaned back against his marble chair and hoisted his shoulders. 'As I told my grandmother—'

But nothing followed. Words unspoken, because blue and purple flames danced across the prince's lips. He couldn't move them; he was simply unable to speak like a drawing in a sketchbook. The words he wanted to share couldn't flow, frozen, still. The eyes of the queen hadn't been as open in years as when they saw fire sway in the boy's eyes, in the windows to the bird's soul too. And then, Tyrus stopped. However, Prince Drec remained speechless.

With that out of the way, providing proof that Tyrus was indeed Owlbound, that he was indeed capable of magic, he continued, 'Your Majesty, the realm, the Wingspan Continent—human territories, The Void Lands, and the Elven Kingdom alike, along with every field, every path, every mountain, every hill, every valley and lake and every soul—bows to a never-ending winter. And while right now, for the most part, your glorious city doesn't appear to brawl with it, I can assure you that the rest of your kingdom does.'

His words were strong like a white peryton or a frost golem protecting their eggs, and sharp like the daggers Lyra had to part with to enter the palace.

Tyrus continued, 'I'm sure you all have noticed it, too. The Eternal Winter seems like it's getting colder every year. And that's because it's true. It *is* getting colder and there is no denying it. Things have escalated to the point where even crops like frostwheat and geluroots are ceasing to grow bountiful harvests, something you have even felt here, no doubt. It will continue to escalate to the point where hot springs, like the one you've built this impressive city on, will lose their warmth.'

Prince Drec sighed and once again rose from his seat. 'For the love of that stupid-looking owl of yours,' he said with a raised his voice. 'Get to the bloody point!'

'Drec!' shouted the queen after drawing a deep breath. 'Sit.'

Defiance lived in the prince's gaze, but his grandmother's command settled it. He retreated into his chair once more.

Tyrus took a step forward. 'I'm the last of the Owlbound and with the help of my friends, I have found a way to bring about spring. My friend Lyra may have spoken out of turn, but she didn't lie. To end winter, I humbly ask for your crown, for it holds an item we need to complete our quest,' he said as he kneeled.

'Blasphemous! Preposterous!' interjected Drec. 'Impossible. Grandmother, don't you see, this is a scheme. They seek to end us, end you!' he spat.

'To the contrary, Your Highness,' said Tyrus. 'We're

here to save *everyone*, including you and your kingdom.'

'What the human says is true,' said Kellan without a single stutter. Everyone, except the queen's council and their guards, turned his way with their mouths hanging open ever so slightly. He stepped forward from behind Cedric's shadow and lowered his hood to reveal his pointy elven ears. He didn't like the idea of revealing himself in a place he didn't feel comfortable, but he figured they were never going to take a human's word for the truth.

'And what is your name, dear boy?' asked Queen Sarela.

'Kellan, Your M…M-Majesty.'

Silence lingered in the air, disturbed only by the heavy breathing of the queen. Even asking that simple question tired her out. She eventually signed the young elven boy to come closer and so, Kellan slowly and steadily climbed the steps up to the throne. Drec watched him carefully.

'You have travelled with this human?' asked the queen.

Kellan gulped. 'Y…y-yes.'

The queen huffed and puffed stale breaths. 'And you believe him?' she asked.

'I do,' said Kellan.

The queen's gaze was on him now. Glassy eyeballs—worn down by time itself—peered right into what felt like his soul.

'What wondrous eyes,' said the queen at last.

'Enough of this, Grandmother!' shouted Drec, leaning forward out of his seat.

Kellan stepped back, back to the safety of standing among his friends.

'We've entertained them long enough,' continued Drec. 'Surely, you're not as naive as to believe them. We should slit their throats for wasting our time.'

'No, Drec!' shouted the queen as she rose from the throne. Even if her body was bent and broken and withering, she stood tall. She tried her best to straighten her back, to take on a truly royal posture but her old bones and fading muscles didn't let her.

'Sit down and keep your mouth shut,' she said, breaths short and following in quick successions. 'As long as I am queen, I shall rule as I see fit…Do you understand?'

A 'Yes, Grandmother…' slithered out of that bitter mouth of his.

The queen looked down, directly at Tyrus.

'Before I am to accept your request. Explain to me what exactly you want with my crown,' she commanded.

'We believe your crown holds a splinter. A magical splinter from a magical key. A key to a sacred and lost place where I can undo the Winter that was cast upon us by the Owlbound of ages lost,' explained Tyrus.

There was something in speaking with royalty that unlocked a fancier tongue for him. Something that made it possible to channel his inner Malum with the guts of his inner Lyra. It worked because his words cast contemplation on the face of the old ruler.

'How the splinter came to be inside your crown, I do not know, but it's there and we need it,' explained Tyrus. 'This could be the start of peace between elves and humans. True peace, I mean.'

'Humans don't know what peace is,' said Drec. 'Look at their territories, divided and restless.'

Tyrus couldn't argue against that; the humans were divided.

'What the crown-prince says is true,' interjected Malum. 'We as humans are divided but if memory serves you as well as me, we can't forget that once upon a time we were one. The entirety of our human race, riding under the banner of a queen and there was peace. This was before the cold; we were a peaceful kingdom then; we can be one again in the future. However, we need a push, and spring could be exactly that. The peace Tyrus speaks of is a tangible and probable possibility.'

Drec spit on the floor. 'Who permitted you to talk?! You lot and your pretty words,' he said. 'Grandmother, let's say we give them this splinter they speak of and let's say they bring about spring, which I still think is ridiculous. Let's say the humans do unite, who's to say they'll unite in peace? What if they unite against us?'

'A gamble,' said the queen.

'A risk,' corrected the prince.

'A risk worth taking,' cut in Tyrus, his jaw firmly set before he continued. 'How many of your people suffer from the cold?'

The gears inside the queen's head turned. Even Drec's mind fired at the question and there was no denying it; ending winter wouldn't only benefit the humans, it would be good for the elves too.

Queen Sarela ignored her grandson and looked at the other members of her council and they all seemed to agree. With that, the queen's trembling hands rose to her head as she clutched her crown and carefully lifted it off of the thinning hairs that scarcely crowded her scalp.

'A risk worth taking,' she said, and her son grovelled in silence as the crown eventually landed in Tyrus' hands.

His fingers explored the golden surface of the crown, feeling every crevice, every nook, looking for a way to get the tail feather splinter loose, to get it out but eventually his patience wore thin, like the hairs on the queen's head. He blinked and his eyes were fire, Flake's too, and with those eyes, his right hand as well. He phased it through the crown, taking the tail feather splinter with it and there it was; the final piece of the puzzle was theirs. Tyrus extinguished the fires in his eyes and the fire that was his hand as he gave Queen Sarela her crown back.

'Thank you, Your Highness. The people of the human territories will know you helped us, they will know the elves aided in our quest. One day, they will unite in peace,' said Tyrus.

The queen sank back into her throne with a smile on her face.

'Good luck, Tyrus, last of the Owlbound,' she said. 'Now, bring us spring.'

His goal, the thing he had dreamt of ever since his parents disappeared, was in reach. He couldn't fully process it. Yet, things were far from over because only the Owlbound of ages lost knew where they'd have to travel next. For the sake of his friends and everyone else's, Tyrus hoped the completed key knew too.

Tyrus and his friends were escorted back out of the royal hall, passing the many pillars and then they followed the royal guard out the palace entirely, passing all the art that draped the corridors, all the exquisite wallpapers that hugged the walls and leaving the checkerboard marble and basalt floors behind.

After they had left, Drec approached his grandmother. 'Have you lost your mind completely?' he asked her. 'On top of entertaining that charlatan's musings, you let that Kellan boy speak in these sacred halls? Despicable.'

The queen drew a deep breath once more. 'He had elven blood…kind eyes…he had travelled with the mage, his opinion…mattered to me.'

Drec growled. 'The opinion of a half-breed?! When I'm king, this will not stand.'

Queen Sarela ignored Drec's hatred, disregarded her own flesh and blood as she pondered the future of the Elven Kingdom.

'Now, bring us spring,' she whispered.

CHAPTER 23

THROUGH THE FABRIC

The last splinter burned in Tyrus' hand as his and his friends' belongings were returned to them by the royal guards outside the palace. Trudy kept tapping her hoofs on the road below at the sight of her beloved old merchant.

'Well, that was at least one splinter that wasn't life threateningly protected,' said Cedric as he threw his arms around Trudy's nose and jowl for a hug.

Lyra scowled. 'You didn't hear how that Drec guy talked about us? We were lucky his old grandmommy was as much of a fan of his as I was,' she said.

She was right, too. If it weren't for Queen Sarela and her distaste for her grandson, things could have gone incredibly sideways.

'Either way,' announced Malum. 'We did it.'

'I feel like we were also lucky that Tyrus basically barfed out a whole fancy dictionary in there,' said Lyra.

Tyrus lifted his hands up, looked at Malum, and said, 'Well, I learned from the best, didn't I?'

They all laughed for a second, except for Malum, who merely smiled and accepted the compliment.

The tail feathers splinter nearly burned a hole in Tyrus' hand and the totem almost melted one into his chest. He couldn't bear it any longer. And so, without much discussing and before anyone could move, he joined the tail feathers with the rest of the owl totem.

This time, the vision was different. Not for Tyrus— as for him it felt the same, only stronger once again—but for his friends. For them, Tyrus started levitating above the ground. The vision manifested itself so intensely that Flake had to fly off of Tyrus' shoulder and hide in between Trudy's long wavy manes. The guards at the palace entrance didn't know what they were witnessing, let alone what to do. Lyra and Kellan tried holding Tyrus down to keep his feet on the ground but it didn't work. The magic was too strong. It looked genuinely scary, too. Every muscle of the sorcerer boy's body tensed up like he was possessed with a foreign entity and yet, there wasn't a thing they could do other than wait for it to end.

Tyrus' vision showed him Mantlecrest. *Tail feathers*. It then took him above the frosty peaks of Talonstead in a flash. *Talons*. He blinked and he hovered over Crownhaven with a view at the sun setting behind Alula Isle. *Wings*. He turned and found himself near Featherburn in front of the entrance to the nightmarish mines. *Chest.* And then, his body folded in on itself like a paper note and he sat in his room at the lighthouse, reading a book. *Head.*

From there, the vision dragged him out the front door. It threw him into the air where his arms changed into wings, where his nose and mouth changed into a beak and his feet became talons. The totem was complete. The key was whole. And it filled him with power, power with which he soared through the sky and where they needed to go next came into view as he dove down.

Far to the Southwest of Featherburn, way out there, you'd find the great city of Beaksworth. And in between the two—closer to the former—thrived a system of caves, and hidden within those caves lurked a temple. One that was erected by the Paragons of the Owlbound Council. The same council that summoned the cold to save the world but ended up dooming it instead. Tyrus saw the place where he could undo it all.

In the real world, Tyrus still hovered over the ground and blood ran out of his nose as if it were evacuating a home that had caught fire. Cedric pleaded to whatever god would listen, while Malum had faith that this was normal and that everything was going to be all right. Kellan couldn't bear to look, and Lyra, who didn't want to look either, couldn't not watch. Flake trembled in fear and Trudy tiptoed restlessly in place too. Then, it stopped. Tyrus fell to the ground, unconscious. However, all was okay. He was breathing, he was alive. That was what mattered most.

Tyrus woke up inside a rocking carriage as Kellan cleaned his upper lip with wet cloth, and Flake staring at him. The curly-haired boy's head spun round, and round and he stumbled to the floor of the coach when he tried to stand. The look of confusion clung to his face like sticky honey to the inside of a jar.

'T…t-take it easy, Ty,' said Kellan. 'That vision you had was…scary. Are you okay?'

'What happened?' asked Tyrus.

Lyra yawned after waking up due to Tyrus' sudden regaining of consciousness. 'You collapsed,' she said. 'For a second, we thought you died, Clever Chap. That's how scary it was.'

Kellan wrapped around his neck and gave him a passionate kiss. Tyrus wondered if he would ever get used to enjoying Kell's lips on his, because every time it felt more like magic than his actual magic.

'I'd say get a room, but that's not an option right now, is it?' said Lyra.

'Wait, are we moving?' asked Tyrus, interrupting his kiss with the handsome elven boy. He tried looking through the tiny window but couldn't see anything. 'Stop the carriage! Stop!'

He flung the door open as the carriage still moved, which made Cedric abruptly halt Trudy from trudging forward. Malum almost fell forward on a direct collision course with the behemoth horse's butt.

'Tyrus, laddie! You're okay!' exclaimed Cedric. 'Wait, are you okay?'

Malum climbed down the front bench. 'Are you out of your mind, young man? My goodness, did you hit your head when you fell?'

'I know where to go!' screamed Tyrus from the top of his lungs. 'I know where to go!' Flake landed on his shoulder. 'We're not heading deeper into the Elven Kingdom, are we?'

'Definitely hit his head,' said Cedric as he got down from the front bench as well.

'Yup,' sighed Lyra in the doorway. 'Relax, Ty. We barely left Mantlecrest.'

Malum no longer cared if he did or didn't hit his head. He wanted to know where they were going next. And when Tyrus explained where he had seen the Owlbound Council temple—where all this started—both Malum's and Kellan's faces soured, while Cedric let his hands travel through his grey hairs, from the front down to the back.

'Between Featherburn and Beaksworth?' he asked. 'But that's…'

Lyra let her head sink as if it could roll off her neck. 'Weeks of travel,' she completed in a groan. 'We're looking at more than a month on the road, right?'

Kellan, utterly defeated, had to go and sit down on the stump of a cut down pine tree. While everyone didn't mind spending time together, the prospect of living in that carriage crammed next to each other for a month wasn't exactly inviting.

'Oh, don't worry. We'll manage, won't we?' countered Cedric. 'Time flies anyway.'

Lyra stepped down the ladder, into the snow. 'I wish we could snap our fingers and…' She leaned into Kellan to scare him. '*BAM!* We'd be there.'

Kellan shot about a foot up into the air, and poked Lyra in her side as revenge. Meanwhile, a candle in Malum's brain lit up and shone bright.

'Lyra, you brilliant soul!' exclaimed Malum. 'Exquisite!'

Everyone looked at each other, thinking Malum was the one who got hit in the head, not Tyrus. But once he explained his idea, it made sense. Malum proposed that Tyrus could cast a gateway to Featherburn, a portal. The boy's amber eyes would have fallen out of their sockets if they weren't somehow attached.

'I can do that?' he asked.

'Under normal circumstances, I'd say no,' began Malum. 'Or at least, not yet. For a Paragon, the spell would still take immense power, but they'd be able to do it. You're still a Learn-ling, which complicates things but, we can't forget…you have an amplifier.'

Everyone looked a bit puzzled.

'The key around your neck! It's a powerful magical artefact after all, and it wouldn't surprise me if it has been slightly feeding your mana pool already,' explained Malum using his arms enthusiastically to support his words. His broad smile spoke volumes. 'With it complete, you should be able to drain more magic from it. Perhaps enough to cast a gateway!'

Tyrus had always felt the power within the splinters, and now—with the key complete—it was more obvious than ever. The thought never crossed his mind to draw power from it. Malum's genius knew no bounds.

'This cool and all,' began Lyra. 'But why does mister mage boy have to cast a gateway to Featherburn. I'm an escaped prisoner there, remember?'

'In all my readings, I haven't come across any Owlbound mage, Paragon or not, that managed to create a portal to a place they hadn't been before, and Featherburn would be closest,' explained Malum. 'That said…now that you mention it…you being a fugitive there is a slight complication, yes.'

Cedric, who took a few seconds to make sure Trudy was okay after the sudden stop, stepped forward and put a hand on Lyra's shoulder. 'Taking the lass back to Featherburn could endanger her life. I'm not sure if we should take that chance.'

'Maybe this too is a risk worth taking?' asked Tyrus hoisting up his shoulders. 'Lyra's parents could help us prepare for heading to the temple, perhaps they can even gather their friends to help us.'

'I could stay hidden until we ride out?' proposed Lyra. Her eyes lit up at the mention of her parents. She hadn't talked about them much, but whenever she did, everyone could tell she missed them terribly. 'Yike doesn't have to know I'm there, right? And when push comes to shove and he does find out, Flake can peck his eyes out.'

Hoot!

In the end, after detailing Malum's plan, everyone voted to see it through. First, Tyrus would conjure a gateway a little outside Featherburn for Cedric, Kellan, and the carriage. Then he would cast a smaller portal, right in front of Xylia's hearth for himself, Lyra and Malum. He'd need the Talonstead traveller to talk him through the spells, and they figured the Watch would suspect Tyrus of orchestrating Lyra's escape. As for Lyra, the carriage would be searched upon entry, and they didn't want to leave her somewhere outside Featherburn either. And so, they chose to go through two different portals, minimizing the odds of anyone being captured while they prepared to save the world.

While the plan sounded relatively straight-forward, in reality, Tyrus needed quite some practice. Back when the world burst with magic, spells like that entirely depleted the mana pools of the most powerful wizards and their owls. Tyrus wouldn't stand a chance to attempt them without an amplifier, without the key; these spells would simply kill him, Flake too. Their lifeforce would give into the magic like a ripe apple giving in to gravity, saying farewell to the tree that nurtured it.

Back when he fought the frost golem in Featherburn, the mana pool of his magic ran out rather fast compared to now. And while Tyrus undoubtedly improved in wielding his magic through training and the different ordeals he's overcome, the key that became more complete over time probably helped speed up both the learning process, as well as deepen the scope of his mana pool. With the key complete now, he felt more powerful than ever before but despite all that power, casting portals did not go the way he wanted it to go as days passed without making much progress on the matter. Malum had prepared an area around camp where Tyrus could practice casting portals from one side of the camp, to the other. He failed, and failed again, on repeat.

'This is bullcrap!' shouted Tyrus on the fourth day, fed up with blundering over and over again. 'I can't do it! Even with the extra power of the key, I can't do it! We should pack up our things and prepare for a month's long journey.'

Tyrus' temper grunted like an enraged frost golem.

He conjured an axe of flames into his hand and threw it, felling three larch trees around them in the process.

'Tyrus, calm down,' said Malum with his hands out in front of him and his eyebrows raised. 'What's the matter with you? Anger won't solve anything.'

'Don't tell me to calm down, Malum!' he lashed out. If looks could kill, Malum would have been dead. 'You're not the one that has to save the world, are you? If I can't even do this, how the *fudge* am I supposed to undo winter?!' He felled another tree, and another. Flake didn't enjoy this version of her human.

Kellan stood by the sidelines. 'Tyrus. Breathe,' he said. 'Come here.' He held out his hands, ready to embrace his boyfriend.

'What if I can't do it, Kell?' asked Tyrus before accepting the hug. 'What if I fail the entire realm?'

Kellan let his head rest on Tyrus' shoulder as they embraced one another. 'Ty, you had t…t-trouble with runes at first too, no? From w…w-what I heard, you had issues learning to phase as well. And now look at you, you can do both with ease. You'll be able to cast these p…p-portals in no time. I know you've got this,' he encouraged. 'I believe in you.'

'That's just it, Kellan. What if I don't deserve the faith everyone's putting in me?' asked Tyrus.

Cedric approached the two lovebirds. He had over-heard their conversation. 'Tyrus, laddie…ending winter, while the ideal outcome, it's not what we expect from you. When we tell you we have faith in you, we have faith in you giving this your all, giving it your best. And in the end, that's all anyone can ever do in their life, their best.'

Malum joined them. 'With everything I've seen you do, with everything you've overcome, I'm positive we can do this,' said Malum. 'And like the old man says, all we can do is try our best.'

Malum shared the story he'd told Cedric that night around the campfire on their way to Crownhaven. About the man he loved, the man he had lost. About his research, about his drive to end the winter.

The snowy environment shimmered in his watery eyes. 'I didn't try my best a long time ago, and I still regret it, but you Tyrus…You've been doing the best you can since the day we met, and I have no doubt in my mind that you'll keep doing so.'

'Thank you, Malum, and…I'm sorry,' said Tyrus.

'Don't be,' said Malum. 'Let's have some rest and practice more later. Agreed?'

Lyra was fashionably late to the conversation but decided to join in anyway. 'Oh, is this a pep-talk moment? Tyrus, even though you can be a huge dork, you've got this!' she shouted.

Laughter ensued.

The next day, after the rest Malum had recommended, Tyrus and Flake resumed their training. By the end of the day, wielding newfound confidence, the boy successfully cast his first tiny portal. And in the days that followed, he kept going at it to perfect this new spell while Lyra taught Kellan how to wield a sword ever so slightly more adequately. In return, he taught her about a plethora of fantastical creatures. Cedric bored himself a little but found pleasure in hunting game and cooking meals for his friends.

Before they all realised it, the day had come to try and return to Featherburn. Through all the training, Mal and Tyrus had discovered that conjuring the portal spells worked best when provided with audio-visual stimulation. And so, the Talonstead traveller would guide Tyrus' mind (Flake's too of course), to the places the portals had to lead. Before starting the spell, he kissed Kellan a long kiss goodbye as the elf joined Cedric behind Trudy.

'You g…g-got this, Ty. I trust you,' said Kellan with a smile.

And then, the moment came. Tyrus and Flake listened to Malum's words carefully, eyes closed, grabbing the owl key tight to draw power from it. They tried their best to take the words to heart; to make them flow through them like the blood and the magic in their veins.

'Picture the road,' said Malum with that butter-smooth voice of his. 'Picture the road outside Featherburn, the one you crossed when you escaped through the wall with

Lyra. Picture it.'

He did, he saw it in front of him like a painting. The rough strokes of the wooden log walls, the soft blotches of white snow and the delicate shadows in the tracks of horses and carriages.

'Good, now hold on to that image,' instructed Malum. 'Hold it close and feel the wind on your face, perhaps even the specks of snow that fall. Can you feel the icy touch of the wind? The pressed down snow underneath your boots?'

If anything, Malum was damn good with words, so good that Tyrus saw everything he described, felt everything too. Down to the finest details.

'Now, that wind you felt,' continued Malum. 'You hear it, you hear it howl, you hear it pass you by as it goes through the curls that peek from underneath your hat. You can hear the townsfolk inside the walls, you can hear a blacksmith clashing the iron for the sword they're forging, you hear the butcher hack into meat, the baker taking a fresh loaf out of the oven, you can even hear that cute bartender we met, pour someone a mug of ale.'

Tyrus and Flake felt like half of themselves were no longer outside Cedric's carriage. It felt as if their other halves stood on that road outside Featherburn. A remarkable feeling, to be split in two across different locations, miles and miles apart. In reality, their bodies were still in the same place they were before, but their minds weren't, not anymore. Malum stepped back a little and circled around Tyrus, until he stood behind him and his owl. All while Cedric, Lyra and Kellan waited in silence and anticipation.

'You sniff the air, and the smell of that freshly baked bread fills your nose,' said Malum. 'The wind carries the faint smell of pines with it but also a scent that is inexplicably, yet unmistakably the scent of winter itself.'

The combination of Malum's eloquent tongue and Tyrus and Flake's stellar magic made sure that the painted picture was utter perfection. And when what Tyrus saw, felt, smelled and heard was as clear as Lyra's hair was white, that's when he knew it was time.

Malum inched closer until his breath tickled the hairs in Tyrus' neck when he spoke. 'Now, raise your hands. Conjure a flame and build a door in your mind between the here and now and the then and there, intend it to burn through the fabric of our world, intend it to connect.'

And there it was. A portal, a gateway formed, born out of blue and purple flames. However, the power he could draw from the key strained. When Tyrus unavoidably fell to his knees, Malum shouted Cedric to hurry through the portal before it would close.

Cedric nodded and rode through. From barely outside Mantlecrest to a little while outside Featherburn in seconds and as fast as the gateway had been conjured up, the sooner it closed up again. The realm stitched itself back together, back to the way it was.

'I have to do that again?' asked Tyrus huffing and puffing his way through his exhaustion.

'Yes, but the next one will be a bit smaller, thankfully. But replenish your powers first, you should be able to draw more out of the key,' explained Malum.

Tyrus clutched the key in his hands once again and Malum was right, even after using it to conjure up a portal, even if its power had strained for a bit, it still held so much more, like a never-ending stream of it.

In the hour that followed, Tyrus held the key tight as he and Flake feasted on its power to replenish their own and then, they were ready to do it all over again. This time Tyrus imagined the warmth from Xylia's hearth landing on his face, the embers going up the chimney and the draft that came from the windows. The sound of the floorboards creaking, the interior of Lyra's parents' home manifested in the form of a perfectly painted picture. The faint smell of medicinal herbs climbed up his nose as the faucet drip in the kitchen crawled into his ears. His portal opened, just about large enough for Lyra, Malum and Flake to escape through, before also jumping through himself. Lyra was home in the blink of an eye. She tried to hide her tears of joy, but she failed miserably at it. Tyrus and Malum couldn't resist smiling, happy for the white-haired girl who finally came home after all this time.

The first thing they heard was knocking on the front

door and a humming Xylia downstairs hurrying to meet it, to see who it could be and like they had planned, there stood Cedric, accompanied by a boy they'd never met.

'Who's this boy? Where's Lyra?' asked Xylia, pushing Cedric back. 'Where is my daughter?! Is she alive?!'

Cedric smirked. 'Why don't you ask her, lass?' he said and he lifted his chin, at which the healer turned round.

Their daughter came home.

Chapter 24

Keep Them Close

Tears streamed down Lyra's face, her ren's arms wrapped around her like gift wrapping around a present. Before all this adventure, Lyra had never been away from home for longer than a day, so naturally, Xylia took great relief in having her back.

Lyra hated the prospect of being cooped up inside the infirmary, Tyrus too, but ultimately, it was for the best. Chief Yike finding out would complicate things, and Tyrus especially wanted to avoid that at all costs. They were beyond close to ending winter. He wanted as few things to stand in his way as possible. And so, after being reunited with her ren, Lyra had to wait to see her father. She couldn't run to the market to surprise him, she had to practise patience and for her, that stung like a nasty insect. Flake kept her company so she didn't have to do all the waiting alone.

Time inched forward so slowly it almost seemed like the

clock above the hearth turned backward any time Lyra took her eyes off of it. In the meantime, Tyrus introduced Xylia to Kellan, and Malum and Cedric filled them in on the plan to venture out to the mysterious caves to the southwest, to find the Owlbound Council Temple and put an end to the pestering cold. Xylia promptly offered their services to aid the quest and they assured them Silas would feel the same. They congratulated Tyrus with Kellan as well, saying he got himself a nice catch.

'Is Father growing that frostwheat he needed himself, or what?' asked Lyra, her right leg restlessly annoying the floorboards.

'Patience, Lyra, he only left for the market an hour or two ago. He'll be here soon enough, although you know what a chatterbox he can be. Gods, I missed you,' Xylia said with sparkly eyes.

'At this rate, I'll be an old lady by the time he gets here,' she said. 'And…I missed you too.'

The front door swung open as soon as she said it, Silas dropped the groceries he'd gotten on the floor. He ran toward his daughter, and they hugged each other tight, as tight as the knots in the nets his hunters used to catch large prey.

'How are you here?' he asked. 'Why are you here?'

'We found all the splinters, Dad. The key is complete, and we know where to go,' explained Lyra with a glint in her eyes.

Silas looked at the rest of them, including the unknown

elven face, for confirmation.

'It's true,' said Tyrus. 'We can end it.'

'Never in a million years would you have thought to ever hear those words, would ye?' added Cedric as he came in for a sturdy hug as well.

This time, since Malum and the seasoned trader had only finished their story with Xylia minutes before, Tyrus explained everything to Silas. As a matter of fact, he would gladly explain it a hundred times more if it guaranteed even more help. After their chat, Silas vowed to convince his troupe of hunters to come with. Apparently, the lands they sought had a reputation. *Perilous* and *Dangerous* were the middle names of the road to the Owlbound Council Temple. The swords and spears of the hunting party would prove a most welcome addition, of that, Malum, Tyrus and Flake were sure.

In the days after the gang's arrival back in Featherburn, everyone prepared to escort Tyrus and Flake toward and into that temple. Cedric stocked up the carriage to make sure that no one could go hungry for weeks. 'You never know what'll happen along that trip, better safe than sorry,' he said.

Silas gathered fellow hunters he trusted for the cause. Not everyone believed him and not all agreed to come along, but enough of them—nine of them—did. Malum helped Tyrus with training, teaching him more magical spells, ones that would help him in combat, while Lyra sharpened daggers and helped out where she could. Xylia and Kellan, on the other hand, got to know each other a little better. He assisted them in making sure there were enough medical supplies for everybody. The elven boy hadn't ever done anything like it, but he enjoyed learning the practical medicinal applications of various plants and animal produce. The infirmary quickly became a base of operations, a place everyone would gather to talk about the mission, to work on weaponry, to gather resources. It took them nearly a week to get everything and everyone together, and considering all that needed to be done, that was impressive.

Sadly, the preparations didn't go as unnoticed as Tyrus would have liked. Everyone went about their way as carefully as they could, but the Featherburn Watch began noticing patterns anyway. And with all clues seemingly converging at the infirmary where escaped convict Lyra used to live, Chief Yike took a personal interest into the matter. So much so, that on the morning the expedition was scheduled to commence, the front door of the infirmary cracked and shattered at the pressure of the Watch's battering ram.

The entire building flooded with guards, while every exit and every window was suddenly blocked by soldiers of the Featherburn Watch. No one was coming in or out unseen, at least not without magic. Unfortunately for Lyra, Tyrus was nowhere near her and by the time she had tried to escape from various windows, two guards held her firmly and dragged her down from her room into the living area where they had been rounding up the rest of the group. For now, Tyrus had decided to stay calm, quiet, and composed.

'You're not taking my daughter away again, you jerk!' shouted Xylia.

'Shut up, Healer,' spat Chief Yike who was out of breath from climbing stairs and opening the door. 'I knew something was up in here…So, what is this, huh? A band of rebels? Plotting to overthrow me?' He turned to Xylia. 'Planning on taking revenge for rightfully imprisoning your daughter?'

Tyrus spoke up as he straightened his back, Flake proudly gracing his shoulder. 'No.'

Everyone else kept their lips as sealed as the settlement gate. 'Pardon me?' asked the chief.

'No,' repeated Tyrus louder.

Yike laughed. 'You're going to have to give me more than that, Mage,' he spat. 'You are all harbouring a dangerous and cunning fugitive who managed to escape captivity! Captivity, I might add, to which she was subjected to after an honest and fair trial! Besides…the mage helped her escape, I'm sure of it.'

No one spoke, but the expression on Tyrus' face said it all.

'It was the mage and the healer who put you all up to this, wasn't it?' asked the chief. 'I will grant immunity to anyone who will testify to that.'

The room remained silent. The only conversation that was had, happened through pissed-off glances.

'Still nothing? Fine, then this is what I will do. You will all face trial for treachery and harbouring a known fugitive. The mage will be burned for mounting a prison break. And Lyra, oh Lyra, you shouldn't have returned, if you ever left that is, because now I will take your life in the name of justice,' said the disgusting ruler as the smell of his rotten teeth laid siege to the noses around him.

Tyrus spoke up even louder now. 'I said…No!' Fire now burned in his eyes, and the guards stepped back; Lyra even managed to get loose and ran into Silas' arms.

'You will do no such thing!' added Tyrus.

'Is that supposed to scare me, boy?' said Chief Yike but at the same time he also inched ever so slowly backward.

'Touch any of these people and I'll burn you to a crisp,' threatened Tyrus eloquently. 'We're not here to plot rebellion, we're not here to have our revenge on you, even though we definitely have valid reasons to. We're here to save Featherburn and every other settlement and kingdom in the realm. We're here to relieve everybody of the never-ending winter and you Chief Yike, you and your soldiers won't stand in our way.'

The fire in Tyrus' eyes became more intense with every word he spoke, to the point where the chief and his guards were afraid the whole place might go up in smoke.

And then, after he was done talking, the boy put the fires in his and Flake's eyes out, extinguished them like putting a glass over a candle.

'Have I made myself clear?' he asked finally.

Chief Yike gulped and everyone heard it. 'Right, perhaps I overreacted a smidge,' he said.

Tyrus sensed he had a million questions about them ending the Winter, but the unfit leader didn't have the guts to say or ask anything else and he ordered his Watch to leave the infirmary at once.

Chief Yike headed out the door but turned around before he closed it. 'One day, you're going to be sorry about all this, Mage,' he said.

'I'm sure he will be, Yike,' spat Lyra sarcastically.

'But know this,' interjected Malum. 'Spring is coming and that won't be thanks to you, it will be thanks to us. Lyra included. Whether you like it or not.'

The chief mumbled grumpy words and incomprehensible sentences before leaving everyone be and as soon as that door slammed shut, everybody in the room felt like they could breathe again.

'All of you m…m-mentioned him being the absolute worst so many times, and even with all that, he m…m-managed to surprise me. What a c…c-cockroach,' said Kellan. 'Ty…that was awesome,' he added and went in for a kiss.

'Genuinely wish I could have seen you two burn the man to a crisp, Tyrus and Flake,' said Lyra.

Everyone couldn't agree more, but Tyrus felt relieved it didn't have to come to that, even if his blood unequivocally wanted to give in to the anger. In the end though, Cedric's carriage—escorted by new and familiar allies—rode out of Featherburn that morning, and the Watch let them. Tyrus hadn't left them a choice.

Silas and his hunting party led the way on their horses while Trudy followed behind, treading on already trampled snow, pulling the carriage. Xylia and Malum also had horses and they made sure everything was in order behind Ced's large coach. The carriage itself held the rest of the crew; Flake (who occasionally went out to roam the skies), Tyrus, Lyra, and Kellan. They all felt a little useless, but they didn't have anything else to do other than spending the majority of the trip safe and sound and warm inside. Besides, everyone agreed they had to save their strength for whatever the temple would throw at them.

Most of the journey went off without much of a hitch, like ice skating on a perfectly levelled frozen lake. A few days went by and every night when the sun fell out of the sky, they made camp and whenever the moons did the same, they'd clean everything up again to continue onward.

Many had called the journey dangerous and perilous, but Tyrus and his friends started to think that was bogus. That was until the hills turned into modest mountains and the fields turned into dense forests. Things abruptly moved slower, the journey became fiercer and harsher. Gradually, the cold started digging into people's skins more tenaciously, seeping into the flesh, on a path to reach their bones. Their situation especially took a turn for the worst when the weather decided there wasn't enough snow around, puking even more of it down to the surface. At this point in their journey, stops were made more often for Xylia to treat frostbitten wounds assisted by Tyrus' magic.

No matter the snowstorm the brave convoy found themselves in, they kept going and before they knew it, they were making their way through a forest Tyrus recognised from his visions. They were on the right track, gaining ground on the road to the temple. The home stretch.

But then, a single sound made them all stop. A sound that made its way down Cedric's spine with an almost stinging shiver. It was a distinct howl. A bleakwolf's howl. It turned out it wasn't alone either. The other howls followed in rather quick succession, an entire hungry pack's worth of them.

'Cedric! Get inside the carriage with me, now!' shouted Xylia. 'Hide!'

'What if they need me?' he asked.

'You can't be out here, and you know it! Now get in, that's an order!' shouted Xylia, and they wouldn't take no for an answer.

Unlike the hunting pack that attacked Cedric months ago, this pack announced their presence because the convoy had unknowingly passed into their territory. An attack was unavoidable by that point.

'Everyone, keep your eyes peeled. They could come at us from anywhere!' ordered Silas. 'Keep your swords and spears at the ready!'

No matter how much they didn't want it to happen, the inescapable attack surrounded them with angry growls coming from behind bushes and trees.

'Silas! I see one!' shouted one of his hunters.

'Another one over here!' shouted another.

After five long and terrifying minutes, they had counted at least one bleakwolf per person. Warm quick breaths alternated and evaporated in the air while the bleakwolves relished in the panic they caused as the growling stopped and for a second. Relief lived a short life, until the bleakwolves, armed with their sharp poisonous teeth, lunged at the hunters. The women and men of the hunting party fought bravely and adequately but the gang inside the carriage could feel their courage waning by every passing second. Tyrus refused to have any of those lives out there on his conscience and stood up, taking Flake with him.

'Tyrus, what are you d…d-doing?' asked Kellan.

'I have to help them,' he answered, and he kissed his elven boy goodbye.

'Lad, no. Stay here!' shouted Cedric but the young talented mage didn't listen.

He swung open the carriage door, bursting with energy and power, and attacked the bleakwolves with his magic immediately and in doing so, little by little, he strayed further away from that carriage door. The bleakwolf pack's numbers ended up being more than double the amount the hunters had counted before. The wolves outnumbered them two, nay, three to one.

Tyrus and Flake didn't see it, but the leader of the pack jumped on top of the roof of the carriage and everyone inside tried to be as silent as possible. The scarred wolf didn't proceed to look inside the carriage though, because its eyes were set on a boy it recognised. The boy that gave him his scar. A scar above its snout and between its eyes caused by burning magical fire. It felt hungry, not only drooling for flesh but also craving revenge. The scarred bleakwolf leapt off the carriage and snuck up behind Tyrus who was fighting off two other wolves. The leader of the toxic wolves jumped at Tyrus and luckily, that jump made enough noise for the boy to leap aside and evade the bloodthirsty beast.

'You,' he said when he saw the scars on the wolf's head.

The wolf growled back at him, dissatisfied with the way their last encounter ended, the way Tyrus had made him flee. The battle between the leader of the pack and the powerful young wizard commenced and the two were remarkably evenly matched until Tyrus activated his secret weapon, the magical key around his neck. Without breaking a sweat, he gained the upper hand and so between all the attempts at clawing away at him, at trying to bite him and push him, the bleakwolf failed to even touch the boy for a single millisecond. Cedric watched it happen through the open carriage door, but he couldn't do anything, could he? Sweat ran down the man's face.

Tyrus stood his ground but comparative to his fight with the peryton, the boy felt invincible. So invincible, he didn't notice another bleakwolf swooping in and knocking Flake off his shoulder. Cedric's heart stopped. Flake fell underneath a bush, and she didn't get back up.

The scarred leader took notice and didn't hesitate to lunge at the last of the Owlbound the first chance it got. Tyrus was on the ground now, his back pressed into the snow as a drooling almost rabid wolf kept him from moving because it held down his arms with its strong paws. It looked straight into his eyes and Tyrus saw nothing but hatred. It opened its mouth and right before it would tear into the boy's throat, someone rammed into the wolf with everything they had. Last time it was Trudy who saved him, this time, it was Cedric.

The trader had most certainly broken a few of the scarred bleakwolf's ribs, and his little intermezzo allowed Flake to get back up and fly onto Tyrus' shoulder.

Together, Ced and Tyrus battled the wolves around them while Flake provided support from the air. She breathed fire, she pecked at eyes, and used her talons relentlessly. The battle ended when the leader of the pack had seen enough. Once again, it fled and like it had last time, it looked back at Tyrus before it ran. Only this time, it smiled like it had somehow enjoyed their battle and then, they were gone. Every single bleakwolf left, except for the ones who had growled and howled for the last time.

Xylia stormed Cedric's way with the frowns of rage draped across their face. 'That was mighty stupid of you,' they said.

'I know, but I'm fine,' said Cedric. 'And the lad is, too.'

'No bites, right?' asked Xylia to make sure.

'Don't ask me how, but no bites indeed,' he answered, catching his breath. He sounded surprised in the best way possible. The alternative would have been disastrous. 'Now, check up on the others, will ye?'

Having reassured them, Xylia went to check up the hunters in Silas' party. Kellan joined them as well, assisting them wherever he could. Miraculously, the healer had to administer only one dose of antidote. With the hunter in question exposed for merely a few minutes, the medicine worked quickly, and they would make a full recovery without complications. A stark contrast to what would have happened to Cedric if he had gotten bitten again. The other wounds Xylia tended to were grazes from claws, or bruises from falling. Without Tyrus' magic, there would have likely been casualties.

Cedric climbed his carriage to continue steering Trudy, and Tyrus joined him for a little while. 'Thank you for saving me,' he said. 'Are you all right?'

Cedric smiled. 'I'm fine, laddie. I guess we're even now, right? You saved me from those wretched things, I saved you?'

Tyrus nodded in agreement and barged in for a hug. Cedric was left with a smile when the boy's auburn curls chased Kellan's charcoal coils. A little while later, the convoy set up camp and after a pleasant night around a campfire, a good night's sleep and a portion of well-deserved rest, the group continued their final trek to find Tyrus and Flake's destiny.

Flake hooted from the sky and as soon as she did, Silas raised his fist high. They had arrived. The whole convoy came to a gentle halt as they saw Lyra's father's raised fist. The caves they sought sat right in front of them, burying down into the earth and stone.

Tyrus and his friends exited the carriage immediately and marvelled upon the several entrances that swam in the reflections of their eyes. Flake came down to Tyrus and hopped around on the shoulder pad below her talons. They could set up camp outside the caves, it was perfect, and a moment of pure ecstasy and relief washed over everyone.

Unfortunately, it wasn't long before the happiness was squashed by Cedric as he suddenly fell off his carriage bench without warning. His skin looked like the snow around him, his breaths as shallow as the many frozen creeks they had encountered.

'Cedric?!' shouted Silas from atop his horse and he sped to the fallen trader's aid.

Tyrus turned and ran too, as fast as he possibly could until he crashed into the ground and the snow with his knees, trying to help Cedric up, but he couldn't.

'Cedric?! What's the matter? What happened?!' said Tyrus. He kind of already knew the answer, but he didn't want to know it. He'd seen Cedric like this before.

'Xylia! What happened to him?!' he asked as the healer joined them. 'Was it the bleakwolves again?'

Xylia's hands retreated up into their white hair, and when they scrunched up Cedric's trousers, they cursed. A bleakbite sat at the bottom of his right leg, right above the ankle. 'Damnit, Cedric!' shouted Xylia, tears welling in their eyes. 'You told me you were fine! Why would you do that?!'

'Didn't…want…to worry…the lad, did I?' grunted Cedric.

'Kellan, grab the antidote!' shouted Tyrus. 'Quick!'

But the elf didn't move. Kellan knew Cedric had been bitten before, how long he was exposed to the bleakvenom, and he assumed Tyrus knew what that meant. Confusion settled in Tyrus' amber eyes.

'Kellan, he needs the antidote! What are you doing?!' he cried, his vision turned blurry from the tears that welled in his eyes.

'Tyrus...' said Xylia, laying their hand on his shoulder.

'Save him!' he shouted as Flake jumped off into the snow to be next to the trader. 'Save him, please!'

'Cedric didn't want to tell you,' cried the healer.

'Tell me what?' asked Tyrus, now sobbing. 'No! Ced?! What are they talking about?!'

Cedric drew a deep breath. 'Tell him, Xylia.'

'With how long Ced was exposed the first time, the antidote wouldn't work again,' admitted Xylia, struggling to get the words out. 'There's nothing I can do to save him.'

Cedric struggled speaking. 'I thought I could hold out long enough for you to...enter the caves, laddie...for you to end the winter...I...didn't want to derail...the plan,' he said in bursts of short breaths. 'I didn't want...to be a distraction.'

'Why didn't you stay in the carriage?!' asked Tyrus as he felt his world crumble. 'Why didn't you stay safe?!'

'Tyrus...I made a promise...to your parents...to keep you safe...so I did,' he said.

'There must be something I can do to save him!'

screamed Tyrus to everyone around him, to anyone who would provide him with an answer. 'There has to be something!'

He looked at Malum but the wise traveller didn't have anything either and so he shook his head. Tyrus' tears kept coming and coming.

'There has to be a spell!'

'Even magic has limits,' said Malum from experience. He gulped. 'I'm sorry.'

'No! This can't be happening!' screamed Tyrus, flames forming in his eyes. 'It can't!' he roared. 'You can't go, Cedric! You can't! I need you!'

'It's okay…laddie. It's okay,' said Cedric, wanting to place his hand on the boy's hand, but couldn't. 'Promise me, Tyrus.'

Tears kept rolling down the boy's cheeks as the flames now disappeared.

'Promise me, that…as soon as I'm gone…you'll go and kick winter's arse. Your destiny is waiting, lad…Your future is bright.'

Tyrus buried his head in the trader's chest. 'Please, I can't do any of this without you,' he pleaded.

'Yes…you can. I know you can,' said the trader. 'Flake? You there?'

Hoot.

'You…take care of this one for me…will you?'

Hoot.

Cedric couldn't hug Tyrus back due to the poison, but the boy knew he would have. 'I love you, Ty,' he whispered.

'I love you too,' and Tyrus hugged him because he knew it was time.

'And hey…those memories…memories of me…Keep them close, will ya, laddie?' asked Cedric, and his amber-eyed boy nodded.

After that, Cedric could no longer speak. No matter how hard he tried. Tyrus stepped back, and everyone said their goodbyes while they still could as he just stood there catatonically. First Xylia and Silas, then Kellan and Lyra, and finally, even Malum as well. Despite their differences, even he knelt down in the snow and whispered inaudible words in Cedric's ear to say farewell.

Lyra and Kellan hugged an inconsolable mage and his bird, as Malum put a hand on the boy's shoulder. Silas and Xylia held each other tight. And finally, Cedric's last visible breath rose to the sky—evading every flake of snow—to meet the dark clouds above.

Those memories of me, keep them close.

CHAPTER 25

ETERNAL WINTER

The wind howled through the cave system, like the structure itself mourned the sudden death of a loved one. Tyrus felt like how that wind sounded. He wanted to howl and scream and shout and cry and sob, but he couldn't. He'd done all that outside and he had to stay focused now. He had to end winter now. Otherwise, Cedric would have died for nothing. A useless sacrifice, and he wasn't going to let that happen.

Malum, Lyra, Kellan, and Flake were right there with him in the caves as Xylia and Silas waited outside with the rest of the hunters, guarding the various entrances to the cave system, mourning their friend. Regardless of how much Tyrus wanted to focus on the quest at hand, no matter how much he wanted to think about unsealing the temple that hid within the caves, flashes of Ced's death kept haunting him.

Your destiny is waiting, lad. Your future is bright.

The caves themselves didn't do anything to guide Tyrus and his friends toward the seal they desperately sought. But they kept going anyway, and Tyrus for one wouldn't rest until they had found it.

'Tyrus, you haven't said a word,' said Lyra as she treaded behind him. 'It would be okay to let things sink in a bit before we continue.' Her cobalt-blue eyes cradled tears.

Kellan and Malum were concerned too, and from the look Flake gave them, as she turned her head around toward them, she was worried as well. He didn't even acknowledge what Lyra had said. He kept going, searching for the temple's entrance. He hadn't spoken to Kellan, either. Tyrus felt cold, distant, and most of all angry.

Promise me that as soon as I'm gone, that you'll go and kick winter's arse.

Tyrus came to a stop and held the key firm. He had had enough. He closed his eyes and listened to it whisper, he figured if the caves weren't going to lend them a hand, the key would, and he was right. He could feel where to go, the magic told him and so he conjured up a trail of fiery breadcrumbs that led the way. Breadcrumbs that illuminated the dark capricious caves a bit alongside the fire in his own hand and Malum's lit torch.

'Tyrus, please, talk to us,' pleaded Lyra.

'This way,' he said, moving forward.

Kellan pulled her back a little. 'Don't worry, Lyra. He n…n-needs time is all,' he said.

The white-haired girl agreed and took comfort in the fact she had at least made sure he knew he could talk to them.

The further they ventured into the caves, the more mushrooms they encountered. Not regular ones though, glowing ones. At first, faintly but as they went on and on and on, they shone brighter and brighter, to the point where Malum extinguished his torch, and Tyrus let the fire in his palm die. They traversed those caves the way blood and magic traversed veins. Here and there the veins were slightly clogged and they'd have to squeeze through, making their way to the heart, to the temple.

After following the breadcrumbs of fire, the gang turned around a corner and it looked like there was a lot of light at the end of the tunnel. At first, they thought they had gotten to an exit, but it being light would have been impossible. It would have gotten dark outside already. But once they stepped into the light, it all made sense. They had made it. They had made it to the sealed temple.

Tyrus, consumed by anger and sadness, was the first to adjust to the light, the light that came from thousands upon thousands of crystals, mushrooms and flowers that desperately clung onto or came out of the cave's ceiling.

'Woah,' let Lyra escape.

'M…m-magic will never get old, will it?' asked Kellan.

'No, it will not,' agreed Malum and for the first time on their journey, he was actually surprised by something.

The walls of the open space they found were the regular mix of limestone and dolomite they'd been seeing for hours now, but that ceiling, it looked like what Tyrus felt when he conjured magic. That being said, the sadness he'd been holding back ever since he entered the caves, escaped in full force, Cedric would have loved seeing this; he would have adored it. Tyrus fell to his knees on the cold damp ground.

'Quite the sight, isn't it, laddie?' he heard Cedric say in the back of his mind.

Tears ran down his face like stars falling from heaven and Flake was there to catch a few. The Owlbound boy's fickle heart couldn't handle it as he buried his eyes in his hands and leaned into his sweet bird.

Lyra and Kellan hugged him as he sat down, his knees shaking at the cold, and he hugged them back. The feelings of being so loved by others, and his heart being ripped out of his chest, washed over him simultaneously. He felt so full and so empty. Malum came down on one knee as Kellan and Lyra backed away, with one hand he held the boy's shoulder, firm like Cedric often did and with the other, he comforted Flake.

Those memories. Memories of me, keep them close, will ya?

'I'm okay,' said Tyrus as he tightened the grip on his

emotions again. 'Thank you all.'

He got back up on his feet, let the last few tears sink away in the fabric of his dark-green jacket's sleeves and he traipsed toward the doors of the temple. Doors that almost sank away into the limestone that surrounded it. They didn't seem like they were in great shape, but they sat tightly sealed regardless. Sealed shut with the power of magic.

Tyrus took the key from around his neck and let it rest in his hand as it surged with power. It knew it was close to the door it was supposed to open, and the moment Tyrus approached the door further, to finally unlock it, he was stopped by an absolutely terrifying scream. A scream he faintly recognised, one he'd heard before but a little different and when he turned around together with Lyra, Malum and Kellan, he knew why it sounded so familiar.

'A f…f-frost golem!' shouted Kellan.

It towered before them, a big one, a giant one. So big that if it were to stretch its arms up high, it would hit the magical ceiling. It had to be twice the size of the one Tyrus had battled in Featherburn back when his adventure began.

The frost golem buried its arms in the rocky floor and hefty strong and sharp crystals of ice erupted from the ground and blocked the path toward the door. It was ready for a fight.

'I think it's g…g-guarding the temple,' said Kellan. 'I

think we trespassed into its home.'

Tyrus set his eyes ablaze, and Flake's burned as well. 'Nothing is stopping me from ending the cold, it has taken enough from me. This one…is mine.'

They all felt it, the rage in his voice. Different from the anger that would occasionally erupt from his mind when things didn't go his way. It was the kind of rage he had felt in the months after his parent's disappearances. A dangerous emotion for a powerful mage, especially one that was amplified by an object of immense power. It scared Kellan especially, this wasn't the sweet boy he had come to know. Lyra agreed. This wasn't Tyrus.

'Remember, Tyrus! F…f-frost golems don't usually attack without good reason!' shouted Kellan. 'We have to show it we m…m-mean no harm! It is only protecting its home!' he added but his magician boy couldn't hear him anymore.

Impressive magic ensued but it was also hard to watch. In Tyrus' anger, he couldn't think. From where Kellan, Lyra, and Malum were standing, it looked like Tyrus didn't merely want to beat the golem or knock it out somehow to stop it from hindering their quest. It looked like Tyrus had it out for a kill.

The fight between the ginormous frost golem and the last of the Owlbound was a showcase of everything they had. The frost golem didn't hold back and unfortunately for it, Tyrus didn't either. He used every single move he'd learned. He blasted fire balls, made his fire into the sharpest speeding bullets to pierce through the rock and the ice of the creature, he phased through attacks, and he even used tiny gateways to portal himself behind, or above, or even below the golem for surprise attacks. The creature didn't know what hit it and Tyrus' friends had their hands full with evading the fallout of the various offensives.

Tyrus' rage made him feel unbeatable. He didn't think; he attacked over and over, drawing strength out of the key in his hand. And that's where the frost golem saw opportunity. While Tyrus and Flake were busy gloating, the golem surprised them with a shattering punch to the chest. Tyrus flung back and crashed into the dolomite, but the key thrusted out of his hands. He screamed out in rage with everything he had, again and again. They were the kind of screams that came with saliva being catapulted from his mouth while tears slid down his face, and then he went quiet.

Without the key, his mana pool was depleted beyond what he thought possible. How utterly crap he had felt after moving everyone from one side of the realm to the other with portals, was nothing compared to how empty and tired he felt now. Flake, who would otherwise have flown to grab back the key, couldn't, and Lyra, Kellan, and Malum were too far away to get him the key in time. Tyrus cried. He fell to his knees on the cold solid ground and looked up at the frost golem before him. He then laid his hands down flat in front of him. Tyrus thought this was the end. Part of him thought he deserved it. He couldn't hack it. Winter would continue to slowly kill Wingspan. He failed. He let his rage get the better of himself and failed. He had relied on the strength of the key, and it had made him careless. It's what had gotten Cedric killed, too. If he hadn't been careless, the trader wouldn't have needed to save him from the bleakwolf. He let Cedric down and it cost him yet another father.

One of the robust fists of the frost golem flung his way. Bang. A loud one. The room was shrouded in dust. No one could see. But when the violent dust settled, they didn't only see the one frost golem that attacked them, they saw two.

Tyrus opened his eyes. He wasn't dead. He should have been, but something saved him. *Kindness* saved him. The guarding frost golem's fist was blocked by a hand made of rock and ice and moss, the hand of another frost golem. One he recognised. It was the one from Featherburn, the one Lyra and Tyrus had showed kindness. The two creatures exchanged a series of incomprehensible deep sounds. The bigger golem backed down. They stepped back and Tyrus swam in confusion.

'No!' he screamed. 'I should die! It was my fault! I killed Cedric! So, do it! I deserve it!'

The golems didn't move, and Kellan sprinted toward

the boy, having heard every word.

'You s…s-stop that, right now!' he shouted, giving Tyrus a push. 'Cedric knew damn well what he was risking w…w-when he saved you! You promised him, Ty. Are you going to break that promise?'

'I'm sorry,' cried the distraught boy. 'I'm sorry.'

'It's all right,' said Kellan. 'Come here.' They hugged, and while Tyrus didn't feel deserving of one, it felt invaluable in that moment like a salve numbing a violent gash.

Lyra and Malum joined them, supporting their friend as he stood upright, bruised and cut from the fight.

Tyrus looked up at the two towering creatures. 'Why did you save me?' he asked.

The female frost golem stepped aside at that and behind her stood another one of her kind, only this one was the size of a human.

'Its orb hatched!' exclaimed Lyra. 'The orb we returned to it!'

The fatherly golem bowed to Tyrus, stepped aside and made the icy spikes in front of the temple door melt away. He was more than forgiven, and a debt was repaid.

The moment he'd been dreaming about ever since winter took his parents was within reach, right there for the taking. Tyrus and his friends approached the ancient temple door with heavy steps, the end of their quest was in sight. The key in Tyrus' hand hummed and vibrated more intensely with every step closer to the seal. Lyra couldn't explain it, but she always imagined a lock. She had dreamed of picking it. But it didn't look like that at all; the shape of the totem was carved into the stone.

'Okay, here it goes,' said Tyrus, moving the key closer to the seal.

The owl-shaped carving lit up with an orange glow and suddenly as the key hovered over the seal, it flung out of Tyrus' hand like a strong magnet near metal. The same orange light from the seal appeared around the edges of the door and the whole cave started shaking. Kellan panicked for a moment, but Malum reassured him it would be fine. Or at least, that's what he hoped himself.

The key dissolved into the seal and the heavy robust doors moved as they folded open, rock chafing rock with bright orange light shining from within. Tyrus covered his eyes with his arms, while Flake closed hers on his shoulder and Malum held out one hand in front of his face to shy away from the light. Kellan did the same while Lyra just turned around, waiting until it was over.

The shaking stopped. The light faded. A sinister corridor lurked beyond the door, dark and dreary. The frost golems behind them curiously took a gander inside while Tyrus lit the fire in his eyes, balled his fists, folded them open, and blew embers into the corridor. They all watched as the embers sailed the waves of the draft toward the torches that graced the walls and marvelled as they ignited them, now carrying the mage's signature blue and purple flames. The corridor stretched as far as their eyes could see, seemingly ending in more darkness.

'That doesn't look ominous at all,' said Lyra.

Malum turned his head. 'To the contrary, Lyra...' He paused. 'Right...sarcasm.'

Tyrus didn't say a word and headed inside. Malum followed, while Lyra and Kellan looked at each other, gulped, and eventually did the same. The air they breathed felt and tasted like it had died of old age. The dust that ruled the corridor forced Kellan into many sneezes as the cracks in the walls around them seemed to lead the way.

In the end, the corridors bloomed open into a gorgeous ceremonial chamber with an altar in the middle, and glowing mushrooms for a ceiling. Nine marble pillars, ending in detailed sculpted flowers, clung to the walls, walls decorated with frescos — wall paintings that depicted a story. They had faded slightly over the decades, but all things considered, between the cold, moist and damp conditions, they had been preserved remarkably well. Tyrus and Malum figured the magic inside the place had something to with that.

The first of the frescos depicted the Paragons of the Owlbound Council of ages lost and how they encountered an ancient being from another world. A dark entity that sought nothing more than to destroy the world and remake it into their image, bending and scrambling the minds of those who were perceptible to outside influence. The blight targeted people who had lost people dear to them, making promises they couldn't possibly keep. The council had named the entity Netheros, oozing out of the cracks of the Nether Realm at the core of the world, a parasite.

'Netheros,' whispered Tyrus.

Lyra went ahead and took a closer look. 'Sounds like a twat,' she said.

'The t…t-twat of twats,' continued Kellan.

Lyra snorted. 'Nice one, Kell.'

On the second fresco, they saw how Netheros approached a powerful Paragon of the Owlbound arts, one that was on track to become a member of the esteemed council. The mage had lost their spouse, and the dark entity led them astray with promises of bringing their lost love back from the dead. The mage came to be known as the Renegade Paragon.

'That mage…again,' said Tyrus.

'The very one your parents must have feared,' said Malum.

'The one t…t-that slaughtered hundreds at Alula Isle,' added Kellan.

'The one that laid waste to Ravencreek,' finished Lyra.

The third wall painting showed the council performing a sacred ritual, a ritual to freeze the world, to starve the parasitic being at the core. Much to the disdain of the Renegade, who was portrayed resorting to extreme measures to find the temple, torturing and killing council members.

Malum moved toward the fourth fresco. 'And then, humans and elves alike, hunted the Owlbound, until there was barely anyone left,' he translated.

The illustrated mages burned, hanged, drowned, died gruesome deaths. Unbound people usually separated them from their owls and killed the birds first to prevent the warlocks from accessing their magic.

The fifth and final piece of art was dedicated to the Renegade Paragon, hooded and hidden, with runic symbols underneath. The symbols wondered, questioning if they were still out there, clinging to the shadows, biding their time. Waiting for the right moment to strike. The symbols also specifically asked to not bring about spring until at least one hundred and seventy-four years had passed. The exact length of time it would have taken to kill Netheros at the heart of the world.

One hundred and seventy-four years.

'Hold on,' started Lyra. 'Has that much time passed already? Because I don't want to be responsible for unleashing an ancient evil upon the world.'

'Yes,' said Malum. 'History books were quite clear on that. The Eternal Winter began a little over one hundred and eighty years ago.'

'So, Tyrus can safely end the n...n-never-ending

winter!' exclaimed Kellan.

Tyrus turned around with Flake gracing his shoulder and approached the altar in silence. Lyra thought it slightly dramatic but figured it was best not to say anything. After all, Tyrus had essentially lost a father, something she knew for sure would devastate her, so she cut him a little slack.

'So, this is it then,' said Tyrus. 'The end of our adventure.'

'Well,' interjected Malum. 'If it is, it has been an honour.'

'Okay, then let's do this,' announced the boy.

Hoot!

'For my parents,' said Tyrus.

'For my husband,' said Malum.

'For all the people that suffer in Featherburn and elsewhere,' said Lyra.

'For everyone,' said Kellan. 'Humans and elves alike.'

'For Cedric,' said Tyrus, a tear escaped the corner of his eyes.

They all agreed. 'For Cedric.'

And so, Tyrus conjured his fire and as with any of the spells he'd learnt, intention was the foundation. This time there was no intention to harm, or to phase through a wall or to attack, or to grant increased speed, or to portal to a place far away, or for flames to become a bridge. This time, the intention was to end, to heal, to restore. To end the Eternal Winter, to heal the seasons and to restore the world.

Before being in that chamber, Tyrus hadn't the faintest idea as to what he was going to do once he was inside, how he was going to do what he wanted to, but in the end, as soon as he stood in front of that altar, surrounded by frescoes depicting times lost, he knew. He couldn't explain it, not in the slightest, but he knew.

Malum, Lyra, and Kellan watched as their favourite mage and his magical bird entered a trance. One that made Tyrus' shoes leave the surface of the floor behind. He floated above the altar, just like Flake now and they glowed, and they kept glowing and glowing, until they both burst into flames. The fire didn't hurt them or Tyrus' clothes. It danced across his body as it dripped onto the altar, which absorbed it, drank it.

The whole place shook, the way it did before when they had opened the doors, but a little more intensely this time, with more vigour and enthusiasm. Kellan and Lyra were worried to their core for Tyrus and Flake, but Malum, he just smiled. He closed his eyes and stood there with his arms spread wide, embracing the miracle before him.

'This is for you, Lux,' whispered Malum underneath his breath.

Bright white made sure no one could see a thing. Bright white followed by silence.

Cedric was about to leave the mortal realm behind him, and Malum watched as everyone who knew and loved him said goodbye. And then, it was his turn. He bowed down and knelt in the snow next to the dying trader. He brought his mouth close to Cedric's ear, making sure the others wouldn't hear what he had to say.

'I'm sorry, my friend,' he whispered. 'I'm truly sorry this happened to you, Cedric.'

The dying man let his eyes wander toward Tyrus for a moment.

'But don't you worry. I will look out for your boy…' he continued, unable to resist. 'He's in safe hands with me. Malum the Renegade Paragon will take good care of him.'

A dastardly smile no one could see formed on Malum's face. Cedric could no longer warn the son he'd never had. Powerless and on his way to the beyond, a single tear escaped the corner of his eye. And as the wolf in sheep's clothing backed away, the villainous grin on his face was replaced by the mask he'd worn since the beginning of their journey. He looked sorrowful, and only the spirit of a man who could no longer speak, breathe, scream, or cry, knew it was all a ruse.

All the torches were extinguished, along with the fluorescent light emitted by the ceiling mushrooms. Darkness enveloped Tyrus and his friends for a few seconds, before the shrooms and the torches alike woke up again. It was as if they had taken a brief powernap.

When everyone opened their eyes, Tyrus was flung back against a now cracked pillar and laid seemingly lifeless on his stomach. His hat had left his head alone after being thrown back and the sweat in his curls—from the straining magic he performed—had frozen in place. Kellan sped his way and sighed in relief when he saw his back moving up and down. After hugging that floor for a second, Tyrus rolled over. He felt like he had aged sixty years in an instant as he struggled to get up from the floor.

'Tyrus, I think you did it!' shouted Lyra with her arms up in the air.

Kellan flung around Tyrus' neck and hugged him tight, their bodies embracing each other's warmth and for a moment they let their foreheads rest against each other as amber ran through dense blue. Tyrus wanted to relish in that gaze a little longer but ultimately, he leaned in for something infinitely better. A kiss.

'Hey, boys, can we get you two a room later maybe?' asked Lyra, pulling them apart.

'Malum…Did it work?' asked Tyrus.

'It sure looked like it did,' answered Malum. 'However, I suppose only time will tell, Tyrus.'

The thought of having to wait to find out the answer tore him apart a little on the inside. Did he succeed? Did he avenge his parents? Did he avenge Cedric? Did he end the cold that stuck to their world like glue?

Only time would tell.

CHAPTER 26

A TASTE AND A DASH

One whole month ran past faster than anyone thought possible. There had been much to do, many things that had kept people busy ever since the moment Tyrus presumably ended winter. An ending that cost a sacrifice, the ending that took Cedric's life, but nonetheless, an ending to a season people didn't think could ever end. The young mage took pride in what he and his friends had achieved, but it didn't cancel out the bittersweetness of it all.

At first, people wondered. Did anything change? Did the kid free the world from the relentless never-ending cold? For a while, doubt ruled like a ruthless emperor. But then, the days brought along a gentler wind and the weeks even made sure the sun felt like it had more to give. Layers of ice across the realm thinned like the hairs on the top of seasoned Cedric's head began to, and crops grew with slightly more ease. Snowfall became less common and even though the white carpet hadn't melted away, everyone knew in their hearts and minds that it would only be a matter of sand grains in an hourglass.

It felt weird going back to the lighthouse. Tyrus took Kellan and Lyra with him, Malum too. Not even Cedric had ever seen it with his own eyes and, if he was honest, that's what pained the boy most. It was the most peculiar thing because Tyrus could clearly see the lighthouse through the trees as they approached it. However, Lyra saw nothing, neither did Kellan, and the frown that buried itself in Malum's forehead, said it all.

'Are you sure you didn't lose the way, Clever Chap?' said Lyra on the way there.

Kellan agreed. 'It's okay if you did, no one w…w-would laugh at you for that. Besides Lyra, I mean.'

'Now hold on,' spoke Malum because as they got closer—much, much closer—the lighthouse finally came into view.

It was like it sat hidden behind a veil. Not until Malum and Tyrus inspected the glass at the top of the lighthouse did they understand why. It seemed as though Tyrus' parents had left him a piece of magic all along. How his parents had managed it, they weren't sure. A mystery for another day. But all this time, Tyrus had lived in an enchanted lighthouse next to a frozen lake. No wonder

Tyrus didn't get any unwanted visitors over all that time, the possible visitors never knew the lighthouse was there to begin with. The runes responsible sat inscribed and instilled within the glass, the glass that held the light he was never allowed to ignite and now he finally knew why, because lighting it made his home visible to all.

The first few weeks, it was only Tyrus, Flake, Lyra, Malum, Kellan, and Trudy. Hunting together, dining together, building together, living together. They prepared the lighthouse and the surrounding area for the arrival of Lyra's parents who would move into the cabin they were building. They even accounted for space to build out an infirmary next to it. Xylia and Silas had both made the necessary arrangements to finally leave Featherburn (and its inhabitants) behind in favour of a new settlement to be. Tyrus' settlement, away from the clutches of Chief Yike, the settlement he and Lyra had dreamed about when they travelled to Crownhaven months before.

When Xylia and Silas finally arrived, their reunion with Lyra was as heart-warming as it was when the group of travelling friends had returned to Featherburn from Mantlecrest, and especially Lyra's ren was excited to start filling up their new infirmary with potions, ointments and concoctions. Silas had already thought out a plan to provide his hunting services to the new settlement and six of the brave hunters in his previous party would join them in a few months' time.

When everyone was there, they decided to hold a memorial for Cedric.

Kellan had a statue of Cedric commissioned—paid for by Malum—with a moderately renowned sculptor in Crownhaven, one of the very few people who had been kind to him there. The statue would decorate the town's square of the, as of yet, unnamed settlement around the lighthouse, serving as a delightful surprise for Tyrus.

'We didn't always see eye to eye, but in the end, I knew in my heart that he always meant well. He was an honourable and respectable man of whom I learned a lot in the short time I had known him,' said Malum during the ceremony.

Lyra, who always knew what to say—for, most likely, the first time in her life—didn't. Or perhaps she wasn't able to say it without bursting into tears. Whatever words she could think of, she swallowed whole. 'Cheers, old man!' she said instead.

'Thank you for always b…b-believing in us, for always protecting us. You'll be m…m-missed, you old sod!' said Kellan.

Xylia spoke for both themselves and Silas when they said, 'It's been an honour and a privilege to have known you, to have cared for you and to have been able to pour my heart and soul out to you. Wherever you are now, I hope you know peace and that you know we're all okay, thanks to you.'

Flake hooted serenely from her magical boy's shoulder throughout the whole thing when finally, Tyrus had prepared a few words to share. He experienced difficulties getting started. It was as if his throat had closed on purpose, barricaded to stop anything from getting out, stopping words from escaping like iron bars imprisoned criminals. He gathered the courage to say what he had to say, even if he wasn't sure he could get through his whole speech.

'Ced, you've always been there for me,' he began, tears rolling off his cheeks. 'Even when my parents were still around, you had my back and every time we met, you'd come bearing gifts. Gifts I had to pay for, but gifts nonetheless.' He laughed. 'And then, after my parents disappeared, after the cold claimed them, I could feel myself slip away. I could feel myself fall. I was so young, but you were there, and you caught me, cared for me, even when I held you at a distance.'

The boy burst into inconsolable tears. He wanted to continue but couldn't and so, Xylia approached him, asking if he wanted them to continue reading in his stead, to not leave the words unsaid. He nodded.

Xylia continued reading the words Tyrus had written down with his magical flames, 'Ced, it's been my greatest pleasure to have had you in my life because not everyone can say they had a mom and not one, but two dads. I love you and I'll always love you, forever and always.'

As Xylia spoke his words, Tyrus felt the seasoned trader's presence. He couldn't explain it, nor did he need to. He could feel it in the breeze, Cedric was with them, and he was proud.

Tears were shed. A lot of them were sad tears but there were plenty of happy ones too, because they all had memories of Cedric. Memories that they would carry with them in their hearts, memories they would hold dear, memories that would shape the way they tackled the future. Memories they'd treasure. Memories they'd keep close.

They exchanged stories that evening, stories that journeyed into the night, tales that rode the smoke of the campfire up into the sky, to the two moons and the stars.

In the days and weeks that followed, Tyrus noticed that for the first time in a long time, everyone thrived. Everyone smiled and laughed and had fun. Everyone didn't merely survive, like many in Featherburn did. No, they *lived*. It meant more to Tyrus than anything because Cedric's sacrifice had made all this possible, his bond with Flake and the magic they shared, made all this possible—not to mention the people around him—and he felt grateful for all of it.

However, his mind was plagued with a feeling he

couldn't shake, and he suffered nightmares about it, too. Cedric's death had scarred him, perhaps more than he cared to admit. During their travels they had encountered warnings and harrowing tales about the Renegade Paragon. They had even seen the results of their dark and twisted powers. But they hadn't even caught a whiff of them, not a single trace. Tyrus had spoken about it with Malum, who tried reassuring him. But the wise traveller didn't lie to him either, or did he? Malum told him the Renegade Paragon could still be out there, but that it was just as possible that perhaps they were long gone. Maybe they were dead? Perhaps they were taken by the cold? But the boy couldn't get this thought out of his head, the thought that they were still out there, lurking.

Tyrus and Malum stood beside of the lighthouse as the sun dove into the lake. Flake's feathers ruffled in a gentle almost lukewarm breeze.

'What if ending winter was only the start?' Tyrus asked Malum, standing in front of the lighthouse. 'What if a greater challenge is ahead of us?'

'Oh, I am sure this is just the beginning,' answered Malum. 'But don't worry about what kind of beginning it'll turn out to be, because we'll be taking it by the horns, together.'

As soon as Tyrus turned his back and no one was watching, Malum smiled from underneath the veil.

Apart from his worries, Tyrus tried to focus on his

plans upon plans for the settlement. They'd have to pick a name, build a wall, and plenty more. He chose to focus on the hope he had for the future. A future full of friendship, full of love. The sun set. Kellan gave him a kiss, and together with their friends, Tyrus and Flake enjoyed a dash of what came after winter.

Together, they enjoyed the first taste of spring.

Acknowledgements

When I first started plotting this novel, the thought of ever publishing it seemed like an unobtainable faraway dream, which is why I feel beyond fortunate to have the privilege of being able to self-publish. To do so with the support of so many, is an absolute honour, and a feeling I couldn't possibly begin to describe. Needless to say, I have a few people I'd like to thank.

First of all, I want to take a paragraph or ten (okay, I'll try to keep it more concise) to thank my wonderful and beautiful partner, Cleo. At the beginning of our relationship, you reignited my passion for reading, something I had lost for quite some time, and for that I'll be eternally grateful. Your kindness and support have meant the world to me. You inspired me to do something with the stories and characters that swirled inside my head, and you always had my back throughout the entire process of making this book a reality. I know better than to claim I couldn't have done it without you, because you'll stop at nothing to deny that's the case, so I won't.

To my mom and dad. Thank you for always being

there for me, for always providing me with everything I needed to pursue any creative paths, and for always believing in me, even when I didn't.

To my brother, Marco. I can count on you no matter what. I'll never forget the stories we'd explore through our plushies and action figures when we were younger. I like to think that sense of exploration is partly responsible for this novel and the many to come.

To my friends Cedric, Jasper, Charley, and Jokke. Thank you for having my back, making me laugh, and for being stoked about my writing, even though not all of you are avid readers.

To my future parents-in-law, Conny and Jean, I will never forget your kindness, your willingness to help, and your often wise advice. Thank you.

To my beta readers Charley, Joy, Joke, Elke, Cleo, Conny, and those who didn't wish to be mentioned, I will be forever grateful a thousand times over. You helped the story and characters in this novel soar to new heights.

To my editor, Caryn Pine. You pushed me to lift my manuscript to the next level and aided me in my battle against my biggest adversary, punctuation. Thank you. Ironically, she had to fix the punctuation in this very paragraph.

To all the backers who chose to support this novel on Kickstarter. No matter how many times I say thank you, it couldn't ever be enough. Thanks to you, I am no longer an author of books to be, as my first novel is here now. I have all of you to be grateful for that. Special thanks to Lia, Joram, and Michaela.

To my Twitch chat. Thank you for keeping me company and accountable during our many focus sessions. I've said it before on stream, but I wouldn't have been able to finish this novel without your support and the good times in chat.

To my cat, Bolin, and my dog, Naga. Thank you both for all the emotional support and being the adorable gremlins you are.

And finally, thank you, my dearest reader. Thank you for going on this adventure through Wingspan together with Tyrus, Flake, Cedric, Lyra, Kellan, and Malum. There are so many magical stories out there, and I'll be forever grateful you chose to spend your time with mine.

ABOUT THE AUTHOR

Wesley E. Joseph (he/him/they/them) is a bisexual author and was born in the Flemish part of Belgium, in 1996. When he's not watching a TV-show, a film, playing Dungeons & Dragons, or reading books—preferably science fiction and/or fantasy—you can find him streaming on Twitch (twitch.tv/cobblewobbles) writing his novels. On Twitch, he shares his passion for creating worlds and characters with their lovely online community. He's a social media and community manager for a game developer by day, and a creator of magical worlds and characters by night. This is his first novel.